A QUEEN'S CONSPIRATOR

by Sam Burnell

First published in eBook and paperback 2023

•

© Sam Burnell 2023

•

The right of Sam Burnell to be identified as the author of this work has been asserted by her in accordance with the Copyright, Designs and Patents Act 1988.

All rights reserved. No part of this publication may be reproduced, stored in or introduced into a retrieval system, or transmitted, in any form, or by any means (electronic, mechanical, photocopying, recording or otherwise) without the prior written permission of the writer. Any person who does any unauthorised act in relation to this publication may be liable to criminal prosecution and civil claims for damages.

Sam Burnell

Thank you for respecting the hard work of this author.

Please note, this book is written in British English, so some spellings will vary from US English.

A Queen's Conspirator

For All My Children

Jules
Saffron
Savannah
Spyke

Character List

The English Court

William Cecil – Secretary of State
Somer – Crown Servant

Fitzwarren Household

William Fitzwarren – Father of Richard, Robert & Jack
Eleanor Fitzwarren – William's wife
Robert Fitzwarren – Richard's brother
Harry – Richard's cousin
Edward – Richard's cousin

Knights of St John

Emilio de Nevarra – Nephew of Philip of Spain
Jerome Sinclair – Knight of St John, expelled from the Order

Other Characters

Jamie – A priest at Burton Village
Mya – A London Pawn broker
Sir Ayscough – Lincoln Sheriff
Master Threadmill – Jack's Lawyer
Myles Devereux – a London Merchant
Garrison Bennett – a London Merchant
Christian Carter – a London Merchant

Sam Burnell

Introduction

It took two weeks. The first horse he stole went lame near Lincoln, and he had abandoned it. The second piebald cob he had led away in the dead of night from a gypsy camp had got him as far as Doncaster. After that, he had walked, doggedly placing one foot in front of the other and heading as far away from London as possible.

"Captain Jerome!"

"What is it, Carson?" Jerome answered as his head drew level with the deck.

"We found another good for nothin' sleeping in the scuppers near the forecastle, Captain. Master Tailor was for rolling him over the side, but I thought we'd best check with you first," Carson finished.

"You did right, lad," Jerome replied, climbing the last steps to the deck, "Come on, show me where."

Carson pointed towards a dark ragged heap that was indeed blocking the scuppers, asking eagerly. "Shall we ditch him over the side, sir?"

Jerome, stepping forward, kicked the ragged bundle.

"No, Carson. I think this is one good-for-nothing knave we might just have to keep. Welcome on board, Master Fitzwarren."

Chapter One

London – December 1558

Froggy's horse clattered over the cobbles, the sound rebounding from the arched gatehouse at Bryke Place.

"There's no sign of him," Froggy announced. Feet already out of the stirrups and dropping from the horse before it stopped, then asked, "Where's Jack? Any news?"

Marc shook his head, a grim look on his face. "He came back a few hours ago, then set out again, but there's been no news of the Master. He's disappeared."

Froggy cursed, looping the reins over the horse's head. He started to lead it towards the stables, Marc falling in step beside him, "Jack should know by now that if the Master doesn't want to be found, he won't be. He's business of his own, and Jack will do just as well to leave him be."

"You might well be right, but that's not going to stop Jack, is it?" Marc said frankly.

"No, you're right," Froggy conceded, then asked tentatively, "How's the lass?"

Marc shrugged. "I don't know. The physician Jack sent for is still with her. More than that, I don't know."

"Who'd do that to her?" Froggy replied, "Jack said it

was arsenic, and that doesn't get onto the Queen's table by accident, does it? Surely it wasn't meant for Lizbet."

Marc spoke slowly, his eyes on Froggy's, "The Master wasn't seated with us, so more than likely, it was meant for Jack."

"That was my reasoning as well. But who would want Jack dead?" Froggy said.

Marc laughed cheerlessly. "You need a list? There's been a time or two when I'd have happily slid a knife between his ribs."

Froggy leaned his head towards Marc and said quietly, "This wasn't a tavern fight in a dark street at night after sundown, Marc. This was the Queen's table. Someone went to great lengths and must have had help to carry this out. The poison was either meant for Jack or it landed on the table by mistake."

"God's bones! You mean it could have been meant for the Queen?" Marc gasped.

"I think that is the question many people will be asking today, don't you?" Froggy said as he handed his horse to a waiting stable hand.

From behind him, he'd heard the sound of approaching riders, the horses' hooves ringing on the cobbled lane that ran towards the entrance to Bryke Place. If he had hoped it was the Master he was soon disappointed. A group of ten riders bearing the Queen's livery slowed as they rode through the open gates and into the yard.

"This looks like trouble," Froggy said quietly, his eyes fixed on the riders.

One of the men brought his horse closer to Froggy and Marc. "Fitzwarren, where is he?"

Marc glanced towards Froggy, who stepped forward and said bluntly, "Looking for his brother and not here."

The soldier turned to those behind him. "Search the house."

"Yes, Captain Amery," came the quick response. Three men dismounted, handing control of their mounts to their companions, and headed towards the house.

"What?" blurted Froggy, protesting, "I told you, he's not here."

The answer from Captain Amery was to press his heels to the flanks of his mount and force the stallion forward to tower over Froggy. "Stay where you are!"

Behind him, several of the men had quickly dismounted. Two men remained, holding the horses. Without a glance at Froggy or Marc, the rest disappeared inside the house.

Froggy's face reddened with anger, but he held his ground, his head level with the bay's broad chest. Behind him, he could hear raised voices from within the house. He said again through gritted teeth, "I told you, he's not here."

"That might be the case, but I'll not leave until I know that. If he's not here, then where is he?" Captain Amery demanded from above Froggy.

"I told you that as well. He's looking for his brother," Froggy growled, standing his ground in front of the horse and refusing to look up.

"And where might that be?" The man demanded.

Froggy's temper flared. "If I knew, I'd not bloody well tell you."

A whip whistled through the air, catching Froggy across the cheek, leaving a long bleeding line on his skin. "There'll not be another warning."

"He's not here, Captain, only the woman," came the call from one of the soldiers emerging from the house behind him.

The whip had been replaced by a sword, and it was levelled at Froggy's head. "You'd better think very quickly of where your master might be."

Froggy forced his shoulders further back. Looking up, his eyes glared into Captain Amery's, who loomed above him, refusing to acknowledge the sword point that hovered between them. "I told you, I don't know."

"You also told me that you'd not tell me. I think you need to revise that opinion and quickly. Your master is out of favour with his sovereign. Protecting him will do you no good," Captain Amery advised, his voice cool.

The soldiers who had emerged from the house had not remounted; instead, they had formed a closed ring around Froggy and Marc.

Captain Amery addressed his men. "You said the woman is here, fetch her. We can see what she knows."

Froggy's temper snapped. "She's ill. The lass can't even stand! You can't drag her from her bed."

A humourless smile crept across the rider's face, and he returned his attention to Froggy. "Then you'd better think very quickly about where your master is, hadn't you?"

Froggy hesitated.

"Fetch her here," Captain Amery commanded.

Men from the ring broke away, moving towards the house.

"Leave her be!" The command came from the gateway.

Looking now beyond the mounted man, Froggy could see Jack on horseback, framed by the arched entrance to Bryke Place.

The sword pointed towards Froggy dropped away, and the mounted man turned his horse towards Jack. "Lord Fitzwarren, I've a warrant for your arrest."

If Jack was surprised, he didn't show it, remaining where he was, the reins loose in his right hand and his left resting on the pommel. His hair stood out in disordered spikes, and the fine clothes he had worn to the celebration the night before were now dusty and crumpled.

Froggy paled and watched as the men remounted and together, with Jack now riding in the groups centre, they left Bryke Place.

"God's bones! What's he been arrested for?" Marc gasped as the riders disappeared through the archway.

Froggy shook his head. "I don't know, but it's got something to do with the Master."

"We need to find him and quickly," Marc said.

"I agree, but it would help if I had a clue where to start looking, wouldn't it?" Froggy growled, his eyes still on the retreating backs of the riders.

"The Master has never run from anything in his life. He can't have just disappeared," Marc continued.

"If Jack doesn't have a clue where his brother might have gone, then I'll ask Lizbet," Froggy said, turning his back on Jack and the Queen's men as they left Bryke Place and headed in the direction of the house.

Master Smythe, the physician, listened to Froggy's argument patiently and spoke only when he had finished. "I am afraid the lady is beyond you."

"My God. What's happened?" Froggy said, his face filled with alarm.

Master Smythe, smiling raised his hands. "Nothing bad, sir, I have given the lady a sleeping draught, and it will be some hours before its effects wear off. Until they do, I am afraid there is little chance of rousing her, and indeed it would not be wise to do so."

That left only one person he could think to ask: Master Carter. He had already enquired at his house earlier that day to be told that Carter was at his warehouse, and there had been no sign of Richard Fitzwarren. However, that did not mean that Carter might not have some idea where Richard might have gone so Froggy took his horse and headed back towards the centre of the city.

Froggy was admitted to Carter's office immediately, Carter closed the door quickly. "What's happened? Coleman was here earlier to tell me that you'd been looking for your master?"

Froggy hesitated momentarily, then said, "It's not my place to say, sir, but I'm looking for the Master and Jack has been arrested."

"Arrested. On what charges?" Carter exclaimed, his eyes wide with horror.

Froggy shook his head. "I don't know, the Queen's men arrived at Bryke Place about an hour ago, and he left with them. That's all I know, and I am trying to find the Master."

Carter folded his arms. "I'm a good friend of your master's, and Jack's. You must put your loyalty to them aside and tell me what has happened if you want me to help."

"I'm sorry, sir, it's not ...."

"....your place. You've told me that. But without facts, I can't help, can I?" Carter said, his back against the door blocking the exit.

Froggy tugged at his beard, indecision clear on his face.

"Come on, man. They sound like they need all the help they can get," Carter pressed.

"Alright. I don't even know where to start," Froggy said, a pained expression on his face. "The Master was to marry, had you heard?"

"Yes, Elizabeth Howard, he'd told me," Carter confirmed.

"Well, the wedding was cancelled," Froggy mumbled.

"Cancelled? Why, what happened?" Carter sounded horrified.

Froggy tugged at his beard again, his face creased with confusion. "I don't rightly know. There was a celebration meal. All of us were there, including Lizbet. She was poisoned and...."

"Poisoned?" Carter interrupted.

"Arsenic, Jack said. Richard found her and picked her up, there was some confusion, and Elizabeth Howard's father accused him of taking another woman to his bed the night before the wedding," Froggy tried to explain. "It wasn't the case. He was trying to save Lizbet's life."

"The woman, Lizbet, what happened?" Carter asked.

"She's survived, but she's gravely ill," Froggy replied.

"No wonder Richard has disappeared," Carter groaned.

"There's more, I am afraid. As a punishment, the Queen decreed that there would be a wedding the following day, only not between Richard and Lady Howard. Instead, he was forced to wed Lizbet," Froggy said, falling over his words as he explained.

"Lizbet is the woman he'd declared as his sister, am I right? Some tavern wench from Southwark if I remember rightly," Carter said.

Froggy's eyes narrowed. "Lizbet is a kind soul, and I'll not hear ...."

Carter held his hand up. "It was not my intention to insult the lady." Carter moved away from the door and paced across his office. "When was the last time you saw your master?"

"Last night. They were searching for the Master, so I took his horse from the stables to make it look as if he had escaped," Froggy explained.

"But I am assuming he hadn't?" Carter said.

Froggy shook his head. "Jack and Richard did what they could for Lizbet. The Master stayed with her during the night in a chapel and in the morning, he was arrested and thrown into a store room by all accounts. Jack told me he was released on the Queen's orders and taken directly back to the chapel. Before the bells had rung for Prime, he was wedded to the lass, and no-one has seen him since."

"Where's Jack? You said he was with him?" Carter asked.

"He was until he was arrested and locked in the store room. Jack was forced to witness the marriage. Afterwards, he said the Master turned and walked from the chapel. When he made to follow, the Queen's guards wouldn't let him. When they eventually did, he couldn't find the Master," Froggy replied.

"Could he have been arrested? Taken by the Queen's guards to the Tower or some other place?" Carter asked, his voice now worried.

Froggy shook his head. "The Queen's men arrived at Bryke Place looking for him, so they've not got him in custody."

"But they do have Jack," Carter said darkly. "What a mess. Those two cannot be trusted alone for five minutes. Right then, let's deal with what we can. The lass, Lizbet, is she safe?"

Froggy nodded. "She's at Bryke Place, and there's some of the Master's men there, but if the Queen's men come for her, then there's not much they can do."

"There is not much any of us can do if that happens," Carter said in agreement, "Where are you going next?"

Froggy looked suddenly confused. "I don't know, sir. Back to Bryke Place, I suppose, hopefully, there is word from Jack or news of the Master."

"Have you tried the Angel?" Carter asked quickly.

Froggy shook his head in reply.

"I'll get my cloak. I'm coming with you. We will go to Bryke Place first, then the Angel if there is no news," Carter announced. It took him only a few minutes to send one of the boys in his office back to his house to let them know he may not return for the evening meal, and they set off across the city to Bryke Place.

Chapter Two

London – December 1558

On his arrival at the Tower Jack was surprised to be met by a man he recognised. Christopher Morley had smiled at him apologetically and led him to his own office. As they made their way along the corridors, they were followed by the Queen's guards, and Jack noted that two of them remained outside Morley's office when they had stepped inside.

Morley must have seen Jack's glace towards the posted guards, saying, "A precaution only."

"Against what?" Jack replied sarcastically as the door was closed.

Morley, sighing heavily, removed his hat, placing it on the desk. "You are awaiting a summons from the Queen; until she is ready to see you, you will remain here as my guest. I don't think, given the circumstances, that it will be a long wait if that is any consolation."

"My brother, have you seen him?" Jack said, walking past Morley to look through the unshuttered window onto Tower Green.

"No, I haven't, and I don't think anyone else has either, not since ...." Morley's words trailed off.

"Not since his marriage," Jack finished for him, his voice acid. "That was a cruel act."

"It was the wish of the Queen that there was still to be a wedding, I am afraid," Morley replied.

"I heard. I've also heard a rumour that my brother was being punished for causing insult to his bride's family and you know as well as I do that's not what happened. She was poisoned and, worse, she was poisoned at the Queen's table. I think that should be your issue, don't you?" Jack growled.

"The episode has raised a few questions, it's true," Morley conceded.

"A few questions?" Jack spluttered in disbelief.

"I accept there seems to have been some confusion ...." Morley tried.

Jack's keen blue eyes were locked onto Morley's. "Your master is Cecil. What I am wondering is what he has to do with this?"

One of Morley's eyebrows arched, creating a series of questioning lines across his brow. "I hardly think Lord Burghley would have a hand in laying poison on the Queen's table, and I would heartily recommend you don't share that opinion outside of this room."

"That didn't really answer my question, did it? I want to know what Cecil had to do with the Queen's insistence that my brother wed. He gave me this, told me it was a wedding gift for my brother, and he was looking particularly pleased with himself," Jack produced the gold coin Cecil had handed him, holding it up between them.

"Oh." The slight sound escaped from Morley's mouth, and he removed his gaze quickly from the coin, returning it to Jack's face.

"Oh, indeed. Why did he give this to me?" Jack moved the coin closer towards Morley's face. "Why?"

Morley reached up and took the gold disc from Jack's hand. Reversing it, he inspected it momentarily before handing it back.

"What?" Jack demanded.

"It is tainted," Morley replied quietly.

"Tainted? What do you mean?" Jack was inspecting the coin.

"A forgery and not a very good one either," Morley said, adding, "the die that has been used on the reverse was cast during Henry's reign; it doesn't belong on a coin with the late Queen's image. I would place a wager that you were aware of the dubiousness of its authenticity but not the error."

Jack was looking at the words circling the exterior of the coin, twisting it between thumb and forefinger so he could read the legend that wheeled around its edge. Morley was right.

"Those coins were brought to the mint as part of your father's estate; I think you can see quite plainly the situation this places you in. It would be wise to be compliant with any wishes of Lord Burghley," Morley stated simply.

"Is that a threat?" Jack's face was reddened with fury.

Morley smiled. "Not at all, simply a statement of fact."

Jack turned his back on Morley, planting his hands on the stonework on either side of the window and staring through the glass. Below him, followed by a not inconsiderable retinue, and heading towards the White Tower was Emilio. Jack watched him pause briefly before climbing them and disappearing inside.

He was trapped.

Again.

Richard, you bloody fool!

When it finally came, the meeting with the Queen was brief, and the bulk of it took place while he was on his knees, eyes fixed on the floor, making only the responses he must. The presence chamber was filled, and Jack realised this was why the wait had been so lengthy; it had taken time to assemble such a large number to witness his humiliation.

On the whole, Jack escaped better than he had imagined he would. He was neither incarcerated in the Tower, nor was he stripped of his land or wealth. Instead he was banished from the Queen's Court and charged with finding his brother and presenting him to the Queen's Constable.

"What has happened to you would have humbled most men," Carter observed later that day when he finally caught up with Jack at Bryke Place.

"I'm not most men," Jack pointed out bluntly from where he was brooding near the fireplace.

"True. You've lost your Queen's patronage and access to her Court that, for many, would be a political death," Carter observed thoughtfully, coming to stand next to Jack.

"I call it a blessing." Jack absently kicked at a log that had rolled from the flames sending it back into the hearth.

"You still have to find your brother, remember?"

"I want to speak to Devereux, but he's still not in London, something that I don't think is a coincidence," Jack said grimly. He had retained possession of the coin that was undoubtedly a forgery; reaching for it, he almost produced it to show Carter then thought better of the act. If he told Carter he would implicate him, the man did not deserve that.

"What do you think Devereux has to do with this? Do you think he had a hand in the poison?" Carter said, disbelief in his voice.

"He might have," Jack replied.

"What makes you think this is Devereux's work?" Carter pressed.

Jack let out a long breath before he replied. "It seems I might have been wrongly informed about

Robert's death, and there's a good chance he's working with Devereux."

"I thought you found out Robert had died in a tavern brawl?" Carter sounded confused.

"I did. It was Devereux who told me that. I've no other proof," Jack replied.

Carter tugged at his chin with a thumb and forefinger and paced across the room, hitching himself up on the end of the table. "That might be the case, but this isn't Devereux's style. He is more one for leaving you with a knife in your back in a darkened corner of London. This is more than likely a mistake, and the poison has missed its mark."

"There's more than just this. The horse I was thrown from, the bit had been wired to make the horse bolt. I bought the horse from Devereux. And I was attacked in an alley by a man I'd swear I'd seen in Devereux's tavern," Jack continued with his list of evidence, turning his back on the fire.

"Do you have any proof?" Carter pressed his arms spread wide.

"The groom. When I bought the horse, it was the same man at the hunt," Jack replied, crossing the room to stand nearer to Carter.

"How sure are you? Did you speak to him?" Carter asked quickly,

"No, not really," Jack conceded.

"Was he dressed the same?" Carter quizzed.

"Of course not. At the hunt, he was wearing livery," Jack replied snapped.

"Well, there's a start. Whose was it?"

Jack shook his head. "I don't know, it was blue chevrons on a yellow background with red, or blue, barrels on this side." Jack indicated where he meant with his right hand.

"Red or blue?" Carter echoed.

"Red. I'm pretty sure it was red," Jack said after a moment's thought.

"On the left or the right quadrant?" Carter said.

"Err …. left …. I think."

"And you are sure this is the same man? Jack, you can't even remember what the livery looked like. Is there a chance you are deceiving yourself? Compiling a picture to fit the events?" Carter asked.

"I remember his bloody face. It was the same man," Jack's temper was rising, "Stop trying to tie me in bloody knots."

"I'm not," Carter soothed. "These are only the questions you'd be asked if you raised this matter with the sheriff."

"I'm not raising it with the sheriff, I'm telling you," Jack said.

"Alright, then. The man who attacked you, are you sure he worked for Devereux? You said you'd seen him at his tavern, the White Hart, that is one of the taverns where pretty much every cutpurse and criminal this side of the river can be found," Carter pointed out.

"I saw him there. He was in the tavern, then again in the alley," Jack said, trying to recall the man's face clearly.

"That's not confirmation that he was in Devereux's pay. What was he doing when you saw ...."

Jack cut him off. "Stop trying to make me doubt myself."

"I'm not, Jack. I'm just trying to make you look at this rationally before you turn up at Devereux's and murder him and end up in even more trouble than you are now," Carter said bluntly.

"I'm not planning on murdering him," Jack said defensively.

"You need some facts, Jack, that's all I am saying," Carter said, then added, "and right now, you don't have any."

"I understand what you are saying," Jack conceded, turning back toward the fireplace, his palms flat on the lintel, staring into the flames.

Carter dropped from the table and came to stand next to his friend. "Look, no one would seek to poison this woman, Lizbet, would they? And even if someone did want to rid the world of her, they would not go to such lengths to do so, agreed?" When Jack nodded, Carter continued, "So the only person at that banquet who it would be almost impossible to strike at any other way was the Queen."

"You think so?"

"Come on, Jack. She's not hugely popular in many quarters, there are plenty would like to bring the realm back to Catholicism and she stands in their way," Carter continued his argument. "Who else could it have been meant for? If you think it was yourself or your brother, then your vanity is getting the better of you."

Jack, still not convinced, said. "Devereux is never out of London, he's too scared someone will move onto his muck heap while he's away. So it seems strange that both he and my brother have disappeared at the same time."

"I think you'll find it is a coincidence," Carter soothed.

When Carter left, Jack's confidence in who was accountable for all that had gone wrong in recent weeks was severely weakened. Maybe Carter was right. Robert and Devereux fitted too neatly.

Jack had only to wait another day before his source informed him that Myles Devereux was once again back in London. Jack arrived at the White Hart in Cheap Street with ten men; he had no intention of being made to wait.

It was Matthew who intercepted him. "Master Devereux is expecting you." Matthew had said.

"He might be expecting me, but this isn't about to be a meeting your master is going to enjoy," Jack replied tersely, striding up the stairs two at a time.

Matthew, above him on the steps, ignored the comment. "If you follow me, My Lord, I will take you straight up."

The door was opened for them at the top of the stairs; the anteroom where Devereux's business was conducted was empty. Beating Jack across the room, Matthew rapped on the door, saying, "I'll let him know you are here."

Jack, pushing by him, shoved the door open. Matthew stepped quickly into the opening, blocking Jack.

"Get out of my way," Jack growled.

"Matthew, just let him in," the bored voice of Myles Devereux drawled from inside the room.

Jack barged his way passed Matthew.

Devereux was sitting on the edge of one of the chairs near the fire, wearing only hose and a loose shirt. In his left hand was a knife, and in his right, a piece of dried meat; sitting on the floor before him was a dog. Its brown eyes switched from the food in Myles' hands to the newcomer to the room. Ears that had been pressed back in pleased anticipation dropped forward. The animal rose, and the sheen of the black coat shifted as muscles beneath it tensed.

"I'm not so sure he likes you," Myles said, leaning forward and ruffling the fur between the dog's ears. The Alaunt, ignoring him, kept its eyes firmly on Jack.

Jack took another step into the room.

The Alaunt growled, a deep guttural sound rising inside the dog's chest.

"Now that's a shame," Myles declared sadly.

"A dog isn't going to save you, Devereux," Jack shot back.

"And why would he?" Myles said playfully, returning his attention to the Alaunt and delivering a friendly pat on its head. "Loki, this is not how great your new master."

"What?"

"Sit down, Fitzwarren. He's a gift from your brother," Myles declared, rising.

The Alaunt's body stiffened as Myles rose.

"You've seen him?" Jack demanded.

"Not exactly," Myles supplied.

"Damn you, Devereux. Tell me what you know," Jack demanded.

The Alaunt's growl increased.

"Will you just sit down," Myles countered, pointing towards the other vacant chair. "And I will tell you what I know. Loki, down," Myles commanded. The Alaunt slowly lowered itself to the floor, its eyes fixed on Jack.

"Tell me, now, Devereux."

"God's bones, Fitzwarren, I will tell you, but just ...."

"I'll not be commanded to sit and beg for you like that damned dog," Jack retorted.

Myles rolled his eyes. "Very well. Bloody stand where you are then." Myles lowered himself back onto the chair, not sitting on the edge of it as he had when Jack arrived, but this time sinking back, the plush fabric almost looking as if it were wrapping around him. "Your brother did warn me you'd be fit to burst like the cork from a rotting barrel of eels. Although, I can't say I blame you."

"You know what has happened?" Jack said warily.

"More or less," Myles let a trace of satisfaction creep into his voice. "There are a few versions of the story, but I prefer the one where the bride and the bride's father caught him naked in the gardens at Durham Place with another woman."

"That's not what happened."

"It might not be what happened, but there'll be more than a grain of truth in there. Come on, your brother is no saint," Myles said, laughing.

"Where is he now?" Jack's voice bore a dangerous edge, and the Alaunt's body stiffened.

Myles shrugged.

"Tell me what you do know."

Myles sighed heavily. Leaning behind him he filched a page from the desk, flicking the unfolded sheet towards Jack. Myles settled back even further in the chair to watch his guest read the missive, retrieving a wine glass and cradling it with his long slender fingers.

Jack caught the letter badly, creasing it in his hand as he snatched it from the air. The moment he opened it, there was no mistaking his brother's handwriting.

"I believe the third line down is the one you need to read first," Myles supplied helpfully.

The message was short, indeed was little more than a list of brief instructions the preamble being only an indication that the writer would pay well for the execution of his wishes. Richard requested that Myles provide men to ensure both Bryke Place and the London house were secure and that the location of Robert Fitzwarren be found. There was, as Myles had indicated, a line directed towards him.

"Jack, you can be assured Devereux has played no part in what happened."

Jack looked up from the page, his ice-blue eyes meeting Devereux's dark ones.

Myles grinned back at him. "I told you."

Jack returned his gaze to the page.

Richard had instructed Devereux to locate Robert Fitzwarren and the lawyer, Geoffrey Clement.

So Richard, too, suspected Robert. "Have you found either of them?"

A grimace twisted Myles' features for a moment. "In a manner of speaking, yes. Clement surfaced but not Robert."

"Surfaced?" Jack repeated, confused.

"Literally, I'm afraid. His body had been tied to two stone anchors from one of the fishing boats and rolled over the bank into the river near the landing stage at Lambeth. One of the ropes around his body came loose and the bloated little body popped out of the river like a frog jumping from a box by all accounts. I am surprised you'd not heard. Stunk like a plague pit in August, so I'm told," Myles concluded.

"Don't tell me you know all this because you were charged with disposing of the corpse," Jack said.

Myles nodded. "I charge the Parish double in cases like this."

"I'm not interested in your dealings, Devereux; do you know what happened to him?" Jack growled.

Myles settled his shoulders back into the chair and steepled his fingers, a furrow appearing between his brows. "I think I can say with a degree of certainty that he didn't take his own life. Tying two anchors to your legs and then rolling yourself into the Thames would be the Devil's work. Oh, and his neck had been broken."

"Anything else?" Jack said.

"He had been in the river a few days at least, not long enough for the fish and the eels to unwrap his turgid guts," Myles provided.

"Has anyone been questioned about his disappearance?" Jack pressed.

Myles shook his head. "Not that I know of, although I do know that his office was being watched by Garrison Bennett's men. Clement worked for Bennett, and he was also working for your brother, wasn't he?"

"I don't know anything about that," Jack answered too quickly.

"You can't dissemble. Your face lets everyone know exactly what you are thinking," Myles retorted then huffed loudly.

"And Robert?" Jack asked.

Myles shook his head. "On that score, I have no news, I am afraid. He may very well have been the cause of your brother's.... problems. I don't know. Richard has a particular talent when it comes to creating enemies, don't you agree?"

Jack looked at Myles closely for a moment before reaching inside his doublet and producing the gold disc. Held up between thumb and forefinger, the newly minted coin caught the light from the fire.

Myles's mouth twisted into a lopsided smile. "Is that for me?"

Jack switched his gaze from the seated man back to the coin, turning it in his fingers. "I know you had a hand in making these, Devereux. It is a shame that you do not have the attention to detail my brother has."

Myles frowned.

Jack continued. "Did you ever look at them closely?"

Myles moved towards the edge of his seat, his eyes on the coin. "Why?"

Jack tossed the gold disc through the air towards Myles, the coin spinning before Devereux's long fingers coiled around it, snatching it towards him.

Jack watched with growing satisfaction as Myles examined the coin, cursing loudly when he turned it to view the reverse.

"Richard doesn't know, and it may be that error that has placed him where he is now," Jack said bitterly.

"Are you going to tell me he didn't notice that either? It could have been reworked. I'll not take the blame for this,' Myles said dismissively and flipped the coin back towards Jack.

It wasn't the response Jack had either wanted or expected. "Don't you think you should have noticed?"

Myles shrugged. He had already begun to settle back in his chair. "It's not ideal, I agree. However the coinage was accepted by the treasury, and both he and I made a profit, and you too, I have no doubt."

"Me?" Jack blurted. "What's this got to do with me?"

"For God's sake, Fitzwarren. You know damn nicely that the gold was turned into the mint as part of your father's estate. Don't tell me you didn't know and don't tell me that you were not profiting from the arrangement," Myles pointed out.

Faced with the accuracy of the statement, Jack knew there was little he could say.

"I doubt if that tainted gold has anything to do with what happened," Myles provided. "Although I agree, it may have helped to fuel Richard's current unpopularity at Court."

"How do you know that?" Jack snapped.

"I have ears everywhere, but that's a chance he took and he knew it," Myles replied coolly. Then, changing the subject, he said, "You didn't finish reading your brother's letter? He even charged me with obtaining a wedding gift for his bride. In my honest opinion, jewels would usually suffice, or lace, or cloth, but rarely...." Myles paused and leaned down to pat the Alaunt's head, "a hound."

Jack looked at the dog and then Devereux before casting his eyes back to the letter he had forgotten he was holding.

Chapter Three

London - January 1558

Jack found his wife in the bedroom seated at a small table. Her long brown hair was unbound and she was pulling a brush through it slowly. A fire crackled happily in the grate, a low winter sun threw its weak rays through the window, illuminating the room in a pale yellow light.

A peaceful scene. So at odds with the turmoil he felt.

Catherine, hearing his entry, turned and smiled, laying the brush down on the table. "Jack, you're back. Any news?"

Jack shook his head, closing the door behind him, "Where is Lizbet?"

"She's resting. Master Smythe has just left," Catherine replied quickly, rising from the chair.

"I need to speak to her. Maybe she knows something more, something I don't know about where Richard is," Jack said, pacing across the room towards the window.

"Jack, she's been badly ill. Please don't vex her more with your questions," Catherine followed him and lay a hand on his arm.

"I am sure you are right," Jack conceded, running his fingers through his hair. "I just can't believe he has disappeared."

"I know, but he is capable of looking after himself, and I am sure he will be well," Catherine soothed, then added, "You know at least that the Queen does not have him in custody. The likelihood is he is staying away until this is forgotten about."

"I wish I could believe that. The truth of what happened has been twisted, and it becomes worse every time I hear it," Jack said, his voice weary.

"Really, how so?" Catherine asked.

"Well, what started as Richard carrying Lizbet from the courtyard where she had collapsed now has him being caught in bed with her by the bride's father and the bride herself. How can such untruths become such common knowledge?" Jack complained, throwing his arms wide.

Catherine shook her head. "I don't know. I think people desire to always think the worst."

"I found out today as well that Robert isn't dead," Jack pronounced.

"Robert? Your brother?" Catherine gasped, taking a sudden step backward.

"The same, yes," Jack replied.

"I thought you said he was dead? You even told that lawyer he had died, remember?" Catherine said, fright in her voice.

"Don't worry. He'll not get anywhere near you, come here." Jack pulled her towards him and held her close. "I thought he was. Indeed I was told that he died over a game of cards."

"Why didn't you tell me?" Catherine tried to push away from him, but he held her fast.

"I honestly thought he was dead until I spoke with Devereux, and it seems Robert's demise was nothing more than a convenient rumour. The house is guarded; he's no money and no men in his pay so there is little he can do," Jack continued, his arms around her, one hand stroking her hair.

"You know what he is like, and he has every reason to want rid of you," Catherine said, her voice worried.

"Don't worry. He's not going to get within striking distance, I promise you," Jack didn't feel the need to tell her that he'd found out that Richard had been in touch with Devereux and that he suspected Robert might be at the root of some of the ills that had befallen them recently. "I will be back soon. Where did you say Lizbet was?"

Catherine shrugged. "I'm not sure which rooms Hanwyn has given her."

Lizbet, sat up on the bed, her back against the wall, and hugged her knees. It was a small room, crudely furnished but warm, having one wall backing on to the bread ovens in the kitchens. The room was used as a dry store, and not all of the contents had been removed. Grain and flour were still stacked in one corner, moved to one side to make space for the simple bed.

Lizbet remembered everything that had happened until unconsciousness had claimed her. The agonising spasms clamping her innards. The stabbing pains, like a blade, twisting in her stomach. Richard taking a knife to her dress.

The beautiful blue dress!

Slitting the material until the dress fell, ruined, to the floor.

Then, drained, hardly able to hold her head up, seated in a chair, she remembered the chapel. The hastily muttered words of the priest. Richard's head close to hers, his steadying words, the gentle pressure of his cool hand on hers as he reassured her.

Quietly, with a calm she found hard to believe, he had spoken the words she needed to repeat, helped her when her croaking voice threatened to fail and coaxed her on stumbling towards the conclusion.
She'd not understood why it was happening. Her head had spun, and her vision blurred.
"Lizbet, just say the words they want you to say. All will be well, trust me," Richard had reassured.
The priest's voice had shaken when he spoke - "Richard Fitzwarren will you take Elizabeth ...."
She had thought they were talking about someone else. Another Elizabeth. Was she at Richard's wedding?
"Elizabeth ...." The priest had cast his eyes around the room; they had even lingered on her for a moment.
"Cropper," Richard had supplied quickly, "Elizabeth Cropper."
It was then that she realised he was talking about her. How had he even known her family name? Had she ever told him?
Then it had been her turn to repeat the words: make her vows.
"I can't," her voice had croaked.
"You can, and you must, for both our sakes," came the steady reply. Her hand tightened in his, he had guided her through the last of the ceremony.
And that had been it.
He had squeezed her hand one final time, and whispered in her ear one final reassurance. Then he was gone.

Where Richard had gone, she didn't know. Froggy had welcomed her back at Bryke Place, and soon after, the physician had arrived. He had given her a sleeping draught, and when she finally awoke, the internal agony had subsided to a dull and persistent ache. Master Smythe could not answer her questions, telling her only that Lord Fitzwarren had sent for him. Then she had glimpsed Froggy's concerned face as he exchanged words with the physician from where he stood at the doorway. She tried to ask him what had happened, where everyone was, but the words wouldn't form in her mouth. All he'd said was, "All will be well," and left.

It was not until another two days had passed and Master Smythe informed her that Lord Fitzwarren had insisted she move to his London house from Bryke Place that she found out more. On her arrival, the house was the scene one of furious activity. Armed men filled the courtyard. Servants moved between them carrying various burdens and, standing on the threshold to the doorway, arms folded and with a look of fury on her face, was Jack's wife.

Just like everything else it was spoilt. All of it remained a visually painful memory.

"I was told to expect you, although I had hoped you would have had the decency not to show your face after the trouble you have caused," Catherine had said bluntly, striding towards her. Then to the steward, Hanwyn, who stood behind her. "Show her to the room you have prepared."

How could all this have gone so badly wrong?

Apart from Master Smythe and the servants who had brought her food, Lizbet had seen no one else since her arrival.

There was a knock on the door stopping her thoughts. Thinking it was Master Smythe she called for him to enter. The knock was repeated, perhaps he hadn't heard her, and Lizbet called out again, but still, the door didn't open. The third knock was accompanied by a voice calling her name; it was one which she recognised.

Moving slowly from the bed to the door she hauled it open to reveal Jack standing in the narrow passageway, a lead in his hand and next to him, watching her intently, was a dog.

"Where've you been?" Lizbet said, her voice hoarse.

"One question at a time, lass," Jack said, raising a hand to still her words. "Are you going to shift over and let me in, or do I have to discuss this out here to entertain the servants?"

Lizbet reluctantly stepped back, allowing man and dog to enter the small room.

"Where I've been is trying to find him, and I am afraid I've failed," Jack said as soon as he had closed the door behind him.

"What went wrong, Jack? What did I do?" Lizbet said, tears in her eyes.

"Christ, Lizbet, you didn't do anything wrong." Jack ruffled the dog's ears before seating himself on the edge of the narrow bed, adding, "What are you doing in here? I had the Devil's job finding you."

"Never mind that no one will tell me anything. What happened?" Lizbet demanded.

Jack met her eyes, his blue ones serious for once. "What happened is that you took a poison which was delivered to our table and meant for someone else."

"Who?"

"In all likelihood, it was meant for the Queen," Jack replied, then added, "Although I've found out that Robert isn't dead, so I can't discount him from having had a hand in it."

"God's bones, it might have been meant for you?" Lizbet blurted, then added, "I thought he was dead."

Jack reached out a hand and took hers. "Sit down, lass, before you fall down."

Lizbet seated herself next to him.

"I thought he was, but it seems I was deceived," Jack said darkly.

"And because of that I'm .... I've ruined the wedding?" Lizbet faltered over the words.

Jack slung an arm around her shoulders and pulled her against him. "You listen to me. This was not your fault."

"It was! It's fate. If I'd taken just a few more steps, he'd never have seen me," Lizbet sobbed.

"Christ, if you'd taken a few more steps you'd be dead." Jack hugged her tightly, resting his chin on her head. "I would never have forgiven myself, and neither would my brother."

"But he was to be married ...."

"Well, it didn't happen, and you are not to blame," Jack said firmly.

"Did you find out who killed your horse? Could that have been Robert?" Lizbet said, sniffing loudly.

"It seems likely," Jack replied, then added, "You are safe here, no one will get through the guard that is in place on the house now."

"Where do you think Richard is?" Lizbet asked.

"I don't know. I've searched but there's been no word from him, no one has seen him, apart from bloody Devereux," Jack grumbled then, changing the subject, he asked. "What on earth are you doing in here?"

"Why do you think I'm in here?" Lizbet asked.

"I don't know unless, of course, you wanted to be housed in the dark with the flour sacks," Jack said, looking round the room for the first time.

"Your wife is in charge of the accommodation, she appointed me the room," Lizbet said.

"Surely not. She wouldn't put you in on purpose. There must be a mistake," Jack replied.

"Oh, there's no mistake, Jack. You ask her. She's made it clear how she feels about me being here and places the blame on me for Richard's disappearance," Lizbet said.

"That is a state of affairs that cannot continue," Jack said.

Outside the room, footsteps rattled the boards in the corridor and the dog growled. Jack placed a hand on his head to stop him.

"What are you doing with a dog?" Lizbet asked.

"He's called Loki," Jack announced a lopsided grin on his face. "He's a fine hound."

"I can see that," Lizbet said, pulling from Jack's clumsy embrace to look at the dog. He reminded her of poor Kells, dark chestnut eyes, almost entirely black apart from a white blaze on his chest, and observing her with the same slightly puzzled expression. Reaching forward, she ruffled the dark fur on its head.

"What are you showing him to me for?"

"He's for you, from ... Richard," Jack said haltingly.

Lizbet's eyes shot from the dog to meet Jack's. "So you have seen him."

"Lord knows, I wish I had. I went to see Devereux and Richard had left him instructions. Amongst them was one to buy Loki," Jack replied.

"He bought me a dog?" Lizbet said, her voice incredulous.

"He bought you one before, remember, and no one could have got within ten feet of you when he was around, and I've no doubt Loki will be the same." Jack replied then, holding out some dried strips of meat towards Lizbet added, "Take these and come and meet him properly."

Lizbet snatched the offering from Jack and glowered at the dog. "You look like a doleful creature, don't you think you can share my bed! Here."

Lizbet held out the meat, and the dog took a slow step forward and then, head slightly to one side, gently took the offering from her. Lizbet ruffled the fur behind its ears, and the dog sat down, its eyes fastened upon her face.

"He's reading your face, he wants to know what you are thinking," Jack said smiling.

"How can he read my face?" Lizbet scoffed.

"Dogs are sensitive animals. They often know what we are feeling before we do," Jack replied. Standing, he leaned down and unclipped the lead from the dog. "When I was a child, my closest friend was a wolfhound."

"Oh, poor Jack, lived in the stables and raised by wolves," Lizbet said, her voice though was not unkind.

Jack dropped to sit back on the edge of the bed. "I know it isn't easy, Lizbet, but please try and make this your home. It is as much mine as it is yours."

"If you check the coat of arms over the door I'll think you'll find it has only one owner," Lizbet said, scratching the dog's ears.

Jack cursed. "Why am I surrounded by such obstinate wenches? You know, as well as I do, I would not be here if it had not been for you, my brother would not have survived and you are as entitled to live here as any other man."

"Or woman," Lizbet said, her voice sullen.

"Is this about Catherine?" Jack asked.

"Jack, she doesn't want me here, blames me for what happened – God only knows how many times I have lived through that night. I didn't want this to be the outcome, I'd never have driven him away, and I certainly didn't try and snare myself a husband."

Jack looked at her aghast. "Is that what my wife thinks?"

Lizbet met his eyes but remained silent.

Jack rose from the bed. "I will be back soon enough."

Lizbet caught his sleeve as he made for the door. "Jack, I bear your wife no ill will, your words will not make the situation any better."

Jack halted for a moment. "Can you honestly tell me they will make matters worse?"

"Well, no, but ...."

"No buts," Jack already had his hand on the door latch and a moment later Lizbet was alone.

Lizbet regarded the dog that was still sat on the floor in front of her. "I hope you are not going to be as temperamental as the other men in my life."

✝

"I said no such thing," Catherine replied tartly.

"And the room Lizbet is in, did you have a hand in that?" Jack demanded.

"Certainly not, it was the servants who selected it for her, it's not my fault if they have recognised her as one of their own and installed her near the kitchens, is it?"

"Oh, so you know exactly whereabouts in the house she is, then?" Jack replied.

"I might, but that doesn't mean I chose the rooms. Also, Jack Fitzwarren, this house is as new to me as it is to Lizbet. I've no idea what many of the rooms are like. If she had an issue with them, Lizbet has a loud enough voice and is capable of complaint. She does not need you to champion her cause," Catherine replied, standing her ground.

"One of their own ...." Jack repeated slowly.

"You know exactly what I mean."

Jack opened his mouth to reply, then stopped himself. He turned on his heel and stormed through the door, leaving it open in his wake. Catherine was still standing in the middle of the room when he returned five minutes later with Lizbet in tow.

"Sit down." The command Jack made was directed at both of the women before him.

Lizbet obliged. Jack turned cold blue eyes on Catherine until she lowered herself into a chair some distance from Lizbet.

"It seems to have escaped your attention that outside these walls, there remains a man, or men, who wish us harm. As a result of that I have lost contact with my brother, a fact that pains me greatly. His absence is not due to anything else; Lizbet is not to blame for what has happened. But it has happened and while Lizbet remains under the Fitzwarren roof she will be treated as the wife of my brother."

Catherine's eyes locked again with Jack's. "You can't expect her to be accepted as his wife?"

"I don't expect it; I demand it. And when I've finished in here I will ensure that every man, woman and child who resides in this house is also left in no doubt as to her position within this family,"

Catherine rose. "She," pointing across the room towards Lizbet, "is a gutter whore, for the Lord's sake. Not only have you slept with her, but half of London Town probably have ...."

Jack took two quick steps towards Catherine. "God woman! You make me want to strike you. My brother, Robert, made you his whore, does that mean I shouldn't have taken you to bed let alone wed you?"

Catherine paled; her voice trembling, she said, "That was different, and you know it was."

"You were known as a servant in this house. For all I know you might have been known as Robert's whore as well," Jack shot back.

"I had no choice."

"And likely neither did Lizbet; there, at least we have found some common ground," Jack growled. Then, turning his attention to Lizbet, he said, "and who I decide to make my wife is my choice, not a decision my wife will be called to question upon. Do I make myself clear?"

Lizbet's hands were tightly wrapped around the chairs arms, her reply to Jack was a nod only.

"Good. Catherine is my wife, and Lizbet, you will respect her as such. Catherine, Lizbet is .... your sister-in-law and you will treat her with mutual respect. My attentions need to be directed to those outside of these walls who wish us dead, and I do not need to be distracted by your squabbling," Jack finished.

The room remained silent for a moment; it was Catherine who broke it. "Sensible words, husband."

Jack grinned. "Well, that's the first time you've called me sensible! And that is what we need to be, sensible and united."

"I thought you believed it was Devereux who was behind this?" Lizbet asked, changing the subject.

"It seems not. Richard, damn him, even left his last instructions with him before he left London and a message for me that Myles Devereux was not involved, which is a shame," Jack said.

"I agree, it is a shame, he's an arrogant bastard by all the accounts you have given me," Lizbet replied.

"But Richard trusts him. Indeed more than me, it seems." Jack had come to stand in front of the window, gazing down at the street below.

"I am sure that's not true," Catherine replied, rising and following him.

"Then why leave his final instructions with Devereux?" Jack said, turning back to face her.

"Jack, Richard disappeared from Durham Place. The Queen's men were looking for him. They followed you; it well might have been that Devereux was the safer option," Lizbet said.

"You might be right," Jack said.

☨

Lizbet returned to her room. Opening the door she found a pair of brown eyes watching her intently. The hound was curled up on her bed, the covers rucked around it – she had forgotten about the dog.

"Get down," Lizbet scolded and pointed towards the floor.

Obediently Loki slunk from the bed and sat on the floor before her. Lizbet smoothed its ears. "It looks like there is going to be another in my life who likes to do just as he pleases when my back is turned."

A few minutes later there was a hesitant knock on the door and Lizbet found Catherine on the other side.

"It seems a truce is in order," Catherine said bluntly, then added, "Whether we like it or not. There are more suitable rooms on the ...." Catherine flew back from the door as the Loki, black, growling and saturnine, appeared at Lizbet's side.

Lizbet caught the dog's collar.

"Where did you get that beast from?" Catherine said from the other side of the corridor.

"From my husband," Lizbet said with satisfaction.

Shortly afterwards Lizbet moved into three rooms that had once been occupied by Robert Fitzwarren.

There was little evidence of the previous owner; Jack told her that Robert had spent little time at the Fitzwarren house. When he was in London, he preferred to lodge with his cousin, Harry. Cleared of the detritus of the previous owner, the solidly furnished rooms pleased her well. The windows had heavy shutters, all three rooms had large fireplaces, and the floors were clad with thick rugs, the panelling dark and aged. It had been Edwin who told her that the rooms had once been the main rooms of the house before it was extended during the time of Richard's grandfather.

On either side of the fireplace in the bedroom hung two smoke-darkened portraits, one of a woman and another of a man. There was something in the woman's face she recognised, the dark guarded eyes, a mouth pressed into a thin line that looked as if it were about to smile. There was no doubting Richard's lineage; he had certainly inherited this woman's features.

Chapter Four

Newcastle 15ᵀᴴ January 1558

†

Richard had no recollection of the end of his journey from London. He woke in the dark, laid on a narrow cabin bed with a coarse blanket over him. Ruined boots were still on his feet, the leather soaked and split, the cobblers stitching barely holding the soles in place. Damper still was the long woollen tunic he wore that he'd stolen from the open window of a cottage north of York, the occupants absent, engaged in trying to round up a brood of piglets that had mysteriously broken free from their pen.

Slowly he pushed himself up on one elbow, joints and muscles stiffened with cold making his movements clumsy and slow. With effort, he hauled his legs over the bedside and sat, elbows on his knees, face covered by dirt-blackened palms. He had made it to the *Santa Luciana,* but that fact produced no sense of relief.

No human sound reached him; there was no thud of feet on the decks, the sound of voices quiet or raised was absent.

But he could hear the ship.

Buoyed up by the tide, there came the sound of her fenders catching on the quayside. A dull hollow knocking that seemed to have no definite source and travelled along the timbres like a sorrowful lamentation. Suddenly a drumming, woodpecker-like noise told of a taught rope stretching around a bollard, the stranded hemp complaining at the extra load as the *Santa*

Luciana tugged at her moorings like a hopeless captive in a cell. As if in answer to her pointless protest, screaming gulls issued piercing warnings, their disapproving vociferous shrieks heralding ill omens from high-up perches in her rigging. Timbres shifted and stretched, clicking and groaning as the tarred oak planking twisted between fixings and the pressure of the water, then settling back against the grasp of the sea: waiting.

Richard dropped his hands from his face, his breath pluming grey in the cold air, and, hands on his knees, he pushed himself to his feet, muscles and sinew throbbing as blood coursed through his frozen body. Emerging onto the deck of the *Santa Luciana,* he found her remaining masts and sail cloth stolen from view, enveloped in a cloud of fog. Grey, insubstantial and cold, it hung like a beggar's mantle over the deck, banishing the prow to obscurity.

Moving toward the guard rail, he could see nothing of the quay, and the water lapping quietly at her sides was blanketed beneath the early morning's doleful veil. Pressured again by the tide, the ship grumbled, rubbing her sides along the stonework of the quay. It was a good ten feet below him, swathed in the ethereal haze and hidden from view, as was the sea another fifteen feet below that. Muffled and distant, the sound of church bells reached him. The clattering chimes signalling the first mass of the day were strangely comforting.

Richard became aware of a cooling in the air around him, that slight drop in temperature that preceded the faint whisper of a breeze. It grew quickly in strength, the herald of rain, bearing an iced edge that set about clearing the fog from the harbour.

Cold, wet planking, dripping rigging weighed down with winter water, ropes rigid with cold, sail cloth solid with ice all began to reveal themselves as the wind gently pushed the fog seawards.

The eyes that viewed the *Santa Luciana* now saw her as a different ship. Robbed of promise and expectation, he saw the ruined aft castle, smashed guide rail, the hopelessness of the missing mast and rent sailcloth. A galleon bereft of her guns, plundered of anything of worth and riding too high against the rising tide rocking beneath his feet. The gulls continued above him with their discontented squall, high-pitched and laughter-like from lofty perches.

What had he done?

He'd fled from London. There had been no fear, no terror snapping at his heels. It had been a deliberate and considered desertion. One so decisive that he had taken the time to close and lock the doors behind him, then discarded the keys ....

The sound of a lock, the levers shuffling, sounded in his mind ...

Stop it.

Closing his eyes tight, he pushed the sound from his mind, banishing the image of a locked door. What had happened after the door had opened he wanted to dwell on even less.

"Fitzwarren!" A voice he recognised called his name across the deck, the tone bright and amused. "Have you gambled with your clothes again?"

Richard schooled his features and turned towards the speaker.

Jerome's assessing gaze ran over him slowly. "You were lucky. When they found you last night, the lads were tempted to heave you over the side. And you can be sure they'd not have wasted time stripping you naked before consigning you to the waves. God's bones, Fitzwarren, what are you wearing?"

"Repair work doesn't seem to have progressed in my absence," Richard replied, ignoring Jerome's comment.

"Were you robbed? That at least would be a reasonable explanation for your current state," Jerome continued, his eyes glittering with mischief.

Richard's dark eyes, filled with malice, bored into Jerome's.

"Not robbed then." Jerome stifled a laugh. "I stripped you of your clothes once over a game of cards. One can only hope it has happened a second time."

45

Richard folded his arms, his cold gaze fixed on the other man.

"So, not incautious gambling then, either?" Jerome's weathered face feigned a puzzled expression.

"Concern yourself less with my appearance and more with the tasks you were charged with completing." Richard delivered the words bitingly.

Jerome's eyebrows rose, and the smile dropped, forgotten, from his face. "If I've a master who appears as if he cannot afford to pay for the repairs or the pay for the lads on board the ship or, come to that, my fee, then it is my concern."

"A fair point," Richard replied but his voice was far from conciliatory. "Be assured that your fee will be paid."

Jerome nodded slowly. "And the lads?"

"As well."

"And I've bills for timber to pay ...."

"The situation, Jerome, remains unchanged," Richard replied scathingly.

Jerome nodded. "And going forward?"

"The *Santa Luciana* will be repaired and sail, as planned to the Indies," Richard's voice bore a warning note.

Jerome chose to ignore the warning and pressed on like a terrier, "And will you be joined by anyone else, or was it a solitary journey from London?"

"I am, unhappily, without a weapon. A fact that you should be grateful for."

Jerome's brows rose, his face a picture of shocked innocence. Palms outstretched towards Richard, he said, "Master, you mistake my intentions."

"Do I?" Richard growled.

"I ask only so that we may know if preparations are needed for more guests on board," Jerome paused adding, "Also, I have had a letter from your brother. He was insistent that I convey the message to you that you should contact him if I encountered you."

"Where is it?"

"It's in my.... your cabin," Jerome corrected a crooked smile on his face.

Pressing by Jerome, Richard headed back below deck. Jerome followed but too slowly, finding himself standing alone in the narrow passageway, listening to the sound of the bolt sliding home on the inside of the door. In Richard's absence he had taken to using the cabin, however it seemed that particular tenure was now at an end. About to retrace his steps, he stopped when the bolt grated once more.

"It seems this is not all you've helped yourself to." Richard thrust an empty flask that had once held aqua vitae towards Jerome's chest. "Refill it!"

Jerome accepted the flask, stepping backwards, a look of grim disapproval on his face, and asked, "Just the one?"

The door slammed shut in his face.

"Two then," Jerome said to himself and, sighing, headed back towards the deck ladders.

Jerome had taken the cabin as it was the only one that had any real natural light. The table was set at an angle in the cabin so that it was best illuminated. Upon it, Jerome's papers sat in ordered piles. Leafing through them, Richard quickly found the message from his brother. It was brief and penned in Jack's hand, the pen strokes decisive, the spluttered ink betraying the urgency of the message. Richard read the first few lines, then sent the page spinning across the table to land on the floor.

Jack .... he didn't want to think about Jack.

Or anything else.

Chapter Five
Newcastle – 30th January 1559

Newcastle was a town in the grip of new ownership. The mining of coal had once been under the control of the monasteries that held title over the lands, but when Henry stripped them of their wealth, the land fell into the hands of the local nobles, and so did the rights to mine them. The monasteries had kept production low and prices high, but now the black seams beneath the ground were under new masters who wished to exploit them for as much as they were worth.

A steadily rising trade was in place now, shipping coal to London and city's appetite for it was increasing. Under the control of Hostmen, who also titled themselves the Company of Merchant Adventurers of Newcastle, their business was booming. And one such Adventurer, Richard Brandling, traded his wares in London with a merchant of some notoriety, Myles Devereux. Hasty yet effective arrangements made before Richard had left London meant there was money he could access in Newcastle.

The letter Richard now had in his possession had come north on one of Brandling's returning ships, the hull filled with coal dust and little else as it sailed empty back to Newcastle. The parchment had been tightly folded, sealed and locked. All that was visible on the outside was the alias Richard occasionally used – *R. Garrett*. The folded and cut sheet of intricately twisted paper was firmly bonded together; threaded through a hole in the pages was a thin slice of parchment cut from the original sheet, twisted and tied tightly around the folded bundle and finally fixed in place with a thick layer of wax.

Richard placed it on the table before him, regarding it for a moment. It was Myles' own work, of that he was sure. His sharp mind and long, delicate fingers would no doubt have revelled in the process of producing the secure letter. Myles understood it would take time and care to open, knew it could not be read the moment it was received, and Myles would have delighted in delivering the painful wait. Somewhere in the back of his mind he could hear Devereux's delighted laughter.

Sighing, Richard broke the wax that held down the thin strip of paper and began the process of unfolding the sheet. The narrow locking length had been cut from the page's centre, twisted and rolled to make it thin enough to pierce the hole through the page and, predictably, it had sliced its way through the centre of Myles' carefully written text. Richard unrolled it slowly; the paper would have been moist when rolled but now dry, it threatened to crack and destroy the sender's message. Finally, the inked slice of paper was free, and he pressed it down to fill the gap in the sheet, supplying the missing words and letters.

Richard, knowing the writer well, started at the bottom of the letter – Myles would not have presented the message he wanted read easily. He was right, added almost as a post-script, the words purposefully cleaved by the knife, Myles had written - *"I can also inform you that you are not a widower."*

Richard rocked back in the chair, releasing the page that curled and twisted back around the creases, the thinly cut slice springing from the desk and rolling back in on itself.

It was all he had wanted to know.

There was more on the page, another dozen or so neatly penned lines in Myles' efficient hand. For a moment, Richard's hand hovered over the sheet, about to hold the loose section of paper in place to read the rest of the message. His eyes snatched at one word on the sheet: Cecil.

"I'll not play your games, Devereux, nor anyone else's." Richard swept the parchment from the desk. White against the dark wood of the cabin floor, it glared up at him.

Tempting him.

From a dark corner of his mind, he could hear Myles' voice ridiculing him.

"Damn you to Hell!"

Swiping the sheet from the floor, he fed one corner to the eager flame of the oil lamp. When it was alight, he let it fall to the floor and watched as the sheet blazed into a moment of yellow and orange glory. When the sheet was as black as the ink that had been printed upon it a booted foot extinguished the last of the flames spreading the letters ash across the floor.

†

With gold in his possession once more and divested of the clothing that had disintegrated during the journey north, Jerome accepted Richard's presence with much more enthusiasm and the distressed state of his arrival on the ship was not referred to again.

Richard also found that, despite appearances, plenty of repair work had been carried out. Broken timbers where the burnt mast had sat had been stripped out, the hull repaired and strengthened, waiting only for delivery of the new mast. The wood for that had been prepared in a nearby workshop, iron hoops fitted along the length. Another week and it was expected that it would be attached to the *Santa Luciana* and the ship would once again be able to hoist a full complement of sails.

The deck of the ship had become a temporary workplace for carpenters and shipwrights. Two workshops had been set up, tented beneath canvas from the ruined sail Emilio had cut free. Their wooden frames were lashed to the galleon's hull, the canvas pulled taught over the top and fastened bow-tight with ropes. Beneath them, braziers burnt, anvils sat next to a shave-horse and tools lay ready on workbenches. Jerome had explained that the arrangement gave him control not only over those employed to carry out work but also over the materials, tools and the physical progress they were making. The mistakes that had occurred in Spain were not about to be repeated under Jerome's command.

Above deck, the *Santa Luciana* had a patchwork appearance. Fresh pale wood had been spliced into the aft and forecastles to repair the damaged structures. Guardrails, smashed by the careless storm, bore lengths of fresh new wood. Grills on the decks, allowing light to seep below, were new and firm fitting and sat in pale contrast with the darker wood of the deck, much of which was still scorched from the original fire. Jerome explained that he wanted the decks weatherproof before he started work on the ship lower down.

Below deck, an oil lamp in his hand, Jerome led the way. Richard followed at a slower pace, treading carefully on the neigh vertical ladders that descended into the bowels of the ship.

The flame, protected by a glass shroud, threw a crescent of helpful light onto the inner hull but did little to banish the endless black night that stretched fore and aft. Richard, casting a glance into the night, knew Jack would have found this cramped dark space nothing less than Stygian. The temperature had fallen as well; Richard watched as Jerome's breath escaped into the hold in a billowing grey cloud.

"All the ballast has been cleared from here, and you can see the problem," Jerome held the lamp closer to the hull in the cramped space.

Richard could indeed see the damage.

The ship was caravel built: the shipwright had begun with laying the keel, attaching to this the stem and sternpost then along the length of the keel a series of skeletal beams and frames reached up over. To these were fixed the horizontal planking that formed the hull; three full-lengths were missing, and two more were staved in, although they remained attached to the vertical supports, they were splintered mid-length.

"That happened during the storm?"

Jerome nodded. "We were close to seeing her smashed on the rocks."

"It's above the water line, though." Richard moved across the bottom of the hull to the damaged area in front of Jerome. Light was seeping through the planking.

"It is now," Jerome chuckled, "but we took on plenty of water through here." Jerome ran his hands along the damaged wood.

"What did we hit?" Richard said, looking at the ravaged wood.

"The sea, nothing more," Jerome answered.

"Christ, I'd not know waves alone could inflict such damage," Richard replied, his eyes on the hull.

"You've a lot to learn yet, lad," Jerome said, then offering Richard the lamp, he said, "Hold that."

Jerome navigated his way along the bottom of the ship with his usual agility until he reached the first vertical support attached to the keel at the end of the run of damaged planking. Pointing he said, "Can you see the vertical supports are varying in their distance along the keel. Towards the front they are closer together, but here, their distance is at its widest. Pressured from the outside, the hull could flex there more easily, and the repeated battering from the sea was enough to smash the wood."

"That water can inflict such damage seems ..."

"Incredible?" Jerome offered.

Richard nodded, then asked. "Can it be repaired?"

"It can, and a horizontal will be added here as well," Jerome waved his arms above his head to indicate what he meant. "That will brace these timbers and add extra support for the hull."

The inspection continued for another hour, Jerome showing Richard everything he wanted, either repairing, replacing or completely rebuilt. Two hours later, they were seated in Richard's cabin on opposite sides of the small table. Weighted down with a dented pewter cup were several drawings of the *Santa Luciana*. Richard slid them from beneath the weight, pulling them towards him. A cresset lamp, the body a highly polished bronze, centred with a fat cotton wick and hung from the ceiling on three chains provided the main illumination. On the desk, another, filled with brown tallow, burned with a steady orange flame little disturbed by draught.

Jerome reached across the desk and tapped a finger on the top one. "This is how I propose to arm her. I want to move the powder room here as well."

Richard examined the diagram. "Why move it?"

"I want it lower down, and when we are repairing the hull here, it is the perfect time to relocate it. The lower, the better, I prefer to keep it as far away from a chance shot as possible," Jerome supplied.

"What about the water? We've just been down there. It's damp, hardly a good place to keep it, surely?" Richard's head was still bent over Jerome's illustration of the ship.

"Copper lined and sealed from below the store will keep the moisture out, and I am guessing you will not be carrying as much black powder on her as she would have had when she was equipped as a fighting ship, so the store can be smaller, and we can access it here, from the gun deck," Jerome's finger end tapped another part of the neatly penned image of the ship, "there's plenty of room, we have Henry's flagship to thank for that."

Richard's brow furrowed, looking up, he asked, "The *Mary Rose*?"

Jerome nodded. "Much was learned from her sinking. Ships like the *Santa Luciana* built afterwards changed in design. It was quite a unique occasion."

Richard said with some sarcasm. "I can't image old Henry seeing it as such. I've heard accounts that he was so apoplectic with rage that those closest to him feared his heart would give out."

"I'm afraid that's why the event was so significant," Jerome replied.

"Because it nearly killed the King?" Richard said dryly.

"No, no...." Jerome paused, seemed to change his mind, and rather than continuing, asked instead, "You've an enquiring mind: why do you think the moment the *Mary Rose* sank was so pivotal?"

Richard leaned back in his chair, folding his arms across his chest. "Jerome, it's late, and I'm too tired to continue this game of master and apprentice."

Jerome smiled. "You said you wished to learn - this is the task you charged me with."

Richard sighed deeply before continuing. "Rarely, I would imagine, have the commander of the fleet and the wife of the captain been afforded the opportunity to witness the sinking of the ship."

Jerome nodded. "You are, of course, right."

"Carew was her captain, and I'm sure you've heard the reports of his final words. They were hardly those to inspire confidence in the ship's newly appointed commander," Richard replied, then continued, "allegedly he shouted to his uncle as he sailed by her that the crew were the sort of knaves that he could not rule."

"And what do you make of that?" Jerome continued with his questions.

"I see your time as the master continues. Afterwards, it came to light that Carew had been given command of the flagship that day; he didn't know the officers, he'd never sailed her before, and he was a man on display before the King – those who knew him alleged he overly indulged in self-confidence."

"True, it was his first naval command, and the crew and officers were expected to carry him, and his words perhaps hint at some argument between his command and those beneath him," Jerome mused.

"The chain of command would have been relatively short, he would only be communicating his orders with his senior officers, and they had been onboard since her refit, so his crew were experienced in handling her," Richard said.

"Then what happened?" Jerome asked.

"She fired a volley from her starboard side, and it appeared she came about to deliver a second volley from her port side. However she heeled over in the wind, turned too quickly, her sails caught the breeze, and she dipped too far towards the waves. The starboard gun doors were still open and once the sea entered these there was little chance for her," Richard supplied matter-of-factly.

Jerome fished amongst the papers on the desk until he found the one he wanted. "Look at the *Santa Luciana*, her betwixt decks are much higher than those of the *Mary Rose*, and her fore and aft castles much lower."

"The *Santa Luciana* is a much smaller ship; she must be ..." Richard paused momentarily, "around a third of the size."

"The *Mary Rose* was six hundred tonnes, the *Santa Luciana* three hundred and fifty, but the same principals of design apply. She'd not seen action since her refit; as the flagship of Henry's fleet, the fore and aft castles were raised in height, and canon were added to them. To support the extra weight, the hull was strengthened; much of this was above the waterline. Her previous Captain, Dudley, described her as 'unweatherly' after the alternations," Jerome explained.

"'Unweatherly'," Richard chuckled. "Blame not the ship, nor her designers, not Henry who oversaw the refit personally but blame the elements. A much safer course of action."

"Indeed. And on her final voyage, Carew had around five hundred fully armed men on his decks. Many of those poor souls were in full armour. The likelihood must be that when the ship turned to bring her portside guns to bear that some of them may well have lost their balance. There were reports of men crashing across her decks and even falling over the side rails long before her full plight was known. Now, if you have the weight of three hundred men, who were at one moment spread evenly across the deck and the next staggering towards her starboard side, that shift in weight alone is going to add to her plight."

"And not just the weight of the men: armed and with half-armour that would be an additional weight per man of around fifty pounds, added to that the weight of each man and the free weight on her decks would have been...." Richard paused, looking up and meeting Jerome's gaze.

"Go on ...."

"Forty-five tonnes," Richard supplied the answer, "But she had carried more than this before. A thousand troops sailed on her to the battle at Flodden in Northumberland and they would have been similarly armed and double the weight."

"Agreed, but that was in 1513, before the refit and the raised decks. It has been argued that the guns came free of their carriages and careered to the starboard side. That will have happened, but not until she was long beyond the point of no return," Jerome replied.

"So this unsecured weight sealed her fate?" Richard asked.

"As you will find out when we go to sea, it's rarely any one action that leads to catastrophe but more a combination of effects. In the case of the *Mary Rose*, it is probable that an inexperienced captain, desperate to impress, turned too quickly to bring his guns to bear for a second volley, eager to secure victory for his on-looking sovereign. The canting decks unsettled the soldiers, decks that were now too high up on a ship that had become overly heavy, and the sudden change in weight distribution along with the tight turn, tipped her towards the waves," Jerome replied.

"The flooded gun deck and the loosened canon would then serve only to take her to the seabed even quicker," Richard concluded.

"Invariably, one mistake alone will not sink a ship. It is only where one leads to another that the problems begin," Jerome concluded.

"Another lesson delivered," Richard replied.

"If you like. But I am rather sure you would not like to be stood in Carew's boots," Jerome admonished.

"Like Jack, I prefer my feet to be dry," Richard replied.

Chapter Six

London 5TH April - 1559

The travel-stained and weary messenger who waited to see the Queen was Colin Campbell, half-brother of the Earl of Argyll. Campbell had held in his possession a letter from Scotland that he had been charged with delivering to the English Queen. It had not been a part of his plans, or those of the writers, to have the document poured over by one of her officers of state; a fact he had made plain since his arrival in Cecil's presence.

"This letter, sir, bears the seal of the Congregation and is for the eyes of Her Majesty. I am charged with its delivery and taking back the answer, should there be one," Campbell's reasonable tone was beginning to slip in the face of Cecil's continued disregard for either him or the importance of his missive. The document in question had been handed by Cecil some time ago to one of his officers and taken from the room despite Campbell's protests.

With two liveried men standing behind the chair he was seated in there was little he could do to prevent the letter from being removed from his presence apart from complain and Cecil, his spectacles fixed upon his nose, and his attention upon other documents before him, seemed quite capable of ignoring his protestations.

When Campbell had finally cursed the Queen's official a threatening hand had been clamped upon his shoulder and a painful squeeze of sinew and muscle had turned his tirade of protest into a feral yelp of pain.

Eventually Cecil's man returned with the folded parchment that had been given into this keeping and placed it before Cecil. The seal, neatly and firmly affixed, had been sprung intact from the sheet.

Campbell could stand it no more and made to rise from his chair. "Sir, that is for the Queen's eyes, not yours."

Firm hands on both of his shoulders forced him back into his chair, the wooden legs thudding on the bare boards of the floor. Cecil, ignoring him, adjusted his glasses and carefully opened the sheet - his attention on the neatly penned lines and the group of signatures that were penned at the base of the letter.

Finally he lifted his eyes from the page and met the messenger's. "No code? No precautions? I am disappointed."

"The letter was delivered under my protection; it was to be read by the Queen. We stand by our intent and have no need to skulk behind codes and ciphers," Campbell spat back.

Cecil tapped his fingers absently on his desk, his gaze unfocussed for a moment, lost in thought, a single deep crease dividing his brows. Rising suddenly he swept the sheet from the desk, instructed the guards to continue in their restraint of Campbell and departed from the room.

†

Somer was about to depart for his home. Swathed in furs, a cap trimmed with a fox's pelt pulled around his ears, he was heading, with his attendants, towards one of the landing stages when Cecil's men caught up with him.

Guards stepped aside as Somer followed Cecil into his outer office, brightly lit, it was a hive of activity. Four blackened finger scribes, industriously engaged, heads bent to their work, didn't even look up as Cecil entered. Apart from a narrow passage to Cecil's own office door the room was full with as many desks as would fit. One wall bore a series of wooden trays, some with documents, some empty, some in use to hold office detritus with jars of pens, ink pots, sealing wax jumbled into them. Two more guards taking up valuable floor space were positioned either side of Cecil's office door, the key holder was the one on the left and at the sight of his master he had stooped to open the wooden door that filled the stone Norman arch.

"Must you really drag me in here?" Somer complained as the door was closed behind him.

Hanging from the roof, a dark metal chandelier, suspended on chains, provided the main illumination above the desk. It was so low that Somer estimated Cecil would need to rise from his desk with care to avoid the iron contraption. Every windowless wall was packed with documents Cecil had no care to share, and before each a tall floor mounted oil lamp, the flame shielded by glass, threw a steady orange light upon the documents.

"You'll ruin your eyesight working in here," Somer grumbled, lowering himself into the purposefully uncomfortable visitors chair, with one eye on Cecil's lighting arrangements to ensure his hat didn't catch fire.

"This is not a conversation for the corridors, Somer," Cecil rebuked seating himself opposite Somer.

"I was returning home. Is there really an issue that could not wait until the morrow?" Somer complained.

Cecil didn't answer, instead he reversed the paper that was set before him and slid it across the desk towards Somer.

Somer leaned over the sheet, reading it slowly.

"Does Her Majesty know?" Somer said at length, raising his eyes from the parchment and looking directly at Cecil, his annoyance at being delayed now forgotten.

Cecil answered with a shake of his head. "It seemed prudent to formulate a response before presenting this news."

"A wise decision. The problem of Scotland is a complex one." Somer reversed the sheet; finding nothing on the back of the note he flipped it back to the side tightly packed with neatly inked characters. "The bloody congregation in Scotland are overreaching themselves. No codes and with little preamble they are practically demanding Her Majesty support them."

"The naivety of the righteous, I agree," Cecil replied, leaning toward Somer, his elbows on the desk.

"How was this delivered?" Somer asked, stabbing the page with an ink stained finger.

"Colin Campbell, the Earl of Argyll's half-brother, delivered it. The congregation obviously thought that he was expendable should we fail to return him along with the reply." Cecil provided dryly.

"If Knox is to return from exile and unite the Scots against their French overlords then that's their business. I find it hard to believe they are asking Her Majesty to offer Knox her protection, to allow him to arrive in London then provide him with a safe passage north." Somer said incredulously, the room was warm and he swiped the fur cap from his head,

"If circumstances were different then he might have proved useful," Cecil grumbled tugging his beard.

Somer laughed, rocking back in the chair and making the aged woodwork creak. "From what I have heard Her Majesty will not even have his name spoken in her presence."

"You've heard correctly, I am afraid." Cecil said, spreading his hands wide on the desk, "If there was one man who could rally the Scots against Mary De Guise, it is Knox. From the nobles to the base born he could gather them to his cause and press them to evict the

French. Unfortunately he is one Protestant not to Her Majesty's taste."

Somer pointed an arthritic finger towards Cecil, stabbing the air between them. "That would be an act of persuasion that is even beyond you. The Queen will never countenance any association with Knox. He is a man who has made his position far too clear. For God's sake he even called for England to rise up against its anointed monarch."

"True, but that was when Mary was on the throne," Cecil pointed out, leaning back in his chair and raising his hands in the air,

"It makes no difference, his opinions on female monarchs have not changed. You would have thought that the man would have seen sense; there was much for him to gain politically had he revised his opinions. He could have drawn English support more readily for the Scots cause but no ... the man continues to stand by his words," Somer complained. "This, however, is proof that not all of Scotland is happy with French rule. We've long suspected that Argyll and Stewart were against sharing their sovereignty with France; now they have drawn to their cause considerable support."

"The Scottish could never recognise a good thing if it were boiled in a clootie pudding and served to them on a platter," Cecil replied sarcastically. "Greed for power is what drives them, Somer, especially men like Argyll. They are in the position to lose the most; they could be ousted from their posts on the council, replaced by men the De Guise's choose. That's why this has come about. Scotland benefited greatly from her alliance; only pig headed men like this can't see it."

"You are in favour of France's hold over Scotland?" Somer said, surprise in his voice.

"Of course not! I am simply pointing out all the advantages the nation has gained through their alliance that the fools cannot recognise. There has been a building programme, French troops offer security and French rule has also offered Scotland a degree of stability it has rarely enjoyed."

"It is often the nature of man to not recognise a gift," Somer replied, the fingers on his right hand tapping on the desk.

"It plays into our hands well, though. We also do not want the enemy lined up at our northern border and if Argyll and his supporters wish to oust the and have asked for Her Majesty's help then she would be a fool to refuse," Cecil's voice was quiet, but clear, and he leaned towards Somer.

"It would be a desirous outcome, no-one would argue otherwise. The risk is that if England assists these rogue Scottish rebels then we risk war with France," Somer pointed out flatly.

Cecil took the letter from the desk and waved it under Somer's nose. "And do you think for a moment that France does not already know of this? I would wager that a copy of this is already in France and another with Mary De Guise. This is a game where England cannot be seen to be in direct support of Argyll and, because of this," Cecil flapped the letter in the air again, "we have little choice but to act. France will suspect we will have a hand in any move against the De Guises. We just need to ensure that they cannot prove it."

"Will Her Majesty risk taking action? She is adamant she wishes to steer a path that keeps England safe from the risk of war with France and I am inclined to agree with the sentiment. War is something the Crown coffers can ill afford," Somer said, slapping his right hand down hard on the desk.

"So England provides support for the ousting of France from Scotland but there must be no proof of it," Cecil replied, his eyes narrowing.

Somer laughed, the noise harsh and without humour. "How can that be arranged? Argyll is not only asking for a safe passage for Knox but also for funds, troops and diplomatic support. How can any of that be quietly provided?"

"What he asks for and what he gets might be two very different things," Cecil countered, the corner of his mouth twitching into a smile.

"I can tell from the tone of your voice that you have a plan," Somer said guardedly, pointing a forefinger that was no longer entirely straight towards Cecil, the joints swollen with age.

"Financial support could be provided, funds to allow Argyll to raise an army against the De Guises," Cecil said spreading his hands flat on the desk.

"Financial support? I wish you luck, Her Majesty will be hardly persuaded to give away gold to fickle Scottish nobles, gold that could end up in French hands," Somer scoffed, rocking back in his chair, the woodwork creaking in complaint.

Cecil inclined his head, saying patiently. "A sum of six thousand pounds would allow Argyll to raise an army, one of sufficient size to allow him to take Edinburgh and hold it from French hands. France will soon know about this plea for help and despatch French ships to bolster Scotland. As soon as they are spotted sailing north it would be only reasonable for Her Majesty to despatch an army to secure our Northern border and once there the moment can be judged as to whether to assist or not."

"If we assist it will be an open declaration of war against France," Somer, flustered, rose from the chair and began pacing around the cramped office. "This is not a safe course of action."

"I agree. But if France is ousted from Scotland and it looks as if this was a rebellion cited by her nobles then there are few grounds to raise an army against England," Cecil remained seated, his eyes on Somer as he strode around the room.

Somer stopped, placing both hands on the desk, he leaned towards Cecil. "That outcome rests upon a lot of uncertainty."

"We are afforded little choice. We must press for an outcome where we can assist the Scots to overthrow the De Guises with as little blame being attached to English blades as possible. For this we need Knox, he could unite Scotland, draw the wavering lords to his cause."

"You spoke of six thousand pounds to back Argyll, can you trust him?" Somer questioned.

"Can you trust any man with that amount of gold?" Cecil scoffed. "Six thousand pounds is the amount he has asked for – it's not the amount he's going to get. Our response, if is to be taken seriously, will need to be backed by some gold but not that much."

"So how to you propose to ensure that the gold is used for the correct means and not pocketed by Argyll? And at the same time make sure Knox steers Scotland in the right direction – turning her against France and not England?" Somer, feeling the heat from the fire, shrugged his cloak from his shoulders and dropped it over the chair back.

"That is, indeed, the crux of the matter," Cecil grumbled. "To find a trusted party that could be distanced from the Crown if need be."

Somer laughed, retaking his seat at the table. "I'd wager you are regretting your treatment of Fitzwarren now."

Cecil's mouth set into a hard line.

"I have to say, it was a rather rash act, not one I would have credited you with," Somer continued, his eyes fixed upon Cecil's.

"All men can weaken when offered such an opportunity as that, I'll agree the temptation was one I could not resist," Cecil said, adding, "there were other issues involved, ones I cannot discuss, and Fitzwarren needed his wings clipping."

"He is a man who often needs to be kept in check, however, he'll need his feathers if he's to be of any use to you. Rumour has it you've lost him, even his brother cannot find him," Somer replied.

Cecil let out a long breath before he replied. "Like the knight on the chess board he is backed into a corner awaiting instructions."

Somer's brows raised and a broad smile spread across his face. "So you do know where he is? But will he work for you, Cecil, after what you did?"

"That might depend upon what choices are placed before him I would imagine. Richard Fitzwarren, is nothing, if not practical."

†

The Gentlemen Ushers outside the Queen's privy chamber informed Cecil that that Her Majesty was taking a later dinner and he would need to wait. Forced to contain his impatience he waited. Dinner was served usually at noon and he'd timed his visit to coincide with the meals conclusion, or so he had thought. There was much on his desk that he needed to attend to, and the loss of an hour waiting for an audience was not welcome. He grumbled inwardly even more when he found out the loss was attributable to something as trivial as Lady Dray's new lap dog that been the centre of attention in the Queen's private garden.

The doors opened at last and a procession of servants laden with trays carried away plates and food, his presence was announced and shortly after the door was held open so he could admit himself. Five of her ladies were still present, entertaining themselves holding out left over pieces of food as the willing dog balanced on its hind legs pawing the air.

"Do we witness the talents of the trainer or the dog?" Elizabeth said smiling, as Cecil bowed towards her.

Cecil forced himself to smile towards the annoying animal. "A combination of both, perhaps."

Elizabeth laughed. "Ever the diplomat!"

"I have a sensitive issue to discuss, Your Majesty," Cecil winced as the small dog began to let out a series of shrill barks.

"It can count, if you were wondering," Elizabeth replied pointing towards the source of the noise. "Hold up your hand, Lilly."

One of the ladies did as commanded, the fingers spread wide. The dog sat and then barked five times, Swapping hands to her left she held up three fingers and the dog obligingly barked three times.

"Amazing, Your Majesty," Cecil said dryly.

"If only all my subjects were as obedient," Elizabeth's mouth was pressed into a thin hard line, and the eyes that regarded him were cold.

Cecil, perhaps a little too hastily, outlined the request that had been received from the Congregation and the need to support the Scottish against the French.

"Six thousand pounds!" Elizabeth's wide eyes regarded him with shock.

"Your Majesty..." Cecil attempted for the second time.

"Six thousand pounds!" Elizabeth rounded on her most senior advisor. "And what assurances can there be that this sum will be used for the purposes for which it is sent? There are none. England's gold could be spirited away, Scotland will be the richer and I shall be viewed as a fool, sir."

"Your Majesty, please, this is an opportunity and we must consider all of the possibilities," Cecil tried again, his voice firm

"You, sir, seem to have failed to consider the possibility that you will make me poorer and for little gain: that is the risk. I cannot send my nobles to Scotland, can I? We have little opportunity, if any, to ensure that these funds would be used as we intend."

Cecil opened his mouth to speak but Elizabeth's small pale, ringed hand raised, stopping him.

"There is more at stake here than the issue of gold. We cannot be viewed as being complicit with the Scots," Elizabeth said, her expression threatening.

"But, Your Majesty, if we do nothing Argyll and his supporters are still likely to rise up against the De Guises and without sufficient backing they are likely to fail. And by their folly, not ours, they have made their plan to ask for English assistance known so we will be blamed anyway for an uprising and, if it is unsuccessful, we will have a French army on our northern border," Cecil's explained patiently.

Elizabeth's right hand balled in a fist and slammed down hard onto a wooden table top setting an ink pot to rattle and threatening to upset a wine glass that sat there. "Don't treat me like a fool, I am well appraised of where I stand in the middle of this."

Cecil, unperturbed by his sovereigns outburst continued, his voice reasoned. "I have a proposal that I think you might find acceptable."

Elizabeth turned on him, her arms folded, and fixing him with a terrible stare, her voice quiet. "Do you indeed."

"If we can send the funds north and ensure that support is provided from another quarter that is not linked to yourself then, should the Scots fail to oust the De Guises, the rebellion will not be linked to England. And should the action be a success it will matter little what the French think because they will no longer be staring at us across the Scottish border," Cecil said matter-of-factly.

"They will still know we are complicit with this plan, no matter what happens."

"Your Majesty, they will blame us even if we do nothing, so having a hand on the tiller and retaining some control over the navigation of this venture is to our advantage. If we do nothing and Argyll fails, we could be facing a war with France, it is to our advantage to ensure his success." Cecil replied.

"And if he succeeds then will we not simply be facing a war with France anyway?" Elizabeth's top teeth were biting into her bottom lip and a deep furrow divided her brows.

"It is a risk, however the more we can distance Your Majesty from the support provided to Argyll the more unlikely it would be that France would be able to call their nobles into action to make a war upon England. War not only drained our coffers but did little for the French and there are many who have no taste to continue the conflict between our two nations," Cecil provided his hands spread wide.

"I too have barely any desire for war," Elizabeth replied. "You have, no doubt, given this much thought. The figure of six thousand pounds doubtless is one that has been costed in detail. And where do you intend to conjuror this support for Argyll, from Ireland perhaps?" Elizabeth quizzed.

Cecil shook his head. "I shall come to the point."

Elizabeth's eyebrows raised a degree.

Cecil, ignoring his sovereign's expression, continued. "Send a small force north led by a man whose loyalty to yourself you can believe in."

"A trusted man would be a man known to be loyal to the crown?" Elizabeth interjected.

"Most would be, however there is a one, recently known to have lost your favour who...."

Elizabeth rounded upon Cecil. "I've been manipulated once, Burghley, do not think I have forgotten, or even forgiven."

Cecil bowed his head. "Your Majesty, I have begged forgiveness, it was a folly for which I am most humbly sorry. But it has provided a few possibilities."

"Only you could see a profit from this," Elizabeth rebuked, then added, "how so?"

"He is a man out of favour; surely acting for Your Majesty on this mission would be something he would readily accept if it would reinstate your favour and his position at Court," Cecil replied quickly.

Elizabeth remained silent and walked slowly towards the window. Her back to Cecil she said, "You know where he is?"

"I don't, Your Majesty. But enquiries can be made; Fitzwarren is not a man to hide away for long," Cecil lied smoothly, "It would be believable that after, erm, recent events, Fitzwarren would seek a new master. He has acted in a mercenary capacity before and it is reasonable to suppose he would take up that role again, especially if a profit were offered."

"And you believe he can be persuaded to carry out this?" Elizabeth replied.

Cecil smiled. "I am sure he would wish once again to be restored to your favour, and what better proof could there be."

Elizabeth agreed in principal with his plan, she did not however agree to the sum of six thousand pounds and the amount that was to be extracted from the royal coffers was a third of that amount. It was a figure Cecil was in agreement with. However, he was wise enough to know that if he had suggested two thousand pounds he would have received little more than five hundred.

Chapter Seven

Newcastle - 1559

After two more weeks of repair work, Jerome had declared the *Santa Luciana* seaworthy once more and had finally been released from the quay and turned towards the sea. Richard had toiled alongside the crew and workmen, the hard work leading to dreamless nights for which he was grateful. Once the ship left port, the workload increased further.

Richard knew that the trials Jerome had put himself and the crew through were to ensure the *Santa Luciana* and the men onboard worked harmoniously. His muscles ached, his hair was crisped with dried salt from the sea spray, and his clothing was perpetually damp. Despite the season and a stiff wind with an icy edge, there had been no time to become cold. Jerome kept them working, there was never a free moment to think of anything other than the task at hand, and for that, Richard was thankful. The ship travelled slowly south for four weeks, her crew practising drills, learning how she turned in the wind and how her sails were best rigged.

Passing Jerome's cabin, Richard headed towards his own to claim his reward of peaceful sleep after a long day. His hand reaching for the door, he stopped when he heard the familiar voice behind him.

"A good day, lad. Have you a moment spare? I've some questions I'd like to put?" Jerome said.

Richard noted that Jerome's voice bore no trace of his own weariness despite Jerome having worked alongside the men all day.

Richard let his hand fall back to his side and turned toward Jerome with a tired smile. "Are they questions that need answers tonight?"

"Tonight would be as good a night as any." Jerome disappeared back inside his own cabin, leaving the door open.

Richard, sighing and resolving that the detour would only be short, entered Jerome's cabin, closing the door behind him.

Jerome had unrolled on the table before him the map that Richard had last seen when he had used it to try and persuade Jack to travel on the *Santa Luciana* to the Indies. An ink pot, a pewter tankard, a trencher and the hilt of a knife were all employed to hold the map flat on the table.

"We are at the start of a voyage, my lad." Jerome had a flask in one hand and two cups in the other.

Richard closed the door behind him and took the cup Jerome held out for him.

"This will be our last stop in England, here," Jerome's finger tapped the map, "We'll take on fresh water and more supplies at Hull before we sail south. And the gallant sail needs repair, there's some minor damage to one of the clews. Easily fixed, but we'll need to bring it down onto the deck to stitch it properly."

"How long before we arrive?" Richard asked, leaning forward to examine the map.

"Tomorrow," Jerome said, smiling.

"I thought we were still much further north," Richard replied, raising his eyes from the map to meet Jerome's.

"We might have spent the last week putting you and the lads to the test, but we've also made good progress along the coast. We have been heading in the right direction at the same time. Did you think we were going around in circles?" Jerome asked, laughing. Lifting the flask from the table, he slopped more of the aqua vitae into Richard's cup before topping up his own.

"You've kept me that busy I hadn't given it much thought," Richard admitted, draining his cup quickly before setting it down on the table.

"Sit down, lad. I've a few questions to ask," Jerome said urgently.

"Can they not wait until tomorrow?" Richard said wearily.

Jerome laughed again. "I've ten years on you, lad, at least. Surely you are not going to concede defeat?"

"You might have more years, but you also spent your day with your feet planted on the deck while you had me climbing the ropes, re-rigging the top gallant twice. My feet, unlike yours, spent little time on the deck today," Richard replied, still standing.

"Well, you'd not have had to do it twice if you'd got it right the first time. You can't captain a ship unless you know how it works," Jerome replied.

"I'm paying you for that role," Richard said dryly.

"And a captain needs a second, and that, my lad, is you, and you're taking some knocking into shape, but we'll get there over the next few months," Jerome replied.

"Was that meant as a compliment?" Richard asked.

"It was. Will you sit down?" Jerome refilled the empty cup, "It would take five years in the Order to learn your skills, five long hard years, and even then, there would be no guarantee that you would receive a commission of your own."

Reluctantly Richard pulled the small stool away from the table and sat down opposite Jerome. "You must have been lucky then."

"Luck was not on my side," Jerome said, putting his cup down solidly on the desk.

"How long do you think it will take to reach the coast of Africa?" Richard asked, his right hand's index finger tapping the continent's northern coastline.

"We are not in a hurry. You told me that yourself," Jerome said.

"I'm not in a hurry. It seems sensible to test the *Luciana* and her new crew in familiar waters before we venture into seas that even you've not travelled before," Richard said in agreement.

Jerome nodded, the flat of his hand smoothing the map, swept over the inlet that was the Mediterranean. "It seems strange to me that we shall sail by this."

"You still wish to return?" Richard said a bemused note in his voice.

Jerome let out a long breath. "Everyone is entitled to identify somewhere as home. These shores, this sea and the islands within it are mine. Familiarity is something we all yearn for on occasion."

"Familiarity, yes, but I don't think you would receive a warm homecoming," Richard replied, his eyes following Jerome's hands where they lay on the map on either side of the small island of Malta.

Jerome looked up and met his gaze, asking, "Did your father not make your homecoming a difficult one?"

"Slightly more than difficult: he tried to kill me," Richard replied darkly.

"Well, I think the homecoming the Grand Master would extend to me would be of the same order," Jerome replied, his eyes on the map.

"De Nevarra told me something of what happened," Richard said.

"He was only speaking the truth as he knows it," Jerome replied, his eyes still on the map.

"De Nevarra is many things, but amongst them I don't regard him as a liar. I'll not pry into your past, Jerome. It's late if there's nothing else...." Richard placed his palms on the table's edge and began to rise.

"What did he tell you?" Jerome asked quickly.

"Not a lot, and it has no bearing on what we are set to do. Your past is your business," Richard said and stood.

"Sit down. We are about to embark on an endeavour that will involve more than a small degree of trust in my skills on your part, and I would prefer to proceed without an element of doubt in you," Jerome replied, his voice serious.

"Jerome, I have faith in your ability," Richard said, his voice tired.

"I would like the path before us to be a clear one," Jerome persisted.

"If you need confession, can I suggest a priest?" Richard replied, an acid edge creeping into his voice.

"I would have you know what happened here," Jerome's finger stabbed the coastline. "I need to know that you have trust in me."

"Oh, very well," Richard conceded, resignation in his voice, dropping back onto the stool, "Entertain me then, at least. I hope the tale is one worth listening to."

Jerome picked up the flask and refilled Richard's empty cup, pushing it towards him. "What happened can only have been God's will, and I beg daily for his forgiveness."

"You weren't listening to me, were you? I'll not take your confession," Richard replied, accepting the cup.

"And I'll not make one," Jerome said, his brow furrowed as he returned his attention to the map, obviously trying to locate some point. "It was here – there were three ships of the Order, and we were caught in a storm. It was a bad one, and the seas were rough. We had some shelter from the headland," Jerome's forefinger tapped the map, "but too little. All three ships were lashed together. There's less risk on a rolling sea of them capsizing when they are riding at anchor. The *Diana,* my ship, was on the outside, taking the worst of the weather. The sea was sluicing through her, and we had every pair of hands on the ship bailing her out."

Jerome's narrative stopped abruptly.

"So what happened?" Richard asked.

"Halfway through the night, the anchor chain broke. Now, remember, I said all three ships were lashed together, and now that the *Diana* was free, she was dragging her weight on the anchors of the other two ships; if all three of them broke loose, we would have all ended on the rocks. On my order, your cousin, Edward and his men axed through the ropes that held her alongside the other ships," Jerome replied.

"Ah, the hallowed Edward Fitzwarren," Richard replied, one corner of his mouth twitching into a smile that bore little humour.

Jerome, ignoring his comment, continued. "When the ropes were cut, she'd turned towards the sea, and the waves had broken over her side. Knights and slaves toiled side by side to bail the water from inside her. The skies were blacker than hell. I'd lost where the coast was, so I pressed her out into deeper waters rather than see her dashed on the rocks."

"I seem to remember a similar night on the *Santa Luciana* before we arrived in Newcastle," Richard said, turning the cup in his hand.

"That was nothing but a rough sea, had the *Santa Luciana* been properly rigged and with all her sails in place, we would not have been at the mercy of the winds," Jerome replied.

"So, what happened then? You headed into deeper water. I know from De Nevarra that the vessel didn't sink," Richard said, prompting Jerome to continue.

"I took her, what I judged to be, a safe distance from the rocks and held her there until the storm lessened. By daybreak, it became clear that we needed to make repairs. We followed the coast and found a small bay sheltered from the seas, a natural harbour had it not been for the high-sided cliffs surrounding it." Jerome's forefinger tapped the map, showing the location of their sanctuary. "It was not the safe haven I had hoped it would be."

Jerome's narrative paused again.

"I'm guessing you had placed yourself in a neat trap for the Turk," Richard said.

"I had: there were three of their ships, and they blocked the entrance to the harbour. We were in no fit state to stand and fight; the powder stores were sodden, the shot spread from one end of the *Diana* to the other, and the men had battled with Poseidon for three days without sleep," Jerome shook his head, his expression saddened as he recalled the event.

"De Nevarra said you agreed to the surrender of the ship; under the circumstances, that might have been the sensible option," Richard said.

When he raised them from the map, Jerome's eyes had narrowed, and his mouth was set into a thin line. "Knights of St John of Jerusalem do not surrender."

Richard leaned toward Jerome, planting his elbows on the table. "Surrender is often an act that takes greater courage."

Jerome sat up straight and slammed his cup noisily on the wooden boards, aqua vitae escaping over the rim and darkening the grain. With one hand, he swept back the long hair from the right side of his forehead, exposing the beginnings of a jagged scar that disappeared beneath his hairline. "That is where part of the mizzen hit me when the first shot fired by the Turk felled the mast. Fourteen Knights died trying to defend the *Diana*, and the rest were captured."

"Amongst those, I assume, was the famed Edward Fitzwarren?" Richard asked.

"He was overpowered, along with two other Knights and taken captive. The rest perished on deck in the fighting, and the Turks hurled their bodies over the side," Jerome said bitterly.

"At least that's what you heard. I assume from the crack you took on the head that you were not a part of the fight?" Richard asked.

"No, no, I wasn't. Edward and the other Knights were taken onboard the Turkish ship as prisoners. There is nothing quite as prized to a Corsair as a Knight of St John. From there they were taken here," Jerome's finger stabbed the map showing a coastal city, "and held there as prisoners."

"And you? What did they do with you I wonder?" Richard asked thoughtfully, his eyes never leaving Jerome's.

"They also took me there, keeping me separate from the others. It was weeks before I came to my senses again. They told your cousin Edward that when I had thought I would die of my injuries, I had begged for help and traded their lives and the ship for my salvation," Jerome said bluntly.

"That would have been quite a confession had it been true," Richard observed.

"Had it been true," Jerome echoed bitterly. His eyes broke from Richard's, and he silently filled both cups.

"So why did Edward believe the lie?" Richard enquired after Jerome had pushed the full cup towards him.

"Why would he not? He had no belief that they would ever gain their freedom. He was expecting a cruel and public cruel end. He'd not seen me since he had been taken prisoner, and it would have only taken a few well-placed words, and he would have begun to wonder where I was and why the Turk were holding me in such high regard," Jerome supplied.

"He escaped, though, didn't he? I feel there is about to be more to that than a simple matter of chance," Richard said.

Jerome smiled. "Public execution of a few members of the Order might have provided a fleeting satisfaction but instead they used the situation far more effectively. Edward's escape was no matter of chance; it was planned, and he was allowed to return to Malta and carry the news of what had happened. News that a Knight of the Order had turned against his fellow Knights, not due to torture or coercion but simply to save his own life. They sent a message to the Grand Master that the vows of obedience his Knights pledged were worthless in the face of fear."

"And you, why did they let you survive?" Richard asked thoughtfully.

"I was the Captain of the *Diana*. Perhaps they hoped to learn more about the Order's fleet from me, and gain information about the defences on Malta. Either way, their physicians handled me with some care, doubtless, I would have died otherwise," Jerome explained, his cup held between his two hands and his gaze fixed on the contents.

"You are here, so I assume you either struck a deal or escaped," Richard said.

Jerome raised his gaze from the cup and met Richard's enquiring stare. "The vows I took to obey and defend the Order until the breath leaves my body remain intact. Edward's escape might have been no accident: mine was. I travelled overland and finally made my way to Venice. That's when I discovered that Edward had reported my failure to the Grand Master."

"You argued against this, surely?" Richard replied.

"It would matter little. I had been used to undermine the credibility of the commanders of the Order, and whether that was based in truth or not didn't and doesn't matter. The fact remained that I had lost one of the Order's ships and survived when I should have died on the deck with a sword in my hand," Jerome swiped the flask from the table and slopped more coarse aqua vitae into the cups.

Richard accepted the cup, then several more, as Jerome finished his tale. When Richard left to find his own cabin, his feet were unsteady, and the effect of the liquor and the hard work delivered him rapidly to a night of deep sleep.

☩

A thump followed by two more rapid ones told him the *Santa Luciana's* hull was running against something solid. Richard rolled onto his back, his eyes still closed. Jerome must have brought the ship into the port at Hull already. The knowledge came with a slight sense of annoyance. He'd slept through the voyage as the ship had moved from the open seas into the relative calm of the harbour, and the change in rhythm had not breached his sleep. Remembering the previous night, he was inclined to forgive himself. Jerome had talked until the flask had been empty, and Richard stayed later and drank more than he intended.

There was one small window in the cabin, but the view from it was blocked by something piled on the quayside. The *Santa Luciana* heeled over, leaning away from the quay, straining against her ropes. Richard could hear the shouts above him, evidently, another vessel was passing nearby. A moment later, the *Luciana* straightened, her hull bouncing off the stone quayside, and Jerome's voice called for the ropes to be hauled tighter.

Did he need to make his way onto the deck?

Closing his eyes, he decided he didn't need to, nor did he have any desire to take one last look at a country that he would shortly be leaving for good. Jerome had told him they would call into Hull, pointing it out on his chart: a small town crowded around a natural harbour well protected by the high cliffs. From what Jerome had said, he intended for the ship to linger only a few hours in this northern port.

The bells, swung by their ropes in a church somewhere in the town, struck for prime.

Richard's eyes snapped open. The peel of bells announcing the time was repeated; other churches, more distant, were ringing the hour and many more than there should have been.

This wasn't Hull.

Bare feet landed on the cold cabin floor, and Richard launched himself at the door. Taking the rungs two at a time, he emerged onto the ship's deck, his breath catching in his throat.

"Jerome! What have you done?" Richard gasped as he rose from the stairs to stand on deck and address the captain where he was supervising the lowering of the boarding plank.

Jerome's gaze on him was cold, his eyes flashing like flint. "Some reckonings we cannot avoid."

Unsteady legs bore him to the ship's side rail. Grasping it for support with both hands Richard stared, wide-eyed, in dismay at the scene before him. The crammed quay, the voices of the men moving the barrels and bales, the other ships tied up to mooring bollards to the left and right of the *Santa Luciana*: all this told him where he was.

London.

Beyond the quay rose the high sides of the customs houses; beyond that, the skyline was pricked with the spires of the city's churches. Further upriver, rising from the water's cool fog London Bridge appeared, seemingly hovering between the banks, the pontoons upon which it was mounted disguised beneath the grey mist.

London. Christ no!

Richard swallowed hard.

Why?

Richard turned on Jerome, sparks of anger lighting his dark eyes. "Tell me now why you've brought her here?"

Jerome stood solidly on the deck next to the lowered boarding planks, his arms folded across his chest. "Your business in London is not completed."

"My business in London?" Richard repeated.

Jerome inclined his head but did not reply.

"On whose orders have you brought me here?" Richard stepped towards Jerome, one steadying hand still on the guard rail.

Jerome stood his ground, remaining silent.

"Damn you, whose orders?"

From the quay, the sound of horse's hooves striking the cobbles rang out through the fine mist, and the bright colours of the cloth of their riders cut through the morning fog.

Richard watched in horror as a dozen men wearing the Queen's livery approached the docked ship.

Chapter Eight

London 1559

Locked and guarded when not in use, Cecil's office was nothing less than a large strong box. All four walls were shelved from floor to ceiling, and along them, ranked and ordered, were the secrets of England. Books, bound sheaves of papers, and rolled parchments were all neatly arranged. Security did not allow for a window, and the light was provided by hooded lamps, and a wheel of candles hung low over the desk.

He had been here before.

Nothing had changed.

Richard examined the dust by running his finger along the edge of one of the shelves. "You really must get a housekeeper."

Cecil ignoring him, rounded the desk that took up half the space in the small room, seating himself in the worn but well-cushioned chair. On the opposite side was a wooden one that offered far less comfort, and he gestured for Richard to seat himself.

Wiping the dust from his fingers, Richard obliged, carefully avoiding the low-slung candelabra.

Cecil's cold gaze never left his guest's face as he reached into a desk drawer; finding what he wanted, he held it up. The lamplight glittered on the surface of a gold coin.

Richard remained silent.

Released from Cecil's thin fingers, the angel skittered across the desk. Richard's eyes remained fixed on the other man's, and he made no move to catch the coin when it rolled off the desk.

"You have disappointed me. I had not thought that you lacked attention to detail," Cecil said, his mouth compressed into a thin hard line.

"You are adopting the role of the saddened tutor; it doesn't suit you," Richard replied coolly.

Cecil, ignoring him, continued, "It was an ambitious plan, I will admit that much, and your father's death provided you with the perfect opportunity to dispose of the counterfeit along with his wealth. The mechanism of the process I already have a good grasp of. What I don't know, however, is where you came by such a quantity of gold in the first place?"

Richard's expression remained blank. "That's surely not a question you expect to be answered?"

Cecil rounded the table, a thumb and finger tugging thoughtfully at his beard. "You may have acquired it overseas before you returned to England. However, my sources have told me that, apart from a sizeable sum gifted by your father, you have been poorly funded over recent years, so I doubt that." Cecil walked behind Richard, rounding his right side before he spoke again. "If you had relieved the Order of that quantity of gold, I think it would be fair to assume your life would have been forfeit by now, which leads me to the only possible conclusion."

"Which is?" Richard asked, his voice tinged with boredom.

"It has to be an ownerless hoard, one lost, forgotten or forfeited," Cecil finished.

"That would make sense if I had been in possession of such gold, which of course, I haven't," Richard said thoughtfully.

"If it had already existed as currency, there would have been no need to re-work it, no... I rather think you manufactured these farthings and Angels from church wealth," Cecil had completed his circuit of the cramped office and was now standing behind his desk, his hands resting on the chair back. "Six and a half thousand pounds, Fitzwarren. What made you think it would not be noticed?" Cecil pronounced angrily, nails biting into the leather, chin jutting forwards; he glowered at Richard.

"As you say, a significant sum but not one I know much about," Richard replied. Leaning back in the chair, he raised his boots to the edge of Cecil's desk and rested them crossed at the ankles.

There was a short silence. Youthful grey eyes, tempered with steel, locked with brown ones surrounded by the wrinkles of age.

"I'll not argue with you, Fitzwarren, and, as it happens, I now have a use for both you and your tainted coinage," Cecil said, retaking his seat at the desk, ignoring Richard's feet.

Richard folded his arms, an image of reclining comfort. "Pray tell, what might that be?"

"A threat remains to the peace of Her Majesty's realm on England's northern border," Cecil stated bluntly.

"Oh dear, are the French not still in mourning after the death of Henri?" Richard quipped, an expression of mock concern creasing his brow.

"This is serious. While Henri lived the French court was a more temperate animal, it had been hoped that his untimely death would have delivered to France problems of her own, too many for them to consider hostilities with England," Cecil's fingers rapped on the table while he spoke.

"But?"

Cecil raised his eyes from the desk and met Richard's. "But the court, and the Dauphine, are now controlled by those fanatical Catholics, the De Guise family. In the hearing of our ambassador to France, they even had Mary Stewart proclaimed Queen of England. 'Make way for the Queen of England,' such words cannot be left unchecked."

"They do remain mere words," Richard pointed out unhelpfully.

Cecil slammed a fist down on the table, his knuckles whitening the backs of his liver-spotted hands. "Such words are a mere precursor to action. Mary De Guise is in Scotland garrisoned with French troops; our sources in France tell us more are to be sent to reinforce them. The numbers are sufficient to indicate that an offensive is being planned."

Richard unfolded his hands and, displaying empty palms, asked, "And what would you like me to do? By your own device, I am no longer in the Queen's favour."

"Her Majesty wishes to support the rebel's cause without being seen to be doing so. It is in England's interest that they succeed," Cecil replied, stabbing a forefinger towards Richard, he added, "That is where you can apply yourself."

"Now we have the crux of it. Will there ever come a time when you will fail to have a use for me?" Richard said, laughing bitterly. His fingers linked, he settled his hands behind his head.

"I am sure we both hope that will happen. However, by your actions you have provided the means to furnish the Scots rebels with support without implicating Her Majesty. I had retained those Angels in the treasury to employ against you, Fitzwarren; however, it now appears they have a more valuable use."

"Go on."

"Out of favour and about to be expelled from Court, you are about to seek out a new master and hope, with the provision to the rebels of a quantity of gold, to secure for yourself a controlling role in Scotland should they be successful," Cecil explained with unnecessary simplicity. "It will soon be known that the gold you supplied, albeit of value, has been poorly fashioned into Angels and was not the product of the Queen's treasury."

"So, in this scheme, am I to act only as a courier? Or did you wish me to become part of the rebellion against the Scottish crown?" Richard enquired, sounding mildly amused.

"You will also present the Scottish Congregation with another gift that should help consolidate their position against the De Guises."

"And what would that be?" Richard asked, his grey eyes locked with those of the statesman.

"Not what, but who. You are to reunite them with John Knox," Cecil stated bluntly.

"Knox!" Richard laughed. His feet dropped from the desk, and the chair tilted on two legs banged down loudly on the floor. "I have to congratulate you. I had not thought you possessed the capacity to surprise me; however, on this occasion, you've excelled yourself."

"He is the one man capable of bringing that ragged Scottish council to heel; they will unite behind him. There are, at the moment, quite a few Scottish nobles who have not declared their allegiances," Cecil explained with a voice that told of a patience well tried.

"How remiss of them," Richard remarked.

Cecil continued as if he had not spoken. "The Earls of Glencairn and Morton are undecided, as are Lords Erskine, Boyd and Ochiltree. If the rebels are to have more than an even chance of success, then they need to attach these men to their cause. Knox will be instrumental in doing this."

"And where is the illustrious Protestant at Court?" Richard asked then, catching the look on Cecil's face, he continued, a slight sneer bending one corner of his mouth. "Not at Court. No, that could never be, could it? Elizabeth would not countenance him in England, indeed could not. He has called for the faithful to throw off the yoke of their female sovereign, and the last time I heard anything of Knox, he had yet to revise his opinions. Very set in his ways is Master Knox. What was it, he said? Ah yes, I remember, 'that female rule is contrary to the Bible.' I've often thought it was not one of the wisest treatises. With one stroke of the pen, Knox directly opposed our Queen Mary, Mary De Guise, her daughter and of course Her Majesty, not to mention a host of other women, including Christina of Denmark...."

"Enough, Fitzwarren."

"....and we mustn't forget Anne of Hungary and even Diane de Poitiers, although uncrowned, she was a woman who wielded...."

"Damn you....Enough!"

"....not an inconsiderable amount of power," Richard continued as if Cecil hadn't spoken. "Did he not say crowning a woman was akin to placing a saddle on an unruly cow? You have to agree that Knox has not left himself many safe rocks to hide under in England or elsewhere."

"And so I am sure he will be delighted to be returned to the Scottish fold," Cecil said through clenched teeth.

"So where is he if you don't have him bound in chains? Under normal circumstances, I might have known, but little news has reached me of late," Richard said pointedly.

"Her Majesty has refused him safe passage to travel through England; he is in Bruges and has complained bitterly in writing that he shall have to make the return journey by sea. I am sure you could help him with that," Cecil said flatly.

"So you want me to deliver Knox along with a quantity of gold? Anything else? Perhaps you would like to add one of the labours of Hercules to my list of tasks?" Richard asked, his voice acid.

"You are an able commander, a mercenary who has had some success. I am sure the Scots can find a use for your services," Cecil replied.

"Some success ..." Richard echoed Cecil's words.

"This is not a time for games," Cecil rebuked.

"I think it is. And what makes you believe that I will play yours?" Richard replied with a hard, bitter edge in his voice.

"I'm sure you will decide to aid Her Majesty," Cecil replied bluntly. "It would certainly be in the interests of your brother and his new wife. They are expecting their first child, did you know?"

†

Richard found himself accommodated after the meeting in the Beauchamp Tower. One of the oldest parts of the London stronghold, constructed originally by William, it had, over the years, housed many notable prisoners. The guards led the way down a dozen steps to the heavy arched doorway at the bottom of the tower. Built for defence, even on the side of the tower facing the inner courtyard, it bore only small windows, which were high up, outlined by a dozen arrow slits framed with white stone. A left turn into a narrow passageway with a high arched ceiling took them to tight spiral stone steps twisting up over. When they reached the floor above, a narrow corridor led to a low doorway. Another guard, waiting for their arrival, unlocked the door.

Stepping inside, the door closed solidly behind Richard. A moment later, the metallic jangle of keys ending with a loud clunk told of the lock being fastened against him.

His prison was three rooms, linked by wide arches, open arrow slits to his left let in the wind and afforded a limited view of the Thames. Palms on the cold brickwork, Richard viewed the slice of the river through the narrow opening. Grey water, raised in patches to white crests by the gusts, led to the opposite bank where poor houses clustered around an empty landing stage; behind them loomed the square tower of a church, and above sat a sky the colour of the river.

Pushing his hands away from the stonework, his eyes found the letter J encircled by a C carved deeply into the stonework. Thoughtfully, Richard's forefinger traced the inscription. It was probable it had been left there by John Collins, an unfortunate who had been part of the only real rebellion against the rule of Henry. To the right of it was another name - William Tyrrel had carved his epitaph in Italian, dating it 1541. Richard read the words slowly.

"Since fate has chosen that my hope should go with the wind, & now want to cry for the time that is lost, and & will be sad and unhappy forever. & wish for time to be destroyed."

A breeze, cold and edged with the promise of winter, came in from the arrow slit caressing his neck as he read; perhaps it was Tyrell's complaint. Richard ran his fingers over the words. It was ironic that he wished time to be destroyed, and yet by leaving his words, he had forever preserved the memory of his suffering.

Opposite the window set a large fireplace. The inscription,

"the just shall be remembered,"

was carved in large cursive script on the smooth lintel above the opening. To the right of the fireplace was an intricately carved memorial left by John Dudley, the Earl of Northumberland. He had been imprisoned here after his failed attempt to place Jane Grey on the throne. A painstakingly carved heraldic device, with a lion and stag facing each other, all captured within the boundary of a shield, decorated the wall. Beneath it the text. Marked out carefully were four lines. Three had been completed, and two more were blank, left as a stonemason's work in progress.

"You that these beasts do well behold and see. May deeme with ease wherefore here made they be with borders eke within. Four brothers names who list to serche the ground."

It seemed such a recent event. Richard's fingers rested on the lion. He had played a part in this; he knew that. He had switched from supporting Northumberland to Mary, but the tide had already turned, and he, like many others, had abandoned the lost cause. The engraving would still have been on the wall whether he had switched sides or not.

Below Dudley's heraldic shield was a cruder carving of a kneeling figure. Next to it was a square niche cut into the stone, where a candle had perhaps once rested. To the right, another name he recognised, William Wynter. He'd been among the conspirators Wyatt had rallied to try and overthrow Mary's rule. He remembered meeting the Welshman at Wyatt's sister's house in London, a serious and yet sensible man who had tempered the fanciful and often ridiculous plans some of the other conspirators had proposed. Winter had fared better than Wyatt. His naval career and his continued usefulness had seen him released from the Tower. So many words on the walls, so many messages from the past. It seemed the inhabitants had been compelled, one after another, to leave their epitaph in the walls.

Final words that told of despair, frustration and defiance.

Richard's examination of the walls was stopped by the rattle of the key and the turn of the lock. Three guards entered, and behind them, two servants carrying a basket of wood and a tray. Eyes downcast and without looking in his direction, the tray was laid on the table, the servant swiftly retreating while the other knelt near the grate and set the fire. One guard blocked the doorway, and the other two paced slowly around the room.

"Checking to see if I've taken to adding to the narrative on the walls?" Richard asked conversationally; he received neither reply nor acknowledgement.

When the fire was lit, the remaining servant retreated along with the guards, and the door closed, a key rattling in the lock on the outside again.

Richard examined the offerings on the tray. Cecil obviously wasn't planning on starving him to death, at least. There was enough bread, cheese and cooked meat for at least two people. An earthenware jug contained good quality wine, and the bread was still warm from the ovens. Breaking a lump off and filling the cup,

Richard returned to examining the walls, the next inscription was in Latin.

"Stand and bear your cross for you are Catholic..."

The words continued on, a ramble of faith in death and a hoped for salvation, their meaning clear, yet the form was incoherent, telling of a mind that was no longer sound.

Richard was reminded of Jack's internment in the dungeons below ground. Damp, wet, dark and filled with the ability to torture a man past any endurance. The souls of the Beauchamp Tower's prisoners might have departed, but their torment remained carved into the stones that were their prison. Careful letters, etched, carved, embellished, and even beautiful, told a story of unimaginable horror.

The inside of one of the arches had provided a blank canvas from the bottom to the top on both sides. Catholic epitaphs stood side by side with Protestant. Edward's brief reign had seen Catholics interred for their faith inside the Tower walls, then, when his sister Mary held the sceptre, it was Protestants who had filled these rooms, and now....

And now he was here.

Annoyingly.

And not for his religious beliefs either, although in keeping with the Beauchamp Tower it was religion that was at the heart of it.

Knox.

Protestant, reformist, outspoken and fanatical.

Richard had no intention of adding his own lament to the walls for history to read. Although it was tempting to record the fact that his current incarnation was attributable to a bloody Scot! He was in the process of mentally composing a stinging statement that summed up his current infuriation with the situation when the door opened again.

Two servants cleared the table, neither of them glancing in his direction. One added more wood to the fire and lit the candles on the table before retreating. A guard advanced into the room and, for a moment,

Richard thought he was about to speak to him, but he dropped a sheaf of papers onto the table before turning on his heel and retreating.

The door shut loudly. Keys jangled.

Richard put down his cup of wine and leafed through the sheets, a grim expression settling on his face. They were copies of Knox's writings and sermons. Some had been printed, others copied out by hand. Cecil was nothing if not thorough; he obviously wished for Richard to be fully briefed about the man he would take to Scotland. Glowing orange and licking delightedly at the fresh wood that had been added, the fire beckoned, and for a moment, Richard considered sending the pages to curl and burn in the flames.

Only for a moment.

Apart from re-reading the walls, there wasn't a lot else to do.

Seating himself at the table, pulling one of the candle holders closer, Richard began to sort through Cecil's offerings.

Chapter Nine

London - May 1559

Jack rolled his eyes, pressing his mouth into a hard line, sealing it tight against the retort he knew would only worsen the situation. Catherine's pregnancy was, as far she was concerned, not going well. The weather outside remained foul and had confined her to the house and the few rooms they used for weeks. Disinterested in domestic pursuits and with no friends and little company apart from Jack, when he was there, Catherine was becoming belligerent. Jack's attempts to distract her were failing; his good humour had become brittle, and he knew that his temper was threatening to snap. The only other woman in the house was Lizbet, but that was hardly of help as the two could not abide the sight of each other.

"...the fault of this is yours, Jack Fitzwarren. If you'd never set foot in Assingham none of this would have happened," Catherine continued with her frustrated tirade.

"There are days when I wish I had not seen that miserable place," Jack said as levelly as he could.

"None of us can be masters of the past, I am afraid," Catherine replied haughtily.

"We can't be, but we can be masters of the future, or so I've been told," Jack said, trying to change the subject.

"Do not try to distract me, Jack Fitzwarren. You've left me here, on my own, for days," Catherine said accusingly.

"There have been ...."

".... anything and everything claims your attention. Was another foal born? Did you buy another horse? Was there another archery event you needed to attend? Or have you been with Emilio?"

Jack's eyes narrowed; Catherine did not like Lizbet, but she detested the Italian.

"I have duties, woman," Jack tried.

The argument circled round once more, and at the next mention of Assingham, Jack flung his arms up in the air in despair, declaring that he had given up trying to reason with his wife, and left the room.

†

Jack set his feet towards the stables. He knew he had spent too much time there, but the familiarity of the environment was not only comforting; it was one he understood. The animals' training, care and temperament were things he knew and relished. The London house had stabling for twenty, with grazing in a field at the rear, two tack rooms, a forge and a workshop. Jack had bought more horses at auction and even some young stock that were wintering in the field at the rear, and this was his destination.

His yearlings were as far away as they could be at the bottom of the field's slight incline, backed against a hedge; the reason for this was immediately apparent. A large black hound was barking happily and running in circles around its owner, Lizbet.

"What on earth are you doing?" Jack, a boot on the fence rail, was soon in the field.

"I was trying to teach the creature to stay, but, as you can see, he's got too excited," Lizbet laughed. Her right hand clutched a lump of bread and held it above her head. "No! Sit down."

The dog jumped once unsuccessfully and then backed up and sat down, its mouth open, breath pluming like smoke in the cold air, tongue lolling over sharp white teeth.

"Training is going well then?" Jack said sarcastically.

"Yes, actually, it is." Lizbet returned her attention to the dog. Holding up her hand, she prescribed a circle in the air with her finger and the dog obliged by standing and spinning on the spot. Her finger reversed direction and so did the dog. Lizbet held her palm up towards the dog. It stopped immediately and sat staring up at its mistress. Lizbet tore a chunk of bread off and held it out for Loki.

"I wish my wife were as well-behaved," Jack lamented.

"Oh God, what's happened now?" Lizbet said, leaning down and attaching a lead to the hound's collar.

"All she talks of is bloody Assingham," Jack rubbed his hands together to ward off the cold, regretting not collecting a cloak when he'd stormed from the house.

Lizbet shrugged. "If she likes it that much take her there."

"I can't now. Her uncle has possession of it," Jack grumbled.

"You told me it was a poor place, fields scratched from the earth, more thatch and wattle than stone. If that's the case, buy it for her and be done with it," Lizbet replied, returning her attention to the hound, "Stay."

Lizbet began to back slowly from the dog.

Jack scowled at her. "It is exactly that, the main hall is stone, but it was in a poor state of repair – the only reason her uncle held on to it so tightly is because of the rights to the timber, and that's what Robert, the bastard, was after as well."

"So why is that a problem?" Lizbet said, exasperated, her eyes on the dog. "Stay."

Jack looked at her, his expression confused.

The dog, confused by the noise of the two voices, began to rise.

"No, stay there. Timber or no timber, Assingham is going to remain where it was when you left it. There is little to stop you from buying it for her, is there?" Lizbet explained, taking two more steps backwards.

"But what's she going to do with it?" Jack shot back.

"For God's sake, Jack, does it bloody matter? It's what she wants. You've more gold than you know what to do with. You can't tell me that her greedy uncle will turn down a quantity of it in return for Assingham?" Lizbet explained patiently. Unsettled by her raised voice, the dog jumped and ran towards her. "Oh, that's your fault! Loki, down. Good lad."

Jack's face brightened, and he clapped a hand on Lizbet's shoulder, making her yelp. "Good Lord, woman, I think you have the answer. I'll give her what she wants."

"Be careful - you great lummox." Lizbet scolded, moving out of his reach, rubbing her arm where his hand had landed. At his mistress's side, Loki growled, a run of spiked hackles gracing his broad back.

✝

Under the watchful gaze of his ancestors in the unused dining room at the front of the house, Jack poured over a map of England. The room provided the only flat surface big enough to unroll it, and he had the corners weighted down with three matched candle holders and a small gold oil lamp. The map had been prepared by a cartographer interested in showing the Fitzwarren lands, but it also depicted other cities, towns and villages in England. He had obviously copied the plan from another map, and on top of the underlying structure, he had superimposed the Fitzwarren holdings in bright red.

Following a summons by Lord Fitzwarren, his lawyer Threadmill had arrived. Black-capped, neatly robed, and recently promoted, he was eager to please and expound the virtues of the legal firm he was a part of. Threadmill was of a similar age to his client, and Jack, who felt that all lawyers should be both aged and learned, was still a little suspect of his ability. He knew this was unfair as, so far, Master Threadmill's performance had been nothing short of excellent.

Jack had found Hazeldene penned on the map next to a small depiction of a fortified manor and, close to it, labelled in neat writing, was Assingham. The pictorial representation was no more than a small square building with a fence around it – this symbol was repeated across the map, and it seemed to represent a small farm, for Assingham was little more than that.

Edwin showed Master Threadmill and his clerk into the room. Luterell had retired from the legal practice, so Threadmill was now the senior lawyer who dealt exclusively with the Fitzwarren estates and legal matters.

"Is there some matter I can aid you with, my Lord?" Threadmill said, coming to Jack's side, his eyes on the map unrolled on the tabletop.

"Yes, there is," Jack looked at the map, his brows furrowing. He'd taken his eyes from Assingham, and for a moment, he'd lost its location. Finding it again he stabbed it with an index finger. "This used to belong to my wife, and I would have it returned to her."

Master Threadmill leaned over the map. Squinting, he tried to find the place Jack was pointing to.

"My wife's name is de Bernay, and this was transferred to Peter de Bernay. Can you make enquiries? Tell him I wish to buy it," Jack said, tapping the map.

"I'm sure that can be arranged," Threadmill replied, sounding mildly confused, "Do you mean Hazeldene?"

"No, Assingham, next to Hazeldene," Jack corrected.

Master Threadmill beckoned for his assistant to come forward, traded brief quiet words with him, and the clerk set to take down the necessary notes.

Jack straightened, his eyes suddenly fastening on the city of Lincoln, and his mouth twisted into a stiff smile. "And while you are doing that, you can also find out about this place."

Threadmill leaned over the map, focussing on the small depiction of a fortified tower house just above Jack's finger on the parchment.

"Burton?" Threadmill queried.

"Burton," Jack confirmed, forefinger tapping the legend. "It was vested by Queen Mary in my brother's name. Ayscough, the Lincoln Sheriff, as far as I am aware, placed it under his control. I would have it back."

Threadmill nodded. "There will be records. I can certainly check these for you."

"Good," Jack folded his arms across his chest. "I will trust you with both of these matters."

✝

Two days later, Master Threadmill returned, accompanied by the same young assistant in a dreary grey legal robe carrying his leather writing case.

Master Threadmill's expression was bright, his tone eager. "My Lord, I have news I hope will be welcome."

Jack hitched himself onto the edge of the long table in the dining room. "Welcome news would be good indeed."

"Burton is still vested in your brother, Richard Fitzwarren. There has been no transfer of the land or the rights attaching to it since it was granted to him. As you rightly asserted, Burton has been taken over by Francis Ayscough, and he has been collecting the rents and dues from the tenants and the mill," Threadmill provided efficiently.

"Has he, by God," growled Jack, dropping from the edge of the table and turning to look at the location of Burton on the map.

"Yes, and he can do that, legally, if he asserts that he was acting by proxy for the absent landowner. Indeed he can charge a reasonable fee for his management of the land while the owner has been in absentia," Threadmill continued to explain, coming to stand next to Jack.

"A reasonable fee?" Jack echoed.

"He would be holding the rents, tithes and dues for your brother, Richard; if he does not offer them, we can call him to account and although he can charge for his services, he would not be entitled to retain them as his own," Threadmill's finger found the depiction of the mill near Burton. "And the tithes from the wheat ground will also need to be accounted for."

One corner of Jack's mouth lifted, the smile malicious, and bright blue mischievous eyes met Threadmill's dark brown ones. "And how do we relieve him of this money?"

"Ah, well, that is not so simple. As I said, the property of Burton, and the land surrounding it, are still vested in your brother, and it would have to be Richard Fitzwarren that placed the claim. Unless you have an agreement with him to manage his affairs ...in his absence."

It seemed everyone knew of his brother's disappearance. Jack's mouth flattened into a hard line then a thought occurred to him. "I do have such an agreement; if I produce this, what then?"

Threadmill brightened immediately. "Then it would be a simple matter of stating your claim."

"It could even be a simpler matter of travelling to Burton and stating it myself," Jack suggested. It would be extremely satisfying to take Burton back from Ayscough by force.

"My Lord, our legal firm are at your disposal. There is no need for you to travel to this place to make the claim; in terms of your Lordship's estates, Burton would be very minor. If I can obtain the agreement from your brother a copy can be made. Be assured that we can resolve this matter to your satisfaction," Threadmill soothed.

Jack leaned towards him. "I will forward it to your offices presently. Then send your papers, Master Lawyer. My satisfaction will be served when I personally extract what is mine from Ayscough."

Jack's sudden intensity had unnerved Master Threadmill, and he broke away from Jack's gaze, rifling through the papers before him on the table. "I will ensure that the papers are served and send word as soon as it has been done."

Jack's blue eyes sparkled with delight. "Ayscough owes me, and it is a debt I would take great satisfaction in collecting personally. It's a shame I won't be there. I am sure you can understand."

"My Lord, that is none of my business," Threadmill stammered, unsure what to say.

Jack laughed and clapped him on the shoulder. "And the other matter?"

"De Bernay does indeed still have possession of Assingham, much of the timber by all accounts has been thinned, but sizeable stocks still remain. De Bernay is actually attached to Sir William Hewett's household," Threadmill replied quickly, clearly happy with the subject change.

Jack looked at him in confusion. "Am I supposed to know who that is? As you know, I've not spent much time in London in recent years. You need to provide me with more than just names," Jack said, his voice amused.

"I'm sorry, My Lord. Hewett is Lord Mayor of London, newly appointed, and Peter de Bernay is one of his officers; as Hewett's man, he is resident at his house in the city," Threadmill explained.

"Good God, he's in London?"

"Indeed he is. There was some coincidence as it happens, the contracts for the opening of the new tannery yard at Brownside Wharf were handled by our firm and one of my colleagues is familiar with de Bernay via those negotiations," Threadmill explained.

"A tannery yard at Brownside? Isn't that a short distance from the Earl of Norfolk's house?" Jack asked.

Confused, Threadmill replied. "I believe it isn't far, a quarter of a mile at most, I would have thought."

Jack chuckled. "When the winds are in the right direction, Norfolk'll have a fine stench meeting his nose."

Threadmill, obviously not wanting to comment on that possibility, said, "It's a new yard, right on the river. They hope to grow trade overseas. English hide remains a valuable export commodity and Garrison Bennett will be ...."

"Bennett," Jack interrupted, "what's he got to do with it?"

"He runs one tannery in London already, and he is to operate this one as well," Threadmill replied.

"Does the Mayor have any idea who he is dealing with?" Jack said.

"I'm not sure what you mean, my Lord," Threadmill said, his voice rising a pitch, obviously regretting the conversation.

"Bennett, he's one of the worst criminals in the city," Jack said, incredulous.

"I can't comment on that, my Lord," Threadmill said, a nervous edge entering his voice.

"Don't worry. I know you're a lawyer and must be careful what you say. Anyway, de Bernay, what happened?" Jack said, changing the subject.

"After your instructions, we have approached him," Threadmill sounded relieved and turned to retrieve one of the papers his assistant was carrying. "He was most surprised by your interest in Assingham, a property that came into his possession after the tragic death of his brother. He has, by all accounts, had little to do with the property, which is currently rented out to a tenant. He is willing to sell."

"Is he now, and what price did he propose?" Jack asked.

"He indicated that a consideration of one hundred pounds...."

"A hundred pounds!" Jack blurted.

"Yes, I did rather think it was quite a lot," agreed Threadmill.

"Offer him fifty and see where that takes us," Jack said, not about to add daylight robbery to his list of misgivings about Assingham.

Threadmill smiled, seemingly satisfied with Jack's response. "I will ensure that your offer reaches him immediately."

Chapter Ten

London - 1559

With Emilio for company, Jack had taken up residence in a quiet corner of the Angel. A fire to their left sent a welcome warmth, and a small table to their right was laden with enough food and wine to satisfy even Jack's appetite. Jack lost the third game of Primero in a row, discarding his cards on the table. Emilio reached forward and collected them, but instead of dealing out a fourth hand, he placed the pack down with a thump on the wood.

"There is little amusement to be gained when you are not engaged in the game," Emilio stated, leaning back in his chair and observing Jack over the top of his linked fingers.

"I've little enthusiasm for anything at the moment; that's true enough," Jack accepted. "I would have sworn Devereux had a hand in what has happened, but it seems I was wrong."

"Something that you are having a painful time accepting," Emilio observed accurately.

Jack raised his eyes from the glass in his hand and met Emilio's steady gaze. "I can never understand why Richard trusts him; he's a corrupt merchant at best and a criminal at worst."

Emilio smiled. "Your brother obviously recognises his traits and aligns them with his own."

Jack looked at Emilio darkly. "Richard is many things, but he is not a criminal."

Emilio's thick eyebrows arched.

"Well, not the kind of criminal that Myles Devereux is," Jack shot back.

"He is your brother, and I am, unfortunately, aware that you cannot see him as others do," Emilio said sadly.

"And I, too, find it unfortunate that you cannot see him as I do," Jack replied bluntly.

Emilio leaned forward, laying a hand on Jack's wrist. "Jacques, this is not the time for argument, and it is not my intent to anger you."

"Are you sure?" Jack's temper had not subsided, and he snatched his hand from Emilio's.

"Sure of what, my pretty?" A female voice said, the accent French. Jack looked up at Nonny's arrival and smiled. She continued, "Has there been any news of your brother?"

Jack shook his head.

"Such an infuriating man! Why did he place himself in such a situation?" Nonny said as she settled down next to Jack on the arm of the chair.

"I hardly think it was his fault," Jack said, taken aback.

Artfully tinted brows rose above eyes that regarded him with incredulity. "Your brother, mon cher, is five steps ahead of the best men I've ever met. Of course, he knew what he had done."

"I'm sure, Nonny, that he didn't. The match with Elizabeth Howard was one he favoured. It would have placed him at the centre of the Queen's court. I don't think he would have thrown that away lightly," Jack replied, irritated.

"Sometimes, Jack, what you see is not the truth of the matter," Nonny said quietly into his ear.

"It seems the world wishes to argue with me today," Jack grumbled.

"This is not the first time Richard has disappeared, and I doubt it will be the last. He will be safe, Jack. Wherever he is, he is there by his own design," Nonny assured, a hand absently ruffling his untidy hair.

"Nonny is right, Jack. It is only you who is suffering," Emilio said brightly.

"You should listen to your friend, Jack," Nonny said in agreement before rising and leaving them alone.

Jack had little appetite for cards and busied himself in emptying a plate of pastries set at his elbow on the side table.

Watching him with interest, Emilio waited until he had nearly finished before asking, "Were you considering sharing?"

Jack looked from the plate to Emilio and then back again to where only two small pastry parcels remained. Collecting them, he said, "If you'd wanted some, you should have said so."

"Perhaps," Emilio said quietly, then asked, "So, Jacques, now you have been released from Court, what are your plans?"

"I am supposed to be looking for Richard," Jack said.

"I think after three months, you've exhausted every possibility, and there is still no sign or news of him; you can't keep hunting for him forever," Emilio pointed out.

"True, I suppose." Jack's brow furrowed, then his eyes met Emilio's, and he said, "I had thought I might go to Burton; I could always argue if anyone ever did ask, that I thought Richard might have taken himself there."

"Boortun?" Emilio queried, his Italian accent twisting the place name.

"Burton," Jack corrected, laughing.

"Boortun. That is what I said," Emilio repeated, adding, "so, why there?"

Jack, grinning, shook his head. "When Mary took the throne, Richard lent her some assistance, and she rewarded him with Burton. It's a small place, a fortified tower house, and the entitlement to the rents from the surrounding land."

"So what happened?"

"We ...Richard lost it when his allegiance to Elizabeth was revealed. At least he kept his life, though," His allegiance to Elizabeth is what made him valuable to the Order in the first place," Jack said, stopping his narrative suddenly.

Emilio shrugged. "I know of his friendship with Elizabeth, his time in Seymour's household, and a little of what came after, but that is all. It was not I who interrogated him on Malta."

"True," Jack conceded. "I liked Burton, and it was mine as much as Richard's."

"You have a thousand times more now than then. Why does it matter to you?"

"Because it belongs to me. My lawyer believes he can return control of it to me," Jack replied. "It was taken from me by force."

"So, a job for the lawyers, leave it to them. I am sure it will be well dealt with," Emilio said. "But now you have so much more. It is not worthy of you to bother with such trifles."

"I don't want to leave it to them. Ayscough, the Sheriff, took it from me. His men tried to murder me," Jack growled, leaning back in the chair, in his mind the memory of a fight on a muddy road playing out.

Emilio grinned and leaned towards Jack. "Well then, let us go and take it back. You need something to occupy you, and if that means chasing a few peasants around the wet fields of England, then why not?"

"Us?" Jack echoed.

"I am also trying to remove myself from London, so it would serve me well to accompany you. You can show me this Boortun," Emilio said.

"Why do you want to leave London?" Jack asked warily.

Emilio groaned, throwing his hands wide. "The Italian Ambassador is arriving, and while he is paying court to the Queen, he will also wish for my company."

"So why do you wish to avoid him?" Jack asked.

"He is a close friend of my father's, and I fear he will wish to terminate my residence in England," Emilio said.

"I thought you were here at the instance of the Order?" Jack said.

Emilio shrugged. "It's complicated, Jacques. I will greet him when he arrives, a formal occasion with no opportunity for more than the briefest exchange. It will afford for the opportunity to fulfil my obligation but nothing more. After that, we can go to Boortun," Emilio replied.

"Burton, damn you."

Four days later, Jack found himself accompanying Emilio towards the Thames and to the ship that the Italian Ambassador had arrived in. It was customary in such cases for the visiting dignity to announce their arrival and wait onboard their docked ship for a formal welcome to the City of London. In this case, there was a delegation sent by the Queen accompanied by a dozen red-liveried soldiers, with Emilio and several of his own men riding at the rear.

Grooms held the horses after Jack and Emilio dismounted, and they moved to join the Queen's guard, who lined up on the quay at the bottom of a boarding plank that Jack assumed was attached to the Italian ship. It was early, and a damp mist still clung to the river. Jack was aware of the cold air on his eyes, and the stones beneath his feet were leaching the heat through the soles of his boots. Before long, he was uncomfortably aware that he had not dressed as well as he could have for a long wait on the quayside. On the other hand, Emilio did not seem similarly affected, wrapped as he was in a thick cloak edged with sable and no doubt lined with the same.

Jack's eyes wandered beyond the Ambassador's ship to where a Dutch Fluyt was being relieved on her cargo by a steady stream of longshoremen. The cargo was stacked on the quay in two separate piles, one made up of barrels, probably wine from the Rhineland, and the second made up of wooden crates, their contents Jack couldn't even guess at. Three darkly dressed customs officials were overseeing the unloading, and a clerk was completing a tally sheet of each unloaded item. As Jack watched, two of the longshoremen were called forward and instructed to open the crate they had been carrying. The lid was levered off, and one of the officials inspected the contents. Satisfied, he waved his arm and the crate was closed and carted away to join the others.

Further down the quay and partially lost in the mists of the morning was a galleon. Riding high in the water, her forecastle towered over the Fluyt. One of her sails was spread along the length of her betwixt deck, and a line of men along the canvas edge were working on repairs.

Emilio suddenly elbowed him in the arm. "I can see your wife has not taken it upon herself yet to attend to your wardrobe?"

Jack returned his attention to Emilio. "I don't need a woman to clothe me."

Emilio stepped towards Jack, saying confidentially, "I think you need someone to assist you, my Lord."

Jack's cheeks reddened. "It is not the English fashion to look like a popinjay."

Emilio laughed. "You can command a good tailor, and yet you are little better dressed than your steward."

"I am starting to regret hauling your arse back to the surface. I should have let you sink," Jack said. Then, in an attempt to change the subject, he asked, "Is that the Ambassador on the deck."

"Jack, all I am saying is that if your wife had seen to her duties, you'd not be stood here shivering, would you?" Emilio observed accurately.

Jack chose not to reply. Emilio might have a point. Lizbet had looked after his clothes and any mending that needed carrying out, while Catherine had next to no involvement with the running of the house. Richard had provided him with the services of a tailor before their father's funeral. He had been through the experience of being measured and fitted for new clothes with poor grace, and since then, he had been wearing the dark clothes made for him on that occasion.

"At least try and wear clothes that match," Emilio had continued.

"What do you mean? There's nothing wrong with what I am wearing," Jack complained.

Emilio turned towards him, folding his arms across his chest, and ran his eyes over Jack from boots to hat. Shaking his head, he said, "Your boots are leaking," Emilio held up his hand to stop Jack from protesting. "Just listen, they are leaking, you've one pair, and it shows. There's a tear in your hose above the right knee; it's been there for weeks. The top buckle on your belt is broken, the pin has come away, your poniard does not fit the belt properly, and you've cut the leather to make it slide over. One, no, two buttons are missing from your doublet, and by the look of it, another is about to follow. One of the ties on your right sleeve is missing, and there is a tear in the lace on your left cuff."

Jack stared at Emilio – speechless.

"And your cloak is a bad match for the rest of your clothing," Emilio finished, and, with a flourish, he detached the button that was indeed about to depart from Jack's doublet. "Have your good wife sew that back on for you." Emilio took hold of Jack's hand, turned it palm upwards and deposited the button.

Jack stared from the button to Emilio, but any reply he threatened to make was stilled; to their left, a fanfare announced the arrival in England of the Italian Ambassador on the ship's deck along with his entourage. They were, to Jack's annoyance, as well dressed as Emilio. Jack's temper subsided when he became aware that, beside him, Emilio was no longer smiling.

Two robed officials from the Queen's household traversed the length of the boarding plank, followed by four liveried guards; the remaining yeoman stood in a solid guard along the quay. There was an exchange between the men – Jack supposed it was no more than a formal welcome and an invitation to the Queen's Court. A few minutes later, the Ambassador descended from the ship, still talking closely with one of the officials. Progress stopped three-quarters of the way down the ramp as another official stepped up to present the Ambassador with something. Jack could not see what. Another exchange of pleasantries appeared to ensue - Jack groaned.

"That's Rodrigo Inez. He's related to the Ambassador by marriage," Emilio provided, leaning towards Jack.

"Do you think they'll be much longer?" Jack asked.

"Surely you are not in a hurry," Emilio said quietly, his eyes full of mischief.

"My boots are leaking, remember? I wasn't overly bothered by them until some pig-headed Italian drew my attention to the fact," Jack said.

"Pig-headed?" Emilio replied with mock indignation.

There seemed to be no urgency for the Ambassador to disembark the ship. Jack considered leaving Emilio and returning to his horse when the Italians finally stepped onto the quay.

Another fanfare.

Jack winced at the sudden piercing noise, and several pigeons that had settled amongst the rigging took flight.

Casting Emilio a sour look, Jack then brightened as it appeared the Ambassador, too, had cold feet and, followed by his entourage, was making his way with haste along the quay towards where Jack and Emilio waited. The Ambassador came to a halt before Emilio, stooping to kiss the ringed hand that Emilio only slightly raised towards him.

"It is good to see you in such excellent health," Emilio said in his native Italian.

The Ambassador, raising his head, smiled broadly. "It is always good to see a Knight of The Order. I trust I can call upon you during my time in England?"

"Of course," Emilio lied smoothly. "I have some business myself to attend to over the coming weeks, but I am sure there will be time for news."

"I have a letter from your father, and, should you wish to reply, you can trust me with its delivery," the Ambassador continued.

"Very kind, but there is no need," Emilio said, waving a hand airily, "I have the Order's couriers at my disposal, and there is no quicker way to send a message in Christendom than that."

The Ambassador bowed, straightened, and one of the Queen's officers intervened to lead him towards a waiting litter to carry him to Whitehall.

"That wasn't too bad," Jack said, watching the ambassador retreat. "I thought you said he'd insist on a meeting with you?"

Emilio, next to him, did not reply.

Looking at the Italian's face, Jack saw that the relaxed expression had vanished, replaced by a look of shock. His mouth was partly open, his hand, released by the Ambassador, was trapped by nothing more than cold morning air and was still stretched out before him. But his eyes, wide and filled with a strange mixture of alarm and fright, shocked Jack.

"What is it?" Jack moved closer to the Knight, his right hand instinctively finding the hilt of his poniard.

Emilio didn't reply.

From the Ambassador's entourage, a man broke free.

Taking three quick steps away from the others, he dropped to his knees before Emilio, grasping his hand and trapping it between his own. Pressing Emilio's fingers to his forehead, he spoke a few quick words in

Italian before rising and rejoining the rest of the men in the orderly procession behind the Ambassador. He didn't look back, and Emilio didn't look at him; his eyes were fixed on some distant point on the opposite river bank. If Jack had not witnessed the brief encounter, there was no evidence that it had happened.

"Emilio?" Jack hissed under his breath when the group of Italians were far enough away.

But the Italian turned, returning to his men and waiting horse without a glance toward Jack.

Chapter Eleven

London - 1559

Richard reflected on the political situation he now found himself in. Knox was openly defiant of the Scottish Queen Mary, a quality that would endear him to Cecil, if not to Elizabeth. The preacher's condemnation of female rulers, of his attacks upon the princesses of Europe were more than Elizabeth would tolerate. Knox had been an adherent of George Wishart, a reformist preacher who had travelled Scotland bringing God's words from the Bible to the people. There had been several attempts on Wishart's life and Knox has acted as his able bodyguard in his final years before he was arrested for heresy. Wishart was a Scottish martyr, burned at the stake for a truth he and much of Scotland believed in. Knox then fell foul of Catholic rule in Scotland and the French sent him to the galleys for nearly two years. It was a testament to his inner strength that he had survived.

England had been, for a while under the reign of Edward, Knox's sanctuary, he had even been chaplain to the young king. A state of affairs that would not last. Knox fled to Europe when the coupe to place Jane on the throne failed and Catholic Mary became queen. England would no longer offer him a welcome but

Scotland would. A Scotland that wanted rid of French rule and Cecil very much wanted to help them.

It made sense, of course. France, camped on England's northern border, was a continual threat. Remove the French and it was true there was still the hostile Scot, but they would not be backed by the military might of France anymore, vastly reducing the risk. Remove the French and there would be a power play in Scotland that would not involve invasion of England. Their young queen, born in 1542, was only fifteen years old. Scotland would need a governor and the members of the so-called congregation would be busy working to secure their own places in the hierarchy.

It suited Cecil and it was, Richard had to admit, on the face of it, a reasonable plan.

But that reasonableness started to disintegrate when the detail of what might happen was considered. France might be a threat to England on her border but it would be doubtful they would mount a southern invasion. The De Guises had more to worry about at the moment than Elizabeth's England. Scotland was politically unstable, with a power split between the Lords of the congregation and the De Guise family. They had a young, and not very able, dauphin, on the French throne and a child on the Scottish throne.

Neither were ideal.

France would be looking to consolidate and strengthen what it had, not implement expansionist policies when their own centres were so weak, Richard reasoned.

Richard tapped his fingers thoughtfully on the desk, considering the situation. That inner turmoil could last for years, years that would suck money from the French coffers. If France were ousted from Scotland then that came with an added risk. France would no longer be spread quite as thinly as it currently was with the De Guise family trying to rule in Scotland and France. Instead they would be united again, their power base would be strengthened as they would no longer have troops in Scotland. Then they might strike at England across the channel.

So Cecil's plan was not without risk.

Richard finished reading and squared the sheets up, placing them to one side of the desk. The words had given him a more than enough to know he would have little personal liking for the man. If there could be one word to sum Knox up it would be 'inflexible'.

Little survived on those terms.

Even God had to be flexible.

For there to be a world where both Catholics and Protestants lived, was this not in itself a testament to the flexibility of the Lord? Mary had been inflexible in her treatment of Protestants. They had fled from England, hid their religion, many that flouted the rule were burnt. But in the end her intolerance had been swept away.

Replaced.

Elizabeth's views were harder to define. In England there were both Protestants and Catholics, both openly practicing their religion. It was not an arrangement without tension but it was an arrangement, an illustration of flexibility.

Knox, on the other hand, was a fixed point.

Then there was another angle to consider. Knox was not welcome in England. Cecil himself had said that Knox had been denied safe passage by Elizabeth and on the subject of Knox the Queen was unlikely to be swayed. Cecil was acting on his own. His plan to move Knox to Scotland was not one that it was likely Elizabeth would be aware of.

Richard sat back in his chair, his eyes wandering across the shadowed walls with their darkly carved words. No-one had ever obliterated them. Indeed when the guard had entered earlier he'd undertaken an inspection of them to see if his latest prisoner had felt inclined to etch his own lament in the stone.

Richard smiled.

Pushing back the candle he cleared a space on the table before him. The wood was oak, the patina dark with age, marks in the surface blackened scars and dents. He reached for the knife that lay next to the cheese.

✝

"Do you have any idea of the trouble you have caused?" The Queen strode past him, skirts brushing his arm.

Kneeling in her privy chamber, eyes fixed on the floor, he gave the expected response. "I am most humbly sorry, your Majesty."

"Sorry! Tell me, and spare no detail, I warn you, my patience is sorely tried. What is your part in this?" Elizabeth demanded, turning noisily, the drapery fighting to keep up with her.

"The truth your Majesty..."

Elizabeth laughed harshly, passing him again, her shoes rattling on the tiles. "A tradeable commodity, it seems, where you are concerned. You swore your loyalty to me and look where you are now."

"I have made no false promises, I assure you."

"You assure me of nothing, sir. Oh for God's sake, get up, before I trip over you," Elizabeth commanded, waving an arm towards him. "Tell me then, why you are hiding in the Beauchamp Tower?"

"I was not hiding, I was imprisoned," Richard provided rising smoothly.

Elizabeth glared at him. "Your brother has been commanded to find you. Cecil, allegedly, has no idea where you disappeared to, then you suddenly appear. How long have you been there?"

"It was only a matter of a few days, your Majesty," Richard replied.

"A few days," Elizabeth repeated then, her temper rising, she demanded. "And why, sir, does my Master of the Tower, bring me news that a prisoner in his keeping has taken to defacing the woodwork with the name of that bigoted Scot, Knox?"

A direct answer was required. For once sense prevailed and he gave it. "I had planned to sail from England, however, Lord Burghley had other ideas and wishes me to use my ship to provide safe passage for Knox back to Scotland. He hopes that the preacher will unite Scotland and aid the Congregation to oust the French."

Elizabeth stared at him.

"It is a reasonable plan," Richard added unnecessarily.

Elizabeth swallowed hard. The fair eyebrows rose towards her hairline and the pale skin drained of the insipid colour it possessed.

The silence was a long one.

Elizabeth turned from him, taking a dozen quick steps across the room before rounding on him.

"Reasonable?" The Tudor temper exploded.

Richard remained silent.

Elizabeth's hand found a plate of sweet comfits and sent it to the floor to disintegrate into an exploded mosaic of sugary shards. A thin, be-ringed forefinger stabbed towards him. "Since when did Burghley rule this realm? And since when did you let him?"

"I was, as I said, under lock and key. It was not my design to aid him. I sent a message to you, the only way I could think of," Richard replied, his grey eyes meeting hers.

"You expect me to believe that?" Elizabeth glared at him.

"Why else would I carve the man's name in foot high letters in one of your tables?" Richard pointed out, adding. "I am not an adherent of Knox, you know that."

"It was only due to the loyalty of the Master of the Tower that this was reported to me, you cannot have known that it would be the case? It was more likely that it would have been reported to Burghley," Elizabeth spat back.

"It was the only course open to me. I hoped that it would be reported to you directly," Richard said plainly, his voice calm.

"So what does that leave me with?" The brown eyes, unveiled, were fixed on his.

"Knox asked of you safe passage through England and he is not to get it. I am to take him by sea. The man will never set foot in your realm," Richard continued, his tone level.

Elizabeth's forefinger continued to stab the air before him. "But you! You are helping him. It matters not how he gets to Scotland, what matters is that I will not assist him."

"I believe he is aware that this is against your will ..."

"Against my will? God save us! Parliament petition but Burghley does as he pleases."

Richard remained silent.

Elizabeth strode across the room, breathing heavily, her shoulders shaking with temper. Richard watched her back as she stared through a window. When she turned towards him she had regained some of her composure. "So my statesman has decided to make policy without me. Is it only this or have you been given further instructions?"

"I have been requested to make my skills available to the congregation and to take your financial support to them. As one no longer in your favour Cecil believes that I can deliver the gold and the assistance and, if the tide should turn against the venture, the blame would not attach itself to your Majesty but to one of her rogue nobles," Richard replied plainly.

"It is true that I demanded of him that he ensure the support we are to provide would not be attributed to England," Elizabeth conceded. "How do you propose to achieve this?"

"I am out of favour. I have some skills and, thanks to Cecil's network, he's made it known that I am looking to abandon England and seek advancement elsewhere," Richard said.

"And are you?" Elizabeth asked bluntly.

"No, your Majesty."

"You made a fool of me Fitzwarren." She held up a warning finger to stave off any protests. "Before you seek to argue against me, I am well aware of the facts of what occurred at Durham Place. Cecil took an opportunity to remove you from my favour. The blame for that lies at your door for gifting it to him," Elizabeth had moved towards a coffer, her back turned towards him, her palms resting on the wooden surface.

"It was unfortunate, I agree," Richard replied.

"Unfortunate?" Elizabeth whirled towards him. "I hardly think that is a term to use when poison has been laid on my table."

That she viewed herself at the centre of the incident did not come as a surprise.

"And I am forever grateful that it failed. Have Cecil's investigations found out how this happened?" Richard asked.

Elizabeth shook her head. "No. Although he has his suspicions."

Richard's expression remained blank; he was sure Cecil would be using it to his full advantage, the Queen's paranoia would provide him with a control mechanism he could exploit.

"And don't change the subject," Elizabeth warned. "Scotland knows of your pending arrival with Knox?"

"They have asked for support. Outwardly I am to provide that along with the additional gift of Knox," Richard replied.

"If anyone should be incarcerated in the Beauchamp Tower it's that intolerable Scot," Elizabeth growled. "And what do you think of Cecil's proposed plan?"

"He seeks to defuse the threat to your northern border," Richard replied.

"I am well aware of the threat, that's not what I asked," Elizabeth said, striding towards him.

"Henri is dead, the De Guise family are split between rule in Scotland and France and the figureheads for both of those countries are children. I am not privy to the information Cecil has, however, I would have thought that they had too many domestic concerns at the moment to consider starting a war with England," Richard said truthfully.

"If that is the case then why proclaim Mary Queen of England within hearing of our Ambassador in France?" Elizabeth said, folding her arms tightly across her chest.

"They were merely words and, if I may be so bold, given Henri's stance, if they did not then it would have appeared that they have decided to denounce Mary's claim to the throne. May I suggest it was uttered in the hearing of the Ambassador for the simple reason of offending yourself and reminding the rest of Europe that France remains behind its policies, despite the death of Henri," Richard provided.

"It is a slight I cannot allow," Elizabeth fumed.

And one I am sure Cecil has embellished and repeated many times, Richard thought.

"It is a statement of intent," Elizabeth snapped, continuing her rant.

It was clear that argument against this premise was pointless. "How would you wish to proceed, your Majesty?"

"I do not wish any of this. It is a situation that has been thrust upon me. If France is to move against us and, indeed, if their accursed Mary is to be closer to the throne then the threat comes from Scotland," Elizabeth said, "and I am persuaded that this should be neutralised."

"I can see the sense in that argument," Richard accepted.

"Can you? Or do you say that to humour me?" Elizabeth turned and her dark brown eyes bored into his.

"No advice can ever be perfect, your Majesty. France on our northern border has always been a threat and one Scotland is apt to remind you of often," Richard provided.

"The De Guises wish to place her on my throne," Elizabeth pronounced, an arm gesturing in an imagined direction of the north.

"They do. However their wishes and their ability are not equally matched," Richard replied, his voice reasonable.

"I accept that but we need to ensure that the scales tip in our favour," Elizabeth replied, her top teeth had found her bottom lip and her brow was furrowed.

"Knox could be a weight that would do that," Richard offered.

"Damn Knox," Elizabeth replied.

"Indeed. I have no liking for the cleric but he would be a tool the congregation would eagerly use to bring the Scots to repel the France," Richard replied.

"And would he not look further south should he succeed?" Elizabeth shot back.

"Surely, if your Majesty had aided the congregation they would be favourably disposed towards you," Richard replied.

"So Cecil assures me. But to trust a Scot is akin to trusting an adder, you may feel you have a firm hold on it but it'll twist back and bite you at the first opportunity it gets," Elizabeth spat back.

"If you command me not to undertake this task I will not," Richard replied.

"It is not a case of will this happen or will it not. I have been backed in to a corner and left with little choice, the dice have already been cast long before I reached the table," Elizabeth's voice was still taught with anger.

"I agree, the issue should have been discussed ..."

"Discussed? What happens in my realm is not a matter for discussion, now it seems it is decided in darkened corridors in hushed whispers. I will not have it, do you hear me?" An unfortunate Italian wine glass with a slender stem and delicate engraving ended its decorative life on the tiles. Elizabeth's ladies, who had taken up position as far as away as possible and were intent on embroidery or the view from the window, jumped at the sound.

Richard remained silent, his head bowed, waiting for her temper to subside.

Elizabeth paced across the room, her shoes crunching on the broken fragments on the floor. Richard sent a fervent prayer to the Lord that the calfskin soles were thick enough to resist the cut glass.

Elizabeth stood with her back to him for some minutes, obviously considering what limited choices she had. When she turned to face him traces of her temper remained, the colour in her cheeks brightened and her eyes shone. "So tell me then, How should I proceed."

"It is not for me to dictate policy," Richard met her gaze.

"I am trapped between my statesmen, France and the congregation. I do not want a war," Elizabeth threw her arms in the air.

"There cannot be a decisive plan that would steer a way through the future that is to unfold, not one that can be made now at least," Richard replied.

"What do you mean?" Elizabeth said stepping towards him, glass crunching underfoot.

"For each action there will be a reaction. If I deliver Knox to Scotland it cannot yet be known what strength he will draw to the congregation, which of the wavering Scottish earls will leave the De Guises. There are too many uncertainties," Richard replied.

"So you expect me to do nothing?" Elizabeth sounded incredulous, throwing her arms wide.

"Not at all. But each subsequent decision must be based upon the knowledge of the outcome of the previous one. Knox might fail. The congregation could collapse if they fail to gain the support they need. I advise that you tread carefully, watch and see what happens before you react or commit," Richard said patiently.

Elizabeth laughed harshly. "Cecil chides me constantly for being indecisive and that is exactly what you advise."

"Better to be indecisive than wrong. Better that than lead a country into war," Richard said plainly.

"Bold words," Elizabeth said, then added, "but true. I once asked you to work with Cecil, it was not an arrangement that went well, and that might be fortunate."

"How so, your Majesty?"

"No doubt he wishes you to report to him once you are in Scotland?"

"I would imagine that will be the arrangement," Richard replied.

"Well, I would like to be kept appraised before him, if Cecil is planning any more independent actions I would like to be aware of them," Elizabeth said, her face still flushed with anger.

Richard bowed towards her. "I will use whatever means I can to keep you informed."

Chapter Twelve

London - 1559

Acutely aware of how cold his feet were, Jack stared in anger as Emilio, surrounded by his men, left the quay. There had not even been a backward glance from the Italian; he had mounted his waiting horse, applied his heels to her sides, and a moment later, he was gone, his men scrambling to join their master.

Something had just occurred, but Jack didn't know what. Emilio had little time for the Ambassador; he had delivered a cool reply when asked if he wished to send a letter to his father.

That wasn't it.

It wasn't the reference to his family – it had been after that when Emilio's expression had changed.

Jack replayed the event in his mind, staring unseeing out across the Thames – in his mind, he watched a man separate himself from the train following the Ambassador and, for a moment, drop to his knees before Emilio.

Who was he?

Emilio had stood frozen, his hand trapped in the other's grasp, his eyes staring through the kneeling man. Whoever he was, Jack was sure he was the reason Emilio had practically run from the quay, ignoring him as he had called his name.

Jack tried to recall the moment, freeze it, and examine the man kneeling on the cold stone before Emilio. But all he could remember was an impression of him, a blue cloak edged with sable fur hung from one shoulder; his face was hidden from view as he knelt, his head bowed, with Emilio's ringed hand caught in his. Jack realised his gaze had not been upon this man but on his friend. He'd seen Emilio's face pale, his eyes widen, and his whole body stiffen – all within that moment when this man had detached himself from the Ambassador's retinue.

It was clear Emilio had recognised him the instant he had laid eyes on him. Jack was aware that Emilio had little love for his family and that he had several siblings – could it have been one of them? It didn't seem likely, not as the Ambassador had mentioned that he carried a letter from Emilio's father, and Emilio had only met that fact with indifference.

What else, then?

The kneeling man had imparted a few words, too quietly spoken for Jack to hear – could it have been a threat? Jack considered the possibility that this had been some form of message from the Order of St John, but he discarded that notion. The Order did not send messengers who delivered their missives while kneeling – they were far more direct than that. No, this was something entirely different – if not his family, if not the Order, then what was it?

☦

The ride home was brisk, and Jack's temper had not settled by the time he arrived. Striding inside the house, his mind preoccupied with what had happened by the river.

Catherine found him, a letter in her hand.

"This came for you while you were out from your lawyer." She held out the sealed letter towards him.

Jack looked between the offered letter and Catherine.

Catherine, confused, repeated her words. "It came from your lawyer. Could it be bad news?"

Jack ran a hand over his face. "No, not bad news."

"Are you going to open it," Catherine pressed, still holding it towards him.

"Yes .... no. Later...." Jack snatched it from her hand.

"And what's the matter with you, Jack Fitzwarren?" Catherine demanded tartly.

"Nothing," Jack said, stowing Threadmill's message inside his doublet.

"Nothing made you slam three doors on your way here, did it? Nothing made you snatch that from my hand, did it? You've a face like thunder. What's happened?" Catherine demanded, advancing towards him.

"I don't know," Jack said honestly.

Catherine frowned. "You went to welcome the Italian Ambassador with Emilio. What went wrong? Something obviously did?"

"Nothing. The Ambassador arrived, and Emilio left ...."

"What do you mean he left?" Catherine said.

Jack shrugged. "He just left. The Ambassador arrived, spoke to him, then ... he just turned and left, refusing to speak to me."

Catherine rolled her eyes. "I don't know why you are surprised."

"What do you mean?" Jack shot back.

"It's obvious: the Ambassador, along with other high-ranking Italian nobles, will be far more interesting to Emilio than you are," Catherine replied, "I always said he was fickle. What's he doing in London? Someone needs to remind him he's supposed to be a member of the Order of St John., Perhaps the Ambassador might, although I...."

"Catherine, stop," Jack barked.

127

"I'm only telling the truth, and the truth is he's no friend to you. The moment his countrymen have arrived, he no longer needs you," Catherine said, then added, "what more proof do you need?"

Jack, fuming, swallowed the reply he wanted to make and instead pulled Threadmill's letter from his doublet and waved it in the air. "A letter has arrived from my lawyer, and, as you say, it may be important. There is a matter I need to attend to about Burton."

"Burton?"

"Yes, Burton."

"But you lost it," Catherine said, confused.

"Well, I am about to get it back," Jack announced angrily.

┼

Jack didn't make his way to his lawyers. Instead, he went to the Angel. Seated alone, his feet stretched out in front of him, crossed at the ankle, Jack regarded the room around him with impatience. He wasn't entirely sure why he had come here. He didn't want company.

A table had been set next to his chair with wine, and Nonny had breezed over, run her hand through his hair, leaned close to him and asked the question quietly. He'd answered her only with a shake of his head. Sensing his mood, she'd left him be.

Jack settled his head against the high chair and closed his eyes. In the room behind him, there was the sound of gentle laughter. Closer to his right was the even noise of wood on the fire and the flames' warmth reaching out towards him. Above, he could hear the creak from the timbres and footsteps as one, no, two people walked along the corridor he knew passed above his head. On the opposite side of the room, he heard the gentle clap as one of the players discarded his hand of cards on the table. They were distant noises, all discordant. They felt loud and dragged along his nerves, driving a pain towards the front of his forehead.

Jack opened his eyes and reached for the wine glass, about the finish his drink and leave.

"And I thought you were asleep," the voice of Myles Devereux said from where he stood beside Jack. His long arms crossed, he was regarding the seated man with idle curiosity.

Jack glanced at him. "What do you want, Devereux?" he said roughly, emptying his glass in one quick stilted motion.

"A little company, and it seems you are alone?" Devereux said, his eyes had drifted towards one of the servants positioned near the door, and, without a word, he crossed the room, bringing a chair with him and setting it close to Jack on the opposite side of the fire.

Jack watched with mounting annoyance as Devereux fitted himself in it, one leg over the arm, his fingers steepled, regarding Jack over them with a smile.

"I don't want company."

"You do. You just don't know it yet," Myles said, smiling brightly.

Jack glared at Devereux.

"I hear...." Myles settled back in the chair before continuing, "Cecil had a visitor."

Jack stared at Myles, blue eyes fastened upon the other man's face.

"Don't you want to ask me who?" Myles said, wriggling his shoulders and making himself comfortable.

Jack still held the wine glass in his right hand; with an audible click, the stem parted from the bowl.

Myles's smile broadened. "Not like your brother at all, are you?"

"What do you know," Jack growled, refusing the let go of the decapitated glass.

"You want to be careful. Losing things is becoming a bit of a habit." Myles pulled a length of silk from inside his doublet. "First your brother, then, so I hear, your knight. What next?"

Before Jack could move, Myles had slithered to the edge of his seat. Reaching towards Jack, he plucked the bowl of the glass from his hand, flicking it into the flames.

Holding out the white silk kerchief, Myles said simply, "I think you might need this. Otherwise, you are going to bleed over Nonny's floor."

Looking toward his hand, Jack saw the stream of blood running down the stem and already dripping from the glass to the table. "Damn you, Devereux." Jack detached his hand from the remains of the glass, briefly examined the neat slice it had made in his palm and balled his hand into a fist.

Myles sighed heavily, waving the silk closer to Jack's face. "Stop being so thickheaded and take it."

Jack hesitated momentarily before snatching the silk from the air and wrapping it around his hand, pulling the strip of material tight.

A satisfied expression settled on Myles' face.

"What do you know?" Jack said. With an effort, he kept his voice level.

Myles shrugged. "You might have lost the knight, but I see you've still got his trinket."

Jack managed not to glance towards the ring on his right hand that twinkled in the firelight. "You said Cecil has had a visitor?"

"I did, didn't I?" Myles replied, his long fingers tapping slowly on the chair arm. "Probably not a willing visitor, though."

"Are you going to tell me or not?" Jack growled.

"Perhaps... So, has Nevarra given up on you?" Myles asked.

"I'll not play your games, Devereux. Either you've got something to tell me, or I'm leaving," Jack's hands moved to the chair arms.

Myles huffed loudly. "You are no fun. I heard, through an .... acquaintance, that Cecil had tasked a Fitzwarren with carrying out some mission or other, and I doubted that this was you, so it does seem to be that your brother is back in his pay, don't you think?"

"He's in London? When did this happen?" Jack was on the edge of his seat.

Myles shrugged.

Jack sat back, elbows resting on the chair arms, and regarded Myles with a cool expression. It was clear that this would take the usual course of a conversation with Devereux - it was like negotiating a maze, so many wrong paths and dead ends needed to be explored before Myles would lead the way to the exit and the information Jack wanted. But he knew from experience that the more he pressed for an answer, the longer it would take to get one.

Jack smiled as a recent conversation sprang to mind, and he decided to steer the conversation down his own path, which led nowhere in particular.

"I hear things as well. Garrison Bennett has secured a nice deal with the Mayor of London to open a second tanning yard near Brownside Wharf." He was rewarded with a fleeting moment of surprise on Devereux's face. "That'll put him in control of most of the leather trade in the city, I would have thought?"

To Jack's further satisfaction, Devereux's face soured. "Your sources are right, it pains me to say."

"Brownside Wharf is fairly close to the White Hart. Bennett must be getting a little too close for comfort?" Jack pressed on, encouraged by Devereux's annoyance.

"I'm in too good a mood for you to ruin it with tales of Garrison Bennett," Myles replied, ending Jack's fun.

Jack asked, "How did you know I'd be at the Angel alone?"

Myles smiled broadly. "I could argue it was an accident, but you'd not believe me, would you?"

"No."

"An easy conquest is one not worth having," Myles replied, still smiling.

Jack laughed. "Is that what you think I am?"

"If I am honest, I don't really know what you are. Your brother, I have a good measure of, however, you are ...."

"Why don't we start there?" Jack interrupted.

"Where?"

"How do you come to know Richard? He'd not tell me, and I don't see how your paths could have crossed before," Jack asked. His broken glass had, by now, silently been replaced, and he began filling it along with another for Myles. "Amuse me. You came here for entertainment, after all."

Myles, delighted, settled himself into the chair. "I thought he would have told you. I am surprised."

Jack lifted one of the glasses and offered it to Myles. "Well, I am not."

"The Piombi, in Venice - he has told you nothing?" Myles asked, accepting the glass.

Jack's answer was a shake of his head.

Myles settled back in the chair, the fabric, accepting him, folded around him. "Such a long time ago. Is it safe, I wonder?"

"Safe?" Jack queried.

Myles smiled. "It would be a confidence I have never shared with anyone. If your brother did not tell you, then you can imagine it remains of some significance."

"Are you asking me for secrecy?" Jack asked, confused.

Myles twisted the glass in his hands. "Secrecy, no. If I tell you of the events surrounding our meeting, that would be assured. But I would have a trade."

"What do you want?"

Myles drummed his fingers on the chair arm.

"How much?" Jack pressed.

Myles met Jack's gaze. "I don't want your money."

"What do you want, then?"

Myles put the glass down, regarding it for a moment before he said, "I'll answer your questions truthfully if you'll answer mine?"

"What do you want to know?" Jack asked, too eagerly.

Myles shook his head. "I will place my question after I've told you what you want to know."

Jack let out a noisy breath. "A deal with you, Devereux, is akin to making one with the Devil."

Myles grinned. "That might be the case, but the choice is your own."

"Very well," Jack said, his voice weary, adding the caveat, "and afterwards, you tell me what you know of Richard and Cecil."

Myles' long fingers twisted the glass, the red liquid swilling dangerously close to the rim. Then, smiling, he said, "Why not."

Jack waited, watching Myles closely; he was looking into the depths of the glass, perhaps considering where to begin his confession.

"We were in Venice. I cut a man's throat - badly," Myles said, raising his eyes to meet Jack's.

"What had he done to you to deserve such butchery?"

Myles' face was unaccustomedly blank. "He tricked me into going to his room, then buggered me until I could barely stand. He fell asleep on the bed. I bided my time, took the knife from his belt and made to cut his throat open with it." Myles stopped.

"So what went wrong?" Jack asked, taking a sip of wine.

"I didn't so much slice as stab. The blade went in and stuck fast in his spine. He was dragged, gurgling, from his slumber for one last time, with me clinging to the knife hilt, trying to silence him. There were no words. He was shrieking like a stuck pig with blood spraying from his throat, both of our hands on the knife hilt. He managed to wrench it out and turned it on me. The blade went in just below my collarbone. Richard heard the noise and forced his way through the door. He tried to pull us apart. The knife was dragged from me, and the blade cut through Richard's doublet and sliced across his chest. In a instant, he had his own knife in his hand and cut through the bastard's windpipe. Christ, the silence was a blessing, we both held him down, and he stopped struggling as his blood let out," Myles finished bluntly.

Jack waited for Myles to continue.

"The disturbance did not go unnoticed, and soon we found ourselves under arrest and interred in a pit in the Piombi. By some happy coincidence, we were to be dragged before the officials in the morning to give an accounting of ourselves and the goaler, housed us with another Englishman already in their custody. He had taken a severe beating, and there was a fever upon him, and he was not going to survive the night. Richard knew him as Myles Devereux, a distant cousin of Edward Devereux's. When the bells tolled for prime, apparently, he breathed his last, and Richard stripped him bare and swapped his clothes with mine. I must admit I had nothing to do with it; the wound in my chest was still bleeding, and I can remember little of what happened that night."

"Hold on a minute, are you saying you are not Myles Devereux?" A confused expression had settled on Jack's face.

Myles grinned his reply.

"But everyone in London knows you are a cousin of Edward Devereux?" Jack continued, leaning forward in his chair and looking at Myles with fresh eyes.

"Even you don't want to disbelieve the falsehood, do you?" Myles said happily.

"You can't just assume a man's name and get away with it," Jack shot back.

Myles leaned towards Jack and whispered. "I can, and I did."

Jack dropped back in the seat, genuine shock on his face. But in his mind, he remembered another man, Andrew Kineer, and the easy deception he had created when he had taken Richard's identity. Christ, the world was never straightforward! "So, if you are not Myles Devereux, who are you?"

"That's a little secret I'll be keeping to myself," Myles said.

"How did you escape justice in Venice? Was that when you claimed his name?" Jack continued, clearly not finished with the conversation.

Myles shrugged. "They had a corpse they could hold accountable for the murdered man. Richard could pay his way out, and I was now a cousin of Edward Devereux, thrown in the Piombi for cursing the name of the Doge. A finable, not a hanging, offence."

"Someone must have known you were not Myles?" Jack pressed.

"I was removed from the Piombi and taken to convalesce in Châteaux Blanc in the Canneregio region of the city, paid for by your brother. It was three years before I made my way back to England. Richard said I bore a passing resemblance to Myles Devereux, so that was helpful," Myles finished.

"But his family? Surely they would know?" Jack stammered.

Myles smiled broadly. "His poor mother died in childbirth, his father followed her to the grave a year later, and there were no siblings. He had been in Italy with only a cleric and a tutor, both easily paid off."

Jack shook his head. "So it was that simple."

"It seems so. My brother was never happy about the deception, but he accepted it," Myles said, a sad note in his voice.

"Your brother?"

"He was a friend of Richard's. He had left me in your brother's charge while he conducted some business in Venice," Myles provided, then switching the subject, "enough of my early years. A deal is, after all, a deal."

"What do you want to know?" Jack asked. When Myles did not reply, he said impatiently, "Come on, man."

Myles smiled. "You are nervous, aren't you?"

"Ask!"

Myles inclined his head to one side. One hand held the thin twisted wine stem, and the other rested loosely on the chair arm. "No, I think I'll wait. I shall keep it to savour later. You wanted to know about Cecil and your brother?"

"I did."

Myles set his wine glass down on the table. "Cecil had him brought back to London a few weeks ago. He's working for the Crown again. That's all I know."

"How do you know this?"

Myles laughed. "Surely, you cannot expect me to reveal all my secrets in one night?"

"Don't toy with me, Devereux."

A hurt expression settled on Myles' face. "You insult me. Have I not been candid with you already?"

"How did you find this out, Devereux? I've searched London; there's never been any sighting of him," Jack, brow furrowed, watched the other man closely.

"He didn't seek me out if that's what's vexing you," Myles said.

"How then did you know he was here?"

"He owns a ship, does he not? And it has been birthed at the dock at St Katherine's," Myles explained, taking the wine glass prisoner again in his slender fingers.

"The *Santa Luciana?*" Myles' words had brought Jack to the edge of his seat.

"The same." Myles raised the glass towards Jack.

"When?" Jack blurted, beginning to rise from his seat.

"Settle your arse back down. He's gone. As the saying goes, that ship has sailed," Myles said, waving a hand towards Jack.

"Where?"

"He's working for Cecil, and from what I know, he's gone to Scotland," Myles said simply.

"Scotland?"

"So I've heard." Myles took a small sip of the wine, savouring the liquid.

"What's he doing there?" Jack said.

Myles shrugged. "Who knows? But you can probably place a fairly safe bet on the fact that there will be trouble, and Fitzwarren will be the cause of it - stirring the pot as usual."

"How do you know this?"

Myles leaned forward. "I've got sources inside the Tower. Surely you know that? I hear he met with Cecil and spent a few days incarcerated in there, then sailed from London to Scotland."

"When?"

"A few days ago,"

"Why are you telling me this now? You know damn well I've been searching for him? Why leave it to tell me this now when it's too late?" Jack said accusingly.

"Calm yourself, Fitzwarren. I just found out myself, and here I am, obediently delivering my information to you," Myles said, sounding hurt.

"Why only this week?" Jack pressed. "I thought there was little that went on in London that you were not the first to know about."

Myles put his glass down so quickly that some of the contents escaped. "I don't have to justify my actions to you, Fitzwarren. Take the crumbs from my table, for that's all you'll get."

Jack bit his tongue and swallowed the retort he longed to hurl at Myles. "Alright, I apologise."

Myles watched him through narrowed eyes. "That's better. Your brother's recent stay was a closely guarded secret. The man I learned from knew his life would be shorter if the information leaked before his departure."

"How do you know he left for Scotland?"

"Ah, now I found that little bit of information for myself. The *Santa Luciana*, as I said, was moored at St Katherine's, she'd taken on supplies, and most of her crew were confined to the ship while she was in London, so there was little to learn from the taverns."

"So, how did you find out she sailed for Scotland?"

"Guesswork. A week before the ship left, another man arrived in London, a godly man who took the time to enquire after my brother. Andrew was a Protestant preacher, and when he was in Bruges, he worked with a man called Knox, John Knox. Surely you have heard of him?"

Jack nodded. "Who hasn't? I'd not thought he'd be welcome in England."

"He isn't, and his presence here was kept secret. In less than a week, he had gone, and so had your brother's ship," Myles said triumphantly.

"What makes you so sure they are bound for Scotland?"

Myle's expression turned to one of incredulity. "Where have you been? Scotland's natives are massing on England's northern border, the Scots' rebellion wants to be rid of French rule, and they don't care who knows this. Of course, Knox has gone to Scotland, he'll be the drum the rebels beat to draw men to their cause, and I'd place money on the fact that your brother has been charged with his safe delivery."

Jack was silent.

"Do feel free to thank me," Myles said ungraciously.

Jack covered his face with both his hands and cursed loudly. He'd been at St Katherine's dock when the Ambassador arrived, and someone had taken a great deal of care to engage him. Emilio had known Jack was about to recognise the *Santa Luciana*, and had begun to berate him for his appearance, even pulling a button from his doublet and forcing him to turn his back on the ship. He could see her now, swathed in mist, a sail spread across her decks.

"Oh, come on, you have to share," Myles said, sitting on the edge of his seat. "What has just occurred to you?"

"Nothing," Jack said solidly, not about to share the betrayal with Myles. Changing the subject, he said, "You have no proof Knox sailed on the *Santa Luciana*; you are, as you say yourself, guessing."

"I don't gamble, but if I did, I'd place money on that as a certainty," Myles replied.

"Maybe you are right. If your brother is working for Cecil, it won't be voluntarily," Jack said slowly.

Myles shrugged. "Probably not. It'll be a penance for foisting that gold onto the crown coffers."

"You had a hand in that," Jack shot back.

Myles shrugged and said, "But there is a positive, is there not?"

"What would that be?"

"At least you know whose side he's on, or, should I say, at least you know whose side he appears to be on," Myles said.

"True," Jack said, the response automatic, his mind roaming backwards. Richard must have arrived on the *Santa Luciana*. How had he not known about that? He'd sent a message north to Jerome to contact him if his brother boarded the ship and left suitable bribes in London on the quays to alert him should the *Luciana* birth on the Thames. The only explanation was that both lines of enquiry had been stopped by his brother. Richard hadn't wanted to be found.

Why Scotland?

And why Knox?

Myle's information had not helped. Indeed it made him feel worse. His brother had been in London, and there was nothing to suggest he had been interred against his will, yet there had been no message for Jack, and he had neatly avoided the traps Jack had set to snare information about Richard's whereabouts.

Chapter Thirteen

London - 1559

Christian Carter's house was the only place he could think of to go; he badly needed to talk to someone, given what he had learnt. Christian was a close friend of Richard's. At the least, he deserved to know that he was safe.

Despite the hour, he was admitted to the house and Christian, a bedrobe pulled tightly around him, hurried down the stairs. As soon as they were alone in the kitchen, Jack said, "I've had news of Richard."

"Really?" Christian pulled the robe tightly around him against the cold of the room. "Come on, man. What news?"

"It looks like he was in London on the *Santa Luciana* and might have sailed for Scotland." Jack provided a limited version of the news he had received.

"Scotland?" Christian said, confused.

"It seems so, and it appears he's working for Cecil again." Jack sat down on one of the trestles at the kitchen table.

"This is good news, surely. If Richard is working for the Crown again, it is a way to restore his favour with the Queen," Christian said, beaming.

This was not the response he had wanted. "Yes, but why didn't he contact me?"

"The situation he has found himself in is complicated, to say the least. It might well be that it was prudent, at the moment, to stay away. Jack, rejoice, you've been hunting for him for months, and now you have news: he's safe and well," Christian said smiling. "And I, too, am relieved. If the *Santa Luciana* was in London, it's obvious that the repairs you talked about have been carried out, and that does explain his absence. I think a drink is called for."

Christian disappeared from the kitchens a returned shortly after with a stoppered bottle. Selecting two earthenware cups from a shelf, he filled them both. "A toast: to your wayward brother, my friend, and his continued good health."

Jack raised his cup but didn't share Christian's elation at the news. He told Christian of his meeting with Devereux, then lapsed into silence, slowly turning the half-full cup in his hand.

"You've been staring at nothing for five minutes," Christian broke the silence.

Jack dragged his eyes from where they had rested on the cup, meeting Christian's. "God, have I? I'm sorry, Christian."

"Come on, Jack, you've been looking for him for months; that's at an end. It's time to find something else to occupy your days with."

"The truth is there is little to do," Jack said gloomily.

"Your father's estates are vast. Surely their management must be a demand on your time?" Carter pressed.

Jack let go of the cup and rubbed his hands over his face, his fingers running up over his forehead and into his hair, sending it to stand in spikes. "I have lawyers and stewards for that."

"Lawyers and stewards?" Christian repeated slowly, shaking his head.

"What?" Jack said.

"For the Lord's sake, listen to yourself." Christian's voice was flooded with anger.

"What am I supposed to do?" Jack retorted.

"Something... anything would be a start," Christian shot back, throwing his arms wide.

"What would you have me do?" Jack exclaimed, banging his cup down and bruising the wood.

"Stop, Jack, for God's sake! You have news of him. Face the truth. If he wanted to be found, you would have found him. Leave him be and be grateful for what you have learned," Christian said.

Jack stood suddenly, turning his back on Christian. "Why did he do this to me?"

Christian dropped back in his seat. "Plenty of reasons, none of which you want to face."

Jack turned around. "What do you mean? What reasons?"

"It's bloody obvious," Carter said wearily.

"It bloody isn't. Tell me." Jack turned back, his temper about to snap.

Christian raised a hand. "I'll not fight you, Jack. I will surely lose. Sit down, please."

Jack remained standing, his back to Christian, rigid, hands clenched at his side.

Christian stood suddenly, the bench scraping backwards noisily on the stone floor. "My Lord, now settle your arse back on that bench, and listen to a few truths or leave. The choice is yours."

Jack whirled around.

Christian continued. "Look at you. You're doing a poor job of being a Fitzwarren."

Jack's eyes widened at the insult. "What's that supposed to mean?"

"Jack, you've wished all your life for a place in the world, and your father gave it to you on a plate, do you hear me, on a bloody silver platter, and what have you done with it? You could have ground his gift in the dirt with your heel for all the care you are giving it. You're little better dressed than the workers on the docks."

Jack moved quickly to round the table, but Christian, prepared for Jack's advance, jumped to the end, avoiding him, and continued, "You've land, wealth, tenants who depend on you, and you've not a care for them. None of them."

"Enough." Jack slammed a fist down on the table.

"You're right, Jack. I've had enough. Enough of waste, enough of seeing you squander these gifts from your father and Richard." Christian dived to his right, pulling a chair over to stay Jack's advance.

Jack's hand fastened around the chair back and flung the unfortunate woodwork towards the kitchen wall, where it collided with a shelf, unhooking the rope support. The wood tipped, earthenware jars fell to the floor.

Christian flung himself further round the table out of reach, throwing more words towards Jack. "And your poor wife, how much longer are you going to ignore her?"

That was the final taunt Christian would throw; the table had been heaved from the floor and was coming towards him. Christian staggered backwards, caught his feet on the overturned chair and sat down heavily on the floor, the table landing on its side at his feet.

"Jack!"

Two jars from the shelf dropped to the floor; splitting with dull cracks, they spilt their contents over the stone flags. A final one, larger than the rest, slithered along the swinging shelf, teetering momentarily before joining the rest. The moment it hit the flagstones, its sides split, the fired clay collapsing to the floor, releasing the contents into the air. A powder as light as smoke plumed around Jack, enveloping him in a yellow haze.

Christian, his hands on the ground, pushed himself backwards.

Jack swept a log from the fire basket.

Christian raised a hand towards Jack.

The yellow haze thickened. Noxious dust found its way into his nose and throat and, a moment later, into his eyes. Mustard powder choked his breath from his lungs. The cloud unrolled towards Christian, where he was sprawled on the floor. Lower down than Jack, he was quickly covered in a layer. Gagging and blinded, he writhed on the floor, gasping for breath. The stinging dust clawed tears from his eyes. Sightless, he groped around frantically, searching for a route to the closed kitchen door. With a solid thud, his head banged against the table that lay on its side. Then he found himself wrenched upright, dragged across the floor and pushed into the darkness of the kitchen garden, where he landed on his knees on the gravel path. Christian tried to rub the dust from his eyes and nose where it burnt like fire.

From across the kitchen garden, he heard the noise of the well bucket falling into water, followed by the sound of the winch handle being turned at speed to raise it back up on the rope. Then it splashed back a second time into the water, and the handle rotated quickly again. Christian tried to spit the clogged powder from his mouth, but it set off another coughing fit.

The water hit him full in the face. The cold shock of it made him gasp, the cleaning liquid clearing his clogged nose, washing the searing dust from his eyes. The rest of the pail was sluiced over his head, sending his hair to lay in flat tangles covering his eyes. Pushing it aside and wiping tears and snot from his face, he looked with bleary eyes at Jack, who was sat next to him, similarly soaked and regarding him with pale blue eyes rimmed red.

"Why did you have to do that?" Christian complained from behind a sleeve he was using to dry his face.

"Me?" Jack said indignantly.

"For the Lord's sake, my wife is going to murder me when she comes home tomorrow from her sisters and finds her kitchens in such a state," Christian said earnestly.

"You goaded me into it. You know you did," Jack replied.

"I did, and I regret it already," Christian grumbled. "You need to find a road to take and set your feet upon it: soon."

Jack was silent for a moment, his knees drawn up to his chest. "I know."

"Well, if you do, why are you making everyone around you suffer? You can't just wallow in your own self-pity, it's not an enviable place to be," chided Christian.

Jack lifted his head from where it rested on his knees and regarded Christian with a searching gaze. "If I could find a road, a direction, I would take it willingly, but everything is circular. I find myself back where I started day after day. Nothing changes."

"Today, you need to make a change, then. Do something different," Christian said.

"Apart from ruining your kitchens?" Jack said, a half smile on his face.

"Yes, apart from that. There's too much energy within you, it's wasted, and it's pulling you apart," Christian said.

"I don't know if I can," Jack said quietly.

"It's not easy, but I am sure you can find something else to focus on. In a little over four months, you'll be a father. Do you want to meet your child feeling like this?" Christian asked.

Jack shook his head.

"Your friend, Emilio, has he no good advice for you?" Christian asked.

"Like Richard, Emilio has also disappeared," Jack said.

"Oh, I didn't know," Christian replied, adding, "has he returned to the Order?"

Jack shrugged. "I don't know."

Christian found a kerchief and blew his nose noisily. "You told me a few weeks ago about Assingham. Your lawyer was brokering a deal. Has that come to aught?"

"He's asked an extortionate sum for the place, a hundred pounds. I've offered him half of that," Jack grumbled.

"But it did belong to your wife, and you did say that you wished to restore it to her. Perhaps it is time to enter the negotiations yourself; leaving everything to lawyers is never a good idea in my experience," Christian said earnestly.

"True, they seem to have a different concept of time to the rest of us," Jack grumbled, then added, "and they were supposed to be restoring Burton to me as well, but I've heard nothing about that."

"Burton, it was gifted to your brother, wasn't it?" Christian asked, stifling a sneeze.

"It was, and Ayscough, the cur, took possession," Jack said.

"So, how are they helping you with it?" Christian asked, blowing his nose on his sleeve.

Jack grinned. "I wrote myself a letter from Richard appointing me as a trustee over Burton."

Christian looked shocked.

"Oh, come now. To that lawyer, one Fitzwarren signature looks the same as the next, and Richard would approve of me wresting it from Ayscough's hands. It's just a shame it has to be done the lawyers' way: without violence," Jack said, sounding disappointed.

Christian seized on the opening. "Perhaps you should oversee this yourself. This fellow Ayscough dealt with you both dishonestly. I am sure you can make his handover of Burton an unpleasant experience for him."

"I could, I suppose," Jack said slowly.

Christian pressed further. "Come on, Jack. It's a start. Take your lawyers with you if you must. How far away is it?"

"Two days," Jack said, scratching his chin.

"It would get you from London for a week. Why don't you go?"

"It's an idea,"

Christian leaned towards Jack. "It's more than an idea - it's a path. Take it. Anyway, I'd rather you knocked seven bells out of this man Ayscough than me."

†

It was later, sitting alone in front of the fire in the room formerly occupied by his father, that Jack considered what he had learned. So much in one day. Emilio had known the *Santa Luciana* was berthed at St Katherine's dock, he was sure of that. His sudden comedic tirade had been designed to draw Jack's wandering attention away from where the ship lay. Emilio had made him turn his back towards it.

How could Emilio have known it was there? Had he been in communication with Richard? Was it the Order who were involved? He'd not seen the Italian since that day, and he was now sure that this was the reason, not some words spoken hurriedly by the man who had knelt so suddenly before Emilio. In the morning, he would try and find him, confront him and find out precisely what he knew.

If, as Myles suspected, Knox was involved, that didn't seem to be in keeping with one of the staunchest Catholic Organisations in Europe. Why would they want to divide Scotland and pull her away from France?

It didn't make any sense.

None of it did.

Christian had not been interested. He was more relieved that Richard was safe and seemingly back in control of his destiny. And who would blame him? Being involved with Richard's schemes rarely turned out well. They were all lucky to be alive after trying to trade in the weapons that Richard had discovered in Christian's warehouse; indeed Christian's son, Harry, had almost lost his life.

Then there was Myles Devereux.

Why was he being so helpful? If there was one person in London Jack did not trust, it was this lawless, so-called merchant. He didn't disbelieve Myles' account of how he had met Richard. It fitted well enough, and he knew Richard had spent time in Venice. To find out Myles was an impostor, though, was a shock. Somehow it made him more dangerous in Jack's mind, and he was sure Myles was well aware of that fact.

Myles also knew his secret was safe; to expose him was to expose Richard as the scheme's architect. But that didn't explain why he sought him out in the Angel. Myles wasn't working for Richard, he had made that clear; Richard had gone to great lengths to ensure that Jack didn't find out he was in London, as had Emilio. So why was Myles taking the time to tell him that his brother had been in London and that he was working for Cecil and probably involved in a scheme to overthrow the current rule in Scotland?

Why?

Myles acted only for gain so what could he gain from this?

Then there was his brother Robert. The silence surrounding him, Jack found foreboding. He was not a man who was endowed with a great deal of patience, so where was he? What was he doing?

There was a light tap on the door, and a moment later, Edwin entered, followed by a servant carrying wood for the fire.

"It is a cool night, my Lord. I've brought more wood. Can I get you anything else, perhaps something from the kitchens?" Edwin asked.

"I am well, my wife accuses me of snoring, and I am letting her get some sleep," Jack said, resting his head back against the chair and watching as the fire was fed from the log basket. "But thank you."

The brief interruption had stalled his train of thought, and it took him a moment to re-trace his steps to where he had been.

He could explain why Richard was working for Cecil; the forged currency was enough to ensure that his brother obeyed the commands he was given. To a degree, he understood why Richard had not communicated with him when he had been in London.

Or had he?

Was that why Myles had sought him out and told him who Richard was working for and where he was going? Jack ran his mind back over the conversation. Devereux had nothing to gain from the encounter. He'd been sufficiently vague when Jack had asked how he had found out Richard was in London, and, tied to this, Richard had used Devereux as his messenger before.

It made sense. Jack drummed his fingers on the chair arm. But what to do with the information?

Jack didn't find an answer to that question and awoke in the middle of the night, the room cold, the fire burnt down. Making his way through the quiet house, he went upstairs to disturb the slumber of his sleeping wife.

The following morning he attempted to find Emilio, but his enquiries at the lodgings Emilio used and the Order's house in the Strand did not unearth the Italian. The only possibility he could think of was that he was at Court with the Ambassador, and currently, Jack was barred from entry to that circle.

Chapter Fourteen
London – 1559

Christian had urged him to do something different. So here he was, doing something very different. Jack stepped through the shop doorway and let out a long breath. He was here, so he might as well get it over with as quickly as possible. It was a task Jack could have given to another, but he was sure that if he did, it would necessitate more of his personal involvement than he was willing to allot to the undertaking. After thinking it over, he had decided that if he took the task upon himself, he could ensure its quick and painless execution and a rapid outcome.

After all, how hard could it be?

The shop was unfortunately not empty. Two women looked up from a bale of cloth they had been examining, the fabric spread out between them; one of Master Drew's assistants was hovering nearby, tape measure in hand and an apron full of pins. A boy was sweeping the floor, the broom stilling as he looked towards the new arrival. Standing on a wooden box, arms akimbo, was Drew's latest victim, surrounded by three young men pinning an elaborate lace ruff beneath his neatly trimmed beard.

Jack cast his eyes around the populated shop and hesitated.

"Lord Fitzwarren! How can I be of service?" Master Drew, one of London's foremost drapers, sounded worried. With speed a scalded cat would have been proud of, he pounced. Between the draper and Jack was a table piled with folded silks; the excited merchant flew round the end, pressed down hard on the top, making the structure shake, and leapt to land before Jack in one of the shop's few clear spaces.

"If now is not a good time...." Jack mumbled, stepping back to avoid being hit by the draper's head as he executed a low bow before him.

"Now is a most suitable time. How can I be of service?" Master Drew asked, rising and beaming wildly.

Jack cast his eyes around the filled shop. Master Drew, ever attuned to the need of his customers, especially his rich ones, snapped his fingers three times and waved his arm towards the back of the shop. His assistants, it seemed, could be as animated as their master when required. The gentleman with the incomplete ruff was practically lifted from his plinth and carried from the shop. The two women were likewise herded in his wake, the bolt of cloth they had been examining left to unroll itself and pool in an untidy heap on the floor. The broom was left propped against a wall next to a pile of neglected sweepings, and the boy who had been holding it vanished. Jack and Master Drew were, it appeared, almost instantly alone in the shop.

Jack cleared his throat and addressed the draper. "I am in need of your services."

"Of course, my Lord, I would be most happy to serve you. Is there something specific that you need?" Master Drew said, eagerly observing his with a bright expectant gaze.

"I am soon to go north, and I require new clothes," Jack said, hoping that would be sufficient.

"I would be delighted to help. What will you require? Is it a Court affair or formal attire for a specific occasion?" Drew ventured, rubbing his hands together.

This was not what Jack wanted to hear. He had hoped Drew would take the lead; he had little idea what he should or should not order. So he tried again. "No specific occasion. It is a matter of my wardrobe, I will need new clothes for the journey."

"Ah, travelling clothes!" Master Drew nodded sagely.

"Not specifically just for travel, you understand," Jack tried.

Master Drew's brow furrowed. "Perhaps you need a new doublet, sleeves, shirt, perhaps hose as well, all in a matched fashion?"

Jack gave in. "Master Drew, I just need clothes, new ones."

The little man took a step backwards. "I do need to know a little more."

"Like these," Jack waved his hands up and down, indicating the clothes he currently wore.

Master Drew still looked confused.

Jack turned and paced across the shop, cursing under his breath. "You are Myles Devereux's draper?"

"He is amongst my esteemed clientele," Drew said happily. His hands clasped together, he stepped around the fallen bale of cloth.

"Well then, make my clothes like his," Jack said.

"Master Devereux has specific tastes. He always likes to pick out the fabric, and he...."

"I don't care how he does it or what his choices are, make me several sets of clothes like his," Jack said bluntly.

"I can show you some fabric. Perhaps you wish to choose...."

"Let me put it to you simply, Master Drew." Jack turned back to face him. "I am sure you know my recent elevation, the rest of London is, so I see no reason why you should have missed that particular piece of gossip."

Master Drew paled.

"Excellent, I see you have. Well then, prior to my father's recent death, I was overseas, I returned with little and it is my intention that you should furnish my wardrobe," Jack said.

Master Drew's eyes glistened, and he asked, "Everything."

Jack nodded. "Everything."

"That's wonderful – I can bring fabric samples and get your measurements....."

Jack held up his hand to stop the draper from continuing. "You have my measurements from the clothes you provided for my father's funeral. Use those. As for fabric, if it's good enough for Devereux, it will suffice."

"But my Lord," Drew practically pleaded, "there are other considerations."

"Such as?" Jack said impatiently.

"Well, like cuffs, which lace should we use, and buttons and the trimmings for...?"

"If I send someone to make those choices, will that suffice?" Jack said, wishing to draw the visit to a conclusion,

"That would be most helpful," Drew nodded, sounding disappointed.

Not feeling like he had achieved much, Jack escaped from the shop.

†

"I'll only be gone a week, no more," Jack said.

Catherine was laid on the bed, bolstered with pillows and covered with a counterpane. "That's good, the weather is fine at the moment, it'll be agreeable for you," she replied.

Jack hadn't expected her to be so happy about his proposed trip to Burton. He'd not told her of what he had learned from Devereux. If Richard was working with Cecil again, then the fewer people who knew about it, the better. It could only be a cause for worry, and he saw no reason to share it.

"I will need new clothes," Jack announced, lying on the bed beside her.

"Well, there's a truth," Catherine laughed then, giving him a playful slap, added, "if you are getting on here, take your boots off."

"I've been to see the draper, but it wasn't as easy as I had thought it would be," Jack confessed, discarding his boots on the floor. Lying down beside her, he helped himself to one of her pillows, earning another punch.

"He came here before. Why didn't you just command him to do that again?" Catherine said, sitting forward and rearranging the remaining pillows.

"Because I don't want him to come here. I don't want half the house turned into his drapers shop just so I can choose which cloth he should use, which buttons he should sew on, and which bloody Italian lace he should use on the shirts. It'll take hours. So I am asking you, as a kindness to your husband, to visit his shop for me," Jack said, reclining next to her on top of the bed, one hand stroking the top of Catherine's already rounding stomach.

"What did you ask him to provide for you?" Catherine asked, settling herself back amongst the stuffed down.

Jack shrugged. "I told him I needed everything."

"Everything? Jack Fitzwarren, that man'll have your eyes out. Why did you give him free rein to spend your gold?" Catherine scolded, sitting upright and regarding him through narrowed eyes.

"Because, woman, I need clothes, and it would be a kindness if you would help me," Jack said, smiling. "I tried. Give me some credit for that. Come on, woman, if I leave it to Drew, I'll end up looking like a popinjay. I just need you to direct him to provide good sober clothing."

Catherine smiled. "Maybe I'd like you more if you looked like a popinjay. I am sure Emilio would."

Jack rolled his eyes and pushed himself up on the bed. "Not that again. He's gone, woman, I've not seen him for weeks. Stop scolding me in front of my son."

Catherine laughed. "Son? It could be a girl."

Jack shook his head, a smile on his face. "God in heaven knows I am surrounded by nags and scolds. Surely he wouldn't be so cruel as to bless me with another to add to their ranks."

Catherine's right hand extracted a bolster pillow from behind her and brought it down on his head. "Nags and scolds, indeed!"

"Exactly. Surely the Lord will have some sympathy," Jack said, deflecting the pillow towards the floor.

"Husband, how many women do you have in this harem?" Catherine sent another pillow towards him.

Jack caught the pillow mid-flight and tucked it under his head, a thoughtful look on his face. "Well, obviously there's you, then Alice, Hanwyn's wife, Lizbet has a tongue in her head she's not afraid to use, Christian's wife, Alice, has little liking for me, and then there's Red Molly." Jack ticked each off on his fingers.

"Red Molly, who's she?" Catherine shrieked, sending a pillow to slap down on his chest this time.

"You must have heard me speak of her," Jack said, retrieving the pillow he fitted it beneath his head on top of the other one, observing her seriously.

"You know very well you've not spoken to me about her," Catherine replied.

Jack settled back. "I should have. She's a beauty. When the sunlight catches her right, she's got the colour of rosehips in her hair, long legs firm and full of promise, fierce as the heart of a storm, taming her will be a pleasure...ouch."

"Stop it." Catherine pummeled him with another pillow.

Jack continued, laughing, "She's willing, and only last week...."

"Jack Fitzwarren."

Jack caught her wrists and pulled her on top of him. "I'm teasing you."

"Are you, indeed," Catherine said, slipping her arms around his neck.

"I am," Jack said, kissing her. "Red Molly has four legs with a hoof at the end of each."

"And that's supposed to make me feel better? It's a fact you love your horses more than your wife," Catherine said with mock hurt.

"That's unfair," Jack said. "Some of them I do, but not all of them, take for example, those two I bought at the auction last week...."

"Stop teasing me," Catherine rebuked.

"The good thing about horses is I can own as many of them as I wish and, unlike a wife, they don't get jealous," Jack said, planting a kiss on her forehead and rolling her back to her side of the bed,

"I'm not jealous," Catherine replied, untangling herself from the counterpane.

Jack laughed, pulling her close and nuzzling her neck. "Yes, you are. So will you go and see Master Drew for me?"

"I will. And I shall make certain your clothes are entirely drab to ensure you don't attract the attention of any more scolds and nags," Catherine declared, wrapping her arms around him.

Chapter Fifteen

Something had been at the back of his mind for days, constantly nagging for attention. After failing to find Emilio, he'd been trying not to think about the Italian and his whereabouts. He was, he had told himself, probably at Court, part of the Ambassador's entourage as Catherine had suggested.

And why wouldn't he be?

It was an opportunity to be with his countrymen. That he had prevented Jack from seeing the *Santa Luciana* when it was birthed at St Katherine's dock was unforgivable – and why he had done that, Jack intended to extract from him next time they did meet.

But there was something else.

Like a neglected child, the moment the stranger bent to kiss Emilio's hand on the quay kept pressing itself to the front of his mind, forcing him to notice it. No matter how often he tried to banish it from his thoughts, it kept finding its way back into his consciousness.

The flames ebbed in the hearth, the fire dying. Jack's eyes closed. He should have been asleep in moments. But sleep wouldn't come. He was being plagued by the image of Emilio on his horse riding away from the quay, his men scrambling to mount and follow their master.

Damn him to Hell.

Why was his mind forcing him to relive the event?

Rising from the chair Jack fed the embers from the fire basket. Reaching for the wine flagon, he refilled his glass. Perhaps that would help him sleep and dispel the images from his mind.

Taking a deep breath and letting it out slowly, he focussed on the new flames and the taste of the mellow wine. Fresh wood, dried over the summer months in the wood store, quickly caught fire from the grate embers. Jack stretched back in the chair, feet towards the warming flames, and watched as the pale wood blackened to the touch of the fire's dancing orange fingers. Sap pressed by the heat bubbled from the ends of the cut wood and dripped, hissing, to the hearth. Split by the heat, a log fell apart, sending a myriad of firefly sparks to launch themselves into the air. Wind yowled down the chimney for a moment, pressing the fire towards the hearth; angry orange flames rose in its wake, and a gust of grey smoke drifted towards the ceiling. A log, alive with fire, rolled towards the edge of the grated confines, dropping embers to the hearth. Jack's boot ended its escape sending it back towards the hot embrace, which welcomed it with a crackling chorus.

Looking down at his right hand, he could see the flames had been caught by the facets of the stones in his ring, deepening their colour; the ring had saved his life, of that he was sure.

Emilio.

Why did everything remind him of that damned Italian? Even Myles had taunted him over the incident on the quay.

Jack stopped suddenly in the act of raising the glass to his lips.

That was it!

That was what his tired mind had been trying to tell him. Only two people knew what had happened that day when the Ambassador arrived: himself and Emilio. The only person he had told about it was Catherine, and he was confident that there was no way Myles could have learnt of it from her.

So this could only mean that Myles had found out about it from Emilio or, more likely, someone who had spoken to Emilio. Jack groaned and pressed his fingers into his eyes. Any desire to sleep was gone.

A few minutes later, he opened the door to the kitchen and dropped down the two steps to the cold flagged floor. Moonlight from the high windows on the west side of the kitchen sent three wide shafts of light to illuminate the interior. The tapers and fires were out and would remain so for another few hours when the women arrived to light the bread ovens. The door closed behind him, and Jack's eyes roamed the empty room.

"Are they not feeding you enough?" a familiar voice said behind him.

Turning, Jack found Lizbet, a shawl around her shoulders, standing in the corridor.

"I can't sleep," he confessed.

Lizbet's eyes widened. "When has sleep ever escaped you?"

Jack stepped down into the kitchen and said gloomily. "Since now, it seems."

Two willow baskets sat on the top of one of the benches near the ovens, and Jack tipped one towards him, looking hopefully inside - it was empty, and so was the second. A moment later, there was a light tap at the door.

"My Lord, I can have the servants prepare you a meal," Hanwyn ventured hesitantly.

"Look what you've done now," Lizbet scolded, "you'll have the whole house awake shortly." She turned to Hanwyn. "Go back to your bed. I'll look after Lord Fitzwarren."

Hanwyn looked towards Jack.

"Yes, go on. There's no need for you to be awake as well," Jack confirmed.

"Sit down," Lizbet commanded, her back to Jack, a poker in her hand. She was reviving the remains of the fire in the grate. Bright orange embers glowed, and shortly afterwards, the flames danced among them. Lizbet had tapers lit and was busily collecting what she needed from around the kitchen.

Jack watched her in silence.

Lizbet disappeared through a door; when she reappeared, she was carrying an earthenware jug filled with cool ale. Without looking at Jack, she thumped it down in front of him. Then, from a high shelf to the left of the fire, she retrieved a glazed pottery cup and slid it down the table. Jack reached out and stopped its progress. Lizbet, now at the other end of the kitchen, opened a tall cupboard and, extracting a tray, disappeared into one of the pantries. She returned a few minutes later, the tray now laden, and heeled the door closed behind her. Jack's eyes were on the tray as she approached him.

"You seem to have a remarkable knowledge of my kitchens," Jack said, reaching for one of the small neatly made pies Lizbet had placed on the tray.

"Hardly remarkable," Lizbet scoffed, battering Jack's hand away. "Can you not wait until I've set it down?"

Jack grinning, snatched the pie and fed it into his mouth, shaking his head.

"You don't change, do you?" Lizbet dropped down onto the bench on the opposite side of the table. Jack reached for a second pie, and Lizbet asked, "Do you like them?"

Jack nodded.

A satisfied look settled on her face. "Good. You've me you've to thank for the fare that's coming from your kitchen."

Jack's brow furrowed.

"Don't look so puzzled. I've spent a lot of time here, out of the way of your wife, and at least I could tell them what you liked on your table," Lizbet replied.

"Oh," Jack said, round a mouthful of pastry, "I didn't know."

"Don't worry, it suits me well. It keeps me busy, and your wife is not especially interested in how your kitchen is run," Lizbet replied.

Jack, who had been in the act of raising the cup to his lips set it back on the table, and said pointedly, "My wife, has a name, Lizbet, and you know well enough that she's not having an easy time with her first child."

"Some people are wont to make their lives difficult or make it appear so," Lizbet replied tartly.

Jack raised a hand. "Stop, woman. I came down here because I couldn't sleep, to try to escape my troubles, and you are just set to add to them."

Lizbet selected another pie from the tray and held it out towards Jack. "I'm sorry, I've not seen you to speak to recently."

Jack took the offered pie, his eyes upon it he turned it in his hand. "All I seem to do at the moment is talk and to the wrong people."

"That doesn't sound good ....Want to tell me what is troubling you?" Lizbet asked, laying a hand on his wrist.

Jack raised his eyes to meet hers, his expression sad. "I cannot share, lass. These are troubles I need to keep to myself."

Lizbet withdrew her hand and, rising, leaned across the table towards him. "Are you saying you cannot trust me?"

Jack shook his head.

"And who exactly, Jack Fitzwarren, do you think I am going to share your words with?" Lizbet thumped her chest with the flat of her hand. "I am full already of your secrets and your brother's."

"Well, that's true enough," Jack said resignedly.

"What trouble have you got yourself in this time?" Lizbet pressed.

"Is it that obvious?" Jack said, meeting her enquiring gaze.

Lizbet laughed. "I know you far too well. Come on. Tell me, what have you done?"

"I've done nothing!" Jack replied indignantly, then added, "I've had news of Richard." Jack raked his hands through his hair, rearranging it into untidy spikes.

Lizbet froze.

"He's well, by all accounts," Jack said quickly.

"Thank God for that," Lizbet said on a shallow breath. "How did you find him?"

"I didn't. I met with Devereux, and he had news of him. The *Santa Luciana* has been in London recently. It seems that Richard was on it, but it sailed before I had a chance to find out," Jack said gloomily.

Lizbet leaned towards him, placing a hand on his wrist. "There is more to it than that. I can sense it."

Jack refused to meet her gaze and helped himself to slices of cold meat from the tray.

"Perhaps I can help?" Lizbet squeezed his arm, then added. "What harm can it do? A trouble shared ...."

Jack relented and looked up. "Devereux told me he's been in the Tower and that he's been forced to work for Cecil again. Have you heard of John Knox?"

"Vaguely. He's a preacher, isn't he?"

Jack nodded. "He is, and one not welcome in England. He's Scottish, and Richard has been tasked with taking him back to his homeland to help raise support for the rebellion against the French."

"None of this sounds good," Lizbet said.

"I know. And I don't know what to do," Jack said gloomily.

"There's not a lot you can do, is there?" Lizbet said bluntly.

Jack shrugged. "I've thought about it for days, and the only way Devereux could have known what he did was if Richard had told him. There was no way he could have found it out on his own. Plus, he does nothing if it's not for a profit, so why would he willingly come and share the information he had with me?"

"So you think Richard had been to see him?" Lizbet asked, her brow furrowed.

"I do. Devereux was acting as a messenger. And there's more ...."

"Go on."

"A few weeks ago, I went with Emilio to St Katherine's Dock when he was to welcome the Italian Ambassador. All of a sudden he started to berate me for my appearance. He did it because he was worried I was about to see the *Santa Luciana* berthed further along the quay," Jack said, slopping more ale into the cup as he spoke.

"Are you sure? Why would Emilio do that to you when he has been helping you try and find Richard? It doesn't make sense," Lizbet said, frowning.

"I know. After the Ambassador arrived, he stormed from the quay, completely ignored me, and left without a backward glance. I've not seen him since. There is no trace of him at his lodgings, and I can only think he is at Court with the Ambassador," Jack finished.

"This is quite a puzzle," Lizbet said.

"I am glad you think so. I told Christian, and he brushed it off as if it was nothing," Jack said, relief in his voice.

"Did he, indeed."

"Yes, he advised me to go to Burton and concern myself with my own affairs," Jack said gloomily.

"Does that not strike you as odd?" Lizbet asked, her brow furrowed.

Jack shrugged. "What do you mean?"

"Maybe Richard has spoken to more than just Devereux," Lizbet said slowly. "If he did, then the message is clear, I would have thought."

"Not to me," Jack said morosely.

"Richard is safe, he's even told you what he is doing and also that it isn't something he's willingly involved in and if he's spoken to Christian as well, then he's telling you to stop fruitlessly looking for him," Lizbet explained.

"You think so?" Jack said dubiously.

"Well, it fits the facts, don't you think? If he has gone to Scotland under Cecil's orders what can you do? It could be too dangerous for you to try and be involved. Richard has told you to go to Burton, which sounds like the best course of action. You know he is well and as safe as he can be, and it's wonderful news that the *Santa Luciana* is seaworthy again," Lizbet finished smiling.

"Alright, if we are fitting events to facts, then tell me why Emilio has vanished?" Jack asked.

"That's not as straightforward, I grant you," Lizbet said thoughtfully. "Did he say anything to you?"

Jack shook his head. "Nothing."

"There was something. I can read it on your face," Lizbet said.

"Fine, but I don't think it's relevant. As the Ambassador's entourage walked by us along the quay, one man detached himself from the rest, and knelt before Emilio. He spoke rapidly in Italian, and the words were meant for Emilio only," Jack recounted the brief incident.

"What happened after this?"

"He left. I told you. Turned on his heel, strode towards his horse and left. I've not seen the bastard since," Jack said with feeling.

"And you think this has little to do with his absence?" Lizbet asked.

"He didn't want me to see the *Santa Luciana*. I'm sure of that," Jack replied.

"Who was this man? What did he look like?"

"I don't know." Jack was resenting being quizzed.

"Same age as Emilio, older?" Lizbet said.

"I don't know, it took place in a few moments. I didn't have time to get more than an impression of the man," Jack said.

"And what was that impression?"

"He was dressed in Court attire, as were all of those who arrived with the Ambassador," Jack provided.

Jack was relieved when Lizbet ceased her interrogation, a thoughtful look on her face as she placed two small apple pies before him. After she'd watched him eat them, she asked. "So you are leaving? Going to Burton?"

Jack nodded. "I am."

"When?" Lizbet asked.

Jack drained the ale cup and, reaching for the pitcher, began to refill it. "As soon as I can."

"Does Catherine know?"

"Of course, and she is happy for me to go. I am hoping that I will not be away for more than a week." Jack met Lizbet's eyes.

"All will be well in time, I am sure. Anyway, going to Burton will take our minds from it," Lizbet said.

"Our minds?" Jack repeated, his hands dropping from his face and his blue eyes fixed on Lizbet's brown ones.

"You'll need someone to keep you clothed and fed," Lizbet said.

Jack leaned across the table, his voice earnest. He said, "Lizbet, I can't take you with me."

Lizbet rose from the table and, looking down at him, said, "That's not bothered you before."

"That's not true; before, I couldn't do much about it, but now I can," Jack said with finality.

Lizbet's balled fists had found her hips, and she leaned towards him. "You can take me with you or leave me here to fight with your wife. The choice is yours."

Jack looked skyward.

Chapter Sixteen

London - 1559

Richard had been returned to the *Santa Luciana* during the night when nobody was abroad to witness his passage through London or his arrival at St Katherine's dock. Cecil had allowed him at least the opportunity to make a few stops on his way, for which he was grateful, even if they had taken place under the supervision of the Captain of the Queen's guard. Their ship's watch crew rapidly lowered a boarding plank, and a contingent of ten of the Queen's men remained on the quay as a guard on the ship. Cecil was keen to ensure he didn't slip unnoticed from the ship.

Arms folded, leaning against the mizzen mast, his face illuminated by a gimble lamp, was Jerome.

"I see Dulos awaits my return," Richard said, his voice as brittle as glass as his feet dropped onto the deck.

"Two men are waiting for your return in your cabin," Jerome supplied, reaching up to unhook the lamp.

"You do surprise me. I would have imagined you'd have taken that over yourself or had it rented to the Order by now." Richard's dark eyes, capturing the moonlight, shone like ice. Jerome, lamp in hand, had turned towards the door leading to the lower decks.

"Lead on, Dulos. Let us find out what treachery awaits in Hades," Richard said, his voice quiet yet as sharp as steel.

Voices could be heard in conversation as they approached his cabin. One he recognized, another he didn't, although a Lothian lilt, backed with a volume that was more than needed in such a small room, gave him an unwelcome idea of who it might be.

Opening the door, he found he had unfortunately been right.

Seated at the small table was Morley, Cecil's man; small, neat, darkly dressed and looking particularly pale in the candlelight. Opposite him, robed, bearded and wearing a black bonnet and a disapproving expression, was Richard's cargo.

John Knox.

"Ah, the statesman and the churchman. Shall I join you?" Richard said. Entering the cabin, he drew a chair to the table, seating himself.

"Aye, the false priest is among us, I see," Knox's steady gaze was upon Jerome, who stood near the door.

Richard leaned back in the chair, a broad pleased smile settling on his face, his foot pushing a stool towards Jerome. "Please, Jerome, join us. You've been in charge of slaves before, our guest has taken his turn at the oars, so I am told. There must be much you have in common."

"Fitzwarren, you have no shame, do you?" Jerome didn't take the stool; instead, he remained standing near the door. If he was annoyed by Richard's comments, it did not show on his face. A sudden irregular jarring noise told of the ship's timbers dragging along the quayside and it was only Morley whose face showed alarm.

"Your Order is a distillation of all that displeases God. The unholy Templar and Popish ceremony is thickened in an ignorant stew in the Hospitallers. It dinnae sit well wi' me," Knox declared, dark eyes housed beneath a canopy of thick eyebrows boring into the captains.

Richard inclined his head towards Jerome. "You have to admit, he's direct. Mind you, the pulpit is no place for delicate debate."

Knox, clearly not finished, extended a long forefinger towards Jerome. "Your kind mock Jesus Christ a' surely as the Romans did aboot the cross. Dressin' the altar and making of it a sham, mocking an' insultin' him further with ya pretense of prayers an' ceremony. God's word demands faith; nowhere, mark me, did he demand ceremony. They are baseless," Knox finished by swiping the bonnet from his head, slapping it down on the table.

"Matthew 27 - and they mocked him," Richard echoed, his brow furrowed, a thoughtful expression on his face, the eyes he fixed on Jerome desolate, offering no friendship. "An apt section if I recall correctly. Slightly earlier in the same text, Judas, smitten by regret, hangs himself. Let me lay the yard arm at your disposal."

Jermone ignored him.

"Perhaps we could re-enact the scene for our visitor's entertainment," Richard continued, "a minor religious drama to pass the time on this noxious voyage."

"I will be outside should you need me," Jerome said levelly. Casting his eyes around the room he held Richard's gaze for a moment before leaving and closing the cabin door quietly behind him.

"You have issues with your captain?" Knox observed, refitting the bonnet to his haze of grey-tufted hair.

"You are observant." Richard drew his eyes from the closed door towards the speaker.

"There's a tension, ye canna deny it," Knox continued. From above him, there came the noise of quick footsteps on the deck, and his eyes were drawn towards the sound. "When you have a keen eye for details, one truth prevails."

"Good. Then you'll also be able to sense that I have little interest in you other than the fact that I am to deliver you to Scotland," Richard replied. "Has anyone ever said to you barba non facit philosophum?"

Morley, who had been in the process of taking a drink, choked. Richard cast a disparaging glance in his direction.

"I am told you are a mercenary. Part of that breed that have little regard for anything other than personal greed." Knox's large hands were knotted together on the table, all of his attention on the man who was to convey him to Scotland.

Richard returned the cleric's stare in equal measure. "If it pleases you to say so."

Knox, not to be put off continued. "Greed is the king of sins an' the undoin' o' the weak," Knox proclaimed. "Ephesians tells us that the path to greed is one that the idolater takes. Luck tells us not to store up treasures on earth where moth and rust destroy and thieves break in and steal."

Rising from his chair, hands clasped behind his back, Knox continued striding backwards and forward in the cramped cabin. Taller than Richard, the Scot's grey-tufted hair, uncapped now, grazed the cabin roof as he paced, his words too loud for the small space. "You canna serve both God an' gold."

Somewhere above them, a rope whined through a shackle block.

Richard cast a glance towards Morley, saying confidentially. "Do you think he'll be like this the whole voyage, or is there a spring inside that will thankfully unwind and afford us some peace?"

Knox stopped, clamping one of his large hands on Richard's shoulder. "At least you have not mocked him by feigned worship, your captain is amongst the leagues of misguided people."

"Of course, and you would be amongst God's most equitable servants," Richard replied. He pushed back against the pressure on his shoulder for a moment longer before extracting himself, causing Knox to stumble over the now empty chair.

"A man wi' God upon his side is in the majority," Knox growled, ramming the chair from his path.

"May I be allowed a moment to speak?" As Richard spoke, the table tipped slightly as the *Luciana* moved on the water; his hand instinctively picked up Morley's cup, placing it into a ringed indent to contain it.

"Of course, if you wish to offer a defense for your actions." Knox straightened to his full height, his bonnet against the low roof.

"No, not at all." Richard then addressed Morley, "I just wish to point out that the worst waste of time is time given to argument with fools and fanatics. Neither care overly much for truth or the reality of the situation; they only wish for the victory of their illusions and beliefs. It would not matter how much evidence I heaped before him for the fool, blinded by ego, hatred and resentment, lacks the capacity to understand. The desire to be absolute, to be right, overrides sense. Take note, Master Morley, I fear this is going to be a long voyage."

Morley, wisely, chose not to reply, his eyes switching between Richard and Knox.

"You are a deceiver, sir. I stand by ma word, an I'll hold the ground tha' God has given me by his grace, I shall not back from principal, do ye hear me?" Knox's fist pounded the table top three times, rattling the cups against the wood.

"I do hear you. However, you certainly didn't listen to me. I'll not argue with you. Nolo contendere." Richard, palms flat on the desk, leaned towards Knox, "If you'll excuse me, Master Knox, I have business to attend to with Morley, not of a religious nature, more a matter of twenty pieces of silver, and I feel it would be an affront to your principles to discuss such blasphemy within your hearing."

Richard walked over and opened the cabin door, calling Jerome's name. "Our guest will require accommodation for the passage, and since the *Luciana* is regrettably not fitted with benches and oars, he can instead share your cabin."

Jerome's composure was finally rattled. "Mine?"

"Indeed. I don't see why anyone else aboard this ship should have to put up with his pointless prattle, you on the other hand, I feel are a just exception," then to Knox, "You can see this as a task from God to point out the error of my captain's ways but please, sir, remember the sixth commandment. The only fit stakes to burn him at are my masts, and the poor *Luciana* has suffered enough from fire already."

Knox brought his face within inches of Richard's, his voice a low, threatening rumble. "Yer a hireling and nowt more, remember that. When we arrive in Scotland, I'll mak it ma duty to extract from ye a payment for ye blasphemy."

A moment later, the door closed with a slam, the noise reverberating around the small cabin, momentarily drowning out the sound of a large chain clanking noisily through its cog spokes.

"Are you sure that was wise?" Morley said, breaking his silence.

Richard smiled broadly. "I have created a microcosm. Let us regard it as an experiment."

Morley ignored Richard's words and, leaning forward, said, "You have been employed to aid the rebellion in Scotland. Why anger their figurehead?"

"As has been pointed out, I am a mercenary. I've little interest in Knox. Causes, in my experience, have the disagreeable practice of attracting men such as he."

"And now you've trapped your captain and Knox in the same room," Morley said, shaking his head.

"Indeed. A twin pointed sword, and both of them clothed in the indignation of the righteous. Who will be the victor, do you suppose?" Richard sounded amused.

"You are to deliver him intact," Morley reminded him.

"I am providing him with the opportunity to hone his skill; when he has sharpened up his sermons on Jerome, the Scots rabble will flock to him like rats round a split grain sack. Cecil should thank me," Richard added, "and Jerome deserves a lot worse than having to listen to Knox. This brings us neatly back to the reason for your presence on my ship."

"I am to be here only until she sails. Lord Burghley has provided a guard on the quay, and I am to ensure you sail with Knox to Scotland," Morley provided.

Richard fixed him with a hard stare and leaned across the table. "What exactly is to stop me from heading into the middle of the North sea, heaving your irritating Scot over the side and sailing to Africa with your gold?"

Morley didn't seem perturbed by the argument. "You went to a lot of trouble a few years ago, even to the extent of blowing a hole in the side of the Tower, to retrieve your brother. Lord Burghley relies on your family loyalty with good reason."

Richard sat back hard, the pegged joints in the chair complaining. Above them, the clattering noise of a capstan turning was accompanied by more footsteps. When the noise abated Richard said, "Family, Morley, are a continual trial."

Morley smiled, his foot tapping a wooden box on the floor. "Here are the funds you are to deliver. Slightly more than twenty-two pieces of silver."

Richard rubbed his hands over his face. "Do you believe this plan of Cecil's is a good course of action?"

"Policy is not mine to make or comment upon," Morley stated bluntly. Then, changing the subject, he said, "your captain was kind enough to give me a tour of your ship when I arrived. I have only ever seen ships such as this from the quay. Truly remarkable. To be aboard something so big that does not sink below the water is incredible."

"It is a matter of science," Richard said, distracted by the sound of the water slapping on the sides of the Luciana's hull.

Morley continued, "The masts alone must weigh many tonnes, and the cannon, of course, will add even more weight." Morley shook his head and added, "Is it possible to overweight a ship such as this? Are there limits as to how much she can carry?"

"Cannon?" Richard repeated slowly.

Morley smiled. "Of course, you've not had time to converse with your captain, have you? The gun deck of the Santa Luciana has been refitted while you were... at court."

"Refitted?"

"Indeed," Morley sounded delighted to be the bearer of such good news. "The cannon from the warship, *Jer Falcon,* have been fitted. Lord Burghley felt there was little point in sending a mercenary ship north to aid the rebellion if she could not lose off a round of cannon shot."

Richard dropped forward in the chair, the front two legs banging solidly back on the floor, his grey eyes riveted on Morley. "Black powder and shot as well?"

Morley nodded, smiling. "There would be little point in providing cannons if there are not the means to fire them."

"It slightly offsets the irksome cargo you have given me to ship. Tell me, how did you get Knox to England? Cecil indicated he was waiting for passage from Bruges," Richard asked.

There was a sudden bang, and the ship tipped. A pen on the desk rolled towards Morley, and Richard quickly stopped it from falling from the table. Some of the colour had drained from Morley's face, and his small white hands had found safety in gripping the table's edge.

"The tide is rising, and her hull is against the quayside, that's all," Richard reassured.

"Yes, yes, of course," Morley said. Swallowing hard, he regained his composure and answered the question. "Knox was brought to England two weeks ago. It was a closely kept secret for obvious reasons. He had hoped, I believe, that the Queen would grant him safe passage. However, that wasn't the case, and as such ....what's that?" A noise like a wounded animal in some deep cave reached up to them from the bottom of the ship's hull.

"She'll not sink," Richard laughed, "the timbers in the hull move against each other. That's what you can hear."

"There has been a lot of weight added. How can you be so sure?" Morley had regained a little of his colour, and his voice had steadied.

"She was designed originally to carry cannon. Without them, she rides too high in the water, which makes her unstable in a heavy sea. So to compensate, her ballast weight was increased. For all his faults, Jerome is a good captain, and he will have removed ballast from her hull to compensate."

"Ah, so that was what was being removed yesterday when I arrived," Morley said, nodding, "I did wonder why they were unloading rocks."

"We might need to remove more, but it can be heaved over the sides when we are at sea. The basic premise is you can't add it back again, so it's better to sail heavy and trim it down rather than to sail light, or so Jerome has told me," Richard replied.

"It seems he has been schooling you well," Morley replied. His hands, Richard noted, were still clamped to the table for security.

"In many things," Richard replied a note of sarcasm in his voice.

The *Luciana* heeled over again, this time further. Alarm widened Morley's eyes, and he rose from his chair. "Surely this is not right?"

"You'll get used to it," Richard said sweetly.

"What do you mean?" Morley said, his eyes widening,

"Jerome's just deployed her topsails," Richard replied.

"Why would he do that on the river?" Alarm added a shrill edge to Morley's voice

"He wouldn't. We left St Katherine's some time ago," Richard said with satisfaction, folding his arms across his chest. "It seems your master feels you need to accompany me."

Chapter Seventeen

Dawn revealed a day that had been made from a dreary pallet. England was a thick grey line along the horizon, a rough horizontal mark dividing the drab ashen sea from a dulled steel sky. The *Santa Luciana* had turned north and was tracking the coast as she headed towards Scotland, an efficient northerly wind pulling her through the wavetops. The air was heavy with moisture, and everything above deck was wet with a chilling combination of sea spray and a fine cold drizzle.

Richard had left Morley, frightened and still trying to deal with the calamity of what had befallen him, and gone in search of Jerome who he found on the aftcastle, a cloak hanging heavily from his shoulders, the fibres sodden. Jerome smiled broadly, unaffected by either the sombre weather or the dark mood of his employer.

"Alone at last," Richard snarled, mounting the last three steps to join Jerome on the deck, his gaze on the captain alive with malice. "Emilio told me I had a traitor on my ship. I must admit I was surprised."

"Were you?" the smile was still on Jerome's face.

"Have I been a part of some peculiar bet? For it feels very much as if I have been treated like a puppet." Richard walked slowly towards Jerome, stopping when he was an arm's length away. "I'd misjudged the Order.

I thought they would have little use for you after you lost one of their ships. You told me before that you wanted the path before us to be a clear one, remember? I actually trusted you, Jerome."

"I know. I was surprised by that. However, it did make the deception easier," Jerome replied honestly. "In my defence, not that I need one, I also told you that I will adhere to the vow I took to obey the Order until the breath leaves my body."

"I would dearly like to hasten that moment for you." Richard's cold gaze locked with Jerome's.

"I am sure you would," Jerome accepted, meeting Richard's glare with steady eyes.

"The moment the opportunity presented itself to ingratiate yourself with Malta again at my expense, you took it," Richard's voice was edged with frustrated anger.

Jerome shook his head. "We are both bound to obey. Surely you know that?"

"Why didn't you tell me?" Richard's words, harshly spoken, told of both desperation and endless disappointment.

"Would you have gone to London willingly?" Jerome asked, his eyebrows raising.

Richard didn't reply.

"I have played my part. You now have work to complete for the Order, I will help as much as I can; after this, your ship will sail wherever you please. I do wish you no ill will," Jerome spread his arms wide.

Richard turned from him, his hands clasped tightly behind his back, the knuckles white. He stared unseeing over the guard rail towards the rolling sea, the battle with his temper nearly lost.

After five long minutes, he turned back towards the captain. "Explain just one thing to me. I can understand why Cecil wishes for the French to be ousted from Scotland. That is a simple matter of national security, but I cannot grasp why the Order wants to turn Scotland over to the Protestant cause and, worse, Knox? This makes no sense to me at all. What am I missing?"

Jerome just shrugged.

"So, you don't know either? Helpful to the last," Richard said bluntly. He'd already put the question to Morley, who couldn't supply a reason, so that left only one person to ask.

†

Knox was seated, reading, his craggy face illuminated by an oil lamp. Looking up as Richard entered, he smoothed the red silk bookmark into the book's gutter before closing it. His oversized hands, resting on the Bible, almost covered it completely.

"Why would the Order champion your cause?" Richard asked, stepping into the small cabin and closing the door behind him.

"They dinnea, an' I would not wish for them to, any involvement would be a sin against God," Knox declared, his voice booming in the confines of Jerome's small cabin.

"Well, like it or not, they have," Richard stated, his arms folded solidly across his chest, his back planted against the door.

"I shallna stand in the same light as this blasphemy, 'tis a sin I cannae countenance. Ye must be mistaken. On this earth it can neve' be that their false ceremony could stand side by side wi' tha true word o' God," Knox pronounced loudly rising from his chair.

Richard regarded the preacher with a grim stare. "The true cold facts are that I have been dragged from the path I chose, by the Order, with the simple purpose of returning you to Scotland. I am as perplexed as you are."

"Dinnae play with the truth, sir! The Order are no friend o' the reformist." Knox took a step toward Richard, filling the small space.

Richard nodded in agreement. "So why would they aid you, Knox, or is it that they wish to lend assistance to Elizabeth?"

"An illegitimate whore, 'tis repugnant to nature that England promotes a woman to bear rule," Knox's forefinger stabbed the air before Richard's face, the look on his face daring the younger man to flinch.

Richard, ignoring the threatening gesture, pressed on with his interrogation. "When you were housed by Cecil in London, did you meet an Italian by the name of de Nevarra?"

"I ken the name. I paid him little regard; he was present during a meeting with Lord Burghley," Knox said. Lowering the threatening hand, he glared into Richard's eyes with a piercing unblinking stare; somewhere in their depths was something a little wild and untamed.

"He said nothing to you? Asked you no questions," Richard paced the questions quickly, ignoring the closeness of Knox.

"I traded not a word with him. Who is de Nevarra?" Knox demanded.

"No one you'd be inclined to like," Richard replied, unfolding his arms. Knox could offer no help as to why the Order had a hand in this. It could be that they simply wanted to offer assistance to Elizabeth, help her with the problem brewing on her northern border, but that seemed too much like a simple answer.

There had to be more to it.

There had to be an advantage for them to have become involved, for them to risk the ousting of the De Guise family from Scotland and watch as a reformist rabble took control.

But what was it?

Knox's loud voice tried to cut through his thoughts, but he ignored him.

Knox seized his arm, the hard grip pulling him closer to the preacher. "I'm na fool, sir, dinnae treat me as if I were one. Who is de Nevarra?"

Richard didn't pull from the hold. His face close to Knox's, he said, "His uncle is Philip of Spain, his brother is the Pope, and he is a member of the Order of St John. You do seem to be attracting a lot of Catholic support. What I want to know is why?"

Knox released him, pushing Richard back against the door. "Any action they would take would be ta overthrow the venture. How can ye possibly try to assert that these blasphemous souls are providing support for a cause that is so irksome to them?"

"I don't know why, but the fact remains that they are. Like it or not, the captain of the ship was tied to the Order of St John, and he has worked to ensure I help you make your way to Scotland," Richard replied, wondering for a moment what Emilio de Nevarra had made of this Scottish rebel when he had met him.

"This cannae be! You attempt to make a fool of our cause. Their very existence is a sin against the Lord God, there can be nay help from this quarter, nor would any be welcome," Knox said. He planted his hands flat on the door on either side of Richard's head, trapping him against the door.

Richard matched his glare briefly before lithely ducking beneath one of Knox's arms, extricating himself from the poor trap. Running his hands through his hair, he tried to focus on the problem.

Think, damn you. Why was this happening?

His train of thought was abruptly stopped.

"The Lord God will see 'em an' their falsehoods fall, crumble an' break like hollow shams made o' sand, 'tis a sin against...." Knox declared, clamping a firm hand on Richard's shoulder, determined to get and hold the younger man's attention.

"For God's sake. Stop." Richard pulled himself from the hold.

Knox didn't. "...God an' he will smite them down. I, sir, will be his right arm an' will aid his righteous cause...."

"Shup up, damn you." There was a cup on the table. Richard threw it up in the air then snatched it as it descended, holding it in front of Knox's face, "Is this a falsehood? A contradiction? A duplicity?"

Knox stared at him.

"No, it's a bloody cup. But in your mind, the simple cannot exist. It must be twisted and extorted until it is exposed as a sin against God." Richard hurled the unfortunate earthenware across the cabin. It collided with the wooden wall and exploded into a myriad of sharp brown shards. Richard's hand found and hefted a bowl. "Oh, treasonous vessel, it's shallow and baseless, and that must be ... go on bloody say it!"

Knox just glared at him, the feral eyes wide.

"A sin against God." The bowl followed the cup across the room. "And now this. It might look simple and without guile. What do you think?" Richard, his voice shaking with fury, held up the small oil lamp that had sat upon the table. "But look, the flame flickers with inconsistency."

"Put it down," Knox shouted, his voice trembling with temper.

Richard shook his head. "I cannot. Its very existence is a sin against God, and it must be eradicated."

When it broke against the wall the room was plunged into instant darkness.

Richard slammed the door on Knox, blindly stumbling to his cabin. Holding his hands out before him, he watched them quiver; his breath choked in his throat, and blood pounded at his temples. He should have known his temper was about to snap. It had been threatening to for days. Richard could remember the last hours of calm, the last day when, like a child, he had falsely believed that there was to be an escape. Drinking with Jerome, tracing their voyage on the charts, talking of where they would take the *Luciana* – it had all been a sham.

Richard's temper had been tried when he found he was in London, again when he'd been interred in the Beauchamp Tower and stretched even further when Cecil outlined the actions he wished him to take. More pressure had been applied when he had been forced to appease Elizabeth, promising to spy on her secretary, with further strain as he had tried to cover Cecil's tracks, preventing Jack from finding him in London. And then, like the tightening of a snare, he'd felt like a trapped animal when he'd boarded the Luciana to find Jerome, unrepentant and indeed eager to help him. The final bloody straw, the final weight that snapped the thin strands of his nerves, had been provided by Knox.

"What's the matter?" Morley, still in his cabin, tried.

Morley's voice seemed distant, and Richard ignored it.

He needed to consider a problem, and somewhere in his tired mind, hidden behind the littered wreckage of thoughts wrought by his temper, was the answer. He couldn't find it now. His head was filled only with the shattered snatches of words, loud noises and Knox's overpowering voice shouting, "'tis a sin," over and over again.

Richard stumbled towards the table, found a cup, slopped the ale that lingered in it to the floor and found a flask of aqua vitae. Unstoppering it, he glugged clear liquid towards the glass, watching as some slid over the rim, pooling on the table.

"A toast," his voice was hoarse, raising the cup in a shaking hand towards an ashen-faced Morley. "To my rapidly departing sanity."

Richard drained the cup in one go, refilled it, emptied it again, and then dropped onto the narrow bed, clasping the flask to his chest. His eyes closed, he put it to his lips and began to empty it.

"Why do you have such a dislike for Knox?" Morley asked, his voice thoughtful, a deep crease separating his brows.

"Can we trade in truth, you and I?" Richard asked Morley.

The little man spoke warily. "I believe I've been honest enough with you, sir."

"Andrew Newry," Richard placed the name carefully.

"An unfortunate case," Morley's face twisted into a sympathetic smile. "I remember that he was a friend of yours."

"It was Carfax who implicated him. Ensuring he was caught with papers that branded him as a protestant rebel," Richard said.

"It did appear that this was the case at the time. All the evidence did seem to be against Newry," Morley's voice had adopted a saddened tone.

"Such a shame that the sentence was irreversible," Richard said bitterly.

Morley didn't reply. From above him, the sound of a ratchet clanked noisily, puncturing the silence between them.

"Just one question, what papers were found? I wasn't especially interested until now," Richard's grey eyes, unwavering, held Morley's until the little man dropped his gaze.

Morley swallowed, his face paling.

Richard pointed in the direction Knox had gone, laughing harshly. "So I am right. Newry was blamed for that shit's Protestant ramblings coming in from Holland?"

"They were printed in Holland, as you say, and shipped in the bottom of empty wine casks. Their weight was right. Only the top of the casks held the wine, this small section was sealed with pitch from the rest of the cask, and the printed sheets were in the bottom," Morley explained. "Quite ingenious, really. I saw one of the ...."

"I don't give a shit about the brilliance of their deception. They arrived in London for distribution, which had little to do with Newry. However, he was marked as a Protestant preacher and tied to the trade in these?" Richard's voice was cold, his temper burning in his eyes.

Morley nodded. "Carfax used Henderson to place papers in his rooms, and the casks were found in his store, no doubt placed there by his servants."

"Newry was a good man. A preacher who cared only for the well-being of his fellow man. He did not deserve to have Knox's putrid ravings foisted upon him," Richard finished.

"It was not Knox's fault. Carfax placed the papers where they would be found," Morley offered, sounding a little confused.

"If Knox hadn't used a pen to create poisonous doctrine, then there would be nothing to fear. If anyone should have burnt for their creation, it should have been the author," Richard slammed his fist down on the table at the exact moment that a loud bang from above echoed around the cabin.

Morley inclined his head, saying quietly. "When you put it that way."

Chapter Eighteen

Opening his eyes on a new day, Richard was surprised to find the aqua vitae flask half full and upright in the crook of his arm. Placing it on the floor, he groaned and swung his feet from the bed. His head hurt as much as if he'd emptied it. Grey light pressed through the cabin window, illuminating Morley, still seated at the desk.

"Have you been there all night?"

"Where else could I have been?" The little man's self-assurance, smart appearance and ready smile were all absent. Creases told he had slept at the table in his clothes, and the lines on his face indicated it had been a long and restless night.

Richard rose, rubbed his hands over his face and stretched. "Now, don't think this is an act of pity. I need the table. Come on, up with you. You'll feel like a new man after a few hours of sleep."

"Sir, are your plans still to deliver Master Knox to Leith?" Morley asked, stretching his back as he sat straight in the chair.

"They are. I'd like nothing better than to divest myself of that raging cleric. The sooner the better," Richard confirmed.

"Can I request, if possible, that I be put ashore at the same time?" Morley requested, his voice serious.

Richard laughed. "Passage by sea is not to your liking?"

Morley swallowed hard and shook his head. "I would rather have my feet back upon the land. I can make my own way back from there to London."

"If that is what you wish. I've no desire to return to London," Richard said.

"I am grateful, sir, you have my thanks," Morley's voice was filled with relief.

A hand under Morley's arm, Richard, helped him up, guiding his stiff legs across the cabin to the narrow bed he had just vacated. Morley didn't object, nor did he reject the blanket Richard deposited on top of him.

Seating himself at the desk, Richard reversed a sheet of paper he had been writing on previously, revealing a blank side. On it, he began to write down everything he knew. Knox, Cecil, Jerome, de Nevarra, the Congregation, Marie De Guise, the Order of St John, Scotland, Elizabeth. Richard tapped his chin with the end of the quill. What else was he missing? He added the Dauphine, Mary of Scotland .... then he stopped. He had been absent for most of the year so far. News of little relevance had reached him while he had been in Newcastle, and he had not involved himself with his network, so he knew less than the common man.

He knew Henri of France had died, that the de Guise family were holding the reins of power, but not much more than that. Cecil had provided him with enough to put flesh on the bones of rumour - perhaps he should have asked more when he had the opportunity?

Richard added Cecil to the names on the sheet. Then, without pause, he added another name – Morley – and smiled.

Five minutes later, the little man had been roused from his poor slumber and was seated at Richard's desk, the blanket wrapped around his narrow shoulders.

"I know you may decline to discuss your master's work, and that I can understand. I have been absent from Court, little news has reached me, and if I am honest, I didn't want it to either. This problem of Knox - if I am to help as your master wishes, I need to understand the situation fully," Richard explained, then smiling he added, "We might even arrive at an assessment of whether it was an accident or not that you sailed with the *Luciana*."

"I am, now, coming to terms with my... situation," Morley replied, his voice quiet. "It has been a reassurance that I am surrounded by so many who do not fear that the vessel will sink."

Richard laughed. "You remind me of Jack, he has an ongoing suspicion of what holds a ship up above the water, and he prefers, indeed, we all prefer it if he travels blind drunk."

"Your brother?" Morley said, his voice thin and ready. He coughed to clear his throat and added more solidly. "It surprises me that he dislikes ships. He strikes me as a man who is afraid of little."

"We all have our weaknesses," Richard replied.

"True," Morley accepted some sadness in his tone. "I would never have believed that Lord Burghley would treat me thus."

"I do find it surprising. He cannot seriously have sent you along as surety for the money he has provided, it can only be to report on my deeds," Richard mused, a thumb and forefinger tugging at his chin.

Morley nodded.

Seating himself opposite Morley, Richard held up the sheet covered in names and words he had penned. "I want to know why the Order is interested in Scotland?"

Morley shrugged. "I did tell you last night I couldn't help you with that."

"Maybe not directly, but you might be able to fill in some gaps in my knowledge," Richard replied, smoothing the page out before him and picking up the pen.

"Perhaps. Ask your questions, and if it is not linked to my Master's work, I shall answer." Morley pulled the blanket more tightly around himself.

Richard did ask, working his way through the words. What did Morley know of the Congregation? Were there any links there with the Order? Did he know if St John's had a significant presence in Scotland? Or even in England? Had the political map changed in the last year?

The interrogation continued and Morley provided a continual supply of answers, Richard adding notes to the page.

Who was the French Ambassador? Had he been to Elizabeth's Court? Did he know who the rebel Scottish Earls were? Have any visited London?

"Sir, if I may interrupt you for a moment," Morley said quickly before Richard could place another line of enquiry.

Richard raised an enquiring gaze from the page where he made his most recent notes.

"A drink, sir, if I may," Morley said, a weak smile on his face.

Richard rose. "Of course, all I have here is aqua vitae, which will not help our current cause."

Fifteen minutes later, Morley was provided with both wine, and a platter of food, which seemed to please him. Among the offerings were pies, cooked meat and warm fresh bread.

"This is remarkably good," Morley said, tearing the small loaf in half.

Looking up, Richard asked, "Which position do you think is the most important on a ship?"

Morley's response was automatic. "The captain."

Richard, smiling, shook his head. "The cook."

"I suppose so. I had always thought the food would be poor, and, of course, you do hear tales of life aboard ship," Morley replied, taking a sip of the wine.

"I'm sure when Knox was aboard a ship chained to the oars, the food was not quite to this standard. I don't feel we need to suffer a diet of maise and biscuits if we don't have to," Richard replied dryly.

"Do you think it wise to antagonise him? I admit he can be a difficult man...."

"Difficult?" Richard shot back, disbelief in his voice. "He's more than that. There might be trouble in Scotland. There is a power play for control of her governance between Mary de Guise and the so-called Congregation. They dress up their rebellion in religious rags to justify their cause, and they are willing to release upon their own people a man like Knox to secure their grip on power. Men, women and children who rightly or wrongly declare themselves Catholic will suffer. Knox is a man who will find and make examples. His fiery preaching will demand a pyre to underline his stance."

Morley paled and put down his ale cup, his eyes on the table before him. "I have witnessed more than I ever care to. It is a horror I would wish on no one. Surely Knox would not torch his fellow Scot?"

"You, of all men, will know that Knox's religious bigotry will lead to violence. There might not be public burnings, but men will be hounded for their beliefs. If he triumphs over the De Guises, then you have released a religious war on Scotland. It will divide the nation," Richard said thoughtfully. Picking up his pen, he found a space on the sheet of paper and wrote down, "religious divide."

Morley, squinting to read the upside-down letters from his side of the table, asked. "Do you think that is relevant?"

Richard sighed the fingers of his right-hand drumming on the table. "I don't know. There are too many possibilities."

Morley continued with his meal, watching Richard as he re-read his notes, crossing out some of the words he'd penned on the sheet and sometimes adding more.

"What are you thinking?" Morley asked.

"I wonder... Was de Nevarra at Court before you left?" Richard asked Morley.

"I believe so. The Italian Ambassador has recently arrived, and he has been seen in his entourage," Morley said. He finished his meal, and a little colour infused his cheeks.

"Knox has told me he was present at a meeting between himself and your master, although de Nevarra didn't speak with him, and he had no idea who he was." Richard tapped his finger on the sheet. "For the Order to be involved, there has to be an advantage to them, be it political or fiscal."

"Or both," Morley suggested astutely.

"As you say ... both," Richard repeated slowly. "The de Guise family have control at the French court?"

Morley nodded, dusting crumbs from his fingers.

"When they took political control after Henri died, were there a significant number of other courtiers ousted from their positions?" Richard asked, leaning back in the chair.

Morley shook his head. "Very much the status quo, the only victim was Diane de Poitiers. There were no wholesale disgraces. Political appointments and posts, on the whole, remained unchanged."

"Changes of policy?" Richard queried, tapping the end of the quill on the page.

"Again, they have continued with the policies of their dead King Henri, little changed, apart from perhaps more enthusiasm for their dynastic ambitions in Scotland, which is understandable as their Queen is Mary de Guise's daughter," Morley replied, adding, "which just brings us back round to your problem."

Richard's finger moved to the word Scotland on the sheet; beneath it, he had written Knox, Congregation and Mary de Guise.

"It has to be Mary de Guise, they want her out of Scotland and Knox, and the rebellion are simply a convenient way to carry this out," Richard theorised, his brow furrowed.

"That would make sense, and many in France feel the royal coffers are already overstretched. They fear Scotland is more than France can afford," Morley said. He had withdrawn his arms inside the blanket again. Wrapped in the grey wool, he looked like a monk.

"Is it indeed?"

"Oh yes, France, my dear boy, is nearly bankrupt," Morley replied almost cheerfully.

Richard added another word to the sheet and sat back, surveying his work.

"Have you arrived at a conclusion?" Morley said, his interest genuine, craning his neck to see if Richard had added anything else to the sheet.

Richard shook his head.

Dipping his pen in ink again, he placed thick lines through words. "It's not to do with Scotland, the Congregation, or Knox, the only point north of the border is Mary de Guise. So we keep her. It's not a favour to Elizabeth, that's only a secondary benefit, so we can remove her along with England and Cecil from our list."

Morley leaned forward to observe the lines that remained.

"There is a link between Mary de Guise, the Order and....." Richard drew a line between her name and that of de Nevarra that ran onto the word France. "There's more here, and I cannot fathom it."

Chapter Nineteen

There was a knock on the cabin door. Richard, still making notes, stopped the pen halfway through the word 'reformist'. "Come in."

Jerome admitted himself. He was dry, so it was apparent he had not come from the upper decks. "I thought you'd want to inspect the armaments before we run some trials."

Richard smiled towards Morley. "In the face of Knox's unpleasantness, I had forgotten about Burghley's generosity," scooping his cloak from a chair back, he added, "Do you want to come and see what protection your master has afforded you?"

"I might as well," Morley conceded, pushing himself up, stretching his back and following Richard from the cabin, still cloaked in the wool blanket.

They headed towards the middle of the ship, along the narrow central passageway, down two vertical ladders to the gun deck. Richard could remember first coming here when the Luciana had been moored in Spain. Stripped of cannon, the gun doors hanging open, and the deck tilted as she sat, keeled over to one side, in the harbour. It seemed like a long time ago.

The ship's carpenter had obviously been busy; a shave horse sat at one end along with ready-cut timber and a bright, newly made gun carriage.

"The cannon came from the *Jer Falcon*, actually," Morley supplied, then went on, as was his habit, to provide the details. "It was only built in 1550, so it was a relatively new vessel. There was some incident off the Cornish coast, and her hull was badly damaged; she had been at the dock for five years, apparently classed as beyond repair. Lord Burghley requisitioned the armaments for your vessel."

Sitting on wooden carriages, secured by ropes to the deck, were ten cannons; half the gun doors on the port side were open to allow light onto the dark deck. At the far end, three men were working, and the gun nearest them was positioned in its carriage before the open gun door.

"We have one ready for firing," Jerome pointed to the far gun.

"One?" Richard said, striding towards the operational cannon. "We had better hope the opposition takes a long time to turn and only attack us from the larboard side."

The cannon looked shabby and old sitting as it did on a white wooden gun carriage, shavings, off-cuts and surplus wood, an indication of the very newness of the construction.

Richard laid his hand on the rusted iron, addressing one of the men, "Do they all need new carriages?"

The taller of the men answered, stowing a hammer in his leather apron that bristled with tools, "Sir, we've had more problems than enough, I can tell you."

"Don't spare me the details," Richard said.

"Them over there, they are English guns on English oak carriages," the carpenter said, pointing at the lashed-down cannon in the centre of the deck, then pointing at the gun door, he said, "and this is a Spanish ship, and the gun doors are a foot too high. Fire one of those in here, and you'll blow a hole in her side."

Richard could see the line of cannons standing on squat carriages with small solid wooden wheels no wider than two hand spans. The one the carpenter had constructed was fitted with wheels twice that diameter, the additional size raising the cannon's muzzle, so it was in the centre of the open gun door.

"So we have one operational gun?" Richard looked at Jerome. "Why does this not surprise me?"

"Aye, and if I may, sir, we've not enough timber on board to construct carriages for them all, and with just me an' Paul here working on them, it's taken us a week to make this one, so to make 'em all is going to take a long time," the carpenter complained.

"A week?" Richard echoed, turning his head back towards the long line of useless guns.

"The wheels are iron-bound, and the carriage has iron reinforcing. I've copied the design, sir, from the English ones, but, like I told the Captain 'ere, I'm a ship's carpenter, and I've never built anything like this before, so I fear it might not be strong enough, there's a fair amount of power in one of these Devil's when they are let loose," the carpenter said.

Richard nodded, remembering a culverin he had once bought that, upon firing, had dug itself a hole in a field. "Jerome, you've more experience than any of us have. What do you think?"

"It's a good job. I got the lads to start on this one, it's a demi-culverin, and she fires an eight-pound shot. If we can get her working right, then we can gauge what we need to mount the eighteen-pounders."

"We've got eighteen pounders?" Richard asked, suddenly animated and looking towards the row of cannons, all the same as the one on the new carriage.

"Oh yes, lashed down on the fore deck, there are eight full culverins. I'd plan to have four aside plus three demi's and the rest on the fore and aft castles. That'll give her good all-round firepower," Jerome replied. "We will test the carriage shortly. I am sure it will be sufficiently strong," Jerome said then to Richard,

"I'm afraid it's not just the gun carriages that are a problem."

Richard hitched himself onto one of the culverins, his feet resting on the wheel. "Go on, regale me with the woes of Lord Burgley's gift."

"We've two sets of loading tools, so that does limit what we can do," Jerome gestured towards the carpenter, "Collins can make us more, but again we need materials, and if we could take on some men to help him that would make for speedier work. We've also got an issue with the ropes."

"The ropes?"

Jerome walked to the open gun door. On either side were two heavy iron loops. He hooked his finger through one. "The breech rope is fixed from here, round the back of the cannon, looping round the cascabel, then to the fixing on the other side of the gun door. When the gun is fired, her carriage is hard against the bulwark," Jerome slapped the wood beneath the gun door, "then the breech rope absorbs the recoil."

"And the problem is?"

"We've not enough of the calibre I need. The breach ropes need to be as thick as a man's wrist. When the Luciana was stripped, all the gun tackle was removed." Jerome pointed to the roof of the gun deck, "Each of these iron loops should have a block and tackle to move and lift the guns; there are non-remaining. We've rigged up a set here using some borrowed from the topgallant sail, but ideally, I need four per gun along with rope and iron securing pins."

"Four per gun," Richard echoed.

"Yes, apart from the eighteen-pounders, and they'll need six," Jerome continued, "each gun station needs a priming horn, sand bucket and...."

"Stop," Richard held his hand up. "You are souring my gift. I'm beginning to feel like a bride who's had her marriage chest rifled through. I will obviously need pen and parchment to make good the list of your demands."

Jerome said, "Hardly demands. These are just the bare minimum you'll need to train the gun crews."

"Are there any positives? Or will this prove a ruinously expensive folly?"

"Perhaps," Jerome said a little too cheerfully, not clarifying which question he was answering.

Richard cast a withering glance in his captain's direction. "Returning to the subject of guns, did you not tempt me down here with the promise of seeing one fire?"

"I did." Jerome turned towards two of his crew standing at the back of the deck. "Carson, get the shot, and, Kildale, bring the powder."

"And which poor soul have you chosen to fire her?" Richard asked his eyes on the two approaching crew.

"Unless you would like to undertake the task yourself, I shall fire her," Jerome said, "we've cleaned them up, but there's always a chance with an old barrel such as this that it could split."

"At last, a positive," Richard said, a malicious smile on his face. "Perhaps I should encourage Master Knox to stand next to you. What a dilemma the Lord would have when he is presented with both of you in the same instant. We shall observe from over there," Richard said, pointing to the opposite end of the deck. "Morley, I suggest we retire."

Collins collected the remainder of his tools, cleared the area and Jerome and his two gunners took over. They ran through the process three times without actually loading the gun. When Jerome was happy, they began again. The cannon, nestling on its new carriage, was in the middle of the gun deck.

"First, we scour the barrel," Jerome's loud voice explained for the benefit of the distant audience as they watched Carson press into the cannon a rod with a wire cage at the end, twisting it as he fed it in. "It clears out any debris from a previous charge and also extinguishes any flames that might be in there."

Carson withdrew the rod, stowing it in the roof in rope loops.

"Next, the charge. Hold it out, Kildale." The charge was tightly packed in a cloth wrap. "We cut the cloth just enough to release some of the powder." The point of Jerome's knife sliced the fibres. "Now it needs to go into the gun the right way up, that's right, lad, and Carson presses it home. Carefully, that's right."

Carson withdrew the ramrod and stowed it in the roof.

"Now the shot, this is the eight-pound one, doesn't look much, but this will go through the side of a ship, and we'll find out when we run some tests on what the range is from these guns." Jerome supervised as Carson placed the shot in the muzzle, the noise of it rolling towards the charge an unmistakable dull rattle. "Now in goes this wad of greased sheep's wool. It's enough to stop the shot rolling from the barrel when we move the cannon to the gun doors." Kildale pushed in a thick grey ball of wool and pressed it home with the rod.

"Now she's loaded. We just need to bring her to the doors," Jerome announced. Kildale and Carson had taken up positions on each side of the culverin and, hauling on the ropes, pulled them through pulleys that drew the carriage slowly towards the gun doors. "That's right, keep going, lads, right to the door. The front of the carriage needs to be hard against the hull."

Once in place, the tackle was disconnected from the carriage, and the heavy breach rope was extended around the back of the cannon, looped around the protruding boss at the rear and drawn tight with shackle blocks. Jerome examined the tension on the rope. Satisfied, he nodded for the men to stop.

Jerome had a powder horn slung across his body; unhooking it, he unclipped the sliver end and poured the powder into the priming vent at the end of the cannon. "Like the powder in the pan in a flintlock, this small amount in here will ignite and then light the main charge. Bring me the match, Carson," Jerome watched as Carson brought him a slow match from the other side of the deck where it had been smouldering in an iron bucket. "Now, lads, it might be advisable for you to stand back while I test Master Collins's work. Go on, wait with the Master."

Jerome was alone, his audience was at the other end of the gun deck, the line of cannon between them. There seemed to be a sudden stilled silence. Jerome waited, the match in his hand giving off a tiny tell-tale line of faint grey smoke. The *Santa Luciana* dipped to her right. Morley, standing next to Richard, for a moment lost his balance and took two lurching, involuntary steps, halting when Richard caught his arm.

Jerome never moved.

The deck of the *Luciana* levelled, and there was a deafening explosion. Morley yelped, and Jerome disappeared from view. The boom resonated along the deck, rebounding from the timbers, ringing in their ears. The smoke was acrid and rolling towards them in ever-thickening plumes.

Richard, coughing, was already striding forwards. "Let us see if God has favoured Knox, shall we, and blown the Knight to Hades?"

A strong sea-born wind was already clearing the smoke from the deck, and Jerome, match still in hand, was examining the gun carriage. "The breach ropes have taken the force well, and the carriage is intact. Collins, you've done a good job."

"I shall contain my disappointment," Richard said sarcastically.

"You need me, lad," Jerome replied grinning. "I think you'd be hard-pressed to find another captain who has trained gun crews before."

"Just be careful, Jerome. One day you may find yourself dispensable," Richard's eyes were cold, his voice serious.

Chapter Twenty

It had taken five days to put in place the necessary arrangements.

Five long days.

Jack had wanted nothing more than to saddle a horse, round up his men, and head towards the North Road.

But it had not been that simple.

The complication had been provided by his lawyers; necessary documents were required that needed drafting then, once drafted, they needed ratifying by a Court official. Threadmill had explained to him at length the legal process that he needed to follow to regain Burton in his brother's name. Still, Jack's mind had fastened onto the unwanted delay like a hound on a rabbit and refused to focus on anything else other than the hated legal hindrance to his plans.

He wanted to be outside London, free of the city, free of the confines of the Fitzwarren house and back on the road. Catherine was actively encouraging him to go and find some freedom outside of London. She had ensured that Master Drew provided adequate clothing practically overnight, the cost he didn't want to think about, but she seemed pleased with the results of her choices.

Fifteen miles outside London and Jack was finally feeling better. He felt as if he could breathe again easily. He had a plan, albeit a simple one, and he would be gone from the city for at least a week. For the moment, he was blessedly beyond the reach of the Queen's Court, his wife and anyone else in London who felt the need to interfere, and he had to admit it felt good.

A dozen of his own men would have been his choice. However, the group also included Threadmill and two of his clerks; soon, he realised they were an unwanted addition.

Master Threadmill, eager to please and with a breadth of knowledge about the Fitzwarren land holdings that Jack was beginning to find alarming, had attached himself to Jack's side. Threadmill was conscious of his status as Lord Fitzwarren's legal representative, and behind him, jostling uncomfortably on top of two horses, were two of his legal scribes, heavy packs behind them no doubt containing Threadmill's legal papers. On top of one pack, securely fastened and wrapped in oilcloth, was what appeared to be a portable writing desk. Jack had eyed Threadmill and his associates with grim dissatisfaction when they had arrived at the London house to join him as he made his way from London. The darkly clad lawyers belonged in offices, squeezed behind desks, their blackened fingers fastened around a quill not wrapped around reins.

Jack was at the head of the party, and Threadmill jostled, trotted and even cantered, in a fashion, when needed to ensure he was as near to him as possible. It was, Jack assumed, out of some sense of presumed hierarchy the lawyer had - a belief in his self-importance- that made him feel he needed to ride at the front of the convoy. They might have been matched in age, but Jack doubted Threadmill had ridden a horse overly much; his clerks, Jack noted with amusement, were slightly better riders than their master.

Threadmill, whose first name Jack had heard and failed to commit to memory, clearly belonged in an office. Summer sun caused him to squint constantly, pale skin was highlighted by his dark riding clothes, and his thin frame worried Jack – if he fell from his horse, and there was every likelihood this would happen, the lawyer looked as if he might snap. Hands that could easily manipulate a quill were unsure on the reins, fumbling the leather straps and seemingly unable to find a comfortable hold. Delicate skin, stretched taught over the bones, with jutting wrists and knuckles, a visual advertisement of a body with little muscle.

The lawyer, like Jack, seemed to have invested heavily in new clothes to accompany his client. The boots, barely creased and newly stitched, were as new as the dark wool cloak that hung from his shoulders. The members of the Drapers Guild, mused Jack, were having a profitable month.

Any amusement Jack had found in Threadmill's riding ability and appearance was soon lost, and Jack's irritation with his new companion began to show.

Threadmill rarely shut up.

The Fitzwarren estates were extensive, and Threadmill wanted to bring each issue to Jack's attention along with any action he felt should be taken. Jack had started by providing full, considered answers, but by the end of the day, Threadmill's questions had worn him down to monosyllabic grunted responses.

A Queen's Conspirator

"The main issue at Harrington Hall is the timber; the steward, Master Hardy, has provided a good breakdown of what you have. Thinning it will provide a good amount of income," Threadmill paused.

"So?" Jack responded.

"Sir, is it the right time? We must consider not just the maturity of the woodland, but the economics of the situation," Threadmill responded.

Economics!

"What do the economics tell us?" Jack grumbled. This was to be another conversation where Jack was about to become rapidly out of his depth.

"Well, sir, this is a new reign, and, as you know, oak is a commodity much used in shipbuilding. The Crown has announced no plans as yet to restore the fleet. It could be wise to wait, sir. If a plan is outlined, we can capitalise on the opportunity," Threadmill provided.

"I hate ships," Jack grumbled under his breath.

"Pardon, sir?" Threadmill said, his brow furrowed with confusion.

"Nothing," Jack said, then, answering the lawyer's question, he added, "wait to cut the timber."

"Good, a wise decision," Threadmill responded, nodding sagely. "Which brings me to the need to review the...."

Jack had taken as much of Threadmill's company as he could stand.

"A hind, ahead and to the right. Did you see it, Froggy?" Jack interrupted his lawyer.

"No, where?" Froggy said, confused, then seeing the stern look Jack gave him, he added, "to the right of that tree, yes."

Froggy and Jack broke ranks, leaving the rest of the men behind, their horses galloping along the track around a slight right-hand bend, slowing when they were out of sight.

"Please, God tell me he's not followed?" Jack said, pulling his horse next to Froggy's.

Froggy, leaning heavily on his pommel, had tears of mirth spilling from his eyes.

201

"It's not bloody funny. He never shuts up," Jack complained.

Froggy wiped the back of his hand across his wet eyes. "Oh, it is."

"I'll unseat you from that horse in a moment if you don't stop laughing," Jack growled.

"You can try if you like," Froggy said. Then, in a more serious tone, he said, "The lad is only trying to help you. By the sound of it, there's a lot of issues you should have given some time to by now."

Froggy's observation was a little too accurate, and Jack, pressing his heels to his horse's side, set the mare to canter, leaving Froggy, and another unwanted conversation, behind.

†

They did not go directly to Burton; first, they went to Assingham. This detail of his journey he hadn't shared with Catherine. Her uncle, Peter de Bernay, had accepted the sum of fifty pounds, and the transaction was now being supervised by Threadmill. Jack wanted to see for himself just how bad a condition the small manor was in. Now four months pregnant, Catherine would not leave London until the following year, so he had around twelve months to make the place into a suitable gift rather than give her something that would only reduce her to tears when she saw it.

When Assingham came into view, Jack was initially not sure he was looking at the same place, but, as the distance closed, he realised that his memory of the manor was poor. Assingham was smaller than he remembered, and the wooden lean-to buildings along one side of the stone hall had collapsed.

Fifty pounds!
Ten would have been too much.

Jack grumbled inwardly as they drew up in front of the rickety fence work that enclosed the yard and several thin-ribbed goats. A dog had detached itself from a sunny step. Scattering the goats, it bounded towards them, barking vociferously.

"What a welcome," Jack announced to no one in particular.

Threadmill had overheard him. "My Lord, I am sorry, we did make provision to ensure the current tenants were aware of your arrival. I can only...."

Jack raised his hand. "I am sure everything is in order."

Now he was at Assingham, he realised that he'd never much wished to come here again. It was not only the poverty of the settlement but also the painful memories that accompanied it. His mind turned back to another summer day when the yard had been piled with bleeding bodies after Geoffrey Byrne's men had descended upon the inhabitants. Catherine's mother had been among them, and, although she knew what had happened, at least she had never witnessed it.

Jack hoped that the mere possession of Assingham would be enough to satisfy his wife. The knowledge that it was once more in her control and not stolen from her might serve to provide her with some peace. Soon she would have a child, and that, he hoped, would provide her with the new beginnings he knew she wanted: needed. Jack knew very well what it was like to feel displaced and was hopeful that Catherine would come to recognise the Fitzwarren house as her own in time. But that said, he knew he couldn't leave the place to disintegrate into a pile of rough masonry, which it looked in danger of doing if action was not taken soon.

They had been offered accommodation at Assingham, but Jack had immediately declined, having no desire to stop there. Their visit had been brief. Threadmill had interrogated the tenants, made quick notes of what was needed, then, after two hours, they were remounted and headed towards Burton. There was, Jack knew, a village with a good-sized inn, an hour's ride from the hamlet, and that was where they were headed.

Chapter Twenty-One

Accommodation had been secured for the horses and men, and Jack, whose stomach had been telling for some hours that he needed feeding, was already in the tavern. When he'd arrived, he'd toed out of his path several white ducks that were waddling around the doorway, and an hour later, he was sure there were two less when a platter with roasted fowl was laid before him.

Froggy sat to his right, dug an elbow in Jack's ribs and, leaning towards him, said quietly into his ear, "Looks like your shadow is back."

Master Threadmill had entered the inn and scanned the room, looking for Jack.

"He might not see us if we are lucky," Jack said hopefully, his head lowered over the platter before him, refusing to look in the lawyer's direction.

"If you leave lad to do all your work, what do you expect?" Froggy said, "Master wouldn't be leaving the managing of everything to his lawyer, would he? Nah, he'd have had the matters dealt with, orders issued, and woe betide anyone who didn't carry them out."

"I'm not Richard, am I?" Jack said tersely.

"Clearly not," Froggy replied, raising an arm and waving towards the lawyer.

Jack scowled at Froggy, who smiled back maliciously.

"A meal, a few jugs of ale and a game of Primero was all I wanted. Was that too much to ask?" Jack complained, watching the lawyer approach.

"Sort your business out with him and tell him to sod off," Froggy said quietly.

"I might just do that," Jack replied.

Master Threadmill joined them, taking a seat next to Jack. "My Lord, I have made a reckoning of works needed at Assingham. If I can get you to approve, I would appreciate it." Threadmill leaned towards his bag on the floor and began drawing out a roll of papers.

"Now?" Jack said.

"If now is not a good time..." Threadmill's voice was uncertain, and he left the sentence unfinished.

"Later, first we eat," Jack said, returning his attention to yet more platters being put down before him.

"Of course. Rest assured, there will be little you will need to do, you have an able steward at your property at Cartersgill, less than an hour's ride away from Assingham, and I would propose that he oversee repair work and potentially find another tenant," Threadmill said.

"Cartersgill," Jack repeated.

"I can fully brief the steward and ensure the costs are adhered to," Threadmill said efficiently.

"Costs, indeed, they are important," Jack said, feeling he needed to say something.

"Certainly, and I can...."

Jack cut him off. "Not now. Enough, peace while we eat, please."

Jack didn't get his desired quiet. Before Threadmill could respond, a screaming child ran into the tavern, tripped over a stool and was flung face down on the floor. His tunic rucked up over his back as he fell, revealing pale legs and a naked backside. The feral ball of rags with arms and legs flailing righted itself, gazed in panic, looking for an exit and, realising its mistake, dived under the table next to Froggy, crawling beneath the trestle and clambering behind the seated men.

Jack looked down at the tear-stained face. The eyes were wide in terror, there was a cut beneath one eye, and it was breathing in ragged, uneven gulps. Before Jack could address the bundle of rags, two men fell through the door. One was wearing a Smith's apron, the leather flapping around his knees, a wool cap clamped over greasy hair cresting a nose mostly on the left side of his face. The other wore a belted tunic, knee-high boots and a leather cap that was too small, ginger frizz escaping in uneven tufts from beneath the edges. His eyes were slightly oversized and emphasised by high protruding cheekbones.

"He's in here. I saw him run in," the Smith announced.

In a smooth movement, Jack swept his cloak from where it lay on the table's edge to land, covering the child.

"You seen a lad come this way?" The ginger-haired man called towards them.

Jack shook his head slowly and returned his attention to his meal.

"Little shit, must have gone through the smith's shop, come on."

Jack waited a few moments before addressing the lump beneath his cloak. "What did you steal?" he asked, his voice amused.

A stifled sob escaped from beneath the cloak, and Jack suppressed a laugh. Catching Froggy's eyes, he asked again, "come on, lad, impress me. You must have done something to annoy those two shits."

The cloak shook, but there were no words.

Jack shrugged and returned his attention to the food before him.

"He looks about five, can't be much older, reminds me of my sister's lad," Froggy said, tearing bread from the loaf on the table.

"Why? Was he always stealing things?" Jack said through a mouthful of food.

Froggy laughed. "No, he just looks about the same size as when I last saw the lad, he'll be fully grown by now. Christ, how the time passes."

"Sir, if he has stolen anything, we really should...." Threadmill tried.

"Shut up." Jack broke off a large chunk from the loaf on the table and, peeling back the cloak, offered it to the child.

There was only a moment's hesitation in the lost face before a filthy hand snatched the offering and pulled the cloak back over its head.

"You know what they say about feeding strays," Froggy said quietly, laughing under his breath.

"Go on, what do they say?" Jack asked, twisting duck meat from the bone and offering it to the child.

"Strays are like sins. The more you feed them, the more they hang around," Froggy said bluntly.

The cloak moved, and the meat disappeared from Jack's hand.

"You are going to cause trouble," Froggy observed, although he didn't sound overly concerned.

"It's a state that seems to follow me like a bloody thundercloud," Jack observed, helping himself to cheese from the yellow slab that rested on the trencher between them.

"Hey, there's three of us at this table," Froggy complained as Jack cut himself a large wedge from the block.

"You know what they say about that, don't you?"

"No, go on," Froggy said, stabbing the remaining cheese and lifting it onto his platter.

"There's the quick and the hungry," Jack grinned. He cut the end off the lump of cheese and passed it down beneath the table.

"There's also the greedy." Froggy placed a defensive arm around his platter as he saw Jack eyeing the remaining cheese.

"That's a terrible accusation you are making," Jack said, his voice full of mock indignation.

"Terrible it might be, but it's also true," Froggy observed.

Jack twisted a leg free from the duck and tapped it on the head beneath the cloak; the hand appeared, and Jack deposited the meat into its keeping.

"Remember what I said about strays," Froggy said through a mouthful of cheese.

Jack, ignoring him, continued to dissect the fowl, placing the greasy meat on his trencher.

There was a gentle pressure on his leg and, looking down, he could see the pale white hand open, hoping for more offerings. Smiling, he dropped a thick piece of duck into it.

"I hope you are going to get another; the rate you are going, I'll be going without a meal," griped Froggy.

A few minutes later, there came another light tap on his leg, and the hand, open, protruded from beneath the cloak.

"Well, lad, I'll need your name before I give you some more. I like to know the names of all the men who sit at my table," Jack said formally.

The hand closed and withdrew beneath the blanket.

"No name, no more food," Jack continued, adding, "which is a real shame as there's another leg here you could have had."

The cloak shuddered, and a head of matted ginger curls appeared from the edge. The eyes were dry, the cut beneath one eye still livid, and the flesh had begun to swell, closing it to a narrow slit. It swallowed and said nervously. "I's Oswyn."

"Nice to meet you, Oswyn. Here you go." Jack handed down the promised leg, and the ginger head disappeared back beneath the folds of the cloak.

"They'll be back for him soon, you know that," Froggy said unnecessarily.

"Aye, I would imagine they will be," Jack accepted, tearing himself a piece of bread.

"He's going to belong to someone. Should we try to find out who?" Master Threadmill suggested. "I could...."

"Still your tongue. I left my wife in London, and I don't need you to take her place as my scold," Jack said, then added, "we will finish here and be off soon, have no worry."

Threadmill returned to his meal while casting nervous glances towards the door.

"So, Oswyn, what did you do?" Jack asked, holding a piece of cheese just out of reach of the boy's hand.

"Nowt," came the quick reply.

The small hand made to snatch the cheese, but Jack, quicker, moved the morsel out of reach. "A trade, lad. A truth for the cheese," he said.

"It's a sin," came the words from beneath the cloak. "Stan says I'm going to Hell."

"What for? Our Lord looked kindly on beggars and thieves. I don't think you'll be going to Hell," Jack chuckled, shocked by the boy's statement.

"I didn't steal nowt," the boy said, "please."

The grimy hand appeared open.

Jack almost relented. Then, leaning down, he said in a whisper, "You can have all the cheese on my platter. Just whisper to me what your sin was."

Jack got his answer at the same moment that the smithy and his leather-capped friend came back through the door.

"Oswyn, you little shit, come out," the smithy called, "we know you are in here, come out now, and we'll not beat you half as hard as we will if we have to come looking for you."

"He's all heart, that one," Froggy observed quietly.

"Oswyn, you know what's waiting for you, now come here," the smithy threatened.

The cloak trembled, and the dirty child's head emerged; tears already welling in his eyes, he crawled back under the table towards the men.

Jack leaned down, wound a fist tightly into the back of the boy's tunic and picked him up from the floor, depositing him firmly on the bench between himself and Threadmill.

"Oswyn is finishing his meal now fuck off." Jack shoved a platter in front of the child and deposited the remains of the duck on it.

Oswyn sat rigid on the bench. The tears had outgrown his eyes and were dripping down his cheeks.

"Who the fuck are you?" the Smith demanded, advancing towards Jack and Froggy.

Froggy groaned. "What did I tell you?"

Jack ignored him and glowered at the Smith. That's where the risk would come from. Hours of hammering an anvil would have given him steel muscles; over them, he wore a thick pig skin apron which would afford him good protection from any attack. Jack, Threadmill and Froggy were seated at the back of the tavern, a table before them, a wall behind. The only way out was forward, and that was blocked by the Smith and his friend.

"Carlton, get the lads," the broken-nosed Smith commanded.

"Friends? You do surprise me," Jack said conversationally as the other man ducked quickly through the door.

"Owyn, come here: now!" Smith spat.

Oswyn made to slither from his seat and drop under the table. Jack's restraining hand forced him back into his seat. "You stop there, lad."

Leather Cap was back already, at his back three more men.

Not good odds.

And between them, the table with the remains of the meal.

Jack looked towards Froggy. "Towards the door?"

Froggy nodded, his hands already gripping the edge of the table.

"Master Threadmill, please take care to remain behind me," Jack commanded quietly before addressing the new arrivals, "Well, gentleman, it's been.... now!"

They lifted the table from the floor between them, turning the top towards the men blocking the exit. They rammed them with the woodwork, trenchers, and ale cups, the remains of the duck flying from the table as it turned. The fowl's carcass hit the broken-nosed Smith in the side of the face, and he battered it away. Two men to the left were knocked from their feet by the impact.

Froggy and Jack, with Oswyn and Threadmill, had reversed their positions and were now nearer the exit, Threadmill a look of bewildered astonishment on his face.

"Gentlemen, we will be leaving now," Jack announced, pushing Oswyn towards Threadmill and gesturing for them to head towards the door.

Stools that had been scattered were thrust out of the way. Cursing, the two men who'd landed on the floor righted themselves and stood shoulder to shoulder again with the Smith.

"You got lucky there, but it'll not 'appen again," the Smith said, pushing his sleeves up to reveal solid forearms.

"Sirs, I do feel I need to advise you that this is Lord Fitzwarren. Your quarrel is above your station. Lay down your weapons," Threadmill had re-entered the inn and stepped up next to Jack.

"Who the fuck is that?" spat the Smith, then to Jack, "Lord of fuckin' nowhere more like."

"I advise you to...." Threadmill tried again.

"I don't want to side with the opposition, but on this occasion, I feel you need to shut up and get out," Jack growled at his lawyer.

"Sir, I trained with the college. I'll stand with you. I may be of some help," Threadmill clearly had no intention of leaving.

"Out!"

Threadmill jumped involuntarily. Froggy's strong hand wound into the lawyer's doublet, hauling him towards the door.

Jack eyed the five men. They would need to make a move quickly. Leather Cap lifted a shattered stool from the floor and armed himself with the leg, twisted nails spiking from the end nearest Jack. Hefting it in his hand, he advanced, sure of himself. Jack stood his ground. The wood shaft sliced through the air when the man took another step forward. The shaft was in reach. Jack caught the end of it, enjoyed the moment of surprise that lifted the man's eyebrows towards his hat then pulled.

Balance lost, he lurched forward, and Jack's fist caught him full in the face. The wooden leg was now in Jack's hand, and he slammed it hard on the side of his neck, stepping backwards as the first of the five collapsed to the floor.

Jack flipped the wooden shaft in his hand, so the nails were towards the four remaining men. "Let us go, and I'll put this down."

If they'd had sense they would have rushed him together, four men would have been more than Jack could handle, but that was rarely the way, and his judgement was right. The man at the far left, wearing a smith's apron like Broken Nose's stepped over Leather Cap and scooped a broken stool from the floor as a shield and a weapon. He moved in slowly, intent on using his strength and the stool to smash through Jack's defence and bring a solid blow to his head. Jack kept the end of the shaft moving, and the man mistakenly kept his eye on it. When he was within range, Jack launched a kick to his groin that the leather of his apron did not protect against, the man's legs buckled, and he dropped to his knees. The stool released clattered to the floor. Jack flipped the stool leg in his hand, bringing the end down hard across the side of his head. Without a sound, he fell to lie on top of the first felled man.

Now there were only three.

The third did not wait for Jack to speak. He rushed forward from the left, in his right hand a knife. Jack took hold of the outstretched arm and hauled it high above the man's head. A good two feet taller than his attacker, the action pulled the man momentarily from his feet, the knife fell into the mire on the floor, and the man screamed as sinew and tendon were wrenched out of place. Releasing the useless arm, a hard punch in the stomach dropped him to the floor.

Then there were two.

It seemed it was the turn of the aproned Smith. His nose had either been rearranged by a fight or a horse. Jack suspected the former. From a deep pocket in the apron, he produced an awl, the end twisted and sharp, and he held it fastened in a tight fist. Between them was a heap of three bodies, two inert and one writhing in pain, a trap for his feet if there ever was one.

Jack smiled brightly and darted backwards for the open door.

The Smith, cursing him loudly, floundered over the bodies toward the door. As soon as his head emerged, he was instantly felled by a plank Froggy had helped himself to from a carpenter's neatly stacked pile.

"Right, stop inside or come out. The choice is yours," Jack called through the doorway.

There was a scuffling sound along with the whimpering from the felled man, but no one appeared.

"Well, that'll be that," Jack said, smiling, ruffling Oswyn's hair. "And where do you belong, lad?"

Oswyn was staring open-mouthed at the felled body of his former tormentor. Jack dropped down onto his haunches next to the child. "Where's your home, lad?"

Oswyn shook his head.

"You must live somewhere?" Jack persisted.

Oswyn looked around and then pointed towards the smithy's workshop behind them.

"You lived with him?" Jack said in dismay, gesturing to the unconscious man.

Oswyn nodded. "Since me ma, died and me sister got took by God."

"Are you related to that sack of shit?" Jack pointed at the Smith.

Oswyn shook his head. "He were my sister's husband."

"Your poor bloody sister," Jack said, nodding.

"That's what me ma said before God took her," Oswyn lamented.

"No other family?" Jack asked.
Oswyn shook his head.
Jack sighed.
"You've got to be jestin'?" Froggy exclaimed.
"Shut it," Jack said, pointing the finger at his companion. The Smith was regaining consciousness, a hand had found the wound Froggy had inflicted in his skull, and he was moaning.

Jack planted a boot on his chest, rolling him flat on his back. "Oswyn, come here."

The boy stepped backwards.

"He'll not hurt you. I'll not let the sack of shit get up. Come here," Jack said again.

Uncertainly the boy came to stand behind Jack's leg. Jack reached round, picked the boy up and stood him to face the fallen man. Clearly terrified, he was crying and struggling to be free. Jack, a boot on the fallen man, had two hands clamped on the child's shoulders.

"Never, Oswyn, let a man get the better of you. Now, spit in his face, and we'll be done," Jack said quietly into the child's ear.

Oswyn did as he was bid.

"Perhaps a kick as well," Jack urged, the child's bare foot connected ineffectually twice with the Smith's leg. "Good lad."

Jack turned to a rather pale Threadmill, fixing him with a solid blue gaze. "There are four men on the floor because of you. I have created a problem. Now solve it. It should be easy for you if you are as good a lawyer as you say you are."

Chapter Twenty-Two

Master Threadmill found Jack in the stables, saddling his horse, pulling the girth strap tight through the buckles.

"My Lord, I believe I have resolved the situation. I hope to your satisfaction," Threadmill's voice held the shake of nerves.

Jack emerged from behind the horse's hindquarters. "Enlighten me."

Threadmill swallowed hard. "The young boy can become a ward of the Parish temporarily. There is a Benedictine Order who will take him from them on the provision of a donation. As for the smith, after you told me what Oswyn accused him of, he will be answerable to the sheriff for his actions at the next assize. There are more than just the boy who are willing to stand witness against him for the crimes of buggery. And, I humbly apologise. Master Tate has told me that "my prattle" was responsible for what happened in the Inn, and I would wish to pay for the donation to the Benedictines in recompense."

Jack folded his arms. "It was probably good that you made me want to hit someone badly on this occasion. Otherwise, Oswyn would still be living with his tormentors."

"My Lord, I only wished to provide you with the best service I can. Please forgive me." Threadmill sounded as if he meant it.

"Perhaps fewer questions in future?" Jack said then, thinking about what Froggy had said, he added, "perhaps a discussion to clarify any matters that need my attention once a day, mind you?"

"That would be excellent, my Lord," Threadmill said enthusiastically.

"For no more than an hour," Jack continued.

Threadmill nodded.

"Tell me, how much are the Benedictines angling for?" Jack asked, changing the subject.

Threadmill blushed. "Five Angles."

"Greedy bastards," Jack said with feeling; that amount would be near enough Threadmill's annual salary. "Negotiate. I'm sure that's within your remit as my lawyer. Tell them they can have two, and I'll pay."

A day later, they approached Burton, arriving in time to avoid a storm that swept up from the south. Jack was surprised by the sense of belonging that settled upon him when he recognised the church spire of St Mary's, the mill and the familiar outline of the fortified manor. He pressed his horse ahead, wanting to take in the scene before him alone.

Little had changed.

Everything was as if he had never been away.

Threadmill had advised him that Ascough had, by now, received the court papers and would be aware of the claim he was to place on his brother's behalf. Which was a shame; Jack would have liked nothing better than to put his claim in person. Ascough had tried to have him murdered, and there was a score to be settled.

Jack had enough men with him to ensure that his admittance to Burton would not be prevented. When they arrived, they found the gates to the manor stood open. However, a wooden fence had been erected between them, and the other side of the courtyard was now a sheep pen filled with mired straw and bleating animals.

"God's bones, what's happened to this place?" Froggy said, leaning on his pommel and staring into the woolly-packed yard.

"Sir, it has been rented out for the last five years. They are probably the tenants' beasts," Master Threadmill provided helpfully.

"Rented out as what? Get them out of here." Already down from his horse, Jack was advancing on the makeshift fencing.

Froggy cast Threadmill a sideways glance. "I'd move over, lad. There'll be a glut of sheep wanting to be by any minute now."

Threadmill clumsily pulled his horse away from the centre of the road but not in time to avoid the frightened sheep spilling from the courtyard at speed. Behind them, using the flat of his sword to persuade the beasts to move and adding loud vocal encouragement, was Jack.

"Told ye," Froggy smirked as the press of complaining sheep headed towards them.

Threadmill, his reins too long, was trying to regain control of his horse as it circled beneath him, its legs lost in the river of wool that was complaining loudly.

Froggy shook his head and muttered under his breath. "Bloody lawyers."

Jack, behind the sheep, was sheathing his sword. His work was done, the courtyard was empty. "Let's see what a mess Ayscough has made of the rest of the place."

It didn't take long to find that Burton had been used for farm storage and as an animal pen since he had left. Stables were full of feed, the courtyard had been a sheep pen, but the main house had not been used. When Jack entered the hall, he was sure some of the smaller pieces of furniture were missing, but on the whole, everything was as he left it, albeit covered in a thick layer of dust, dirt and shit.

The only residents were a family of collared doves that had made their home in the hall's roof, their droppings laid in a thick covering on the top of the long table. The messy remains of the last fire still sat blackened in the hearth.

Upstairs he found the bed was still in his room, the covers mouldering. Several doors were unaccountably missing, but apart from that, Burton was intact.

When Jack returned from his tour of the upper floors, Froggy was standing in the hall. "What are you going to do with it?" he asked.

"I am going to do nothing. Ayscough, on the other hand, is going to make good, isn't he, Master Threadmill?" Jack announced, looking towards his lawyer, his arms folded across his chest.

†

Jack lay on his back on the bed listening to the rain, staring at a ceiling he remembered. The beams were painted with leaves, and in between them the wood was decorated with crude repeated images of deer and rabbits. The ceiling had always amused him; the painter had obviously not planned his work, and the repeated pattern did not quite fit into the space, resulting in the final rabbit on the left-hand side being half the size of the rest.

It was obvious he had started to apply the paint in the middle of the ceiling; here, the images of the deer and the rabbit were crisp, well-executed and mildly lifelike.

As the eye moved away from these, it would find rougher, more hastily painted creatures, their bodies contorted, antlers askew and with oversized eyes. Not that he thought he could have done any better if he had been laid on his back with a brush in his hand.

The wind rattled the closed shutters to his right, and he turned his head towards them. Suddenly an image of Pierre standing before them wandered into his mind.

"God's bones," Jack said and smiled. He could still remember the order of those first cards Richard had shown him. Pierre, standing in front of the shutters, had been the five of diamonds; Dan, the six, had been sitting on the coffer; leaning against the fireplace had been Harry, the eight of diamonds; sat in the chair was Carter, the six; on the other side of the door was Master Scranton, the four; and halfway along the corridor was the ace of diamonds.... the ace.... Emilio.

The image of the Italian riding away from him in London flitted unwanted into his mind.

Damn him!

Jack scowled and pushed himself up off the bed. Below him, somewhere, a door slammed shut and shortly after came the distinct sound of raised voices in the courtyard. Jack approached the window and peered down on those causing the disturbance.

"I demand to speak to whoever amongst you is in charge. Now," commanded an angry man at the gates, a long walking pole in one hand, a bag slung over one shoulder and the dark cassock that declaring his calling belted up around his waist to expose a pair of white bony knees.

"I told you, give me your name and I...." Froggy tried.

"My name is of no importance. I demand to speak to your master or whoever it was that expelled Crispin's sheep out into the fields to trample their way through Mathew Riley's wheat field," the cleric continued hotly.

Hearing the man's voice, Jack emerged from the hall into the yard. "Jamie?"

Jamie, wide-eyed, crossed himself. "May the saints preserve us. God seems to love you, lad."

Jack dropped down the steps into the yard two at a time, smiling. "I wouldn't be so sure about that."

"When I heard that someone had loosed Crispin Wood's sheep, stabbing them in their arses, apparently, with a blade, I should have thought it would be you," Jamie said, crossing the yard, limping badly on his right leg.

"God doesn't look like he's been overly kind to you?" Jack said, frowning.

"Ah, that's nowt. I cracked my ankle last winter falling down the church steps in the snow, nothing that a bit of sense on my part couldn't have avoided. And you, lad, you are looking well," Jamie said, grinning. "Indeed, last time we met, I think I accused you of looking little better than Martin, the blacksmith's simple son. Well, that's certainly changed."

"Aye, things have changed," Jack accepted.

Jamie waddled to stand before him. "You look like you should, lad. I am pleased. And your brother?"

"He's well," Jack said too quickly.

Jamie lent close to him. "If you've time for an old man, perhaps let me know how you fared after you left here. I wouldn't say no to getting out of this foul weather."

"I owe you that much," Jack accepted, leading the way back up the steps to the hall.

Jack provided an edited history of the last five years, missing out much, especially Andrew Kineer, Malta and the recent exploits that had led Richard to fall foul of the Crown - again. He kept his narrative to his father, his new wife, and when asked of Richard's whereabouts, he told Jamie he was working for Lord Burghley in the north.

Jamie turned the conversation back to Burton. "Ayscough has been a poor landlord. Bled the village dry he has, rents neigh on doubled, and when tenants didn't pay, he turfed them out. There's a fair number of grievances that need to be addressed."

"I've not seen Ayscough yet, but I am assured that control will pass back to me, and I will do what I can," Jack accepted, then a spark lit in the back of his mind, "Indeed, I have just the man with me who can begin by trying to make a summary of the grievances."

Jamie's brow furrowed.

Jack, rising from his chair, smiled broadly. "Let me find my lawyer, Master Threadmill will be more than happy to hear the tenants' complaints and redress their grievances."

"You brought a lawyer with you?" Jamie said, sounding shocked.

"I did, and it seems it was a wise decision," Jack replied, grinning.

†

Ayscough, unfortunately for Jack, had been forewarned by his lawyers. Threadmill had served the papers on him requesting that he relinquish his stewardship of Burton and return it to Jack Fitzwarren, who was acting as a proxy for his brother, Richard.

It had dampened the occasion somewhat.

Threadmill, armed with papers, his lawyer's robe and a mantle of legal rhetoric, was turning the occasion into a farce. Ayscough had attempted to kill Jack, and he had nearly succeeded.

Ayscough, knowing well that he was on the wrong side of both the law and Jack, was solicitous, spouting falsehoods about his stewardship in Richard's absence. Threadmill had told Jack that as long as Ayscough provided the rents and tithes that had been gathered in their absence, he was, unfortunately, exempt from any further legal recourse. Although he could raise the matter in the assizes, he doubted that Jack would get a remedy to his liking.

Jack strode across the room, preparing to leave. His hand on the wooden door, he was in the process of pressing it open when Ayscough spoke to Threadmill.

"It is customary, I believe, to charge a fee for the management when the owner is absentia," Ayscough said, his voice having adopted a business-like tone.

Jack turned. "In absentia!" He sputtered.

Ayscough was holding out a sheet towards Threadmill.

Jack paced back and snatched it from Ayscough's hand. "I'm not in bloody absentia now. Let me see what you've charged me for."

"My lawyers have prepared it. I am sure it's in order," Ayscough was saying.

Jack's eyes travelled down the list of items and numbers until he found what he wanted.

The total.

His eyes widened when he read it. The shit Ayscough had the temerity to have placed a figure for his services at almost precisely the amount Threadmill had estimated that the rents and dues would have been for the period that Richard had lost control of the manor.

Jack slammed the sheet back on the desk before Ayscough, his hands on either side of it, leaning towards the man. "Did you think that you could cheat my brother?"

Ayscough's voice remained level. "Sir, it is an honest account of the money I have had to spend on your brother's behalf while he has been absent."

"An honest account," Jack growled across the desk, his eyes dropping back to the sheet momentarily.

"It has been agreed between our lawyers already," Ayscough continued.

Jack looked towards Threadmill, his voice incredulous, he said. "Did you know about this?"

"My Lord, with respect, we have refuted Master Ayscough's claim. As you say, it is significantly higher than we would expect," Threadmill said defensively, adding nervously, "I had hoped that a degree of negotiation could take place and that a satisfactory figure for all parties could be agreed upon."

Jack laughed, his cold sapphire eyes humourless. "Of course, you should have told me. I am only too happy to negotiate with Master Ayscough."

For a moment, only Ayscough looked relieved. The moment ended quickly. Jack, hands fastened into his doublet, dragged him over the desk. Hauling him through the ordered piles of paperwork, sending some to the floor and upsetting an ink bottle.

Threadmill yelped, leaping backwards.

Ayscough, unprepared for the sudden assault, found himself released and falling headfirst from the edge of the desk.

"Negotiations have begun," Jack announced. When Ayscough landed on the floor, he rammed a boot hard across the back of his neck, pinning him to the boards. A harsh splutter emerged from the man's mouth, and his hands desperately tried to reach the boot trapping him against the floor.

"Master Threadmill," Jack's voice was conversational, "I believe Ayscough has had a change of heart and decided to waive the charges."

Threadmill, pale and looking between Jack and the man on the floor, stammered, "Does ... he?"

"I think I heard him say as much," Jack said, pretending to listen to the man beneath his boot.

"He ... would need to ... sign ... to affirm ... this," Threadmill stammered.

"That'll not be a problem, will it, Ayscough," Jack said, bringing more weight to bear across the back of his neck.

A high-pitched screech emerged from the man on the floor.

Jack grinned. "There, he agrees. Negotiations are complete. Now, find the sheet he needs to sign, and we will be on our way."

Threadmill, suddenly jolted into action by Jack's words, began a search on the floor for the paper he needed.

"Here ... I have it ... My Lord," Threadmill smoothed the page flat on the desk.

"Are you ready to sign?" Jack directed the question to the man on the floor.

A noise that could not be translated as any particular word emerged from Ayscough.

"Good," Jack released him, stepping neatly back.

Ayscough pressed himself from the floor. One side of his face was grazed, blood ran from his left nostril, and a tendril of drool hung from his open mouth. He glared at Jack, standing out of his reach with a poniard in his right hand and cold blue eyes fastened upon him.

"Sign, you bastard, and we'll be gone," Jack growled.

Chapter Twenty-Three

Jack, returning through the rain to Burton, recognised the standard immediately.

Five red lions, one pierced through the mouth with an arrow, sharing the escutcheon with crosslets and chevrons. The pennant that fluttered in the cold air was that of the Duke of Norfolk, Earl Marshal of England, the bloody Queen's lieutenant in the North. It was held aloft near a group of a dozen mounted men waiting outside the manor.

What did Norfolk want?

Jack's grip on the reins tightened as he entered the open gates of Burton, ignoring the harsh glances of the men standing there.

What the hell was he doing here?

Evidently, they'd been watching for him. Froggy Tate, with a worried expression, took hold of the Jack's horse's bridle. "They're in the hall. We couldn't stop them."

"It's alright," Jack growled, heading towards the steps. It looked like he might get the fight that Ayscough had denied him.

"Jack, wait..." Froggy tried to grasp his arm and stop him but failed.

Jack, stepping into the poorly lit hall, had expected to find a messenger, not the Duke of Norfolk surrounded by his men.

One of the large chairs from near the fire had been hauled onto the dais, and the Duke was seated in it sideways, one arm slung over the back and the other resting on his knee, resplendent in saturnine black, a high-collared, neat, black-edged ruff with a double looped chain of gold links drooping around his neck. Polished knee-high riding boots were crossed at the ankle and a riding whip, with a gold and jewelled hilt, rested on his knee.

Norfolk didn't get up.

His eyes had never left Jack as he walked towards him.

Jack stopped halfway across the hall, performing a poor stilted bow towards the seated man.

"Well, if it's not Lord Fitzwarren, at last," Norfolk said, his tone arrogant. "You ignored the message to return to London."

Jack's brow furrowed, and he shook his head slightly. "I've not received any message."

Norfolk, ignoring him, peered past Jack, looking down the length of the hall. "Not got your Italian Knight in tow, or is it the other way around?"

Jack bestowed an icy blue stare on Norfolk, asking, "Do you want to tell me why there was a message?"

"You've been summonsed to aid the Queen's expedition to Scotland," Norfolk provided.

Jack was silent for a moment.

Scotland!

"If you need my assistance, I will gladly join you," Jack said carefully.

Norfolk laughed. "Fitzwarren, you're not needed. Good God, what have you to offer? By all accounts, you've been your brother's lackey for years and had a somewhat poor, mercenary career. You are hardly a leader of men. Why could you possibly ever think you could be needed?"

"If that is the case, why have I been summoned to travel to Scotland?" Jack said flatly.

"You might not be needed, Fitzwarren, but you are required. There's a difference, you see," Norfolk explained, leaning forward in the chair and pointing towards Jack with the whip.

"Is there?" Jack asked.

Norfolk laughed again, pulled an open letter from his doublet, and spun the thick page towards Jack. "It's all in there."

The letter landed at his feet.

Jack slowly pulled a glove from his hand and picked up the letter from where it sat amongst the filth of the rotting floor rushes.

"You can read, can't you?" Norfolk asked, fake concern in his voice then when Jack didn't reply, he turned to the man on his left, "Hurley, it looks like the poor fellow is struggling, do him a kindness and offer to help him."

The men around Norfolk laughed.

Jack lifted his eyes from the page and met those of Norfolk. "I read well enough." Jack folded the sheet back up slowly, aware of the stares of the other men, careful to avoid meeting them.

You can't win, Jack, so don't try.

Jack heard his brother's voice quite clearly as he folded the final crease in the parchment. Norfolk outranked him in every respect. To defer was not to lose.

But Jack couldn't help himself.

Stepping forward he placed the letter on the table next to Norfolk. "Thank you for acting as a messenger."

Jack turned and began striding back towards the hall door.

He heard the curses from behind him, the angry scrape of the chair as Norfolk rose.

"Fitzwarren, get back here."

Jack didn't break his stride. In two more steps, he had reached the door, hauled it open and exited, slamming it in the frame in his wake.

You never bloody well listen, do you? – The exasperated voice echoed inside his head.

He was at the end of the corridor before the hall door opened. "That's the last time you will turn your back on me, Fitzwarren. Do you hear?"

Jack ignored him.

Fifteen minutes later, he watched from his room as Norfolk, at the head of his men, left Burton.

The message had been short, to the point and signed by Lord Burghley. He didn't doubt its authenticity but doubted whether following the instructions was a wise idea; not that he had much choice. The Queen commanded that he join Norfolk, who was taking men north. What for and what they would do was not clear in the missive, but the instruction to place himself under Norfolk's command was.

※

When Jack heard the noise of horses in the yard, he thought Norfolk's men had returned. However, when he made it to the hall, he found that the source of the disturbance was standing in front of the fireplace dripping wet, a pond spreading from his fine boots to darken the stone floor. Clumsy fingers, stiff with cold, unclipped the buckle that held the soaked cloak at his shoulder; releasing the sodden fabric, he hauled it free and dumped it unceremoniously on a nearby bench. His clothes below were as saturated as the cloak had been.

Jack glared at him, eyes as cold as ice.

The Italian sneezed, and when he had recovered, he said, "Jack, it is good to see you."

Jack folded his arms across his chest, his mouth pressed into a thin line. "Why are you here?"

"I was trying to arrive before Norfolk, but it was not to be," Emilio had found a delicate square of yellow silk inside his doublet and was about to dry his nose when he realised it was as wet as the rest of his attire and cast it on top of his cloak.

"I don't give a shit about Norfolk," Jack declared.

Emilio, rubbing his hands up and down his arms in an effort to revive some feeling, said, "Are you going to leave me here to freeze?"

"You do not appear to have had a pleasant journey," Jack observed, making no effort to move.

"Pleasant?" The Italian retorted loudly, "this country knows nothing of pleasant."

"You have men with you?" Jack asked.

"Just three," Emilio waved a hand in the direction of the hall door before
sneezing loudly. "So this is the Burton you wanted to get back?"

"It is."

"Why?" the Italian asked, moving closer towards the poor remains of the fire.

With Threadmill behind him, Froggy was standing halfway across the hall and trying to catch Jack's eye. Jack, abandoning Emilio, strode towards Froggy. "Find his men good quarters and stabling for their horses. And clear everyone from the hall. Master Threadmill, I know you are eager to help, if I need your services, I will let you know."

Jack returned across the damp hall to his shivering guest. "Why are you here?"

Emilio fastened his dark eyes on Jack's blue ones. "I told you. I had aimed to arrive before Norfolk. You deserved some warning."

"I am to join his men. They are in Lincoln now and bound for Scotland," Jack added. "Something I think you know quite a lot about, don't you?"

Emilio was doing an excellent job of ignoring Jack's rising temper. "Jack, I am half frozen. I've not eaten for two days, and neither have my men. We've changed horses five times and ridden without stopping. We came here to help...." Tired and cold, Emilio was stumbling over the words and switched to Italian. "Stop being so damned petulant. If it pleases you and God, I will explain when my teeth stop chattering...."

Emilio was stopped from speaking by a coughing fit that ended with another almighty sneeze. His right hand had found the arm of one of the high-backed chairs near the fire, and he dropped into it. Jack looked at him. He was indeed soaked, water running from him, his hair was plastered to his head, and dark stubble on his face confirmed his story that he had not stopped for days. Jack had rarely seen Emilio dishevelled. If the remnants of his temper were not still running around his mind like an annoyed child, he would have smiled at seeing the Italian reduced to such a shadow of his usual sartorial self.

"The fire, if you please," Emilio's teeth were audibly chattering.

Emilio was seated near the stone fireplace, and, although it was sizeable, it was barely filled with flames. Emilio scowled at it, and Jack, kneeling, began reviving the fire from the store of wood stacked next to it, feeding the flames until a bright orange blaze was alive in front of them.

"Gazie mille," Emilio said with feeling; his hands outstretched towards the heat trembled.

Despite wanting to interrogate the Italian, Jack realised sourly that he would have to deal with the practicalities of the situation first.

"Do you have dry clothes?" he asked brusquely.

Emilio shook his head. "There wasn't time."

"You can't remain in those."

Emilio sniffed loudly.

Jack had some spare clothes in his room. As yet they were neatly wrapped and unworn as provided by Master Drew and still in the pack that had been slung across the back of his horse. He pulled out a shirt, hose and a doublet and hoisted a woollen blanket from the bed before returning to the hall.

"Get up. If you don't get out of those clothes, you'll be dead before morning," Jack commanded.

"That might be a blessing," Emilio said and, rising from the chair, began to fumble with the double row of buttons down the front of his doublet.

"I can't stand to watch." Dropping the dry clothing he was holding onto his chair, Jack began to twist the buttons, pressing them through their loops. "I bet you wish there were fewer of these now, don't you?"

Emilio sniffed even louder. "Never."

The front undone, Jack took hold of the neck at the back, holding it firmly while Emilio squirmed from the grip of the soaked cloth. Beneath this, the water had glued the fine silk of his shirt to his skin; what had been delicate Italian lace at the cuffs was now a twisted wreckage of threads ensnaring his wrists. Emilio tried to shrug the shirt over his head; the material stayed fixed to his body. He tried again, attempting to pull his right arm back through the sleeve, the material twisted around his arm, trapping him fast in the folds.

"Jacques, please," Emilio's dark eyes met Jack's.

Jack, relenting, pulled the shirt over the other man's head, and when it stuck, he tugged harder.

Emilio yelped as the stitching gave way, and the shirt finally tore enough for Emilio to free himself.

"You can afford another one. It's just a shirt, for God's sake," Jack said, discarding the soggy mess on the floor. Emilio accepted the blanket Jack held out, wrapping it tightly around his body and cowling his head. Seating himself, Emilio began to try and extricate his feet from wet riding boots. Knee-high, buckled three times, and with straps swollen with water, they provided another frustrating challenge.

Jack's cool blue eyes watched the Italian struggle.

The buckles undone on the right boot, he kicked it free. The left proved a greater challenge, the buckle at the ankle stuck fast, the wet leather refusing to navigate back through the silver framework. Emilio, exhausted, dropped back in the chair, the boot undone to the ankle, the leather flopping to the floor.

"I give up," he said, his eyes closed, his face shadowed by the hood of the blanket.

Sighing loudly, Jack knelt on the floor. His strong fingers forced the prong from the leather; released, the strap slid through the clip, and Jack pulled the boot free.

"Grazi," Emilio said, his eyes still closed.

There were wooden cups and an ale jug on the table. Jack filled two of them, holding one towards Emilio. "Here, take it."

Emilio opened his eyes, and a hand appeared from the blanket folds, accepting the cup. Emilio sniffed the contents tentatively, asking, "Please tell me this was not made here?"

"It was, and it's good," Jack said.

Emilio took a sip, his face twisted in distaste, and he lowered the cup to rest on the chair arm. "Would a good wine be asking too much?"

"Why are you here?"

Emilio pulled the blanket tighter around him, twisting his feet inside the wool.

"Well?" Jack broke the silence.

"I did not want you to meet Norfolk... unprepared. I know what a hot temper you have, and I would be ill-advised for you to lose it with him," Emilio said.

"Shame you didn't get here earlier then," Jack said dryly.

Emilio dropped his head back against the chair. "Jacques, what have you done?"

Jack grunted. "The man's an arse. He was spoiling for a fight from the moment I stepped into his sight."

"Please tell me you didn't give him one," Emilio said, his voice quiet, the dark tired eyes fixed on Jack. "He is the Queen's cousin and one of her favoured courtiers. I think it would be fair to say that neither you nor your brother are enjoying your sovereign's good wishes at the moment."

"Nor do I want them," Jack said curtly.

"And you are about to be under Norfolk's command, am I not right?" Emilio said, his voice weary.

Jack's expression clouded. "I am. How do you know this?"

Emilio shrugged.

"I am to join his force and go to Scotland to lend support should the need arise," Jack's words echoed those in the letter, "But you already know all this, don't you?"

"Do not be angry, Jacques," Emilio replied, closing his tired eyes.

"Why not? It would be nice if you shared your information with me occasionally ahead of time," Jack grumbled.

"If it helps, I have only recently found out," Emilio said quietly.

Jack glared at Emilio. "You have no idea how much I dislike being the last to know. That was Richard's usual gift, and now it seems to be yours."

"If you've no wine, would a little food be too much to ask?" Emilio asked, changing the subject.

Jack rose abruptly, the chair sliding back noisily on the wooden floor, and headed from the hall. He found Froggy in the passageway that led to the kitchens.

"Can you find what food there is and have some sent to my bloody guest? Only Emilio could make such hard work of the journey from here to London," Jack grumbled.

Froggy frowned. "They've not come from London, Jack."

"Where then?" Jack said, confused.

"Meaux," Froggy said. Jack stared at him, so he added, "near Paris."

"I know where it is. What were they doing there?" Jack said.

Froggy shook his head. "I can't help you with the answer to that question."

It transpired that Emilio couldn't either. When Jack returned with what he could find in the kitchens, his friend's head had lolled against the side of the chair, eyes closed, and he was fast asleep. Jack's attempts to revive him failed, so he settled back in his chair and demolished the platter he had fetched from the kitchens.

Chapter Twenty-Four

Jack had slept in the chair opposite Emilio, feet balanced on a stool, the doublet he had brought for the Italian laid across his chest for warmth. The feeling of it being pulled from him, tugging on his elbow, woke him.

"Thank you," Emilio said as Jack raised an arm, releasing the trapped material.

The Italian held up the doublet, frowned, and shook it hard, trying to remove some of the creases before raising it for a second inspection. Shaking his head and with a look of distaste, he began to slide his arms into the sleeves, a slight grimace twisting his face as he pulled the front closed.

Jack, still not fully awake, watched, amused.

Emilio was already wearing Jack's shirt and hose. Everything the Italian wore was definitely two sizes too large. Shirt sleeves fastened at the cuffs to his wrists were too long, the linen ballooning around his elbows. His hose were loose around his legs, the excess fabric sitting in a series of uneven wrinkles resting on his boot tops. Hanging from his shoulders was Jack's doublet, the material slack across his chest and the sleeves hiding his hands.

Emilio's sharp eyes, noting Jack's amused expression, said, "The key, Jacques, is not to care."

Jack yawned, stretching his arms wide, his eyes sliding over the other. "You look ridiculous."

"My father's brother, the Marchese of Padua, fell from his horse while hunting. He was forced to commandeer a doublet from his servant. The man was a foot shorter, and the sleeves ended here," Emilio indicated where on his arm. "My uncle made no excuse, provided no explanation for his choice of clothes, and within a week, the tailors in the city were making doublets with sleeves that ended just after the elbow."

Jack's eyes rested thoughtfully on his companion, watching Emilio fasten up the doublet in silence. It was an unfortunate fact that Emilio would look good in sackcloth. No matter what he wore, his manner did not change; his power of personality was the same regardless of his appearance.

"Have you slept there all night?" Emilio asked, his fingers arriving at the last button.

"No," Jack lied.

Emilio smiled, his eyes alive with delight. Swirling the woollen blanket from the floor, he settled it back over his shoulders before seating himself and pulling it around his body as if it were a royal mantle. "It is a poor place. You even seem to want for firewood."

Jack's eyes were drawn to the cold hearth by Emilio's comment. "I don't remember inviting you here."

"But you did! When we were at the Angel," Emilio said reproachfully.

"Did you really intend to arrive here before Norfolk?" Jack rested a questioning gaze on Emilio.

"Yes," Emilio said, his expression now serious. He asked, "What do you know of Norfolk's orders?"

"Not a lot. I am to join his command today. He is taking an army north, towards the Scottish borders." Jack pushed the stool away, screeching on the floor, and leaned towards Emilio, "It's not Norfolk I'm bloody interested in. Why are you here?"

"I said I would come and see Boorton with you," Emilio replied innocently.

"Burton," Jack corrected, glaring at the Italian.

"That is what I said, Boorton," Emilio's smile broadened, his eyes luminous.

237

Jack shook his head, not about to be sidetracked, pinning the other with a cold stare. "I'd like the truth." Emilio's eyes widened. "Wouldn't we all?"

"Stop playing games with me," Jack, already irritated by the Italian's flippant manner, was getting angry.

A mock, hurt expression creased Emilio's features. "Is this any way to treat a guest?"

"You are trying to raise my temper. Stop it," Jack's icy blue glare met Emilio's sardonic one.

"Jacques, please ..." Emilio spread his hands, and the neglected blanket slid from his shoulders.

"Stop calling me that!" Jack had risen and stood over Emilio. "Why don't you tell me exactly what is going on? Why is my brother bound for Scotland? Why even Devereux seems to know of my affairs? Why did you prevent me from seeing the Santa Luciana when she was docked in London, and why did you leave me on St Katherine's quay?"

Emilio, looking up into the angry face, grinned mischievously. "I have missed you."

"I will not miss you with this fist if you don't start and provide me with some answers," Jack retorted, truly livid with him.

Emilio ignored the threatening hand close to his face and instead laced his fingers together, elbows on the chair arms, and regarded Jack with a level gaze. "That is a lot of questions, Jacques."

"I've got all morning," Jack's cold blue sapphire eyes locked with the Italian's dark ones. Clattering back into his chair, he glowered at Emilio. "Get on with it."

"Where would you like me to begin? What is it you wish to know first?" Emilio enquired.

"Why don't you start with Scotland? Richard is bound there, and so now am I," Jack stated.

"Alright," Emilio accepted, rearranging his wool mantle, his face, for a moment, thoughtful. "While I find it amusing that your brother fell foul of Burghley's good graces when he foisted fake gold on the English treasury, it wasn't entirely sensible when he tied you to this folly."

"How do you know about that?" Jack said hotly, annoyed that Emilio knew of his brother's failed plan.

Emilio shrugged. A blanket fold slithered from his knee, and a ringed hand flicked it back over his legs. "Such transgressions are rarely kept secret for long."

"He was forced to find a solution to a problem that Devereux had created," Jack's tone was defensive. He wondered exactly how much Emilio knew of the gold that his brother had planted in Elizabeth's treasury.

"I am sure you believe that to be the case," Emilio soothed, settling back in the chair, looking very much at ease.

Jack could feel his temper mounting again. "If you have arrived here intending to raise my anger, the door is behind you."

Emilio ignored him. "I am simply trying to answer your questions, one at a time. So, out of favour, your brother had little choice but to act as Lord Burghley directed, and he has chosen to use Richard to transport Knox to Scotland. Can I assume you have heard of the Scot?"

"The reformist preacher," Jack answered, wondering exactly what his brother was caught up in.

"The same," Emilio replied, enjoyment plain in his eyes.

"Why Richard?" Jack quizzed. A furrow had appeared between the fair brows.

"Why not? The Scot is not welcome in England. He is an opponent of your Sovereign. There can't be many men who would wish to anger her by aiding him. Lord Burghley wishes him in Scotland for his own devices. Should this all go wrong, he can become like one of the Israelites' sin-laden goats."

Why would Burghley want Knox in Scotland? Why would England aid the preacher? And whose scapegoat was he this time? Burghley's or the Orders - or both?

"Why are you here? Why is the Order of St John interested in a heretical Scottish preacher? Surely you have not begun to involve yourselves in a bloody religious inquisition?" Jack's tone was sarcastic.

"It is simply the fact that we are also keen to ensure his safe passage and arrival in Scotland." The fingers of Emilio's left hand idly twisted one of the rings on his right.

"By 'we', can I assume you mean the Order?" Jack placed the question carefully, observant eyes fixed on the other.

Emilio inclined his head. "Indeed."

"Why?" Jack demanded, flinging his arms wide, "he's opposed to the Order and the Catholic Church. This makes no sense at all."

"Sometimes religion is not the cornerstone of every decision the Order makes." Emilio laced his fingers together and regarded Jack closely, resting his chin on them.

Jack laughed harshly, dropping back hard in the chair.

Emilio's eyes glinted brightly.

"You are not known as God's bankers for no reason, are you?" Jack scoffed, shaking his head.

"The security of Christendom has a price," Emilio said coolly.

"So we know the why, then: money. Explain it to me," Jack's hands had found the finials on the chair arms and were wrapped tightly around them.

Emilio smiled broadly. "Henri of France borrowed substantial amounts. While he lived, this was not an occasion for concern; certain pledges in place offset the sums. However, after his untimely death, there has been a power shift that was not foreseen – Scotland is not a prize that France can afford."

"Not one they can afford if they are to have sufficient money to honour their debts to your Order?" Jack's gaze was speculative.

"Exactly. War is a costly endeavour, but maintaining peace can be even more so," Emilio explained. A hand had escaped from beneath the rough blanket, the thumb and forefinger pinched together.

"So... tell me if I have the scent of it. France owes a lot of money, and Henri borrowed heavily from your Order. You are about to help terminate their rocky tenure in Scotland to ensure they have enough to make their payments as you feel this is an unnecessary drain on their coffers?" Jack summarised.

Emilio grinning, spread his arms wide, palms towards Jack. "I could not have put it better myself."

Jack shook his head. "Why am I stuck in the middle of this?"

"I agree. It is unfair. Your Lord Burghley would like nothing less than to remove you from the ranks of Elizabeth's nobles. There is no one to inherit the title. It would be a simple legal matter to collate everything you own and claim it for Her Majesty," Emilio's eyes held an ironic glint.

Jack was about to point out that there might be an heir before the year was out. However, he thought better of it and simply nodded in acceptance of Emilio's words.

"You are being sent to join Norfolk with the express hope, on Cecil's part at least, that you will not return," Emilio said simply.

"And Norfolk knows this?"

"Of course," Emilio said, then added, "you have three choices."

"Only three?"

"I think even three is too many," Emilio said quickly, smiling.

"Go on then."

"Firstly, you could run," Emilio ticked off the choice on his hand.

"I'm not running from that shit!"

"Alright then. Secondly, you make yourself indispensable and ensure your survival," Emilio held up a second finger.

Jack observed him with cold eyes. "And the third option?"

"You discredit Norfolk," Emilio held the three fingers towards Jack.

"Jesus! You are making the first option look credible," Jack said sarcastically.

Emilio smiled.

"I have only ten men with me and a bloody lawyer," Jack spoke his thoughts out loud.

"That's why this order to join Norfolk arrived here, giving you no opportunity to pull a larger force together," Emilio explained slowly, "I had hoped to arrive in time to persuade you to move elsewhere and avoid his orders; all I can do now is offer my help."

"Your help?" Jack's eyes held a mixture of confusion and anger.

Emilio rearranged the blanket as if it were a cloak of office. Extending a foot, he drew the stool Jack had used towards himself, resting his feet upon it. "Yes, my help. The five Knights I have with me will join Norfolk, but I will remain with you."

Jack leaned forward. "How will that work? Norfolk is going to identify you amongst the ranks of my men? Surely he has met you at court? You are not exactly a man who is easily missed."

Emilio smiled, cowling his head in the blanket. "Dourly dressed like a peasant, I doubt he would spare me a glance."

"You, dourly dressed!" Jack's sudden laughter exploded loudly in the hall.

A thoughtful expression settled on Emilio's face. He rose, the blanket still over his head. "The best place to hide anything is in plain sight. Perhaps as your lawyer's clerk, I shall be at your side."

Jack leaned back in the chair, his loud laughter genuine.

"I can see you like the idea," Emilio said, peering out from beneath the blanket hood towards Jack.

"Don't think I've forgiven you," Jack advised, stopping laughing.

"I have covered questions one and two. Now to your third and fourth questions – Devereux and the Santa Luciana," Emilio paraded along the dais before Jack, the blanket fluttering from his shoulders.

"Go on," Jack remained seated, watching the other pace before him.

"I will admit I met your brother in London. He didn't want you aware he was in the city. He knew you had placed several... traps for him, and with good reason. He didn't want you to find out that they had been sprung. There wasn't time for him to communicate with Devereux, so that unpleasant task was one I undertook. And, yes, I ensured your back was turned to the Santa Luciana when we were standing on the quay. It was a bit of bad luck that she was berthed near the Ambassador's ship," Emilio finished coming to a halt before Jack.

"Why does everyone wish to keep me in the dark," Jack complained, glaring up at the speaker.

"What would you have done? Any action you took could have jeopardised Cecil's plan and your brother's mission that he has been tasked to get Knox to Scotland," Emilio spread his arms wide.

"But I am going to Scotland now. I've been commanded to go. What difference to your plans would it have made?" Jack looked up into Emilio's face.

"There was too much risk that you would draw attention to what was being planned. Half of London knows you were looking for your brother. It was better if it appeared you were still hunting," Emilio explained, retaking his seat.

Jack accepted the argument but asked. "And you, why are the Order here now?"

"Outwardly to ensure the delivery of Knox into the warm hands of his devotees, but truly I am here to ensure my friend's safety. It will be much harder for Norfolk to put a knife in you if he has to go through a Knight of St John first," Emilio said bluntly, crossing his arms.

Jack knew the words were spoken with honesty, and to deny them would seem churlish, so he asked instead. "And my fourth question?"

Emilio smiled broadly, closing his eyes momentarily, a look of pure delight settling on his face. When he opened them again, he said, "There was someone in the Ambassador's entourage I had not seen for a long time. Indeed I did not expect to ever meet them again. It was, how you say," Emilio switched to Italian, "Una sorpresa."

"An unwanted one?" Jack asked hopefully.

Emilio shook his head. "No. Be pleased for me, Jacques."

Jack wasn't.

Chapter Twenty-Five

Despite Jack's misgivings, Emilio was still intent on taking on the guise of Jack's lawyer's clerk; indeed, the prospect seemed to delight him.

"It would be wise to take your lawyer with you should any questions arise," Emilio continued.

"You said nobody would give you a second glance?" Jack wanted Threadmill to be separate from those who went north.

"Well, if they do, his presence might be helpful," Emilio continued, not put off by Jack's tone. "And it would seem too strange to have a clerk with you without your lawyer, don't you think?"

"No," Jack said solidly. "He's not going."

"Alright, then I will take on the role of your lawyer. At least let me talk with him. It will give me some idea of what I need to know." Emilio leant towards Jack, laying a hand on his arm.

Jack laughed, pulling from Emilio's touch. "In an hour, you think you can learn enough to adopt the role of a lawyer?"

"Just send him to me," Emilio said bluntly.

Jack, an evil smile on his face and aware of how much Master Threadmill could talk, complied.

When he returned an hour later, it was not the scene he had expected. Emilio was perched on the end of the table laughing, and Threadmill, standing on the dais, his arms spread wide, was in the middle of recounting a story – in Italian.

"....and so, after five hours of legal argument, the sheep were released," Threadmill finished.

Emilio, laughing, wiped a tear from his eye.

"I am pleased to find you so well entertained," Jack said bitingly, gazing between his lawyer and the Knight.

"You did not tell me your lawyer had spent time in Milan," Emilio slid from the end of the table. "I will enjoy his company on our journey north."

"He's not going," Jack said with finality, folding his arms.

"My Lord, Signor Martino has explained the situation to me," Threadmill's tone was earnest.

"Signor Martino?" Jack echoed, his eyes fixed on Emilio.

"Indeed, and I feel that as your lawyer, I should accompany you," Threadmill continued.

"Do you, indeed," Jack asked, a steel blue gaze on his lawyer. "And who is going to look after you?"

Threadmill drew himself up to his full height, his cheeks flushed. "I have had training. Indeed, I was Captain of the College arms brigade."

Jack's eyebrows rose, and his words were laden with sarcasm. "Captain of the college arms brigade. That's quite a position. I'm impressed. And the poniard you have in your belt, an artful blade."

"A gift from my father," Threadmill confirmed, sounding pleased.

"Can I see it?" Jack asked.

Threadmill obliged, drawing the knife he held it towards Jack.

"Have you ever used it in anger?" Jack's eyes studied the gilded hilt in the lawyer's hand.

Threadmill looked confused.

"I thought not. And wearing that, with your skill, you are asking to be robbed," Jack pronounced, meeting the man's eyes.

Threadmill blushed. "My Lord, I do not think it would be taken from me easily."

Jack smiled. "I am sure you think that to be true. However..."

Jack took two quick steps forward, taking hold of Threadmill's wrist in an iron grasp. The man yelped, his hand opening automatically, the poniard rattling on the wooden boards of the dais.

"Leave the fighting to me," Jack, stooping, retrieved the blade from the floor. "Put it away before you have someone's eye out."

"That was unfair," Emilio said, stepping between Threadmill and Jack.

"You think so, do you?" Jack threw the words towards Emilio.

"I shall ensure your lawyer's safety," Emilio pronounced, standing solidly before Jack.

Threadmill looked confused, as a man wearing borrowed clothes and with a blanket as a cloak championed his cause. Jack, catching the look on the lawyer's face, laughed. "I don't think Master Threadmill believes that to be a serious offer."

Emilio loosed the makeshift cloak from his shoulders, whipping it through the air. He wrapped it around Jack's hand and the knife he still held.

Jack had not been ready for the attack.

Forced to drop the knife, he hauled his hand from the folds, directing a fist towards the Italian's face. Emilio ducking beneath the blow, fastened both his hands around Jack's arm and brought them both staggering to the edge of the dais. Jack lost his balance as he fell and wrapped his hands into Emilio's doublet, hauling the lighter man over his head to land behind him.

Emilio regained his feet awkwardly, turning to face Jack, who had already righted himself but remained crouched. He had the opportunity to plant a kick to the side of Jack's head, and he did.

"My Lord! Sir ...." Threadmill's voice was unsteady.

Jack caught Emilio's booted ankle, forcing the Knight to lose his balance, and the pair rolled in a heap on the floor.

Threadmill, stepping towards them, thought the fight was over, not realising that both men were trying to secure a better hold than the other. With his arms fastened around Jack's neck, Emilio attempted to pin Jack's leg to the floor with his own. Jack's thumbs slipped another inch, pressing into Emilio's eyes.

The Italian swore, releasing his grip for only an instant. But it was enough. Using his advantage of greater weight, Jack hefted the other men over, bringing himself onto the top. Emilio, beneath him on his front, his hand hard on the back of the Italian's neck, fastening him to the floor.

"Enough!" A voice shouted from across the hall.

Jack pressed harder, his knee also now in Emilio's back. He grinned as he heard the smaller man grunt in pain.

"Stop!" There was the sound of footsteps running towards them.

Jack didn't, increasing the pressure.

Suddenly, from behind, a hand fastened in his hair hauled his head back, and he found himself staring at an angry face, the cold steel of a knife cutting into his neck.

Emilio, released, crawled a few paces away, breathing heavily. He waved his hand towards the man with a knife to Jack's neck. "Let him go, Alphonso. It was my fault I angered him."

"Only an English dog would fight a man with broken ribs," Alphonso spoke with utter disgust. The knife pierced the skin, and a fine line of blood ran down Jack's neck.

"Let him go. Now!" Emilio's voice, no longer soft, had adopted the tone of the commander he was.

"He tried to kill you." The hand in Jack's hair tightened.

"I angered him. Let Lord Fitzwarren go, Alphonso," Emilio said.

"Fitzwarren?" Alphonso said, confusion in his voice. He let go of Jack, stepping backwards.

"Yes, he is a friend of mine. He just has difficulty remembering it sometimes," Emilio said, laying back on the floor, his face pale.

Jack looked between the two as he rose from the floor.

"My Lord, are you alright?" Master Threadmill said, concern apparent in his voice.

Jack brushed him away. Staring between Emilio and ...Alphonso.

Jack's mind reeled.

He'd seen him before. More clearly than he had thought. He could recall him now clearly. Slender, a sword belt buckled tightly across narrow hips, a little taller than Emilio, his long neck accentuated by the high ruff collar, the slashed blue doublet revealing the shirt's dark blue beneath. Boots, black with the same rose buckle design as the buttons running down his doublet's front. One of the rings on his left hand, an oversized broad band of gold boasting an enormous sapphire set in a star-shaped fitting.

Jack swallowed hard.

Alphonso was kneeling next to Emilio, his hand on his arm, concern on his face. Emilio smiled back, one corner of his mouth raised higher than the other, his eyes holding a spark of mischievous delight. It was an expression Jack had seen a thousandfold times.

Jack knew he had seen him clearly, and his mind had blocked the image.

"My Lord? Are you sure you are alright? Your neck – it's bleeding," Threadmill's voice shook.

Jack slapped his hand to his neck. Pulling it away, he saw the thin line of blood across his fingers. "It's just a scrape."

Threadmill proffered a linen square. Jack took it - his response was automatic. His eyes were still on Alphonso, who was helping Emilio up from the floor, the Italian had his hand on his right side, and he was moving with care. Emilio had yelped the previous night when he'd yanked the shirt over his head and savagely accused him of becoming soft.

They were coming towards him, Emilio leaning on Alphonso's arm.

Emilio smiled. "Jack, let me introduce you properly to the man who just tried to cut your throat. Alphonso Masartio, may I introduce you to Lord Fitzwarren."

Jack, the linen still pressed to his neck, stared at Alphonso.

Alphonso, detaching himself from Emilio, performed a perfect court bow and, rising, laid a pair of inquisitive pale blue eyes on Jack. "I cannot apologise enough. I misread the situation, My Lord. Please forgive me."

Realising that the silence was becoming uncomfortably long, Jack said haltingly, "No, it was my fault for letting that idiot Italian anger me."

Jack wished to be somewhere else, anywhere. He wasn't going to get his wish.

"Jack, send for wine, or if you've none, some of that cloudy ale you forced on me last night. We have much to talk about," Emilio announced, making his way back towards the table on the dais. "Master Threadmill, join us, please."

For a moment, Jack was left alone in his hall as the rest of the men moved to the table and began to take seats at Emilio's direction.

"Bloody unbelievable." Jack threw a disparaging glance towards Emilio before he left the hall to procure whatever Burton could supply that would not offend his guest.

When Jack returned, the vacant seat was next to Alphonso. He was sure by design. Grudgingly he took it, pulling the chair out and seating himself a foot further away.

Master Threadmill asked, "Is this your first visit to England, Senior Masartio?"

"Indeed, I have travelled little outside of Spain and Italy," Alphonso replied, his liquid blue eyes, the colour of a winter waterfall and about as warm, fixed on the lawyer.

"Don't feel you need to tell us how pleasing you find it. I am already well acquainted with an Italian's view of England," Jack said, raising his cup towards Emilio, "isn't that right?"

Emilio, seemingly relieved, smiled. "It is different from Italy, that is all."

"In many things, not just the weather," Jack said darkly.

Emilio smiled brightly, choosing a new route for the conversation. "True. Do you remember that card game with Devereux where the deck was one you had never seen before?"

Jack rolled his eyes. "Don't remind me. If it had not been for you, I would have possibly been branded the worst card player Christendom."

"You are the worst card player Christendom," Emilio laughed, raising his cup towards Jack.

✝

There was little time left for argument or planning. Jack and his men needed to join Norfolk, and they would move north together. It was agreed that Threadmill's clerk would remain in Burton; Jack had a use for him there. He had promised Jamie redress for the tenants, and this was an opportunity to provide this. The clerk could document the complaints and wrongs during Ayscough's tenure. It also removed one more man from Jack's group, who he regarded as a liability. Threadmill was more than enough. Jack was unsure about Alphonso's capabilities and was pleased when Emilio indicated that he would ride north with the other knights and wasn't about to join Jack's group.

They would separate when they arrived at Lincoln. Jack was sure Alphonso would not have received the same arduous training that Emilio had been subjected to.

They left Burton and headed towards Lincoln to join Norfolk's forces. Jack, for once, was thankful for Threadmill, who rode silently at his side. In front of them rode Emilio and Alphonso. Jack examined the man in minute detail. The hands that housed the garish rings were smooth, the skin devoid of the white marks of scars. Jack and Emilio's hands had knuckles thickened with skin that had healed over repeated cuts.

Jack looked down at the back of his hands as if seeing them for the first time. On the right, he wore the ring Emilio had given him. The back of his hand was crisscrossed with scars. Where they had come from, he had little idea. When the cuts healed, the memory of how they were received tended to fade. One he did remember was a deep cut across his left palm when he had been forced to grasp his blade and use it two-handed to deflect a blow when he escaped from Ayscough's men. Luckily, it hadn't cut through the tendons, but the blade had bitten deep into the flesh, leaving him with a thick white line across his palm. But most of the rest he could not remember; many were scars on top of scars, his hands were rough, the skin on his fingers thick and resilient.

Jack glanced at Emilio's hands, where they held the reins lightly. Hidden inside leather gloves, he was denied sight of them. It didn't matter; he knew they were equally scarred, lined by taught tendons and strengthened sinew. A swordsman's hands.

Unlike Alphonso's.

Clean skin, the colour and texture of a newly peeled horse chestnut; light brown and flawless.

Emilio's face was not as battle-scarred as his hands were, but it was markedly different from Alphonso's. He assumed they were close in age, yet Alphonso's face still seemed to possess the roundness of youth. Jack noted that his mouth seemed to settle into a line of petulant

disapproval whenever he thought no eyes were upon him.
As if Alphonso was aware of his minute scrutiny, he suddenly turned in his saddle. Pale, depthless blue eyes fastened onto Jack's and one corner of his mouth twitched to a half smile before he turned back. Involuntarily, Jack's hands found themselves clamping the reins a degree tighter.
An hour later, they arrived in Lincoln. Jack was relieved that most of the men who accompanied Norfolk and the Duke had already departed. Orders had been left for them to follow, and Jack was more than happy with the arrangement. The group split. Alphonso now rode with the knights, and Emilio took up a position next to Jack as they rode north.

Chapter Twenty-Six

Christopher Morley was pleased to find he possessed "sea legs" and that the constant movement of the *Santa Luciana* did not significantly affect his stomach.

"I prefer to be busy. It is the habit of a lifetime, I am afraid. If I can be of assistance, it would be appreciated," Morley said, leaning over the table and looking at the notes Richard was examining.

"What did you have in mind?" Richard asked, glancing up from where he was seated at the desk.

"Well, sir, you are planning a scheme of works to make the ship ready to run with the canon. I overheard your conversation with your captain. You are hoping to make port shortly and purchase the materials you need. If I may say so, those notes you have are fairly poor. Perhaps I could be of assistance," Morley pointed towards the crumpled, watermarked sheet Richard had been studying. "I've been watching you for the past few minutes trying to figure out if that number is a three or an eight."

Richard laughed. "You don't miss much. The page got a soaking. It was an estimation from Collins of the timber needed for the carriages for the demi-culverins," Richard held the sheet near the candle. "I think, in all honesty, I might have to redo it. Either that or go with the higher numbers. Too much would be better than too little; there won't be an opportunity to obtain more."

Morley smiled. "Let me help you. It is to my advantage that the *Santa Luciana* is as well-equipped as she can be. I wish nothing more than to be back on shore myself, and if I can hasten that, I am willing to do anything, and with the French ships sailing for Leith ...."

Richard's eyes snapped up, fastening on Morley. "French ships?"

"I thought you knew?" Morley's voice had risen a degree.

"It seems it was something else that your master failed to tell me," Richard began to rise. "How many?"

"Err.... well," Morley stammered, stepping backwards from the table.

"How many?" Richard's voice was firmer, eyes riveted on Morley.

"The Lords of the Congregation, as you may know, have suspended Marie De Guise's regency and ...."

"How many?" Richard demanded, palms flat on the table leaning towards Morley.

"The French have dispatched their fleet to aid her in...."

"The fleet!" Richard's words exploded in the small cabin. "For pity's sake! We have one working gun, no carriages for the rest and no trained men to wield them. No bloody wonder you are keen to assist."

"I had assumed Lord Burghley would have informed you that the French were sending aid to Scotland," Morley swallowed hard, "hence why he wished for your ship to be suitably equipped should we meet them at sea."

Richard pressed his hands to his face. His voice had an angry edge when he spoke. "Lord Burghley, and I am sure you agree, shouldn't even be trusted to provision his wife with spindle whorls. What arrogance made him believe he had the experience to provide armaments for the Luciana? Not only has he failed to alert me to this possibility so I could ensure a suitable watch was deployed. His idea of equipping a ship is equally effective as dropping a blind pheasant into a cock fight."

Morley had paled. "When you put it like that, it does rather seem that we are in a poor position."

"If we run into the French, the pheasant would have a better chance of survival," Richard growled. Clothed only a shirt and hose, he ran barefoot through the ship, across the deck and up the ladders to the aft deck where Jerome was.

Jerome frowned at his appearance. "Is the powder store on fire?"

"There is an issue that is more serious even than that," Richard said without humour. "Behind us, or in front, is the French fleet."

Jerome's eyes widened. "And you thought to tell me now!"

"I have just found out. It seems neither of our masters thought to share this information," Richard found himself addressing Jerome's back. The other man was already on his way to send men to the mast tops.

†

Morley made himself useful by helping with planning the materials for the gun carriages they needed and completing an itinerary of the munitions that Cecil had provided. Morley had arrived on the ship with only the clothes he wore, so he had adapted a thick woollen blanket, slitting the middle to fit over his head. He wore it belted around his waist to provide some degree of protection against the weather. When the gun doors were open, the wind howled through the deck, bringing with it unwanted sea spray.

Morley flattened a piece of parchment on a wood offcut balanced on top of one of the demi-culverins to study it. Further complications continued to reveal themselves as they assessed what was needed to turn the Luciana back into the fighting vessel she had once been.

Another spray-filled gust pressed its way into the gun deck. Morley turned his back to the wind, clutching the wooden board to his chest to keep the sheet dry, the other hand on his hat, clamping it onto his head.

"And twenty-five more shot for the demi-culverins," Richard announced, rising from the wooden case he had been examining, dropping the lid back into place. "How many does that give us?"

Morley added a note to the sheet before adding up the tally. "One hundred and forty-three."

"Well, that's something, I suppose. Are there any more cases?" Richard asked Jerome.

Jerome shook his head. The expression on his face was dark.

Richard, reading his mind, said, "There's no shot for the full culverins, is there?"

A wave pressed hard against the ship's hull, and she rose over it, rolling to the larboard side. Morley, robbed of his balance, staggered a few paces across the deck. Jerome's feet stayed where they were, firmly planted on the planking, a look of resignation on his face.

"If they are not here, then we don't have any. This is the only supply of shot we have," Jerome said, exasperated, empty hands extended towards the cases packed with the shot.

Richard exhaled noisily through pursed lips. "So the culverins are useless?"

"For the moment, it would seem so," Jerome replied grimly.

Richard turned towards Morley. "Another small hole in Burghley's planning," then, addressing Jerome, "For the Lord's sake, please tell me we can make enough charges for the shot and the demi-culverins?"

"The charges are not ready-made. I know we have black powder, but we will need to make sure there is enough cord and cloth as well. Given what has happened here, I suggest we check that immediately," Jerome answered, a deep frown dividing his forehead and casting Morley a disparaging glance.

Richard also looked coldly at Morley, "I hope you are taking note, Morley, of your master's shortcomings."

"The black powder and materials to manufacture the charges are all in the powder store to keep them dry. Shall I take Morley there, and we can make a reckoning of the amounts or would you prefer to go?" Jerome asked.

"Better if you do it. I don't know how much of each is needed to make a charge," Richard said, deferring to his captain's experience.

Jerome left with Morley, Richard remaining on the gun deck with the cold line of culverins. Looking through the open gun doors to the sea beyond, he wondered where the French ships were. If they were in front, that made their arrival at Leith dangerous, but if they were behind, that could be even worse. It increased the risk of going to Newcastle, allowing time for the ships to catch them.

The news from the powder store was mixed.

Jerome was the first back on the gun deck, Morley trailing in his wake. "After we found no shot for the culverins, I thought it best to check all the powder kegs. The one I used to make the charge we fired the other day is much newer than the other four we've been given. The tops of the older barrels are all just charcoal."

Jerome held out his palms, both blackened.

Richard ran his hands through his hair. "Dare we remix it on the ship?"

Morley was looking between the pair. "Remix it?"

Richard glanced in Morley's direction. "The powder kegs are old, the contents have separated, the lighter charcoal is at the top of the kegs while the heavier saltpetre will have settled at the bottom. In one respect, it means it's safe, but we can't use it straight from the kegs to make charges. It needs to be mixed together again."

"Not on my ship," Jerome said. "Do that in the powder store, and you'll create an explosive dust that could ignite and tear the ship in half."

"Can't you do it on the deck? The wind will carry away any dust produced," Morley suggested.

"Have you seen the weather? Black powder, sir, needs to be dry. If it gets damp, it stays damp. That's why it's in the powder store," Jerome's arm was outflung toward one of the open gun doors admitting a steady stream of drizzle and sea spay.

"We have one cask that has not separated. How many charges can you make?" Richard asked, hopefully.

Jerome laughed humourlessly. "That one was already partly used and has a third remaining, so I would estimate about ten charges if we are lucky. And luck is not a commodity you seem to have an abundance of at the moment."

Richard's eyes travelled over the useless cases of shot. "One gun, ten charges and a one hundred and forty-three shot. It does seem that we have a few problems to overcome."

"We can remix the shot in Newcastle," Jerome ventured, a hand tugging thoughtfully at his beard.

"Will they let us do that?" Morley said, his tone doubtful, "There are rules on black powder on the quays in London. I would imagine that they will have similar ones in Newcastle."

Jerome leaned closely to Morley, a glint in his eyes. "Surely you know by now how resourceful Fitzwarren can be. I expect he can secure somewhere out of sight to carry out the task."

Richard ignored Jerome's comment. "It is probably better to focus on the demi-culverins. Collins has produced a working carriage he can easily copy. How should we best distribute what we have?"

"I'd say three aside in here and two forward and aft. Do you have the blocks and the rope I want on your list," Jerome said, trying to see what was on the parchment Morley was in charge of.

"Don't worry, we have a note of everything you have requested, Jerome, to plug the gaps in Lord Burghley's provisioning," Richard said dryly. "Although I am not sure we will be able to obtain all of it quickly in Newcastle, I'll not wait there while the merchants make us promises of supplies that will take weeks to arrive. We will buy what is available and leave."

Jerome nodded. "That seems sensible. It will take only another two days from there to deliver your passenger."

"My passenger and your companion. How is Master Knox? I see he has decided to remain in your cabin and out of my way," Richard asked, malice gleaming in his eyes.

"It is a sin against God and the beauty of creation. However, you will be pleased to know that I have been wishing for a loss of hearing," Jerome admitted.

Richard breathed deeply and let out a long sigh, a look of satisfaction on his face. "Knox is nothing if not persistent. He would find another sense to assault if he realised you could not hear him."

†

The *Santa Luciana* headed for Newcastle, where her owner bought the supplies he could have quickly brought aboard. Quick enquiries for another ship's carpenter failed, and none of the men Richard spoke to was awarded a paid passage on the Luciana. What able-bodied men there had been in the local area had been offered paid work to bolster Norfolk's army. What was left were the scrapings from the bottom of a very poor barrel. It had been a fair plan on Norfolk's part to add to his army once in the north. These were men he didn't need to feed and pay from the south of England, and they offered a relatively inexpensive addition to his ranks. Unfortunately for Richard, it left Newcastle short of men and materials. They sailed from Newcastle with no timber and no additional crew. However, it had been a quick turnaround, and the Luciana was heading from the Tyne and turning north the following day.

The powder remained in the store, unmixed, and the Luciana sailed north - undefendable.

┼

Richard was woken by the unmistakable sound of the chains running through iron loops.

Morley, wide-eyed, sat up abruptly on his bed, still shawled in his blanket. "What's that? Have we hit something?"

"Calm yourself. That's the noise of the anchors being lowered," Richard was on his way to find Jerome.

The decks were in darkness, and all her lamps were out.

"Up here," Jerome, with better night vision, called quietly.

Richard found the ladder to the aft deck and stepped up the rungs quickly.

"Over there," Jerome pointed.

Richard's eyes studied the darkness, but there was nothing to see. The moon, hidden behind a shroud of thick clouds, provided no night light, and there was no easy division between the sky and the sea. Richard could only guess where one ended and the other began.

"Tomlinson spotted them, one ship at least, and there may be more out to sea," Jerome said, standing close to Richard.

Richard still couldn't discern anything that might be a vessel in the dark of night.

"There, can you see them?" Jerome leaned his head closer to Richard's.

Richard continued to peer into the night. His eyes adjusting to the dark began to make out a darker immobile and irregular shape.

"Not there, you fool! That's the bloody island. That way," Jerome, a hand on Richard's shoulder, twisted him in the right direction and, raising an arm, pointed. "Look there."

"Are you sure?" Richard could still see nothing.

"Yes, I am, and so was Tomlinson," Jerome said confidently.

"He must have good eyesight," Richard remarked.

Jerome chuckled. "Aye, eyesight that has been sharpened by a keg of beer. I offered one as a prize to the first lookout to spot a ship on the horizon."

"What do you propose?" Richard asked.

"It's too dark to see what flag they are flying. You've told me the French fleet was either in front or behind us, so I am going to run with caution and keep us this side of the island," Jerome said, adding, "The land is behind us, and Lindisfarne is between them and us, it will be hard for them to make out the Luciana in the dark. We can be sure they have missed us if they don't turn. What we can't be sure of is whether the fleet is together. There is a good chance there could be a second wave behind."

"In daylight, they will be able to clearly see us," Richard said, hands on the rail, his eyes still trying to identify the other ship.

Jerome nodded. "I know, so it's a careful game of following but at a respectful distance. From now on, we'll keep two lookouts, one forward and one aft."

"If the French fleet is ahead of us, it means landing our precious cargo near Leith is problematic. We could end up accidentally delivering him into French hands. Imagine your master's ire if that happens," Richard said dryly.

"It is in both of our interests if we ensure he makes it to Norfolk as arranged," Jerome's voice chastised.

Richard ignored Jerome's comment. "We will have to make landfall before Leith, contact the congregation and find some safe place to transfer Knox to them."

"It does appear to be the case," Jerome agreed.

"Any suggestions where?" Richard asked.

Five minutes later, they were in Richard's cabin, the shutters closed to stop the lamp light from escaping. Jerome had fetched charts and unrolled them on the small table.

"We are here," Jerome placed a finger on the small shape of Lindisfarne Island. "Just south of the castle, you mistook for a vessel. The other ship, or indeed ships, are here, to the north of the island. We keep the castle between them and us, and there is a good chance they will not see us. However, if more ships are sailing north, we will provide a fine view of ourselves as they round the coast near Bamburgh as soon as it becomes light."

"Could we not move further inland? There's a bay here on the island's west side," Morley said, leaning over the map.

Jerome shook his head. "The tidal causeway is here, and the waters to the south of this are far too shallow for the Luciana. It's also mud ridden, and there's a danger we would find ourselves stuck fast."

"Alright, so we wait here. I hope no ships are following, then where?" Richard asked, raising his eyes from the chart to meet Jerome's

"North to Berwick," Jerome tapped the map, "We could be there tomorrow, and you can go overland from there to Leith."

"Berwick would be ideal. I can make my way south from there very easily," Morley interrupted.

Richard, still looking at the map, ignored Morley. "Two days ride at most, I would estimate," he nodded.

"First, we need to wait for the ship on the eastward side of the island to head north, then we will follow. Keeping enough distance between us so that she can't see us," Jerome said.

Richard didn't return to his own cabin. Instead, he went to Jerome's, intent on discovering their passenger's thoughts about disembarking from the ship at Berwick.

Knox, a pen in his hand, head bent over the table, looked up at Richard's entrance.

"Ye back are ye. I see yer captain is tryin' to hide," Knox said.

Richard closed the door behind him and crossed the small room to sit on the edge of the narrow bed. "Morley has told us the French fleet has been issued orders to sail to Leith, so Jerome is being cautious."

"Ha! Cautious is it now? We've been at anchor between the coast and the island for most o' the night, and I canna see any reason he'd do tha' unless it was to hide the ship," Knox scoffed.

Richard inclined his head. "Of course, I did forget. You have had quite an education aboard ship. How long did you serve at the oars? Was it two years?"

"Ye've na' right ta ask. Ma life is between me an' the Lord," Knox pronounced, discarding the pen dramatically on the desk.

"Very well, I won't," Richard said, his voice light, his eyes clear.

"He sent me there, and he delivered me. Twas a test he set to show me the heart of the unbeliever, to allow me a view of their souls," Knox thumped his own chest twice.

"What a shame. I thought you weren't going to bore me with details of your life," Richard said, resting his back against the wooden planking behind Jerome's bed.

"I can see their thoughts. I know haw they think," Jerome tapped his temple with an extended forefinger and leered at Richard. "An' I know how we can defeat them. Tha's why you need ta get me ta Leith."

"Delightful. However, as I did say, I'm not interested," Richard said, crossing his legs at the ankles.

"Yer an impudent cur," Knox growled.

"Perhaps. I want to know if you have had contact with the Lords of the Congregation; if we don't take you to Leith, how might we find these rebels of yours?" Richard asked.

"Ye've been tasked wi' takin' me to Leith, and that is where ye'll go. Do you hear me?" Knox boomed, rising from his chair, his cap close to the low ceiling.

"Well, as much as I would like nothing better than to be rid of you, Leith may not be a destination of choice. So I am asking if there is anywhere else that we could land?" Richard enquired, his voice level and calm.

"I'll not ha' yew takin' it upon yerself to vary the path that the Lord has laid before me. Ye'll tak ma to Leith and nowhere else, do ye hear?" Knox boomed, an angry finger stabbing the air between them.

Richard rose. "I'd like to say that this conversation has been interesting, entertaining, or possibly even useful. However, it's been none of those, so I shall, my disappointment complete, withdraw."

Exiting the cabin, Richard closed the door smartly, resting briefly with his back against it, his eyes shut. There wouldn't be any help from Knox. That was clear. He was a zealot with a mission, and he'd not vary from his imagined true cause by so much as a hair's breadth.

Chapter Twenty-Seven

Sieges were the curse of the soldier. Their lives became expendable as commanders sought to break them. A battle had a start, a middle and an end. But that was not the case here; the camps had already existed for months.

When Jack arrived, he passed a cemetery for the conflict's dead. Wooden markers for headstones on some graves with freshly turned soil marking the burial sites. The older internments were further apart, the new ones closer together. As they rode by, he watched bodies stripped to their shirts, being lowered in, one on top of another. His cassock mired with mud, a preacher watched as the dead were stored away. Space surrounding Leith was becoming cramped for not only the living.

"I am beginning to regret that you didn't arrive before Norfolk," Jack said quietly, leaning towards Emilio, who rode beside him.

"I am sorry too," Emilio's voice was grave.

Orders awaited his arrival; he had been instructed to present himself to the Duke. Jack waited for two hours, forced to stand outside, before being admitted to Norfolk's presence, watching while plenty of other men were allowed into where the Duke had made his headquarters.

He waited alone as he had been instructed.

Jack observed Norfolk's carnage on the hillsides around the coastal town. One side of Leith was bounded by the sea, and the other three were now surrounded by the attacker's earthworks. Jack estimated a deep trench ran for a mile around the town, and the excavated earth had been used to make raised mud ramparts. The mound was an easy thirteen to fifteen feet high and topped with a wooden fence that added another ten feet. The ring was fortified with four wooden forts equally spaced out. Norfolk had made his headquarters in the eastern fort. It was also, Jack noted, the fort that was furthest from the city and probably out of range of the guns on Leith's ramparts.

Unannounced, cannon blasts, followed by the rise of smoke to the west of where he was, told him of gun emplacements on the ramparts. The explosions were irregular in timing and weren't part of a sustained attack.

What had been farmland behind the siege wall was now given over to husbanding the machinery of battle: pens for the workhorses; tent villages; some wooden structures, where timber had been available before it had been consumed in the construction of the forts; animal pens and mudded thoroughfares churned with the passing of boots, wheels and hooves.

Finally, he was admitted to the temporary fort and Norfolk's company. The Duke had transported enough of his household furniture north to make his rooms look like the Palace at Whitehall. Red, blue and gold tapestries flanked each wall, the floor was thickly rugged, and the middle of the room was dominated by a huge oak table that would easily seat twenty. It was now given over not to plates and glasses but to maps and papers. Chairs that would have been drawn up to it were arranged out of the way along one wall, allowing easy access to the instructions of war laid on the polished top.

"Fitzwarren, got here at last, did you?" Norfolk said from where he stood at the table, palms resting on either side of a large map depicting Leith and the surrounding defences that had been constructed. Next to him was a man Jack didn't recognise. In pointing towards Jack, Norfolk said, "Grey, this is the man I was telling you about."

The name was all Jacked needed to hear. Lord Grey of Wilton, the notable military commander, had fought in France against the De Guise family. He was back in Scotland, the foe a familiar one.

Grey viewed him critically from across the table. "By the accounts, I heard you have arrived on a battlefield with your lawyer and his clerk. Is this so they can negotiate your freedom when you are taken prisoner? Or are you readying to place a suit against your superiors if you find their commands erroneous?"

"Neither. They were with me when the Duke commanded me to move north and join his force," Jack replied, wondering exactly how that information had arrived before he did.

"And there was no option to leave them? We've enough problems here without adding unwanted mouths to feed," Grey said. "I've heard of men packing many things to take the battlefield, but never before his lawyers."

"I am sure they will not be a burden," Jack assured.

"It'll be your job to ensure they aren't," Norfolk sneered. "The men you brought, we've positioned them here."

Norfolk's finger stabbed the map, and Jack moved forward to better see where exactly "here" was.

"Under Captain Clarke, we've some pioneers. They are currently twenty feet down and only days away from laying mines under the bulwark," Norfolk drew a line across the map to the jutting ramparts on the west side of Leith. "There has been pilferage of materials. Your men are to provide a guard. The entrance is now enclosed in a palisade."

"I am sure we can do that," Jack said, surprised by being allocated such a simple task.

"They are already there. Captain Clark has taken charge. Lord Grey has another more crucial task for you," Norfolk's eyes were lit with a malicious glint.

Here it comes.

Grey settled glasses on his nose and leaned over the map. "We have a gun emplacement here and another here," his thin fingers stabbed the map, "both are in range, and we are securing good hits against the bulwark here."

Jack examined the triangular-shaped defence on the west side of Leith, the most imposing compared to the east walls. It was also the most well-defended side of the city.

"We are to start firing in earnest tomorrow morning at 4am. Cuthbert Vaughan needs to measure the depth of the ditch at the foot of the ramparts. Then he can judge the length needed for the scaling ladders," Grey finished, straightening and fixing Jack with a solid gaze.

"Your lawyers, learned men, I assume?" Norfolk asked.

Jack, wary, said carefully, "I believe so."

"Good, we had enough trouble with your literacy last time we met. Your legal servants can join you in the morning and provide a notation of the measurements," Norfolk said, smiling.

Jack stared at him.

"Now, leave. Vaughan is waiting for you outside, along with your bloody lawyers," Norfolk laughed, waving an arm towards the doorway.

Jack felt numb as he left the wooden fortification. A cannon sounded east of the fort, another thick grey plume of smoke rising in a cloudy steel sky. Outside, waiting for him, were indeed his lawyers. Threadmill was pale and fidgeting with his hat, and Emilio was hitched up on a wall
behind him. ☐

When he saw Jack moving quickly towards him, Emilio dropped back to his feet. Taking his arm, he steered him away from Threadmill. "My men, along with yours, have been taken elsewhere."

"I know. Did you tell anyone you were my lawyer?"

Emilio shook his head. "No. I assumed you had sent for us when they brought us here."

Jack shook his head, glancing towards Threadmill. "It is as you said, Norfolk is keen to be rid of me, and he is sending me with...."

There was no time for more words. A man introduced himself as Vaughan arrived. "Fitzwarren?" Jack inclined his head and noted that his title had not been conveyed to the Captain. "I'm told Lord Wilton is sending you to provide intelligence on the defences."

"It appears so," Jack said dryly.

Vaughan was looking beyond Jack at Emilio and Threadmill.

"Are these your men?"

Jack nodded.

Vaughan shook his head, a look of bewilderment on his face. "You'd better follow me."

They traversed the entire length of the rampart from the fort towards the bulwark at the western end of Leith that Wilton had prodded on the map. Dropping down into the field behind the ramparts, Vaughan led them to a line of tents, where he handed them over to a shabby-looking man named Cydric.

"Find Fitzwarren and his men space in the camp. I'm sure there'll be a few empty beds," Vaughan said before retreating.

Cydric led the way along the line of tents. The first he stopped at, he indicated Jack to take.

Lifting the tent flap back, Jack surveyed the interior. One small low bed, a hessian cloth pack, a worn pair of boots, the laces tied together and, hanging from the roof, tied with chord, a large bunch of dried purple heather.

"Belonged to Lieutenant Firth," Cydric announced. "He'll not be needing it anymore. Poor bastard. His coat is nailed up on the east side of the bulwark."

Threadmill paled.

"Come on, you two, I've space for you at the end," Cydric said, leading Emilio and Threadmill further along the canvas line.

Jack, ignoring him, entered and pulled the canvas flap closed. It wasn't particularly quiet; the encampment's noise invaded the tent's interior, but at least it was still. Jack threw the worn boots to the other side of the tent along with the pack replacing it with his own.

Pulling his boots off, he stretched out on the bed.

†

Captain Vaughan had wanted them to go just after midnight.

Jack refused. Gauging that the best time to cross the waste between Norfolk's defences and the Leith walls was closer to 4am and Emilio agreed.

Jack held out a small flask towards Threadmill. "Have some of this. It'll help."

Threadmill hesitated momentarily, so Jack thrust the flask closer to him. "Take it."

Threadmill accepted it; unstoppering it, he tipped it to his mouth.

"Whoa," Jack rose and snatched the flask back from Threadmill. "Steady, lad. There are three of us here, and I wasn't planning to carry you to Leith and back."

"Sorry," Threadmill said quietly.

Jack offered the flask to Emilio, who shook his head. Shrugging, Jack put the flask to his lips and tipped it upwards. Then, regarding Threadmill's place face, he offered the flask again. "One more, then that's it."

Threadmill took it this time without hesitation.

"I could tell you that you are here by your own doing, but I've had enough in my life of being told the outcome was my own fault, so I'll not," Jack said, accepting the flask back from Threadmill. "I'm not calling you Master Threadmill all night, either. I've heard your given name once before. Remind me what it was."

"Angharad- Dafydd," Threadmill said, then seeing the look on Jack's face, added, "My mother was Welsh."

"Thank God for that. At least they had a reason for saddling you with it, and it wasn't just from spite!" Jack laughed.

"Say it again," Emilio leaned forward, frowning.

"Angharad-Daffydd," Threadmill provided.

"Argurran…"

Jack laughed again. "No, you Italian idiot. Angharad,"

"That is what I said: Angurran," Emilio retorted.

"No – listen to yourself, it ends in 'arad' and not aran," Jack said, still smirking.

"That is exactly what I said. Angurran," Emilio said, an edge of irritation in his voice.

"It's close enough," Threadmill said, adding, "You speak excellent English, sir."

"He owes that to me," Jack replied, "he didn't have a word of it when we met. It was all hand signals and shouting. But with some patient tutoring, he's come along quite well."

"Hah, you had peasant's Italian and serf's French. It was a wonder I could understand a word you uttered," Emilio said. Then, to Threadmill, "It was a poor mix of French, Italian and Latin, not a happy concoction."

"I can imagine," Threadmill said. Jack offered the flask again, and he accepted it. "Thank you, My Lord."

"Jack will do tonight," Jack said, taking back the flask and gesturing towards the Knight, "And you can call him Emilio."

Reminded of the task ahead of them, the smile on Threadmill's face fell away, forgotten.

"Don't worry. I've no intention of dying tonight, so we'll have a few simple rules, alright?" Jack said, his voice calm.

Threadmill nodded.

"Keep yourself close behind us, don't let us out of sight, don't drop behind, and don't call out our names. It's half a mile, no more. Keep your head down and your feet moving," Jack advised.

Threadmill nodded.

Jack pulled on a woollen cap, tucking his tell-tale yellow hair out of sight.

"I heard Captain Vaughan say they were stripping the bodies they found in the ditches of their coats. That's what's fluttering from the walls along the bulwark," Threadmill's voice held the high pitch of nerves.

Jack leaned towards him. "I paid far too much for this doublet; I am not planning to be parted from it soon."

Threadmill produced a weak smile.

"Come here," Jack said. Threadmill rose and stepped towards him. "One last thing."

Jack bent down; his hand was wet with mud when he rose. "Let's not give them something to aim at."

Before Threadmill could pull away, Jack had smeared mud across his cheeks and forehead, doing the same to himself afterwards.

"Don't bloody wipe it off!" Jack slapped Threadmill's hand away from his face as he made the automatic move to rub the dirt off.

Jack looked over to see if Emilio had finished. For the past few minutes, he had been on his knees, head bowed, in prayer. When he rose, he picked up a bundle that had rested on the wall next to a bow and shook it out.

Jack looked skyward as Emilio dropped the tabard of a Knight of St John over his head.

"You can't wear that?" Jack hissed under his breath.

"Why not? If, as Angurran says, they will strip us, then I do not intend to be found dead wearing anything less," Emilio said hotly.

"You can't," Jack spluttered for a second time.

"Sir, he's right. If you are caught wearing the garb of a Knight of the Order, it could be considered treason against the Order," Threadmill said, his voice adopting a lawyer's tone.

"That's not the reason," Jack said to Threadmill before advancing on Emilio. "It's far simpler than that. You cannot cross that field wearing that tunic with a bloody target on the front."

Emilio straightened, glaring at Jack. "I am, and I will."

Before Emilio could move, Jack had snared him in a quick hold. To Threadmill, it looked like they were about to fight, but Jack quickly released the Italian, stepping back out of his reach.

"Now you can wear it," Jack pronounced.

Threadmill looked and understood. Jack had wiped his muddied hands over the white cross on Emilio's front, not obliterating it but breaking up the symbol.

Emilio glared at Jack. "If it...."

Captain Vaughan appeared before Emilio could complete his complaint. "Are you lot going tonight or not?"

†

A starless cloudy night suited their purpose, blanketing them between the dark shadowed earth and the blackness of night. The distance was half a mile to the bulwark. They had been instructed to review the right-hand side of the defences.

The first half of the journey was relatively easy, moving over flat farmland outside the city walls. The occasional stone wall allowed them to stop and assess if they could see any movement along the Leith defences. Once they were halfway across, the inaccuracy of Grey's gunners began to impede their progress. The fields were pockmarked with shallow craters, the rains had filled them, and the clay layer beneath the fertile soil had retained the water.

Threadmill felt an iron grip on his left arm as Emilio clamped a hand on him, stopping his progress. Looking forward, he realised his next step would have taken him onto the slippery edge of one such depression in the field. The grip didn't lessen until he was led around the edge and felt, rather than saw, Jack's presence on his right again.

"Be careful," an accented voice whispered near his ear a moment before the hand let go of his arm.

They came up behind another stone wall, all three taking cover behind it. Leith's defensive wall rose in front of them. They now risked the greatest chance of being spotted by the defenders above.

"Stop here," Jack whispered in Threadmill's ear. The bow on his back was now in his hand, keeping it out of sight below the wall. "No matter what."

Threadmill eagerly nodded, hunched down immobile behind the wall. A moment later, his companions were gone. His back to the wall, his head a good foot below the top of the dry-stone pile, he waited.

Threadmill's fear had lessened, and he was becoming aware of the cold from the ground working its way into his feet and through his clothes. There was no sound, and on the distant horizon, the first faint line spoke of dawn, preparing to announce a new day. If he was here for much longer, the blackness of night would be gone, and his return across the half a mile to the siege line would be in plain sight of the defenders.

The fine grey line had doubled in thickness.

Should he go?

Where were they?

With his back to the wall, he had the perfect view of the sudden appearance of a small orange ball of flame. In the dark, it was hard to judge the distance. He had only just turned towards it when two more appeared and instantly arced high in the sky.

Fire arrows.

He couldn't see where they landed, but he counted eleven silent flaming white lines arching into the blackness. The silence of the night was gone moments later. Shouts, calls to arms, and the noise of a hackbutt erupted from the defences on the other side of the dry stone wall. The noise from the walls grew even louder. There were more shouts, screams and the unmistakable sound of an argument.

Threadmill crouched even further down.

He didn't even hear them return.

Darkness had still not lifted when he was hauled and pulled back across the waste towards the defences by Jack. As they arrived, climbing up a ladder to the ridge behind the palisade, he turned and saw the land now painted in lightening grey tones. He could see the wall where he had crouched, the pockmarks in the fields made by Lord Grey's gunners, beyond the dark rising walls of Leith and, above them, the contrasting orange of a building on fire.

Jack and Emilio were creased in laughter, and Threadmill regarded them with worried eyes. Emilio had removed his tabard and held it balled under his arm.

"I hit his helmet?" Jack had tears streaming down his face, making white tracks on his muddy face. "I couldn't bloody resist it. Idiot stuck his head up after the first few went over." Then to Threadmill. "It hit his helmet and went vertical, straight up in the air."

"And like a line of ducks, every one of the men on the wall stood up to watch it," Emilio said, laughing. "I hit two."

"And look, we've warmed the city for them," Jack pointed across towards Leith, where a fire sent a plume of smoke into the morning air.

"But did you not make a target of yourselves?" Threadmill said, confused.

"Not really. A good archer can fire eight arrows in a minute. The lit ones are a little slower to lose off...." Jack said.

"And Jack managed five to my six," Emilio cuffed Jack on the arm.

"One wouldn't light ... I had to discard it," Jack replied hotly.

"Still five to my six," Emilio said happily, "Even with my broken ribs."

"They can't be that bad if you can pull a bow," Jack retorted. Then, turning to Threadmill, he continued with his explanation. "So it took only a minute, then the fire is out, and we are gone. By the time they have roused themselves, it's too late. It was never meant to be anything more than a diversion. However, it does appear that we have set something on fire," Jack said, observing the growing glow inside the Leith walls.

"Then you went round the other side of the Bulwark to review the walls?" Threadmill asked, his voice incredulous.

Jack nodded. The flask was back in his hand and, tipping it back, he emptied it.

Captain Vaughan arrived, a sour look on his face. "Lord Grey's bloody furious. I'm to take you to him now."

†

"Dragged from my bed by your actions, you, sir, thought fit to launch an offensive against Leith without authorisation," Grey wasn't dressed. He wore a fur robe over a nightshirt and was seated at the table.

"A small diversion before we reviewed the walls, that was all," Jack explained.

"A small diversion!" Lord Grey's voice had risen a pitch. "The roof of a church is ablaze, or had you not noticed that? It is such a significant fire that the defenders have yet to extinguish it."

Confusion clouded Jack's face. "I can't see how this is a bad outcome."

"Can you not?" Grey rose. "We are attempting to convince those inside the city that there will be an assault from the east. From there, they can observe lines of troops and artillery readying for an attack. A ruse. We wish them to focus their defenders in that direction whilst we attack from the west. And now, damn you, you have launched an attack from the west that will have them doubling the watch in that direction tonight."

"It was only eleven arrows, hardly an assault," Jack said.

"The bloody damage is done. Provide Captain Vaughan with what information you have gleaned, if any," Grey growled, pointing towards the door. "The failure of this offensive, sir, if it does fail, will be laid at your door. Get out."

Jack stepped from the room, resisting a strong urge to slam the door behind him.

He was tired.

The brief interview with Grey had stretched taught nerves a degree too far, and all he wanted to do was sleep. Lifting the tent flap, he found he was not alone.

"What are you doing here?"

Alphonso shrugged. "I was looking for Emilio. Is he with you?"

"No," Jack shook his head.

"You do not like me, do you?" the soft Italian voice asked.

"I do not know you," Jack replied, his voice weary.

"And have no wish to either, I think?" Alphonso continued.

Jack shrugged. He was too tired for this.

"I could be a friend of yours also if you wished," the Italian said, his voice purring, eyes fixed on Jack's.

"Friendship should not be a gift given lightly, I was once told," Jack replied.

Alphonso smiled. "And I do not give it lightly."

Jack observed the man critically before him. A few years younger than Jack and slightly built. The wrists that protruded from the delicate lace cuffs were thinly boned and narrow, leading to slender fingers, each singled out by the line of rings that rested beneath the knuckles. His doublet, slashed to show the shirt below, was thickly padded, giving the wearer a stockier form. Below the clothes, Jack could see a slightly built man, the sword belt tight across his body, accenting his slender hips.

Alphonso, misinterpreting the gaze, smiled. Raising a slender finger, he laid it on his lips for a moment, a thoughtful expression settling on his face. "I can see why Emilio holds your friendship in such high regard."

"Can you?" The response was automatic and harsh. Jack regretted it immediately, it had been an ill-considered reply, and he tempered it quickly, adding. "His friendship is important to me."

"I hope you do not feel I have stepped between you. It was not my intention," Alphonso's pale blue eyes glinted with a cold light.

Jack shook his head, forcing a smile to his lips. "Not at all, I am sure Emilio would be heartened if I extended my friendship to you."

Alphonso's smile increased. "He would. I am sure."

Jack extended a hand towards Alphonso. "Come here."

Alphonso's eyes widened, a look of delight brightening them, a cold slender hand slipping into Jack's light grasp. Jack increased the pressure on the grip, slowly drawing Alphonso towards him, the Italian's free hand reaching his neck as the gap closed. Jack felt a feather-like touch as the long fingers slipped behind his neck, nestling in his blonde hair and began to draw Jack's head towards his.

Jack, breathing steadily, forced himself to endure the embrace. Softening his body as the Italian's began to press against him, Alphonso's breath caught on his face. The large pale blue eyes were wide open, the lips close to his, parting slightly, the invitation clear.

Jack waited a moment longer, feeling the man relax against him, surrendering himself to Jack's embrace.

The sudden movement caught the Italian off guard. Alphonso yelped with sudden surprise as he found his body lifted from the floor and thrust against the solid oak pole in the middle of the tent.

"You are nothing more than a fetid alley cat," Jack growled in Italian.

The look of shocked surprise dropped from the lighter man's face, replaced by an evil sneer. His hands, still behind Jack's neck, dug their nails hard into his skin. "I can have claws if that's what you want."

Jack felt the body he had trapped between his and the pole attempting to mould itself to his again.

"Let me make this very clear," Jack tightened his hold on the younger man. "I will rid Emilio of you, one way or the other."

Alphonso smiled widely, saying solicitously, "You are making a grave mistake, my Lord."

"The mistake was made by you. I can see you for what you are," Jack growled.

Alphonso dug his nails in harder. "And I see you. I can read your desires at the back of your eyes."

"You might think so, but I very much doubt it," Jack said with finality. Releasing Alphonso, he sent him spinning through the tent doorway; tripping up, he landed on his back outside the tent. There was a satisfying squelch and a shriek from Alphonso as he fetched up in the mire beyond the doorway.

"The cat is back in the gutter," Jack announced, laughing, and dropped the tent flap back into place.

Chapter Twenty-Eight

When Richard awoke, dawn was making its way into the cabin; Morley had opened the shutters, and the lamp was out. The weak grey light illuminated Burghley's man, who had finally fallen asleep, head pillowed on his arms, still seated at the table.

Richard lay still, listening.

After a minute, he was sure the Luciana was still at anchor and not heading north as they had planned. Richard pulled on his doublet and rammed his feet quickly into his boots.

"What's wrong?" Morley's voice croaked, his throat dry with sleep.

"I don't know. The Luciana is still on her ropes." Richard, rising, pulled open the cabin door. Morley, quickly on his feet, grabbed his hat and followed.

Jerome was on the aft deck, elbows resting on the guard rail, staring at the sea beyond the island.

"Why are we not sailing north?" Richard said as soon as he clambered up onto the deck.

"Ah, there you are, lad. I was just about to send for you," Jerome didn't turn but extended an arm seawards. "That's why we're still anchored here."

Richard looked. The other ship was on the other side of the island, beyond the castle, closer than the vessel they had seen during the night. "Is it headed north?"

Jerome shook his head. "It's heading nowhere."

"Nowhere?" questioned Richard.

"It's the same ship we saw last night. Seems she's got a good watch crew on her as well. They saw us, turned back, and they've been close to the other side of the island for the last hour," Jerome said thoughtfully, a finger and thumb tugging at his beard.

"French?" Richard inquired.

"I don't think so," Jerome said slowly, shaking his head, "there are no pennants attached to her masts, and she's not flying any colours. Interesting, don't you think?"

"They could still be French, trying to avoid detection?" Richard's gaze was on the distant ship.

"True. But I would place a hefty wager that her hull is English built. She's certainly not of French design," Jerome pointed towards the ship.

"Are you sure?" Richard, hands on the guard rail, asked.

Jerome cast him a stern glance. "You need to ask? Look at the way she's sitting in the water. The betwixt decks are too low, and the aftcastle is not high enough to be of French design."

"So you think she's English, with no colours, no flags to proclaim her nationality, and probably wondering exactly the same about us," Richard said, turning towards Jerome and folding his hands across his chest.

"Highly likely," Jerome replied, scanning her decks again.

"It might be Wynter," Morley offered from behind Richard.

Richard and Jerome turned towards Morley, who was tying a cord beneath his chin to prevent the wind from taking possession of his hat. The brim, deformed by the chord, stretched on both sides of his head, covering his ears.

"Wynter?" Richard repeated the name.

Morley nodded.

"William Wynter?" Richard asked.

"The same," Morley nodded, finishing tying the knot beneath his chin. "Lord Burghley has been in touch with him for some time. He sailed north, bringing supplies and men to Norfolk's army at Leith. He sails without a commission, just as you do."

"That would explain the lack of flags," Jerome said, "Come over here and take a look."

Morley held up both of his hands in protest. "I'd rather not get that close to the edge if you don't mind."

Jerome was looking towards the ship again. "Well, your chance to find out might be about to present itself. They've lowered a boat, and it's heading towards the island."

"Do you know him?" Morley asked Richard, his voice hopeful.

"We've met," Richard confirmed, sounding distracted, looking toward the land.

"Let me guess, he's not among your devotees?" Jerome laughed.

Richard ignored his comment. "Have a boat readied. I'll take Morley with me."

"Sir, I'd rather not," Morley's voice was squeaky.

Richard placed a firm hand on Morley's shoulder. "Don't worry. I'll make sure you don't take a ducking in the sea. If that's Wynter, and he's sailing under Burghley's orders, then you, my good man, could be useful in assuring him that we are on his side."

"But, sir, I am sure ...." Morley tried again, but it was too late. Richard had already left the deck.

"It doesn't look like Richard is inclined to grant your request," Jerome chuckled, "What did you do to him in London, I wonder? You've certainly spoiled his humour."

"I can only assume he regrets the commission imposed upon him to go to Scotland. As far as I know, he was to sail for the Indies, set on leaving his brother, his country, his Queen and even his new wife behind," Morley said, pulling his blanket tighter around him.

"Wife?" Jerome turned on Morley.

Uncertainty crossed Morley's face. "It is not my place to discuss it, sir."

Jerome stepped closer to Morley. "Tell me more."

Morley swallowed hard, moving backwards three paces until his reverse was stopped by the aft deck rail against his back. He realised he was trapped. Morley twisted his head, looking behind him, instantly wishing he hadn't. The drop from the ship's side to the sea weakened his knees. "Sir, please."

"I'll let you be when you tell me what I wish to know," Jerome said, blocking his exit.

"It was not an ideal arrangement .... I can understand if he has not spoken about it," Morley stammered, his hands holding the rail tightly behind his back.

"Not ideal! What creature has tied herself to him? Come on, sir, tell me," Jerome said, his voice delighted as he leaned over the shorter man.

"I'd .... err ....rather not," Morley stammered, his weight on the rail increasing as the captain placed a hand on either side of his and towered over him.

"Come now, such news as this you cannot keep from me," Jerome said, Morley, trapped now between his arms.

"It's not my place, sir ...." Morley took a quick, nervous glance behind Jerome, wondering if he might manage to duck beneath one of Jerome's arms and effect an escape.

Jerome grinned, reading Morley's mind. "Don't even think about it. I'll not be denied this entertainment. What unfortunate woman has bound themselves to him?"

Jerome caught the look on Morley's face, and his eyes lit up, "Is she old?"

Morley leaned a little further back.

"Fat and round and poor then?" Jerome continued, chucking.

Morley shook his head frantically.

"Hmm. Ugly and rich then?" Jerome mused. He loosed a hand from the guard rail and fastened it into the woollen blanket acting as Morley's cloak. "Alright, if she's not upstanding, rich and titled, then did he find himself a gutter whore?"

Morley paled, his eyes widening.

"By God! He did, didn't he?" Jerome laughed. "How did he manage to bed and wed himself to a whore? That's careless even by his standards."

Morley stood motionless in front of Jerome, one hand on the rail and still pinioned by Jerome's hand, but his eyes were no longer on the captain. They were looking now beyond him to someplace over his shoulder.

Jerome read his face correctly and, whirling around, found Richard standing on the deck. There was no pause, no words from Richard, no time for Jerome to step backwards. The blow connected with the right-hand side of his face, rattling his teeth and sending him across the deck.

"Not one more word, Jerome," Richard growled, standing over him.

Jerome, a hand to his jaw, looked up and eyed Richard.

There was apparent indecision on Richard's face. Fury burned in his eyes. He stepped toward Jerome, stopping only when the call from below came to tell him the boat had been lowered.

"Master Morley, if you please," Richard spoke through gritted teeth.

Jerome sat on the deck, rubbing his aching jaw, and watched him leave, Morley scuttling quickly behind.

†

Morley was more nervous on a small boat than on a large ship. The boat that took them to the island was not too bad. The water was shallow and calm, and the passage was not unlike that of one of the ferries on the Thames. The journey after that was quite a different matter.

It wasn't De Wynter who met them on the island but one of his officers.

"Fitzwarren?" The name was placed as a question.

"Indeed," Richard affirmed.

"This way, if you will, sir," the man had replied. In the end, only he and Morley left the island, the other men waiting with the Luciana's small boat.

They boarded a second boat that took them into the open sea and towards where De Winter's ship rode at anchor. As her capable crew of four rowed her towards the vessel, waves broke over her bow, spray soaking Morley's face. It dripped from the bent brim of his hat and penetrated the woollen blanket. His boots in the bottom of the boat began to let water in from the sea, sluicing from one end to the other. One hand on the wooden side and another clamped to the seat, Morley endured the passage with his eyes shut. When the boat rose or more cold spray slapped his face, an involuntary yelp escaped from Morley.

"Master Morley, you must open your eyes. We cannot get you on board with them closed," Richard said reasonably, a hand under the little man's arm, attempting to prise him from his seat.

Morley opened them and looked up in horror at the height of the ship rising above them, the small boat rebounding off her sides. Rope ladders had been lowered. Morley, seeing them, exclaimed loudly, "I can't, sir!"

"Oh, but you can," Richard pulled him up. "You are a precious cargo. I'll make sure you don't fall."

A rope under his arms, and with his feet barely touching the rope rungs, Morley was hauled onto the deck before Richard arrived at his side.

Richard cast his eyes around the ship. She was about the same size as the Luciana but with markedly more crew. Barrels and crates were lashed efficiently to the decks; casting his eyes upward, he found twenty men, at least, observing his arrival from the rigging. De Winter's cabin sat at the back of the ship, and he was taken there with Morley.

The Welshman was little changed from the man Richard remembered. A round head fitted with demanding eyes sat on top of a solid square frame, hair efficiently cut, beard neatly trimmed, and with solid broad hands, each finger crested with a heavy ring. If De Wynter remembered Richard, he paid him no attention. Instead, he was regarding the bedraggled figure of Morley next to him with nothing short of contempt.

"Master Morley. Welcome aboard," De Wynter's sing-song voice held a distinct note of disgust.

Morley, next to Richard, didn't reply but affected something that looked like a bow. The ship moved at that moment, robbing him of his footing; he staggered two paces to the left, making the gesture clumsy. Richard, catching his arm, stopped his progress.

Wynter shook his head, taking in the sea-soaked boots, the belted blanket and the ruined headwear. "What a bloody sorry state you are in."

Morley's voice squeaked when he spoke, saying weakly. "It was not a voyage I had planned."

De Wynter laughed, banging down a solid fist on the table. "You've been disposed of by your master? There is some justice in that."

Morley swallowed hard but remained silent.

"I'd had news you were headed north with a cargo for Scotland," De Wynter addressed Richard, his hard eyes still on the little man.

"You are in communication with Burghley?" Richard asked, frowning.

De Wynter nodded then, pointing a meaty finger at Morley, he demanded, "What's he doing here?"

"Burghley sent him, I assume, to ensure the safe delivery of my cargo," Richard's eyes rested on Morley for a moment.

De Wynter laughed. "What, exactly, was he going to do?"

"I agree, he was an unlikely choice, I brought him here as Burghley's man to attest to our mission, but it seems you are already aware of it," Richard said thoughtfully.

"I am." De Wynter rose from behind his desk, walked by them and, opening the cabin door, spoke to the man waiting there, "I have a guest. He'll be waiting outside, on the deck, until we have finished here. Make sure it's somewhere bleak, will you, Atkinson."

Richard watched as Morley was escorted from the cabin. De Wynter retrieved a bottle and two heavy flat-bottomed glasses from a high-sided silver-gilt tray. Dropping both down before Richard, he served a good measure of golden liquid into each before setting the bottle down. Collecting one of the glasses, De Wynter retook his seat, gesturing for Richard to take one.

"Morley stood by and watched as I was dragged from my house in '52. Gave me no chance to walk out as a man, had me bound and hauled out while my wife and children watched," De Wynter said bitterly, his large hands wrapped around the glass dwarfing it. "I owe my release to John Somer. He did mention your name at the time."

"I did what I could. Wyatt's uprising should have succeeded. The odds were in his favour, he had good support. If it hadn't been for one man's stupidity, England might have been a different place," Richard conceded, lifting the glass and sipping at the contents. "Those who rose against Mary were faithful to her sister's cause. Somer recognised that some of those men had an important role in England's future."

"And you helped him to recognise that fact?" De Wynter's hand deserted the glass, one of his thick fingers pointing towards Richard.

Richard inclined his head. "Some, like Carew, deserved what befell them, but others, like yourself, had motivations other than increasing their personal riches. Somer knew that."

"Carew! How that man became involved is beyond me." De Wynter leaned towards Richard, "I have always suspected that he was responsible for Wyatt's failure. Is that true?"

Richard let out a long breath. "I am afraid it is. Carew was not a careful man; he took no security over the messages, which were intercepted and passed to Derby. Because of that, the risings outside of London failed, and the messages were never received."

"Derby! No wonder Wyatt failed," De Wynter sat back heavily in his seat. Emptying the glass in a single gulp, he abandoned it on the table. Richard, reaching forwards, drew it towards him, refilling it from the bottle.

"His messages to coordinate with the uprisings outside of the city were intercepted, so he was isolated, lacking the support he needed," Richard confirmed, pushing Wynter's glass back to the captain. "I cannot be sure, but I believe Carew had been accidentally feeding Derby with information for some time."

"I was questioned by Morley and interred in the Beauchamp Tower for four months. I've a mind to ensure that man never makes it back to dry land," De Wynter accepted the refilled glass that held now twice its original measure.

"He is a man, who, I have no doubt, has made a lot of enemies," Richard agreed, cradling his glass in his hands.

"I would imagine you are among them," De Wynter pinned Richard with a clinical stare. "So, sir, whose side are you on this time?"

Richard smiled. "My own. This was not a task of my choosing. Burghley can influence the fortunes of my family. I had little choice. I am to deliver my.... cargo to the Congregation. We were heading for Leith. However, that might not be the best course for us to take, and my captain considers Berwick a preferable option."

"You'll be damned and go straight to hell if you try and sail to Leith. It's not a good course. The Forth has the French fleet sealed within it, unable to get beyond my ships that are patrolling the waters west of Berwick. Leith is not your destination, sir," De Wynter took a lengthy draught from the glass.

"The fleet is north of us? That I didn't know and it is a reassurance. Morley had led me to believe they could be behind us," Richard set his glass down carefully on the table.

"Did he indeed?" De Wynter said shortly, his mouth set into a thin line, the solid fingers on his left-hand drumming on his desk. "Have you any reason to trust him?"

"None other than the fact Burghley duped him into sailing with us. It was not his choice," Richard replied, suddenly sensing there was much more to Morley's presence than he might have guessed.

"Burghley has known for a month, at the least, that the French fleet is riding at anchor near Leith, and I would assume Morley also knows this. So why would he tell you that they might be behind you? That's the question you need to ask yourself?" De Wynter planted his elbows on the table, balancing his round head on top of folded hands, fixing Richard with an enquiring stare.

Richard shook his head, a thoughtful expression on his face. "Allegedly, to speed our way north. He wishes ardently to be back on land and wants me to put him ashore with Knox."

De Wynter laughed loudly, the sound rolling around the small cabin like a cannonade, his palms slapping the table. "I have no doubt he does."

Richard's grey eyes remained humourless. "Why?"

De Wynter, still laughing, pulled open a desk drawer, lifting out a sheaf of papers. Flipping through them, he found the one he wanted; returning the others, he flattened the sheet and leaned over it. "Here we are....

'... the Giliant, Spanish built, and showing no colours is to sail to Leith. It is imperative she be allowed passage north, but on her return south, all efforts should be made to prevent her from completing the journey....'"

Richard was silent.

"Now, you know why that snivelling shit wants to be put off at Leith," De Wynter picked up the sheet and cast it towards Richard. "See for yourself, the message is two weeks old, and we've been looking for you. It is not an outright declaration that I am ordered to sink your vessel, Burghley would want to avoid stating that directly in case his message went astray. But I doubt there is a second Spanish-built ship within three hundred miles of our current position. The seas around the Lindisfarne are such that captains choose a passage close to land, and this was the easiest place to find you. I've been waiting for you, Fitzwarren."

Richard pulled the parchment towards him. Lord Burghley's orders were written in a scribe's neat hand and he quickly found the lines De Wynter had read aloud. Richard looked up. "What are you going to do?"

"Follow orders, for the moment. It is imperative, apparently, that you complete your journey north," De Wynter restated his orders, then added, "You'll not get to Leith, mind you. The French ships in the Forth will prevent you from making landfall near the city. I have connections at Berwick, bring the Luciana in behind us, and we can take you there safely."

"And Morley?" Richard replied.

"Don't let him off your ship. He'll shit his breeches on the return journey, thinking he'll end his days at the bottom of the sea. Or leave him with me. I'd be happy to accommodate him and eventually return him to London," De Wynter said, a malicious grin blighting his features.

Richard leaned back in his chair. "Will you let my ship return south?"

De Wynter nodded. "It says I've to use all efforts to prevent you returning south. Burghley is not here, so it would be hard for him to know whether I did or did not. If I have Morley, he can report to his master on how we attempted to prevent your return journey."

Richard, considering the proposal, didn't reply.

"I'd have that man suffer, and he can attest as well to my attempt to carry out Burghley's orders," De Wynter reached across the table, hefted the bottle in his right hand and slopped a good quantity into his glass.

"Very well. I'll keep him until I have delivered Knox. That way he can serve us both," Richard's grey eyes met De Wynter's.

"A fair deal. I'd heard the name Fitzwarren in dispatches. When I first read them, I thought it must be you who was with Norfolk. I had no idea you were on the Spanish ship mentioned in Burghley's dispatches," De Wynter replied.

"What news did you hear?" Richard slowly asked, his hand reaching for the bottle, stopping mid-air.

"There's a Fitzwarren with Norfolk at Leith. That's all I know. I had assumed that it would be you," De Wynter replied, emptying his glass and thumping it down.

"How did you receive the news?" Richard's eyes were fastened on De Wynter.

"The name was mentioned in passing in a dispatch from Norfolk about a week ago. I am instrumental in conveying messages from London to Scotland, they come to me then I send them on to London using the Eagle and the Blackfriar, the fastest two ships I have, they also bring back any replies, it's the quickest method to get news to the capital," De Wynter replied, his brows knitted. "You know this man, don't you?"

"Do you have the message?" Richard asked quickly.

De Wynter shook his head. "Passed it south, I'm afraid."

Richard's eyebrows raised a degree. "Are you usually in the habit of reading Norfolk's communications?"

"The recent past has taught me a lesson, and I find comfort in being appraised of the political situation. Like you, we also sail without a commission and without flying Her Majesty's colours. I wish to ensure that I have not been outlawed and sacrificed to the French," De Wynter finished bluntly.

"A wise precaution, no doubt. Was it just the name? Were there any orders attached to it?" Richard placed the questions quickly.

"Just a line, if I remember correctly, informing Burghley that Fitzwarren was now stationed at Leith. That was all," De Wynter explained.

"I suspect it may be my brother, and I doubt he has voluntarily joined Norfolk's ranks," Richard replied. A throb of pain was already starting to settle at his temples.

"Was he, by any chance, part of the 'family' whose safety you are working to secure? Because it seems to me that you are both about to be neatly disposed of, wouldn't you agree?" De Wynter leaned forward, wrapping a large hand around the neck of the bottle and emptying the remains into his glass.

"It does seem that my usefulness has come to an end," Richard said, dark coals burning in the depths of his eyes.

293

"Not just yet, though. You're still useful at the moment. You've got Knox, I assume?" De Wynter asked.

"I have both the Congregation's moral and fiscal support," Richard replied, turning the glass in one hand, "The question now is how best to play those two cards?"

†

Two more hours elapsed before De Wynter sent for Master Morley. When Atkinson returned with the little man, retrieving him from whatever bleak place he had been left, he was beyond communication.

Half frozen, soaked to the skin, he had to be manhandled into the small boat. On his return, Richard gave orders for him to be taken to the galley, the only warm part of the ship, giving orders for Morley to be dried, re-clothed and fed.

It was several hours later when Richard sought Morley out. He was wrapped in a dry blanket, his naked feet soaking in a bowl of hot water and a cup of warmed spiced wine in his hand.

"Thank you, sir, for your kindness. I thought I was to be left on De Wynter's ship to freeze to death," Morley sniffed loudly before taking another sip of the warming concoction he held nestled between his two hands.

"I've regularly been told that our past exists only to haunt us. It looks like I am not the only one to have made a few enemies," Richard replied dryly, seating himself opposite Morley in the narrow galley.

Morley swallowed hard. "I was only...."

"Executing your master's orders. Weren't we all?" Richard interrupted him. "Wynter, I am afraid, hasn't forgiven you. But it does look like you've received little more than a soaking. It could have been a lot worse."

"And, sir, Captain Jerome, I had no idea he did not know of what had happened in London. It was a mistake; I am usually a lot more careful with what I say. But the strain of being aboard the Santa Luciana has tried my nerves," Morley said, an apologetic look on his face.

You are about to recompense me for that - Richard didn't voice his thought, fixing Morley with an unwavering gaze. He said instead, "No harm has been done."

"Thank you, sir," Morley replied, his face pale.

"You are most welcome, Master Morley. Had I known that De Wynter had such a dislike for you, I would not have subjected you to that journey," Richard said, his voice heavy with sincerity.

"Your concern is heartening," Morley's smile was genuine.

"Good," Richard placed the palms of his hands down on his thighs, preparing to rise. "Your safety on the return voyage will be ensured, have no worries."

The cup in Morley's hand tipped, red wine slopping over the rim, staining the water around his feet.

"Careful!" Richard leant forward and righted the cup.

"I thought I was to go ashore with Master Knox?" Morley's voice shook.

"It would be safer if you remained with me. I've no men to spare to ensure you make a safe journey south, and we are a long way from London," Richard rose, "De Wynter's ships will shadow us on our return to ensure we do not fall foul of the French."

Morley trembled visibly. The water in the bowl around his feet was disturbed, sluicing over the bowl's rim.

"Is something wrong?" Richard asked, concerned and beginning to lower himself back to the bench.

Morley shook his head rapidly. "Nothing, sir. It has been a day my nerves have found it difficult to endure, that is all."

Richard clapped him on the shoulder. "Good. I'll ensure you are returned to Lord Burghley as soon as possible."

☦

Richard had told De Wynter he had two cards and needed to work out the best way to play them. The problem was he couldn't find a path through the maze. Morley was still in the galley, and he was alone in his cabin for the moment.

Unlocking the coffer in the room, he extracted the strong box that held England's financial support for the Scots rebels. Opening the lid, he looked at the coins. Picking one up, he examined it – it was true that Devereux had done an excellent job of making the currency appear worn; shame he had not ensured the dies for the front and back of the coins were matched. Flipping the coin into the air, he watched it spin, catching it as it descended and, with a chink, re-united it with the other coins.

Richard deposited the strong box on the small table and dropped into a chair, gazing at the gold. It had been responsible for so much. Without it more than likely that Jack would not be in Lieth, and he would have been wedded to a different Elizabeth.

Richard let out a long breath.

Pondering on 'what might have been' was the preserve of fools. He found it deplorable in others, and wasting time now, when he had so little available, was unforgivable. Picking up a handful of the cold metal, he closed his eyes.

His brother was in a precarious position; he might now be one of Elizabeth's nobles, but he had not one single ally at her court. Without some support some protection, he would find himself continually in situations like his present one. He was an obstacle to placing their father's wealth in Elizabeth's coffers. Anyone who could give her that would probably fair well and benefit handsomely from the transaction.

He did have one supporter. If he could extricate Jack, then it might be time to persuade Jack to exploit his friendship with Neverra. There was, after all, little point in having wealth if you were not alive to enjoy it. That, however, was a problem for another day. The immediate issue was how best to use Knox and the two thousand gold Angels.

Those were the cards fate had placed on the table.

But how to play them?

If Norfolk had Jack, he could trade. That was undoubtedly the easiest option but not the safest. Alienating Norfolk was not a strategy that would provide for any future stability, especially not for Jack.

The gold was a hefty sum. He was sure he could use it as payment for Jack's extraction from Leith, but again, that didn't provide any form of long-term security.

He needed to find another way.

And he did have a third card - Morley.

So how to combine all three?

Morley, Knox and the gold.

Morley, Knox and the gold.

Richard rubbed his hand hard over his face, pressing the heels of his palms into his eyes.

Think, damn you!

Morley, Knox and the gold.

Placing his palms flat on the table, Richard tried to still his thoughts. He needed a course of action that did not simply buy Jack's freedom.

It needed to be more.

His breathing slowed, his mind finally stilled and the tumbling thoughts circling around inside his head, begging for attention, stopped. Like a series of doors in a long corridor opening one by one leading him forward slowly to the last one, he found the path.

A course of action planned, albeit a rough plan, and Richard's mind turned back to the preacher. He'd be rid of him soon, and the chances that he would ever see him again were, thankfully, very remote.

Richard opened the door without knocking and stepped inside, closing it behind him.

"Do ye have news for me?" Knox said, pinning Richard with a dark gaze.

"In a way," Richard replied. "We'll be in Lieth, at your request, soon, and after that, I hope to never be in your company again."

Knox straightened his back, his large hands flat on the table on either side of an open book. "A situation tha' would serve us both well."

"Indeed," Richard pulled a stool close to the table and seated himself opposite Knox. "Before we part, I would ask you a question."

"You are an impudent dog," Knox growled.

"Undoubtedly. I've been told it's part of my charm. Do you remember Andrew Newry?" Richard asked, his voice conversational.

"Newry?" Knox repeated the name.

"Yes. Do you remember him?"

"Why?"

A candle burnt in a small pewter dish, the wax had pooled in the bottom and only a short stump of wax remained upright. Richard absently turned the dish, his eyes on the flame. "Just answer me."

"I'll na' talk with ye, yer an insolent creature, Fitzwarren, and when the fires o' hell are set to yer heels, I hope ye have the sense to beg fer forgiveness," Knox's voice boomed, overly loud in the small cabin.

"You should have told me what you know. It would have been easier," Richard produced a piece of parchment from inside his doublet. It was tightly rolled, the centre bound neatly with cord.

"A message? Who from?" Knox asked, his eyes fastened on the parchment.

Richard picked it up and began tapping one end on the table. "I've an obligation, that's all, and if I don't carry it out, I'm not sure I'll be able to face my conscience again."

"Ye dinnea have a conscience," Knox spat back.

Richard propped the paper tube against the candle flame, and before Knox could react, he had a knife in one hand levelled at the preacher's chest while the other had a tight hold on Knox's left wrist.

"Let's have an earthy taste of the fires of hell, shall we?" Richard forced Knox's hand towards the dancing flame.

Knox tried to rise from his seat, pulling his arm away, but the knife's point spiked through his clothing to his skin, stilling Knox.

"He didn't scream, so his brother told me," Richard pressed Knox's hand closer to the flame.

Colour rose to the Scotsman's face, his eyes wide with loathing, the hand in Richard's steel grip shaking.

"It's only a taste. Mind you, a physician in Venice once told me that a man feels more pain in his hands than in any other part of his body. What do you think?" Richard asked. The smell of the burning flesh rose between them. Knox tried again to haul his hand from the flame but the knife point slipped beneath the skin, "No, I don't think so. Still yourself, Master Knox."

"Newry is a martyr," Knox growled. "Tha good Lord will shepherd him to tha fold."

"So you do remember him," Richard growled, slamming Knox's hand down on the flame.

Chapter Twenty-Nine

There had been no warning.

One moment Morley had been asleep on his narrow bed; the next, the ship heeled over so far that he was flung to the floor, the cups from the small table bouncing off his head.

"What's happened?" Morley shrieked in fright, trying to right himself.

"Stay there. I'll find out," Richard was already opening the cabin door, disappearing through it, wearing only hose, boots and a shirt.

The ship levelled out. Morley scrambled back onto the narrow bed on his hands and knees. Dragging his covers around him, he wedged himself into a corner, the hands holding the blanket trembling. From below, he heard a rumble followed by a series of solid bangs that he recognised as the gun doors opening.

Morley's terror was complete.

The Luciana began another tight turn, the deck canting in the opposite direction. The cups and a bottle that had found themselves on the floor skittered past him, bouncing from the wooden panelling. One of the cups, arriving first, was smashed into pieces when the bottle, spinning end over end, found its journey suddenly halted.

Pebbles, usually employed as paperweights, dropped solidly like musket shot, joining the other detritus slewing past him. Charts, released from the weights, rolled themselves back into tubes, falling silently to bounce and jostle with the rest of the dislodged clutter. An ink pot, with a firm stopper, already on the floor and sitting inside a pewter candle bowl, slid across the wooden boards in front of Morley.

Morley tipped his head back; from above, there came a sudden rush of footsteps on the deck and the shout of orders. It sounded like the captain's voice, but what the orders were, he could not comprehend. Then something he understood all too well ...

Cannon shot.

The explosion seemed to come from behind him; a moment after the noise the Luciana reacted. Every timber along her side seemed to quake, and a noise clawed up from beneath him, a guttural yowl as if some vast creature were caught deep within the hull of the Luciana. Another cannon blast shook the ship, the noise this time coming from below him, and he was sure it was the ship's own canon replying to the assault. A series of irregular blasts came in quick succession. The Luciana turned again, the ink bottle in its silver tray being overtaken by the bottle as everything shifted to the opposite side of the cabin.

Morley felt sick. Fear pressed bile up into his throat, and he retched. The acidic drool ran from between his lips, burning his throat and hanging in sticky tendrils from his chin.

Before the ship levelled out, the first faint curl of smoke crept beneath the door. Grey fingers poked their way into the cabin, bringing the scent of fire with them.

Above, more footsteps and then the sound of pistol shot. Morley jumped with each loud crack; clutching his knees to his body, Morley begged the Lord for salvation. There were more shouts and solid thuds from above, and then two piercing screams met his ears. Morley's heart pounded, and the air caught tight in his throat, threatening to suffocate him.

Silence.

Morley, his eyes closed, listened carefully. There was little to be heard, and the Luciana had ceased her erratic movement on the waves. Had they escaped? Had they been boarded?

There were footsteps but not the hurried drum of feet on the deck; this was ordered, and there seemed to be more. Morley swallowed hard and tried to take a steadying breath, but it caught in his throat as his nostrils filled with the scent of burning.

From beneath the door, the smoke was thicker and now more acrid.

"Oh Lord, help me!" Morley's voice squeaked. An image of Mistress Harrington scythed into his mind, the faggots alight, clothes burnt from her, pleading with the Lord to end her suffering.

Should he go to the door? Try and escape. Morley's hands trapped the blanket to his chest, his fingers kneading the wool. His eyes tight shut, body shaking, he silently pleaded with the almighty for salvation.

From above, he heard the sound of shouted orders and a drum of boots.

If the ship was indeed on fire, they would have deserted her, wouldn't they?

The sound of a dozen musket shots made up his mind. He'd stay where he was. If he emerged, it sounded like he would be their next victim. Whoever 'they' were.

Morley returned to his silent prayer on his knees, hands tightly grasped and hose soaked where his bowels had failed to contain the piss when the canon had sounded.

†

After what seemed like an age, Morley heard footsteps coming towards the cabin and the sound of voices in the corridor.

"He's in here," it was Fitzwarren's voice outside the cabin door, and the language he used was French.

"Well, get him and bring him up to the deck. Now!" a louder voice ordered.

The door was flung open, slamming round, and it hammered into the wall.

"Morley? Come on, up with you. Now!" Richard's voice was harsh.

Morley looked up at Richard's filthy face; blood ran from a cut near his hairline, and his shirt was ripped open. Richard caught Morley under the arm, hauling him from the bed and pushing him towards the door. He was shoved and dragged along the narrow passage towards the deck ladders.

"I've told them you are Lord Burghley's envoy, bound for Leith. Keep your counsel, Morley, and tread very carefully," Richard hissed in his ear as he steered him towards the ladder leading to the deck.

As Morley reached the bottom of the ladder, smoke was pouring down from the deck. His eyes ran with fresh tears, fear as well as fumes bringing them to his eyes. Richard's hands over his guided them to the ladder, and he felt himself being lifted up, his weakening legs being forced to take his weight on the rungs.

"Oh, my God!" Morley gasped, his face sweat-streaked, shaking hands barely clinging to the ladder, the man behind him forcing him upwards.

Morley made it up two more rungs before someone reaching down fastened a tight grip on his doublet and hauled him to the deck. Morley was deposited, coughing and shaking in a heap.

"This is him?" demanded a second French voice.

Morley tried to twist his head to view the speaker, but a thick black layer of smoke wafted down over him, and he was reduced to a coughing fit, his hands clamped over his blinded eyes.

"It is. Master Morley is Lord Burghley's aid on a diplomatic mission to Leith," Richard answered in French, coughing when he had finished.

Morley heard more footsteps and muted words he could not make out. He was aware of Richard standing next to where he crouched on the deck, the smoke still robbing him of air and sight.

"Master Morley, I have a message for your master," the French voice announced above him.

Morley tried to reply, but all that emerged was a raking coughing fit.

The man cursed. "Can he hear me?"

Richard knelt beside him, fastening a hand in Morley's arm and pulling him to his knees. "Answer, damn you if you wish to live."

Morley tried to open his eyes; bleary, tear-filled, he could see little. "Please, sir ... what ... message do ... you ..."

"It's a simple message. Are you listening?" the voice asked again, closer this time, evidently leaning over Morley.

Morley nodded quickly.

"We have your Knox, and we will take him to Leith for you. Do you hear me?"

Morley's head bobbed up and down faster.

"Good. You will go to Leith and tell your masters of his impending arrival, and they can watch their accursed heretic hang from a mast outside the city on the feast of St Isadora. Do you hear me?"

A vicious hand had fastened itself into Morley's thinning hair, forcing him to kneel, his face downcast towards the deck.

"I hear your words, sir," Morley managed weakly.

"Tell me, what is to happen to Knox?" the voice growled at him again.

Morley coughed, drool running from his mouth. "He is to hang ... outside Leith ... on one of your ships."

"When?"

"On the feast of St Isadora," Morley replied.

"Good. The good citizens of Leith will know of the entertainment we are to provide, as will your masters. Get him from my sight," the man released his hold on Morley, and wracked by another coughing fit, Morley dropped to his hands and knees.

Acrid smoke caught in the back of his throat, dark plumes of it were rolling along the length of the deck, he could hear the shout of orders and running feet, but there was little to see. The deck beneath him tipped again, and Morley found himself rolling, wailing, towards the gunwales.

"Help me!"

"Get him over the side, for God's sake!" It was Richard's voice in the smoke. A rope was dropped over his head and pulled painfully tight around his chest. A moment later, Morley was screaming and hanging from it as he was lowered towards the sea. The rope dropped quickly, and he felt helping hands grabbing his boots, steering his descent into the small boat. Smoke was pouring over the side of the Luciana, and the hull was stolen from view. Coughing, Morley was freed from the rope and deposited on the bottom of the boat. There were more shouts from above him and two more cannon shots. Morley curled up into a tight ball, his hands clamped over his ears and sobbed.

†

"Master Morley, I believe we are safe," Richard laid a hand on the small man's shaking shoulder.

Morley looked up. His eyes still stinging with smoke, he found Richard sitting on a bench. Behind him, two of the Luciana's crew worked the small boat's oars, one he recognised as Collins.

"What happened?" Morley's asked.

The look on Richard's face was grim. "We fell foul of the French ships. Damn Burghley to Hell. Look."

Richard's arm was extended over the side of the boat. Morley scrambled to his knees, hands on the side of the boat, tears running down his cheeks; he looked in that direction.

From behind a low rocky promontory rose a black pall of smoke.

"She's on fire!" Richard's voice cracked with emotion, and his head dropped into his hands.

†

It took two hours before the small boat made land. They had rounded a headland only to find the welcome one of high cliffs with nowhere to beach the boat. Richard swapped with Collins, who was tiring, and the other rower changed places with the man near the rudder, and the boat headed back out to sea. Rolling waves made for a slow and hard passage. Rounding the promontory, Collins called out that he had seen a safe bay for them to head towards.

The beach was in sight when the waves turned to breakers, and the boat was thrust high in the air to come crashing down a moment later, the undertow pulling them backwards. It was hard and slow work. Eventually, judging the depth, Richard and Collins jumped over the side and lent their strength to haul the boat ashore. Morley, beyond helping them, remained kneeling in the bottom, arms wrapped around one of the wood seat slats.

"Where are we?" Morley asked when he was hauled from the boat onto the wet sand.

Richard shook his head. "I don't know. We were between Lindisfarne and Berwick last time Jerome checked his maps, where exactly I don't know."

"The captain, Jerome, where is he?" Morley looked around, realising for the first time how few of the Luciana's crew there were on the beach.

"There are only us left," Richard said, his voice taught.

"Oh, my God!" Morley said, his knees sinking into the soggy sand, the moist stuff coating his wet hands. "How do we get from here to Berwick?"

Richard pinned him with a hard stare. "We walk, Master Morley, and we pray it isn't far."

As it happened, Morley did not need to pray. The small inlet was less than a mile from Berwick, and as soon as they had hauled themselves from the beach and up the rising dunes, they could see the town clustered around the harbour.

Chapter Thirty

†

Jack had been woken from a sleep that had robbed him of any sense of where he was. Sitting bolt upright on the bed, his surroundings unfamiliar, the voice that had breached his slumber was one he couldn't recall.

"Did ye hear what I said?" the voice spoke again.

Jack recognised the tent he was in. His voice, clogged with sleep, mumbled, "Yes ...err... no. Tell me again."

"Captain Vaughan wants ye to go to the east side of the Bulwark tonight. Peaceably, this time, no fire arrows. He wants an assessment of the damages to the defences," Cyrdic dropped the flap back in place.

Jack, groaning, dropped back on the bed. He had a few hours left before night. Closing his eyes, he listened to the noise around him. Two cannon blasts, one after the other, sounded to his right. The pattering of a dozen squelching footsteps stirring the mud in the narrow path outside his tent was accompanied by shouted orders. They had reloaded, and the cannon fired again.

Two more blasts.

In his mind, he could see the swirl of grey gun smoke twisting upwards into an overcast sky.

Hammering from behind him. The almost musical sound of metal on an anvil. Tap, tappety tap, tappety tap, tap, tap. The hammer bounced on the iron. There was a line of smiths' workshops, sharing fires, working on shoeing the horses, repairing armour and fashioning the iron implements of war; arrowheads, spears, lances and swords. And the prices would be high. Where else could you get armour repaired at short notice? Or the blade from a sword replaced, a hilt reset or your horse re-shod on the battlefield? And if you couldn't afford their fees, it mattered little as there would be another dozen in the queue wanting the smith's services who did have coins to pay.

It was lucrative work.

Tap, tappety tap, tappety tap, tap, tap.

He'd even considered it himself once. The smith who had worked at Harry's father's house, Walt Wyttle, had travelled England in his day behind the lines of fighting men, providing his services to knights and men-at-arms. Jack could remember listening to his tales when he was a small boy. Walt had been present at old King Henry's assaults on Scotland from England's northern border, the rough wooing as they'd called it later. He'd earned so much money, he told them, been paid in gold and silver to mend swords for the lords of the north. And, of course, they'd believed him. They'd been too young to question why old Walt was still striking iron with a stooped back and working in the Fitzwarren house if he'd made a fortune in gold on the borders.

Tap, tappety tap, tappety tap, tap, tap.

For a time, Jack had worked with Walt. Long enough to learn how to shoe a horse, temper iron in the forge, and make nails but not long enough to learn all the skills he'd need to become a smith. He'd been stopped, forced to spend more time with Harry, joining him in his lessons, Harry's father hoping that Jack would provide the competition Harry needed to succeed.

It hadn't worked.

Harry had remained lazy, even more so when he saw that there was someone else to distract his tutors' attention. He had let Jack take the lead, complete the tasks and succeed, then stood by and watched as his father had beaten Jack for it.

And that had made him worse.

The more he was beaten for besting Harry, the more he wanted to. Sometimes success had been easy, and sometimes the victories had been hard won.

Tap, tappety tap, tappety tap, tap, tap.

The sound dragged Jack's mind back to Walt again. Thick corded arms, hands like shovels, scarred with the burns of the trade, a felt hat with nails tucked into the brim and a blackened pig skin apron, as tough as armour and almost as hard. He'd told Jack iron had a heartbeat, and you could hear that magical musical sound when the hammer struck the hot metal on the anvil. He could hear it now.

Tap, tappety tap, tappety tap, tap, tap.

The noise of the men, the cannon, the shouted orders he could block from his mind as he focused on the sound of the iron ringing under the strike of the hammer. Perhaps it was the distance, maybe even the canvas, but the ring of the smith's hammers was a familiar and peaceful sound amongst the raucous clamour of war. Jack fell asleep with the ring of iron in his dreams.

†

The three of them were gathered again by Cydric and told to ready themselves for another venture across the wasteland towards Leith.

"What time do you propose to go?" Emilio asked.

"It would seem foolish to go at the same time. In fact, it seems foolish to go at all. They will be looking for us tonight," Jack spoke resignedly, gazing through a break in the palisade towards Leith.

"I agree," Emilio moved his head close to Jack's, sharing his vantage point.

"Why send us again? Surely there can't be more to learn?" Threadmill spoke from behind them.

"Probably not. Grey's guns have been active all day, so it's unlikely they will have dispatched men to deepen the trenches surrounding the walls," Jack said in agreement, turning away from Leith and towards the lawyer.

"Grey just wants to strengthen a belief that there will be an attack from the west, and we are part of the mechanism being sent to convince them of that. Ideally, he'd like us to be witnessed by the defenders," Emilio replied, turning towards them and folding his arms.

"That's ridiculous. We'd be killed!" Threadmill's voice was reedy and incredulous.

Jack caught Emilio's eye and smiled without humour. "He's starting to get an understanding of the situation."

"Surely they don't want us killed?" Threadmill said. His voice had risen another notch.

"We are serving a purpose for Norfolk and Grey at the moment, and if it leads to our demise, then, I am afraid, that would also be considered a satisfactory outcome," Jack said dryly.

"Why? I don't understand," Threadmill looked between Jack and Emilio, confused.

"Just sit down and listen."

Threadmill lowered himself to sit with his back against the wooden defence, and Jack dropped down next to him.

Speaking quietly, he said, "You know of my recent past; my inheritance of my father's wealth has not sat well with many."

"Sir, it might not sit well, but legally you are ...."

Jack cut him off, laying a hand on his arm to still his words. "Just listen. What lawyers think and what the law may say is irrelevant. I am not in favour at the Queen's Court, and if I don't return from Scotland, her coffers would undoubtedly benefit."

Threadmill's eyes widened. "I cannot believe that, sir. To send you all the way north, to serve Norfolk, seems too contrived, and the outcome, if that's what they want, too uncertain."

"I'm glad you think it's uncertain. I was beginning to be assured of it," Jack asked bluntly.

Threadmill paled. "You really believe this?"

"I am afraid so. And that is why this idiot," he gestured towards Emilio, "has tied himself to my worthless cause."

"Don't brand yourself as worthless, Jacques, hapless perhaps, but not worthless," Emilio said in Italian, a genuine smile on his face.

"If you can think of a way out of this, then please let me know," Jack said, looking up into Emilio's face from where he sat.

"It is a little difficult. I've no idea where my men are, or yours, come to that. Desertion comes with the risk of capture and swift justice, and if I were to go to Norfolk, I am not sure if that would be of help," Emilio's voice was solemn.

"You don't think you could convince him who you are?" Jack asked.

"I am sure I can. The risk is that he will not look upon the duplicity kindly, and I feel that all it would do would be to strip you of my help. He would not let me return to you, and I doubt he would release you," Emilio said, adding, "I wouldn't."

"Those were the conclusions I had also arrived at," Jack said morosely.

Threadmill was looking at Emilio closely.

"It's better if you don't know," was all Jack said.

†

They headed out from the defences shortly after midnight. The sky was starlit, and the moon had, for the moment, drifted behind the clouds, the extent of which could not be seen.

The route they took was the same, heading towards the cover of the stone wall that crossed the field before the rise of the Leith defences. Moving as quickly as they could, the trio crossed the abandoned fields.

"Shit!" Jack hissed under his breath.

The veil of night shifted. The moon, emerging from beneath a canopy of clouds, bestowed a white light upon them.

Jack grasped Threadmill's wrist to stop him, pulling him down towards the ground. Immobile, they watched the walls ahead of them. The moonlight picked out the metal helms of those on guard duty along the ramparts, and there were plenty of them.

Leith was prepared.

Jack was sure that eyes were looking out towards Norfolk's defences, seeking any movement in the dark. All three of them were laid, face down, in the middle of a field, the sanctuary of the wall another one hundred paces at least in front of them.

Jack found Threadmill's arm and clamped a hand around it. "Don't move," he whispered.

Threadmill's face was turned towards him. "They'll see us. For God's sake, we can't stay here."

"Move, and they'll see us for certain," Jack said. He could feel Threadmill shaking with fear. "Close your eyes, just breath slowly, and stay still."

"I can't," Threadmill's voice choked in his throat.

Jack felt the muscles in his arms tense and, a moment later, he was pulling against Jack's hold.

"No!" Jack growled, his voice louder than he wanted it to be.

"Move, and I'll kill you here and now," the quiet threat, in Italian, came from Threadmill's right. Emilio had a hand wound in Threadmill's hair and was holding his face hard against the cold ground, the moonlight playing along a short blade he held in front of the lawyer's eyes.

Threadmill's terrified gaze linked with Jack's.

Jack answered his silent plea. "Be still. It will be dark again in a moment. Just wait."

Threadmill's breathing was laboured, irregular and, above all, loud. Satisfied he was not about to bolt, Emilio withdrew the knife and slackened his hold.

"Hush, for God's sake," Jack muttered close to his ear.

A voice from above them on the rampart drifted down to where they lay, clear and sounding deceptive closely. "Aye, laddie, another hour, and we'll change the watch."

Jack looked to his right, his eyes meeting Emilio's.

The sky was pricked with starlight; what cloud there was drifted north, exposing them in the moonlight. The only chance to move would be when the guard changed, which might afford them enough time to make it to the sanctuary of the wall without being seen. Jack knew he had the patience to wait, his face against the damp earth, and Emilio would have a similar fortitude.

The question was, could Threadmill?

The sound of a blade on a whetstone made it across the waste to them, along with the low mumble of conversation punctuated with occasional laughter. They must have been behind the ramparts, the stonework muffling their words, rendering them indistinct no matter how hard Jack tried to listen.

Somewhere inside Leith, a bell tolled.

Threadmill's body trembled even more.

"Wait," Jack said, his eyes closed. He was straining to listen to the noise on the ramparts. Were they changing the guard?

The grate of metal on stone, footsteps and sudden increase in the volume of the conversation told them that men were moving on the top of the defences.

Jack looked up. Between the crenulations, the moonlight no longer glinted off steel helms.

"Now!"

Threadmill did not have a choice. The other two men held his arms fast, and he was hauled to his feet and into a stumbling run faster than his numbed legs were ready for. If the wall was a hundred paces away, Threadmill was sure he made it in fifty.

Jack, his back against the rough five feet of stone, stretched his neck and titled his head skyward. The moon smiled down at him. Bright, white and casting a faint glowing light across the field.

There was not a cloud in sight.

"Shit! It's five times the distance back. There's no way we can make that without being seen," Jack's words were meant for Emilio.

"We've an hour until dawn as well. I agree. We are somewhat marooned," Emilio replied.

"What do you mean?" Threadmill gasped.

"Exactly that. If you want to be shot, then head back to the defences. If you don't, then stay here," Emilio was in the process of lying down close to the wall.

"How long for?" Threadmill asked, panic mounting in his voice.

"You tell him, Jacques," Emilio said. His eyes were already closed, and it was apparent he was settling himself to sleep.

Jack fastened a hand on Threadmill's arm, a precautionary measure. He was pretty sure what he was about to say wasn't going to be welcomed, so he tempered it with a lie. "We'll wait here until the moon clouds over. When it does, we'll make our way back."

Threadmill nodded, his eyes fixed on the white disc in the sky.

Jack had failed to tell him that it might be the following night before that happened. And even then, that was not guaranteed.

"Get some sleep," Jack advised, adopting the same position as Emilio, his spine against the stone wall.

†

Jack was awoken by the sun. The bright disc had made its way over the horizon, and, in a cloudless sky, it was poking light into his eyes, making its way around his closed lids. Shielding his eyes with his arm, he gazed across the wasteland towards Norfolk's raised siege line.

"That's perfect!" Jack muttered, his words laden with sarcasm.

Emilio was also sitting up, his knees drawn to his chest and his arms wrapped around them. The expression on his face mirrored Jack's.

Sitting with their backs against the wall, they were gazing towards two black eyes that stared at them from behind the wooden defences: the darkly gaping muzzles of two of Grey's guns.

"Let's hope their aim improves," Emilio said dryly, pointing to the wall ten feet from where Jack was sitting.

Jack swivelled his head in the direction of Emilio's arm. The top three feet of the wall were missing, where one of the guns had sent a ball to carve the wall in half.

Crouched down, they had moved along the wall length as far as they could to a point that Jack estimated was between the two batteries. There they waited. There was a break in the wet weather that had plagued the battlefield since they had arrived, and a clear sky allowed the sun to cast warm rays on them throughout the morning.

Jack, too warm, had stripped to his shirt, knowing only too well how thirsty he would become as the day wore on. His hope for rain did not look like it would be granted. Shortly after midday, there was an improvement in their situation as the sun travelled behind the wall, and they were finally in the shadow cast by the ragged stonework.

Jack had tried to sleep, but Lord Grey did not allow that to happen. His guns had begun an assault on the Leith defences early in the morning, and, although it could not be described as a sustained attack, it was constant. There were four to six shots an hour, and no sooner had sleep claimed him than he found himself dragged back by the sound of the cannon fire.

As the sun dipped below the horizon, the besieged and siegers alike turned their minds towards other things and smoke, laced with the scent of cooking meat, began to drift across the untended farmland.

Jack's stomach complained at the lack of attention he had shown it, and his head pounded, telling him he needed to drink. Emilio had spent the day quietly, either asleep or on his knees, head bent in prayer, but mostly he had slept. The rough sound of the cannon fire didn't disturb him as much as it did Jack. Jack knew he was conserving his strength for their return to Norfolk's defences.

"Not too long to go now," Emilio had pushed past Threadmill and settled himself next to Jack.

"Let's see what the night brings us first," Jack said, adding, "that sky over there looks promising."

"I agree. Let us pray it comes our way," Emilio's eyes fixed on the dark cloud to the west.

The silence between them lengthened.

It was Emilio who eventually broke it.

"In London .... it was bad memories, Jacques. I am sorry," Emilio said quietly, his words for Jack alone. Threadmill on the other side of Jack was out of earshot.

"Bad memories made you leave me on the quay?" Jack sounded incredulous.

Emilio stared towards the horizon for a moment, his fingers twisting a ring on his right hand. Without meeting Jack's gaze, still looking towards Norfolk's siege wall, he said again, "Bad memories, that was all."

"They must have been very bloody bad! I've not seen you for weeks," Jack leaned his head towards Emilio, his voice rough. "I tried to find you. I left messages for you at your lodgings and with Tresham, and you just ignored them?"

Emilio grinned. "An admission at last - you did miss me?"

Jack clamped his right hand hard on Emilio's forearm. "Don't play games with me."

Emilio looked at Jack, indecision clear on his face.

Jack released the hold on his arm. "You know me well enough to know I will not judge you. Who is he?"

"Alphonso?" Emilio asked.

"Of course, Alphonso. Who else do you think I am talking about?" Jack's words were brusquely spoken.

"Alphonso is the second son of a wealthy merchant who was friends with my father. He joined our house, and it was a great honour for him to be raised with us," Emilio stopped suddenly, and Jack was unsure whether he was going to say more.

"He was ... we were ..." Emilio spoke haltingly, for once a little uncertain.

"I understand," Jack said quietly, the muscles in his stomach tightened. They were not words he wished to hear.

"Then he disappeared. One day he was there. The next, he wasn't. No one knew where he had gone or why. Senor Orland, one of my tutors, warned me not to ask, and that was when I knew he had been sent away, taken from me," Emilio's voice was strained and quiet.

"How long ago was that?" Jack asked.

"Years. Ten, maybe more. I've stopped counting," Emilio's voice was weary.

"And you hadn't seen him since?" Jack turned his head towards Emilio. He was having difficulty keeping the annoyance from his voice.

Emilio shook his head. "Not until I saw him in the Ambassador's entourage. If I am honest, I thought that they had murdered him, so that at least was not true."

"Christ! No wonder you have little love for your family," Jack turned his gaze back towards the palisade as the guns spoke again, the noise forcing a halt in the conversation. For once, Jack resolved not to speak his mind. If he did, he doubted Emilio would continue to tell him about Alphonso.

The nose abated, and Emilio continued. "It was not unlikely. My sister, Francesca, had her heart set on an unprofitable match, and the poor boy was found floating in the river. So I believed for a long time that there would eventually be news of his death; when it never came ... I just assumed they had hidden his body well."

"I'm sorry," Jack said.

Emilio smiled sadly. "It was a long time ago; soon after, I joined the Order. Since then, they have been my family. Alphonso confirmed what I had thought: they had forced him from me. They were careful in their planning; he was taken to a ship, and from there, he sailed to Spain. By the time he made his way back to Italy, I had left to join the Order, and there was little he could do."

"He could have joined the Order," Jack pointed out.

Emilio cast a sideways glance towards Jack. "He is the son, the second son, of a merchant. It would be doubtful if his family could provide anything that would tempt the Order to offer him a place. Anyway, he tells me that he was abandoned in Spain, penniless, and worked for a physician for several years. When the physician died, it was then that he made his way back to Italy."

"How did he end up with the Ambassador?" Jack asked. Alphonso was clearly not loyal to Emilio, and after whatever he could get for himself, Jack had no doubt.

"When he returned to Italy, he came looking for me; it seems my father, troubled by what he had done, recommended Alphonso to the Ambassador, and he has been with him for five years," Emilio said.

"And he didn't think to seek you out?" Jack asked, trying hard to keep incredulity from his tone.

Emilio shook his head. "He had heard that my military career had met with some success, and he feared his presence might have prejudiced that."

Emilio couldn't see the sceptical look that descended on Jack's face. He asked. "Why now, then? What has changed?"

Emilio let out a long breath. "Time has swept away so much. And it was I who found him. It is hard to replace the pain of loss with the joy of life. But I shall try. Perhaps it is time I left the Order. Anyway, I miss Italy."

"Why are you telling me this now?" Jack asked.

Emilio turned towards Jack, smiling. "It is a long way back to Norfolk's lines, and that dark cloud may not endure."

We'll get back, and when we do, I'll show you just how loyal that Italian whore is. Jack silently fumed, his face turned away so Emilio couldn't see his expression.

✝

However, Scotland did not disappoint. As dusk descended, a layer of thick cloud headed towards them from the west. Ahead of it rushed a current of cool air, pressed ahead of the weather front, and Jack guessed correctly that it was the herald of rain. At first, a light and fine drizzle, welcomingly cool, then harder, more determined rain which plastered their hair flat upon their heads and worked its way through seams and stitching to the skin beneath. A distant flash, someway to the north, lit the field, followed by a dull thunderclap.

Emilio leaned towards Jack and Threadmill. "My prayers, it seems, have been answered rather well."

"If it's lightning, then they will see us as plain as if it were day," Threadmill's voice was worried, his eyes on his cupped hands capturing rainwater as it fell.

"We shall have to avoid them then, won't we," Jack reassured.

"But how? You never know when they will come," Threadmill argued.

"They rarely follow straight on. We will gauge our time," Jack said.

"But what if we are struck?" Threadmill said.

"If you are, then you'll no longer need to worry about Grey's guns or the Leith defences," Jack said gruffly. His head throbbed, and he was becoming tired of Threadmill's questions.

They watched as the storm came closer. The lightning struck over the Firth of the Forth, the rain becoming torrential, and Emilio made the decision, shouting against the noise of the rain and wind.

"We go now."

And they did.

They picked their way on stiff legs across the soaked ground towards the raised ramparts. The rain had turned the surface to a mire, Threadmill slipped to his knees twice in the mud, finding himself hauled back to his feet and dragged onwards. An explosion of pure white lit them when they were halfway across, and they doubled their speed.

There were no shots from the defenders.

A ditch, five feet deep, was on the Leith side of Norfolk's defences, and the trio slithered into it. The bottom of the now held a foot of water. Soaked and muddy, they made their way laboriously up the slippery side to where one of the gun emplacements allowed for entry to the palisade.

"Where the Hell have you been?" Captain Vaughan was furious.

"Took a little longer to get back than we had hoped," Jack said, wiping mud from his hands.

Vaughan brought his face close to Jack's. "Lord Grey should have turned his guns on you, sitting there, staring at us all day. You didn't make it to the defences last night, did you?"

"No, we didn't. As you know, there was a moon. We'd have been picked off by the defenders," Jack shot back.

"You can bloody well get back out there again and get the assessment you failed to obtain last night," Vaughan said.

"Again?" Jack repeated.

"Yes, again. And now," Vaughan said.

"It's an hour until dawn. For God's sake, you can't expect us to go now," Jack said.

Vaughan stood his ground. "It's an order, and Lord Grey expects nothing less than for it to be obeyed. So if you want darkness, then you and your fucking lawyers had better get a move on before the sun rises over the hills and both sides start shooting at you."

Four armed men had moved to stand behind Vaughan. The threat was clear.

"He'll slow us down, he stays here, and we'll go," Jack said, pushing Threadmill away.

"My orders are clear, all of you or none of you. It's your choice," Vaughan said.

Jack felt the hold on his arm. "He's right, sir. If we don't go now, we risk the dawn," Emilio said quietly.

Five minutes later, they were slithering back down the ditch outside the palisade, slopping into the rain-filled trench at the bottom.

"Who's bloody side are you on?" Jack said through clenched teeth as he began clambering out of the ditch onto the other side, one hand clamped on Threadmill's arm, pulling him up the slope.

"Ours, of course," Emilio grinned. "One more minute, and you, Jacques, would have lost your temper with him, and that would have ended badly. Come on."

Rather than heading through the rain-drenched night towards Leith, Emilio took a path to the right across the wasteland. Jack and Threadmill had little choice but to follow. The torrential rain hadn't lessened, so it was doubtful if anyone could see in which direction they went.

Chapter Thirty-One

The ride from Berwick to Leith should have taken Morley five days, but he was forced to make it in two, arriving tired, bone-sore, hungry and disorientated. He'd travelled with Richard, who had taken charge of the journey, hauling him into his saddle, helping him down, and providing him with water when he needed it. Morley had been grateful for the care, and the arrival in Leith was the end of a torturous ordeal for him.

His admittance to Norfolk's presence, with Richard at his side, had been a matter of a few well-placed words. Burghley's servant was privy to his master's code and knew which words opened doors immediately.

One of the chairs had been drawn from the wall, and Morley seated upon it, a glass of Norfolk's best malmsey in his hand. Behind him stood Richard, a hand resting lightly on the chair's back. Norfolk and Grey stood before him, a little too close for Morley's liking.

"Tell me again? Why were you on a ship bound for Leith?" Norfolk said, interrupting Morley's not particularly coherent account of recent events.

"As I said, Lord Burghley sent me to the Santa Luciana to ensure that it would sail north to Scotland, or so I thought," Morley offered, the hands holding the glass shook, threatening to spill the wine into his lap.

"That doesn't tell me why you are here, now?" Norfolk continued, glowering down at the little man. "For what does Burghley want that he has sent you to us?"

Richard squeezed Morley's shoulder. "My Lord, let me help. Master Morley has had a traumatic journey. I was charged with bringing Knox to Leith along with money to support the Congregation's cause. Is this not so, Master Morley?"

Morley nodded.

"Master Morley, as Lord Burghley's officer, was accompanying me to ensure the safe delivery of both the gold and of Knox," Richard explained.

"And?"

"Just before Berwick, we ran into two French ships; we were boarded, and Knox, I am afraid, was captured," Richard paused. "We were outnumbered. There was little we could do. Lord Burghley's provision of men and munitions was poor. Was it not, Master Morley?"

Morley lowered the glass from his lips in a shaking hand. "It was."

"And now Knox is in French hands?" Norfolk raged, storming across the room.

"I am afraid the news is worse than that," Morley's voice was bleak. "They plan to hang Knox on one of their ships in front of Leith."

"What!" Grey blurted.

"They plan to hang him tomorrow. It is the feast of Saint Isadora, and they are going to hang him from a mast while the citizens of Leith watch," Richard replied, providing the rest of the message that Morley had omitted.

"My God!" Grey exclaimed, "That explains why there is a new vessel closer in the Leith than the rest of the fleet. My men have been trying to train their guns on her, but she's just out of their range."

"I've seen it," Norfolk agreed. "Flying the French colours and with smoke rising from her decks."

"How do you know Knox is on this ship?" Grey pressed, leaning over Morley.

"It would not be a spectacle if you did not know what was to happen," Richard supplied. "Morley was allowed to escape with the express intention of him communicating this fact with you and the congregation."

"And you, sir, why did they let you live?" Grey regarded Richard with a cool gaze.

"I was tasked with bringing Morley to you. Does he look capable of making such a journey on his own? I have lost my ship and my crew, sir, in my efforts to aid England's cause in the north, neither of which I am overly happy about," Richard's voice was cold.

"For the Lord's sake! If they hang Knox on the morrow, we'll lose their support," Grey boomed. "Like it or not, it was the Queen's ministers who transferred him north, and the blame for his demise will be placed at her door, have no fear of that."

"Why did Burghley trust this blaggard with the task? For the Lord's sake, the name Fitzwarren is untrustworthy," Norfolk had come to stand before Richard.

"It doesn't matter where the fault lies. It matters now how we mitigate it," Grey continued, "and we don't have a lot of time."

"What do you propose?" Norfolk growled.

"That ship is out of range of my gunners. We can't launch an assault on it from the land," Grey provided.

"What about De Wynter's?" Norfolk snapped.

"Possibly, but it would take time to get a message to him. His vessels are at the mouth of the Forth, we'd need to send a rider, and it is unlikely it would reach him in time," Grey said, tugging at his beard. "Plus De Wynter has six vessels at his disposal but, outside Leith, there are twenty-five French ships. It's not feasible he could mount a successful assault."

"It would be better to sink it, even with Knox on board. Better that than allow his supporters to watch him hang," Norfolk paced across the room.

"Agreed," Grey said.

"Swift action. There can be no other course. I need ten men. I believe my brother is here as well, we can take the galleon with Knox tonight, and if we don't, then the blame will lie at my door," Richard said.

"If Knox hangs, it won't be blame that will be a problem," Grey said.

"We would lose the support of the Congregation, and this offensive will collapse overnight. Everything we have worked towards will be in tatters because ...You ...you can't comply with one simple damned order," Norfolk's fury was about to boil over.

Grey laid a hand on his arm. "In war, there are setbacks; how we deal with them defines the campaign."

"Setbacks!" Norfolk spluttered. "He's lost the bloody one man the Scots regard as their saviour."

"I agree, it's not ideal," Grey continued, then to Richard. "We can't mount an offensive from here. We've no sea power to bring to bear. Tell me, how exactly do you propose to mount an attack on one of their fleet carrying a man they wish not to lose?"

"The French ship is anchored off Leith. There may already be a fire on board. I don't know. I've experience with black powder, spare us some from your store, and we can take men and either successfully extract Knox or sink him along with the ship. Either is a better outcome than an execution for the entertainment of the citizens of Leith," Richard finished.

Grey turned to Norfolk. "Give him his men. We, too, can attempt to mount an offensive. There is a chance to reposition one of the guns and bring it within range, but it's not guaranteed, so this will at least double our chances of ensuring that Knox isn't publicly hung."

"How do we know he'll not take his brother and his men and desert?" Norfolk said.

Grey pinned Norfolk with a hard stare. "In all truth, we don't. However, he is offering an action that would go a long way to returning himself to favour at court, and I doubt that is an opportunity he would wish to miss. And if I am wrong, and he does, then his brother's title and land would be forfeit. It's a high price. Of course, there is the final possibility that they could both perish in the attempt."

Norfolk shook his head. "There's more than a passing chance your brother and his bloody lawyer are dead by now, but I shall find out."

"Lawyer?" Richard's brow furrowed.

They had been found only because one of the gun crews had been watching their slow passage across the ruined farmland. The youngest and fastest lad from the crew was despatched to get them before they moved within range of Leith's gun defences.

The three men returned to the ramparts, puzzled but thankful. The summons back to Norfolk was one Jack was happy to comply with.

All three were soaked, plastered with mud, and were left waiting outside Norfolk's rooms while their presence was reported. Why he was there, he didn't know, and Jack had a feeling he probably didn't want to know either. It was unlikely to be a reprieve. It was likely that some other foul task had been found for them, even more, dangerous than the one they had already been dispatched on.

And Jack was right.

A door opened, and light poured onto the dark ramparts of the palisade. Two men emerged, and, behind them, a third carried a lamp. Jack's night vision was now lost, and he could see little apart from their outlines.

"Jack?" a voice he recognised asked uncertainly.

Jack fixed his eyes on the speaker.

"Jack, is that you?" the voice said, filled now with genuine concern.

"Christ! Richard," Jack couldn't keep a stupid grin from his face.

"I almost didn't recognise you," Richard stepped forward. Reaching out, he grasped Jack's arm.

Jack took in the man before him. A sword in his belt, wearing a jack, hair plastered to his head with rain, but whole and well and alive: his brother. The relief was palpable. "Where the hell have you been?"

"Can I make my peace later? Right now, we have a fight on our hands," Richard said, his eyes sliding beyond Jack to the two men standing behind him.

Jack, following his brother's gaze, said quickly. "Master Threadmill, my lawyer, and his clerk."

"Of course, your lawyers," Richard said, nodding his head in agreement.

"Dawn approaches. You don't have long," Grey advised from where he stood behind Richard, adding to Jack, "Your men are near the quay at your brother's request. I suggest you make the best use of them and what little time you have left."

"He's unfortunately right. We need to go to the quay now. I'll tell you on the way." Richard, with a firm grip on Jack's arm, was already guiding him quickly in the direction he wanted them to go.

Jack, more than happy to be leaving the defences, matched his brother's quick pace. When they were far enough away not to be heard, Jack leaned towards his brother, asking, "Are you going to tell me what's going on?"

Richard grinned. "I'm not sure where to start."

They weren't quite running but they were not far from it.

"At the beginning is usually best," Jack advised.

"Is that Nevarra in sackcloth?" Richard asked, casting a quick glance over his shoulder.

"Yes. Your story first," Jack said, not about to be diverted.

"Alright. My story," Richard laid heavy emphasis on the word 'story', well aware that his words may be heard by more than just Jack and hoping his brother would recognise his need for duplicity, "is that I was transporting Knox north for Lord Burghley. He should have been delivered to the Congregation at Leith along with a quantity of gold to bolster their support. Unfortunately, we were boarded by the French, who took possession of their valued preacher and intend to hang him from the masts of one of the ships in the Forth for the entertainment of the citizens of Leith tomorrow."

"Christ!" Was all Jack could manage.

"Exactly. So we are to prevent this from happening," Richard said.

"How?" Jack said.

"Well, ostensibly, we are to take a small boat and row it out under cover of darkness filled with black powder. We attach the boat to the ship's hull and blow it, and Knox, to the hereafter," Richard replied.

"And us?" Jack asked, striding quickly to keep up with his brother.

"I intend for us to be elsewhere when the powder ignites," Richard replied, smiling.

Chapter Thirty-Two

Froggy Tate, Marc and Pierre were waiting on the quay near the small boat, along with Alphonso, Jack noted with annoyance.

"Well, I'll be! It's the Devil himself ...." Froggy's words trailed off as he recognised the master.

"Indeed, Master Tate. Back from beyond and with a taste for blood," Richard said. His voice grave, he issued orders that had the small laden boat in the water and heading silently towards the shadow of the ship anchored nearest to the Leith stronghold.

All her deck lamps were out, and no light crept through any of the stern windows. On first inspection, she appeared deserted. In front of Jack were three small kegs of black powder wrapped in sacking and raised from the boat bottom on wooden blocks to keep them dry.

"The only way you can sink her is if we tie this boat to her hull, set the charges and swim back to shore. Do you have fuses?" Jack's voice was a quiet whisper near his brother's ear.

Richard, ignoring him, leaned towards Froggy. "Bring the boat round the other side. Keep the ship between Leith and us."

Rounding the other side of the ship, Jack could see in the moonlight a ladder had been lowered.

Jack caught his brother's arm, receiving a grin in answer to his questioning look. He asked, "What's going on?"

"I'll tell you when we are on board," Richard replied, adding, "I think you might recognise her."

The small boat's hull bumped against the ship's side, and five minutes later, Jack lowered himself onto a deck that reeked of familiarity. The face Jerome, smiling in greeting, confirmed his suspicion.

"Jack, welcome back onboard. It's bloody good to see you," Jerome said, beaming.

Behind Jerome, a haze of smoke was rising from the decks, the prevailing wind sending it over her sides away from them. Concern creased Jack's face. "Is she on fire?"

Jerome grinned. "Only for the benefit of the French fleet and the observers near Leith."

"I'll explain that later," Richard said hurriedly, "What you need to know now is that I have Knox below decks, secured in the rope store behind the galley. He was sailing to Leith on the Luciana. He believes we were boarded by the French, the Luciana sunk, and he is currently a prisoner on a French ship."

Jack shook his head, confused. "How did ..."

"It doesn't matter now. What matters is that Knox believes he is in French hands, and you, my dear brother, are about to provide him with his liberty," Richard said. "He's blindfolded, and the ship is covered in a blanket of smog. Should he get any view of her, we'll keep him bound and blindfolded until we get him over the side. Once there, I will take him to Norfolk, and you can return to the Luciana, then Froggy will make her disappear for a second time."

"Do you not remember the three choices I said you had?" Emilio stood behind Jack, sounding amused.

Jack turned to look at him, a moment of confusion on his face. "Choices?"

"Exactly. You are about to be able to perform the third," Emilio said, smiling.

"Make myself indispensable?" Jack said slowly.

Emilio threw his arms wide, a look of delight on his face. "It seems you do, after all, listen to me."

Alphonso, who had attached himself to Emilio's side, flashed a feline smirk at Jack.

Ignoring him, Jack looked at Jerome. "Norfolk said this was a French ship? How did you arrange that?"

"Not my doing," Jerome said, "Your brother supplied the flags, bounty from a ship Wynter had taken near Berwick, and I supplied the message to the French that we were a powder re-supply ship and that we had a fire onboard. There's been a charcoal brazier warming the decks all day with a good covering of greenwood. I had the message rowed over to their flagship, and they've kept a healthy distance since then."

"You are a crafty bastard," Jack laughed, shaking his head.

"It is not a situation that can continue. Their curiosity might get the better of them; hence Froggy's intervention is needed before they do," Richard warned.

"Agreed," Jerome replied. "They'll expect us to have dealt with the issue by dawn at the latest, and when we haven't, they'll be wondering why."

Richard nodded. "We get Knox off the ship, you come back to her and, smoking like a chimney fire, we turn her towards the sea. Once out of the line of sight, we will reward everyone with several exceptional detonations. The French will believe the powder store has exploded and the ship lost. Norfolk will believe we have destroyed an enemy vessel, which is what we want him to think. Froggy, I am hoping I can trust those to you. There are the three kegs we brought from the shore, plus what's already onboard in the powder room. Jerome can show you what there is. And just remember, I want a ship left when you've finished."

Froggy grinned. "Don't you worry, master, I'll give 'em a show they'll not soon forget."

"Which brings me to your legal counsel," Richard said, catching both Threadmill and Emilio with a quizzical gaze.

"Master Threadmill is actually my lawyer," Jack gestured to where Threadmill, pale-faced, was leaning against a guard rail, his mouth slightly open as he tried to understand what was happening. "He's still fighting to comprehend that he's alive after having made two-night sorties to Leith's defences."

"And Neverra? I had heard you'd left England," Richard said.

Emilio shrugged.

"He's here to ensure Knox makes it safely to Scotland," Jack said quickly before either of the other two could reply. "We have an hour, no more before it's light. I suggest we use it."

"Agreed. We have a few more theatrics to complete before our departure. Master Knox is currently in the rope store, neatly bound and blindfolded. We need to get him off the ship as part of his rescue. I want you to be attributed with his redemption. Once he's off the ship, we'll introduce him to you fleetingly, and then I'll be waiting on the land to take him to safety." Richard added, "Jerome, lower the Luciana's boat on the Leith side. There we will stage an audible coup to convince Knox he has been delivered into the hands of his rescuer."

"That's me?" Jack said, pointing to himself.

"Who else? We'll make certain Knox is aware of who his rescuer is," Richard said. "Then you can disappear on the Luciana. Hopefully, they will think the French ship had been sunk and that you have engineered that as well. I don't think it's entirely sensible for you to return to Leith."

"Neither do I," Jack agreed wholeheartedly.

"Then Froggy can 'scuttle the French ship' while I deliver Knox. Do the crew know my orders?" Richard asked Jerome.

"The lads are ready when you need them," Jerome confirmed.

"Good. Jack, I'll come with you. All you need to do is get him off the ship, bring him to the side here. Collins has a rope ready, and we'll lower him into the boat. You join him in the boat, and we'll take him ashore. We'll keep him blindfolded until he is in the boat, and then we will let him see who has rescued him. Ready?" Richard asked.

"What, now?" Jack asked.

"Yes, now. Jerome, more smoke, if you will. It'll be easy. Let me give the crew their cue," Richard disappeared round to the back of the aftcastle, and before he reappeared, the sound of a pitched fight had erupted.

"Come on," Richard tugged Jack's arm and disappeared down the ladder towards the rope store. "It'll be fun – just try not to laugh!"

Richard quickly told Jack of the role he was to play, and a few moments later, they had squeezed through the narrow gangway near the galley and were close to the rope store.

"He's in 'ere," Richard squealed in French, his voice shrill and nervous. "Please, master, don't!"

Jack took his lead, shouting. "Get the bloody door open. Now!"

Jack realised that the crew's mock battle was directly above their heads, and it was convincing. The sounds of swords clashing, screams of agony, and thuds of men dying on the deck were the backdrop to the rescue.

Richard pulled the wooden securing pin from the door. "Please, sir! No ..." Richard's words ended with a guttural scream that almost made Jack laugh. Richard flung himself noisily against the panelling in the corridor, confirming to the imprisoned man the demise of Jack's French assistant.

"There he is," Richard's voice was now filled with the rich tones of a Newcastle accent. He shoved Jack hard.

"Get him. We need to make it to the boat before they send reinforcements, come on," Jack said, urgency in his voice.

"We've got yer, sir. 'ave no fear," Richard added as assurance.

Knox's arms were bound before him, his elbows jutting out as inviting handles. Richard had one; Jack took another.

"Come on, sir, we need to hurry," Richard urged, pulling Knox from the store.

Crammed in the narrow passage, they ran, pressing Knox before them. Alarm showed on Jack's face as he realised what was about to happen, but Richard on Knox's opposite side shook his head. Richard and Jack ducked, but Knox, running blindly, smacked his head solidly off the low door beam, sinking immediately to his knees.

"Sir! Are you alright?" Richard was already pulling the staggering man along the passage towards the deck ladders.

"Get him up, come on, we need to leave," Jack said, getting into his part, "Hurry, we've no time to waste. On your feet, man."

Knox was hauled to the deck, the sound of the fighting increasing. He was shoved bodily to where Collins waited, a thick loop of rope in his hands. He dropped it over the preacher's head, tucking it beneath his arms and pulling it tight.

"We've a boat to take you ashore. We'll have you on her in a moment. Haul lads!" Richard commanded and stood back as Knox's feet left the deck. He was swung out and lowered hastily over the side. Richard and Jack quickly dropped down the rope ladders to the waiting boat, arriving first.

Richard called up to the deck, his voice urgent. "He's there, lads. Let him go."

Knox wasn't in the boat. He was a good six feet above it when the rope was released, the preacher dropping the last distance, crashing into the bottom of the boat. Knox, hands tied, blindfolded, was unable to save himself and landed over one of the boat's wooden seats.

Richard grinned. Jack winced.

"Lord Fitzwarren, take my knife to cut his bonds," Richard said from where he sat behind Knox.

Jack took the offered knife. He left the hands bound but slit the sacking covering Knox's head. When the hole was big enough, he used his hands to wrench the material apart. "Master Knox, I am at your service."

"Who are ye?" Knox's voice was a pitch higher than usual. Blood poured from a split lip.

"Jack Fitzwarren, it's a privilege to have been able to...."

"Get down. It's not safe. They have archers," Richard declared from behind. He roughly pushed Knox into the bottom of the boat.

"Sir, watch your head," Richard warned, his voice concerned, before delivering a blow to the back of Knox's head, sending the battered preacher into unconsciousness.

"Right. One rescued preacher. I'll take him ashore. You get back on the Luciana, help Froggy load the powder," Richard said, the wooden marlin pin he'd used on Knox's head still in his hand.

"What if he comes round?" Jack asked.

"I will make sure he doesn't," Richard hefted the wooden pin. "Mind you. I'm almost hoping he does."

"Where will we meet you?"

"Berwick, I'll see you there. Jerome knows where to take her. Go on, get your arse up that ladder. I want the Luciana gone before we get ashore," Richard said, readying to push the boat from the ship's side.

Chapter Thirty-Three

The plan was simple. The Luciana would round the point, out of sight of Leith, then Froggy would set a fuse, cut the small boat free, and the powder would ignite, heralding the end of the newest addition to the French fleet.

Jack and Froggy were in the boat when the last cask was lowered. Both men had their hands on it, extricating it from the net it was secured in.

Something clattered, unseen in the darkness, on the top of the keg.

"What the Hell!" Froggy exclaimed.

Jack felt whatever it was grazing his shoulder before falling into the water with a slapping splash. Froggy staggered, his hold on the keg now uncertain. Catching his feet on a wooden spar on the boat's bottom, he lost his balance, falling backwards.

Jack had his hands under the bottom of one side of the small barrel, and he watched in horror as it fell from his grasp, following Froggy into the bottom of the boat.

Froggy yelped in pain.

"Jesus! Froggy ... Froggy! Are you alright?" Jack dropped to his knees, trying to find him in the near darkness.

The boat rocked wildly.

"It's on my arm. Christ, Jack, get it off me," Froggy spoke through gritted teeth.

Jack found the wooden keg on its side. Wrapping his arms around it, he lifted it away from Froggy and set it down next to the others in the boat. Froggy groaned loudly as he moved his injured limb.

"Are you alright?" Jack leaned down, a fist wrapped in his doublet, he pulled Froggy upright. The small man released another gasp of pain, his arm hanging limp at his side.

"I'm sorry, Jack!" Froggy managed.

"It wasn't your fault," Jack said when two feet landed lightly next to him in the boat.

"Lower a rope. You can lift him on board," Emilio's soft Italian voice sent the order back to the Luciana's deck.

"But ..." Jack said uncertainly.

"Between us, we've as much experience as Froggy with black powder. Get him back on the Luciana. We will set the fuse," Emilio said, calling up to the deck before Jack could complain. "The rope, pass it here."

A rope landed between them. Emilio tied a quick knot. "Sit him up."

"Sorry, Froggy," Jack apologised as he lifted Froggy and helped secure the rope under his arms.

Emilio tugged hard on the rope twice, the signal for those above to haul the injured man back up. As he began to rise from the boat, Jack kept a hold on him for as long as he could to help him avoid banging into the Luciana's hull. Froggy's body had become limp, and Jack guessed he had fainted as they secured the rope around him. In the dark, when you were in a hurry, it was hard to be careful.

"Lift him slowly, lads. His right arm is broken," Jack called up as loudly as he dared, holding onto Froggy as he was hoisted to the deck.

Emilio had already taken Froggy's seat. "Come on. We've little time. It will be light soon."

The Luciana was moving already. Knowing there was no time to waste, Jerome dropped her canvas and silently began to creep away from her mooring outside Leith. The small boat, hidden under the dark shadow of the aftcastle, rolled on the waves, towed behind the ship. On the horizon, the first grey light was rising, dawn would not be far behind, and their plan needed the shroud of night to work.

"What fell from the deck?" Jack asked.

Emilio shook his head. "I didn't see what it was."

"It could have been worse," Jack said, "I'll set a long fuse. When we cut her loose, we can climb back up the rope."

"Can you set the fuse?" Emilio asked.

"I might not be as good as Froggy, but I am sure I can produce a loud enough explosion," Jack said, settling himself on the bench. "Pass me that canvas bag. The fuse is in it."

In the prow, charcoal burnt inside a small square glass case, their ignition. A bag that held the length of fuse sat next to the glowing ember. Emilio reached for it. "Jack, this is not good."

"What do you mean?" Jack asked, concern in his voice. Emilio handed him the bag, and his hands immediately told him the problem. "For pity's sake! It got soaked when the keg fell."

"All of it?" Emilio's voice was filled with concern.

Jack fished in the bag, retrieving a dampened coil of cord. He looked at the fuse in his hand. This had definitely not been part of his brother's plan. Feeling along the length, he found where wet became dry and cut away the soaked portion, discarding it.

What was left was not much.

"Is that all we have?" Emilio said, his forehead creased as he looked at the short foot of fuse in Jack's right hand, moonlight picking out the white length.

"The rest is soaked. It's useless. This is all we have left," Jack began to roll the remaining useful length back up.

Emilio rolled his eyes. "We might as well drop a match on the top of the kegs. That fuse is not going to burn for more than a few moments."

"And we are too close to the Luciana," Jack said, looking up at the ship that loomed above them, "if we set that fuse, it'll take the ship with it."

†

It was even worse. To make the fuse effective, Jack knew that at least half of the cord would need to be buried in the powder, meaning what was left to burn would bearly last long enough for them to jump clear. That was if the act of lighting it so close to the powder did not instantly ignite it.

Jack stared between the fuse in his hand and the kegs.

They were round the headland now, out of sight of Leith and the French ships.

Emilio, a knife in his hand, began to apply it to the rope, attaching them to the Lucainna.

"No!" Jack's protest was too late.

The rope fell away.

Emilio, dropping to the bench, took up one of the oars. Jack, cursing, joined him and lowered his own oar into the water.

"You fool, you can't swim," Jack hissed into Emilio's ear.

"We have managed before," Emilio replied coolly.

"We!" Jack's voice was incredulous. "'We' didn't do anything. You nearly drowned. It was me who hauled you from the sea. Or have you forgotten that?"

"And I shall trust you to do so again," Emilio replied. "This is the only way. Otherwise, we are too close to her, and we will risk the ship."

They worked together at the oars. Jack could see little, the Luciana had disappeared against a black sea. There were no deck lights. Even the scent of smoke from the brazier was gone. Where she was, he didn't know. Where the land was, he didn't know either. Behind them, a light grey line was appearing over the hills, but where the coast was, he couldn't see, not yet anyway.

They didn't have long.

Once the light poked over the hills, there could be a witness to their deception; the explosion needed to happen in the darkness. And there wasn't much to it left.

Emilio, drawing his oar to a stop, said, "Give me the fuse here. I cannot swim, as you so regularly point out, and it would be a waste for both of us to remain in the boat."

Jack met the Italian's eyes. Pulling the dry length of fuse from his doublet, he looked at the ridiculously short length. "Let me think."

"We don't have time, Jack. Set the fuse. I will light it," Emilio's voice was an order. "Do it, Jacques. And while you do, I need to tell you something."

Jack shook his head.

"Jacques, listen to me. It's important," Emilio persisted.

"Tell me later. I'm trying to think, for God's sake!" Jack retorted.

Emilio took a tight hold on Jack's arm, his head close to Jack's. "Please, a moment only...."

Jack pulled roughly from the hold. His eyes had dropped to the fuse in his hand. Rolling it tightly, he stowed it back beneath his shirt. Pulling one of the barrels upright, he dragged the knife from his belt and began using the hilt as a hammer. "I am not going to let you arrive in the hereafter filled with righteous bloody indignation on my behalf."

"What are you doing? Stop!" Emilio began to rise from the bench, his voice filled with concern. "If you cause a spark, we will be arriving together."

One more solid attack with the hilt broke the top of the barrel. Jack thrust the knife back into his belt and hauled the keg over. Emilio watched in horror as black powder began to pool in a glistening pile around Jack's feet.

"Jack, are you mad!" Emilio exclaimed, standing now, his hands on the barrel. He tried to right it.

Jack met his eyes, grinning. "Too late."

When the keg was a third full, he rolled it over, pouring the rest of the contents out. The boat was filled with a thick fog of dust from the black powder. Emilio was coughing as Jack heaved the keg over the side into the water.

The expression on Emilio's face changed as he suddenly realised what Jack's intention was. Jack released the cask, and, before Emilio could lower himself back to the bench, Jack struck him in the chest. Unbalanced and cursing, Emilio disappeared over the side of the boat.

"Grab the barrel," Jack commanded. Leaning over the side, he wound a hand in Emilio's shirt and pulled him towards the floating keg.

Emilio thrashed and spluttered in the water.

"Get hold of it. There, can you feel it? Wrap your arms around it," Jack commanded before releasing him.

"Jack, don't do this," Emilio spoke between coughs. He had pulled himself from the water, his arms fastened to the barrel.

"Stop there, and don't you dare fucking drown," Jack ordered. Dropping onto the bench, he grabbed the oars and set them in the water. Emilio watched in horror as Jack and the boat disappeared across the water.

Jack drove the oars into the water hard and as evenly as he could, hoping he was taking the small boat backwards in a straight line away from Emilio. Twenty hard strokes – would that be enough?

Jack wasn't sure.

There was a swell on the water. In the darkness, as far as he knew, his efforts might have been enough only to keep the boat in the same position. If that were the case, he would be too close to Emilio.

The grey line in the sky was now twice the width.

Shit!

Jack drove the oars into the water and pressed the boat through the waves, counting. Another forty solid strokes.

He had to be far enough away now.

Jack hauled his doublet from his body. Ripping the front open, the buttons jettisoned themselves, pinging off the wooden boat sides; he used it to dry his hands. After pushing Emilio into the water, he was soaked, and his hair was dripping. If he dampened the short fuse, then there was no chance it would light. He had the boat where he wanted it now; there was no reason to delay. Emilio, he hoped, was between him and the land. Glancing back to where he thought the Italian was, he could see the grey first light of the day showing him a church spire rising in the distance marking the direction he needed to swim.

"God's bones!" Jack looked down at his feet. His boots were covered to the ankles in black powder. Trying to light the fuse without setting it off was almost impossible.

Jack set a barrel on the boat's bench. Twisting the point of his poniard between the staves, he opened a crack in the wood, and a fine stream of black powder ran out. Jack fed half of the fuse through the hole into the barrel. There really wasn't much left, and what there was had come from the centre of the coil of cord, and it was refusing to lay flat on the bench, rolling back up on itself.

How could he hold it straight?

The keg sat on one of the boat's wooden seats, the other two on the floor next to it. He was sure if he ignited one, the others would join it. Pulling the fuse out, he tried rolling the cord against itself to straighten it – but it refused to uncurl.

Bloody hell!
There was nothing to hold it down.
Nothing!
The pre-dawn light caught in the ruby on his ring.

Pulling the knife from his belt, he ripped the ring from his hand and slid it over the blade. Using the edge of the seat, he forced it down the blade until it split, the band shearing at the back. Twisting the broken band back and forth, it broke, and he had two golden halves. The edges were sharp and rough, where the metal had fractured.

Jack gently tapped the small gold hoops into the planking, a hand's width apart. The hoops of gold, standing proud, were high enough to thread the cord through, forcing the fuse to lie flat on the bench without stilting the flame's progress.

Jack leaned back and looked at his handiwork pinned with gold and jewels to the boat's seat. That he could see the white cord now told him he was running out of time.

Opening the glass box, he breathed gently on the charcoal, bringing it back to life. The embers glowed orange. Satisfied, he set it down at the end of the fuse and lay the cord across the hot charcoal, blowing steadily to coax a flame. It took a second only for the fire to take hold. Jack waited only a moment until he was sure the flame was steady and bright before lowering himself over the side of the boat. He didn't dare dive for fear of dousing the flame.

He made ten solid hard strokes, then ducked beneath the water, praying he had judged his moment right.

Chapter Thirty-Four

Jack lay in an untidy heap, leaking water over the deck. Kneeling next to him, pale-faced, was Emilio.

"Is he alright?" Jack heard Jerome say, the words quickly spoken, dismay apparent in his tone.

Jack was going to reply when another cough stole his voice. He tried to press himself from the deck, but the strength had drained from his arms; unable to rise, he slumped back. Jack watched, unable to move, as Emilio reached up, wrapping a fist into Jerome's doublet, pulling the captain's head close to his own. He couldn't hear the quick exchange, but a moment later, Jerome wrenched Emilio's hand from him and stood upright, glowering down at the knight. Jack tried to lift himself again from the deck, but his arms still refused to take his weight. Groaning, he dropped back. Next to him, Emilio clambered from his knees, rising to stand before Jerome. His voice, when he spoke, pitched to be heard across the deck. "Get you from me, traitor."

"This is not your ship, De Nevarra," Jerome growled in reply.

Jack tried to speak, but all that emerged was a gurgling cough. Why was Emilio, the bloody fool, set on angering Jerome?

Alphonso, in soft leather boots, fetched up between them.

Jack groaned inwardly.

That's all I bloody need!

"You're hurt!" Alphonso exclaimed, his voice a little too shrill.

Rolling onto his side, Jack watched as Alphonso reached out, placing a ringed hand on a cut on Emilio's forehead that was still leaking blood.

"It's nothing." Emilio moved from the touch as if stung, his voice for a moment harsh with a mixture of impatience and something else Jack couldn't quite place. Then, fixing an apologetic smile on Alphonso, he said quickly, "Mi spiace."

Jack saw what Jerome meant to do.

Before Alphonso could respond, a hard grip had been fastened around his arm. Jerome's head close to Alphonso's, he snarled in his ear, "I don't remember giving you leave to be above decks! Get this shit out of my sight. Then come back and haul this one away as well."

Jerome, a good hold on Alphonso's arm, slung him toward one of his crew, who looked only too pleased to take charge of his removal. A smile crept onto Jack's face as the protesting Italian was dragged from the deck. Jack, casting a glance in Emilio's direction, saw the Italian's dark gaze was upon him, not Alphonso.

"Angering Jerome ... wasn't sensible ... was it?" Jack finally managed to speak, his voice hoarse and weak. His arms shook with the effort, but he finally made it onto his hands and knees.

"Just wait! We'll help," Emilio dropped back to his knees next to Jack, fastening a tight hold around his arm.

"I don't ... need any ..." Jack didn't finish the sentence, his other arm was taken by Jerome, and a moment later, he was vertical, supported between the two men.

"Be careful with him. We'll take him to his brother's cabin," Emilio was saying, then he started to talk to Jack, but Jack couldn't hear him properly.

His head was spinning, and it felt as if the ship had suddenly lurched; if Jerome hadn't shouldered his weight, he'd have been back on the deck. Jack wanted to tell Jerome that he should go and make sure the Santa Luciana was in capable hands, but the words wouldn't form, and darkness flooded over him.

✝

Opening his eyes, Jack looked for Jerome, but the captain was missing. He was in Richard's cabin, lying on the bed at an awkward angle. Jack had forgotten just how short the narrow bunks on the ship were. He'd always had to sleep with his knees bent or risk banging his head on the wood panelling at the end. His head was still spinning, his mouth impossibly dry, and he was propped up in one corner.

He wasn't alone, and he watched as Emilio performed a quick and efficient review of all the cupboards and drawers. Any clothing he found he flung on top of Jack, then he produced a bottle of aquae vitae and two cups. Jack watched as Emilio, his hands shaking, poured two full glasses, a quantity of the liquid slopping over the edge of one of the cups and running to drip from the table. Jack tried to raise his arm towards Emilio, but it felt trapped beneath the cloth Emilio had dumped on top of him.

Unwanted, rising suddenly from with him, a loud sneeze convulsed the muscles in his chest.

Bloody hell! That hurt!

"Dio ti benedica," Emilio held the cup to Jack's lips.

"I'm not ..." He wanted to tell Emilio to just give him the cup. He wasn't a bloody child, but the words, if they ever would have emerged, were stopped when the warming liquid was tipped into his mouth.

"Ahhh Chooo .... Christ ...." Jack's eyes were tightly shut; the pain was like a knife blade in his back. Maybe he'd broken a rib.

"Careful, Jacques," Emilio's voice, close to his head, said.

His body stopped shuddering, and Emilio brought the cup back to his lips; slowly, he emptied it. Jack tried again to move his arm, but it remained unresponsively trapped beneath the blankets. Maybe he had broken that as well.

Jack watched Emilio refill the cup and then bring it back to him. More of the warming liquid slid down his throat, like a fire coursing its way towards his stomach.

Emilio attempted to fill the cup from the bottle, but the bottleneck chattered on the cup, so he gave up. Taking the cup, he put it on the table next to his own and, using both his shaking hands, he refilled them. Jack watched as he crossed his arms; clamping his hands under them, he walked around the cabin, his teeth audibly rattling. Emilio must be freezing.

"You don't …. have to …. stay with me," Jack's voice emerged as a hoarse whisper.

Emilio, who was rubbing his hands together, stopped pacing and regarded Jack for a moment. "If the fires in the galley are alive, I will get them to bring some hot stones."

It was a pretence, and Jack knew it. Emilio would need to find out where Alphonso had been taken. Jack hoped it was deep in the hold. Somewhere nice and damp, tar black and icily cold, a slight smile drifted across his face before he closed his eyes.

A moment later, the door banged open, and the tramp of feet filled the cabin. Emilio was giving concise orders where he wanted everything put.

Christ – just shut up!

Jack's head ached. The noise of the voices, the footsteps and the furniture being moved all seemed overly loud and held an edge that dragged against his nerves.

Then his head was being lifted, and a cup pressed to his lips. A frown crossed Jack's forehead. He'd expected aquae vitae; instead, it was a sweet warmed wine thick with honey. It left his lips sticky and didn't do much to alleviate his thirst. Jack was going to say as much, but somehow he forgot ...

†

Richard dropped onto the deck, a smile on his face as his eyes swept the scene.
No Jack.
Jerome was striding towards him. The expression on his face was one Richard couldn't quite unravel. Was it a concern? Annoyance perhaps? Or an unhappy combination of both.
Jerome spoke quickly. "He's in your cabin."
The smile, forgotten, fell from Richard's face. Richard pressed past the captain and ran, dropping down the deck ladders and, landing on unsteady legs, made it to the cabin quickly.
Then he paused.
The hand reaching for the door handle shook. Whatever news awaited him on the other side, he knew it was bad.
Just how bad?
Swallowing hard and taking a steadying breath, Richard pulled the door open, stepping inside.
The movement that stole his attention was Emilio rising from a chair. His brother was lying on the bed. On the floor next to him was a basin filled with bloody water, white cloths soiled with blood lay next to it in a tangled savage heap.
Jack was immobile. His face was paler than it should have been, his body covered in a sheet, with only his head showing, eyes closed, laid on his left side.
"Is he ...?" Richard stammered.

"No..." Emilio's voice had a desperate edge. "It was my fault."

"Jesus! Jack, what have you done?" Richard dropped to his knees next to his brother. There was no response. Jack was asleep, or worse. Richard took hold of the sheet and drew it back.

"Christ! What happened?" Richard gasped, looking at the puckered burnt skin running from his shoulder down his arm and across his back, the livid purple scorch marks heightened by the parlour of the rest of his skin.

"It was my fault. The fuse was too short, and he didn't have time to get away before the explosion," Emilio's words were spoken with harsh anguish.

Richard rocked back on his haunches. "Good God! There must be something we can do." Richard rose and turned on Emilio. He swiped a rosary from the small table. "You're a bloody Hospitaller! Surely, there is something more you can do than pray for his eternal fucking soul?"

Emilio, pale, his eyes on Richard's, said, "I have no skills. We have just arrived in Berwick. It was my hope ...."

Richard didn't let him finish. "Your hope! Is that all we are left with? Your bloody hope?"

"Richard. Enough. We have to think, you have to think, how can we help him?" Emilio reasoned.

Emilio easily evaded the fist aimed at him, ducking beneath it quickly. "Please, Richard, listen to me. We don't have time for this."

"Time!" Richard's voice was incredulous. The word was spoken as he dived across the cabin, the small table flung sideways as he shouldered Emilio into the opposite wall.

"Very well!" Emilio hooked Richard's leg from beneath him; he fell, pulling Emilio with him. Both were locked together, fighting to obtain the hold on the other man that would give them the better position.

"Stop. Now!" Emilio commanded. His right hand held Richard's knife, and the point of it, within Richard's sight, hovered near his neck. "Are you listening to me?"

Richard's eyes flicked back to the blade.

"Together. We work together. Do you hear me?" Emilio tried again.

Richard released his hold on the Italian, pushing him roughly away.

"We are in Berwick. We must be able to get him some help, some respite, more than wine can give," Emilio began to rise from his knees.

Richard wasn't looking at Emilio. His eyes were on Jack. He heard his voice as clearly as if he were in the room with them.

"Goose fat mainly, with clove oil and lavender."

"I remember," Richard said, then to Emilio, "I burnt my arm on a kiln. Jack had a salve he'd made from fat with cloves and lavender."

"Did it work?" Emilio pressed.

Richard nodded. "Yes, he dried the blisters and sealed them with the salve."

"What are you waiting for?"

†

Emilio watched Richard leave.

Reaching down, he retrieved the rosary, then, seemingly making up his mind, he approached the bed, kneeling next to Jack. He found one of his hands looping the beads around it, pressing the crucifix into his slack grip. "Whether you want to or not, you will listen to me."

Emilio spoke in quiet Italian. When he was finished, he released Jack's hand, leaving the rosary wrapped around it.

"Che Dio mi perdoni."

The Mercenary For Hire Series

A Queen's Spy
A Queen's Traitor
A Queen's Mercenary
A Queen's Knight
A Queen's Assassin
A Queen's Executioner
A Queen's Champion
A Queen's Conspirator
A Queen's Rebel – release date 2024

The Tudor Heresy – Short novella prequel to the series

Printed in Great Britain
by Amazon